Coming Up for Air

Sarah Leipciger

BLACK SWAN

TRANSWORLD PUBLISHERS
Penguin Random House, One Embassy Gardens,
8 Viaduct Gardens, London SW11 7BW
www.penguin.co.uk

Transworld is part of the Penguin Random House group of companies
whose addresses can be found at global.penguinrandomhouse.com

First published in Great Britain in 2020 by Doubleday
an imprint of Transworld Publishers
Black Swan edition published 2021

The quoted lines on p. 290 are taken from 'In the Operating
Room', a poem by Alden Nowlan.

A CIP catalogue record for this book
is available from the British Library.

ISBN
9781784164676

Typeset in Adobe Garamond by Jouve (UK), Milton Keynes.
Printed and bound in Great Britain by Clays Ltd, Elcograf S.p.A.

The authorized representative in the EEA is Penguin Random House Ireland,
Morrison Chambers, 32 Nassau Street, Dublin D02 YH68

Penguin Random House is committed to a sustainable future
for our business, our readers and our planet. This book is made
from Forest Stewardship Council® certified paper.

For Eve, for Ali and for Kieran

'The thing about women from the river is that
our currents are endless.'

Terese Marie Mailhot, *Heart Berries*

Prologue

L'Inconnue (The Unknown Woman)
Paris, France, 1899

THIS IS HOW I drowned. I stood beneath the arch of the Pont Alexandre III, on the Left Bank of the slick and meandering Seine. Moon-silver, cold. I took off my coat and boots, and folded my coat neatly, and laid it over my boots, which I lined up side by side with the tips pointing down to the water. I stood quietly for a few minutes, watching the surface of the river form soft little peaks that folded into themselves again and again and again.

I took a step closer to the water so I could peer down its throat. But this was the gut of night, and even with the moonlight, the water was an opaque, bottomless thing. Not for the first time, I climbed into the underbelly of the bridge, and shuffled along the arch, hugging the pillars, towards the middle where the river was deeper. There was the smell of rust and cold steel and there was the smell of the river and there was a chance that, in this moment, things could have gone differently. A small sign from the world to tell me it would rather I stayed than left. The nasal call of some rook. A shooting star, a whistling boatman, a change in the wind. Nothing happened. So. I leaned forward, expelled my last breath, and let myself fall. The black water closed over my head like a toothless mouth.

The cold was a shock, and so was the burden of my heavy clothes.

1

I opened my eyes to oblivion. What I thought had been my last breath was not my last breath – I had been wrong about that. For a few seconds, I was as calm as music, but then my body pedalled and thrashed; it didn't want to drown. This wasn't a new-found desire, after all, to live. This was about air. Oxygen. And my lack of it. My lungs, each of my muscles, hung suspended, seized in pain. I kicked until my head broke the surface, and in that moment I saw the bridge passing above me. I sucked a breath of sweet air before I went under again and wheeled my arms, looking for something solid to hold as I was carried downriver. My suffocating limbs became blocks of stone.

Eventually my body gave up fighting and began to sink and, beyond my control, my throat drew water. Water and river silt entered my trachea, my lungs. Something popped deep inside my ear. I vomited and, with a violent rush, more water, silt and leaves filled the evacuated space inside me. At last, a tingling started in my fingertips. It was remote, pleasant. I opened my eyes (though they may have been open all along) and there was something pale and dead floating very close to my face. My hand. And then darkness surrounded me, like steam from a hot bath clouding a mirror, and a feeling grew too; it was as if I'd been handed the universe in a glass jar. All I had to do was open it. Just as my heart was pumping its last beats, I was hooked at the waistband by a pole and lifted on to the hard deck of a grain barge. And this is where I died.

1

L'Inconnue
Before Paris

I HAD BEEN LIVING in Paris for a year and a half before my death, having gained employment as a lady's companion to an old friend of my grandmother's, a Madame Cornélie Debord. Before receiving Madame Debord's letter requesting I come to live with her in Paris, life for me, in my home of Clermont-Ferrand, had become empty, and I was adrift.

My birth had been the death of my mother. In 1880, in Clermont-Ferrand, this was not a shock – it sometimes happened. Nonetheless, death due to childbirth was horrific. It was bloody, sweaty and exhausting, and happened either during labour or days later from blood loss or infection. My mother's death was attended by three women: her older sister Huguette, the midwife, and my grandmother on my father's side. Tante Huguette always held me responsible for her baby sister's death but my grandmother did not, and this conflict was waged between them from the moment I took my first breath, and lasted for eleven years, ending only when my dear grandmother expelled her last.

I grew up knowing things about my birth that I probably should not have. For example, Tante Huguette told me that after two days of labour without progression, my mother's green eyes turned as black and flat as the eyes of a pigeon. She sweated and shat and vomited and bled until her body was dry. In the end, the midwife ripped me from my mother's body by my feet and I entered the world ass-first, tearing my mother from flower to anus.

Tante Huguette told me that when her pain was at its greatest, my mother begged them to kill us both. I believed this for most of my life.

My father, who was an apprentice baker in the Compagnons and away in Nantes when I was born, came home for one week to meet me and mourn the death of my mother. The Compagnons, a guild of masters, a society of artisans – bakers, carpenters, shoemakers, plasterers, locksmiths – with secret ceremonies and rites of passage, had strict rules and he wasn't able to stay longer. He had just begun his Tour de France, a five-year apprenticeship that would take him all over the country, and he didn't see me again until I was almost two years old. Because he couldn't afford to pay a wet nurse, I was fed for my first few months on goat's milk or pap sucked through a knob of cork, looked after by a loving grandmother and begrudging aunt.

Those last seconds on the grain barge, moments from my life reeled through my mind. And they were condensed. They defied time.

There I was, aged four, in a bed in a too-dark room. Shadows in the corners making the room smaller still. Calling, calling for Tante Huguette to come, to come. The good smells of stewed venison, of bread.

There I was, aged six. My father home for a whole month to visit. Just us two, working together, performing magic in a ceramic bowl. Weighing scales dusted with flour and the smooth passage of a hand-warmed wooden spoon against the bowl's edge, and then the kneading on a kitchen counter greased with oil. My father pinched a wad of dough from the mixture and showed me how to stretch it, without it breaking, to at least the length of my forearm to ensure the kneading was done. A slow rise, he said, before we knock it back, will give us the most delicious taste. Everything in the room, everything in the world, flour-white.

There I was, aged seven, my unkempt hair snagging on branches as I picked my way through the forest behind our town, up the hill to a clearing where I could look down on the houses of Clermont and the volcanic-black cathedral at its centre, Notre-Dame de l'Assomption, where I could gain at least a little height on the hills that hemmed me in and dream of a place where the withering looks of my aunt couldn't burn me. There I sat with my back against the trunk of a larch tree, picking bouquets of myrtille and saxifrage for my dead mother.

And there I was aged twelve, during the first of two happy years (and the only years) when my father actually lived with us in Clermont-Ferrand until he, too, less than three years after my grandmother, also died. Pneumonia. Fluid in the lungs. There I was, waiting for him to finish his dawn shift at the boulangerie, an airless brick building at the back of one of the grand hotels. There I was, watching him and his two companions at their work, their faces wet from the relentless heat of the three ovens, their white aprons like long skirts. One whole wall taken up by the three brick ovens, topped with stacks and stacks of wood. Another wall taken up by trays and copper pans, and cloth-lined, woven baskets as barracks to armies of hot baguettes. Racks of shining implements, copper and steel sieves, spoons, funnels, graters and spatulas. All hung neatly from nails. There was my father, turning the bread with a long wooden paddle while it baked. And I. Sitting on an upturned bucket next to a water tap coming out of the wall, wetting my finger with the drip, drip falling from its mouth. One of the other fellows was knocking back dough on a wooden table under shelves stacked with white sacks of flour. His back and neck shone and when he looked my way over his shoulder, he kept his eyes on me while his arms pumped the dough. He winked. I immediately crossed my arms over my chest and looked directly at my father, who was bent towards the oven.

And there I was aged thirteen, sitting on a bench in the Jardin Lecoq with the girl I thought I would love for ever, Emmanuelle. I had promised her a cream bun from the boulangerie, but when we went to beg some, my father had sent us away empty-handed and I was embarrassed. So I told her to wait for me on the bench. There I was, crossing an empty market square and slipping between the chestnut trees that lined its edge. I crept down a small street behind the orthodox church and was pleased to find what I had been looking for, the old woman who sold little squares of bergamot in paper bags. Each year she hid herself away in the cold months and wouldn't be seen again until the smell of lavender and thyme filled our streets, until the hills were purple and blue and white with wildflowers. And there she was, sitting in a chair next to her little folding table, the table lined with small brown bags of bergamot sweets. Asleep. This was not the first time I had stolen from her.

And so there we sat, Emmanuelle and I, sharing the stolen bag of sweets, sucking each lemony amber square, daring each other not to chew, until they were reduced to sticky dots in the middle of our tongues.

And there I was, aged fourteen, standing over my dead father where he remained in his bed. Tante Huguette was there, or she was not there. She was in and out of the room, and for the most part we ignored each other and I pretended not to hear her when she told the priest that the child – I – was the weight she was cursed to bear. This was just after dawn, in winter, and I was trembling in a nightdress and shawl. Dead a few hours, but he had been gone for days, lost in delirium, drowning within his body and asking for my mother.

6

His eyes would not shut after death, so I weighted the lids down with two coins. I sat by my papa's side and carefully studied his face, every pore and hair and wrinkle, trying to make an impression that might last because I knew he would soon be gone, kept in a crypt until the ground was soft enough for digging, and my only record of this face would be from memory. His cheeks and the sockets of his eyes had become sunken in; I wondered what it was in life that kept them so plump because now, only hours after death, its absence was obvious. He was missing a good many teeth. I put my hands on either side of his cheeks and held them there. A long and winding tweep emitted from his backside, like something falling.

Later, I washed him, all of him except for the parts he wouldn't have wanted me to see, and covered him with a crisp white sheet, pulled only to the shoulders. On his knuckles and strong arms, on the insides of his wrists, the shiny white scars of a dozen oven burns, evidence of who he had been.

And there I was, aged nineteen. Tante Huguette standing in the salon clutching Madame Debord's letter. Always neat and starched, Tante Huguette. Not a hair out of place.

'She says the girl she currently employs is to be wed. She needs someone as soon as possible.' Her eyes scrolled down the letter. 'She'll post the train fare as soon as she receives your acceptance.'

'My acceptance?'

'The money your father left is nearly gone. Your grandmother's money too, spent. There is little opportunity for you here.'

'But this is home.'

'You should find Paris to be very agreeable.' She looked out of the window.

'What will you do?'

'What do you mean?'

'How will you manage? Without me here?'

There was Tante Huguette, raising her chin, pursing her lips. 'I'll manage. I can rent out your room; it will help.'

And there I was on a train, the enormous, gleaming bulk and steel and steam of it bearing me forth to the unknown, the unknowable. Bearing me forth to you.

2

Pieter
Åkrehamn, Karmøy Island, Norway, 1921

I USED TO SPEND the summers with my grandparents on Karmøy Island. I was salt. I was sea. I spent these languid days swimming at the beach, though the North Sea, as my grandfather would have said, was as cold as a witch's tit. I splashed and kicked and dove to the white sandy bottom where the world under the surface of the water was untold, unknowable and ever-shifting.

Each time I swam, when I first leapt into the sea, the cold reached into my chest with two hands and squeezed my lungs, and I was forced to bellow as if I were a musical instrument. The temperature got my blood pumping and my skin tingling. When the sun shone and there was no wind, the water was a marbling of blue and topaz and emerald, but when the wind was up and the weather rough, the surface of the water swelled and folded and galloped, and the colour changed to steel, to fighting green. And on these rough days, the sea sprayed foam against the beach boulders, which resembled the rumps of sleeping elephants.

I could hold my breath underwater for over a minute.

I could dive down several metres before my inner ears pulsed and ticked.

After swimming, I would climb to the top of my favourite

boulder, hot and rough as animal hide under my feet, and dry off in the sun. My hair dried briny and brittle and crusty with salt.

After swimming, I was fiercely hungry. I wanted to eat everything in sight.

My grandfather was a fisherman, and was usually gone before I woke up in the mornings. He was very tall and thin, and had thick black, wiry hair that sprouted from his head as if the salt-strong wind had sculpted it that way. He often smelled of fish innards, and told stories of gales and ice and the moon rising over the sea like a distant fire in the dark. In his pocket, he carried a sharp knife, which he used to carve off bites of chewing tobacco from a plug he kept in a tin. It was he who taught me that the sea was never too cold for a swim.

My grandmother: she was something else. Long, tangled hair the colour of sea foam that she wore wavy and loose over her shoulders and down her back. Eyes like crescent moons when she smiled. Her skin had been toughened by a lifetime of North Sea wind. She lost two babies in childbirth, my father being her only child who lived, and her skin had been toughened by that, too.

For breakfast, she fed me as much salami, eggs, smoked salmon and leverpostei as I could eat. She wanted to fatten me up before sending me home to my mother and father in Stavanger. When she could, she would come with me to the beach, but she was busy at home. There was wood to split, and there was the baking and the painting; there were vegetables to tend, chickens to feed, various dogs and a one-eyed cat.

Most days, I came home with shells and stones, a piece of driftwood, or a sweaty clutch of the pale wildflowers that grew in the grassy dunes that backed on to the beach. Once, I returned with a washed-up glass bottle, scratched and tarnished and chipped at the mouth. I believed it must have, at one time, contained a paper scroll. A message from Denmark or England or France. I kept this collection on the windowsill in my bedroom, which had a view of the sea. It was a very small room with a very big view, in a red-roofed house of white clapboard.

In the front room there was a basket of wood next to the stove. There was a comfortable sofa, two armchairs and a low table. If there was a windstorm, which there often was, the windows shook in their frames. On the wall hung a few paintings: a dry-docked fishing boat, a vase of daisies, the koie my grandfather built up at the lake, with its grass-covered roof and tin chimney. My grand-mother painted these and I never considered whether they were good or bad.

Also on the wall: a clock manufactured in England. An oval mirror, speckled. And a plain white plaster mask, smooth as butter-milk. So milky that I often thought about licking it. The face was a young woman's and it was very realistic, almost alive. Her eyes were closed, with matted eyelashes, and her cheeks were high and round and youthful. She smiled, a little. She smiled a little and it was one of those smiles that could not be contained, as if she were on the cusp of telling me something.

3

Anouk
Ottawa River, Canada, 2017

IT'S SEPTEMBER, ANOUK'S birthday. She's turning forty. Her mother Nora has come with her up north because it's a big deal for Anouk, turning forty. When she was born, doctors predicted her life expectancy to be far shorter than that. They've come north, away from the city, because Anouk would like to see the river, the place she was born, before she's called for surgery. She's on the donor list for a new set of lungs.

The conversation with the specialist at the cystic fibrosis clinic went something like this:

'The indicators are telling us it's time we think about transplant.'

'I know.'

'Your last few FEV1 readings were less than thirty per cent.'

'My lungs have had it.'

'How long has it been since you've been able to work? Have you been writing?'

'I've been trying. It's hard to concentrate.'

'All the medication.'

'Yes, ya. There's that. It's just. Nothing interests me.'

'You're spending more time on IVs than not.'

'I haven't got any ideas. For stories.'

'Half your day is taken up with extra physiotherapy. I'm not surprised.'

'So.'

'If we stick to your current treatments, you haven't got a lot of time left. Maybe a year.'

'A year.'

'And it'll be a lousy year.'

'You're telling me.'

'A successful transplant could give you six. It could give you more.'

'Or less.'

'We don't know. But you can stop using supplemental oxygen. And you won't be coughing. Imagine that, no coughing.'

'I can't imagine that.'

'Post-op, you'll still be on a lot of medication, but what matters is your quality of life will be better than it is now. And right now, it's not very good.'

'No.'

'I think we should refer you to the transplant team. Get your name on the list. But it's up to you.'

Up here, in the last days of September; up here, by this river banked on both sides by trees, a few houses and cottages; up here, the air is crisp and smells something like hope. Though everything is dying, death here is sweet and it smells like hope. Anouk and her mother have rented a cottage (the house just up the river from here, where Anouk was born, where her father lived until he died, now belongs to someone else) and it's evening, and they're sitting on the floating dock in two fan-backed, wooden chairs. They share a wool blanket, draped over their legs, and they share a cold beer, and there is the rustle of wind in the trees and the lap and suck of water against the gently rolling dock and the quiet, ubiquitous hiss of Anouk's oxygen concentrator.

September is an ending and a beginning, both.

The trees are turning and the river reflects purple, yellow, orange burning. The loons haven't yet flown south and they're out there now, yodelling to each other.

'Loons,' says Anouk, more an exhale than a word. She leans back and sighs, content.

'I always thought they sounded like a pack of crazies,' says Nora. She squints across the mouth of the beer bottle, stares at the water. 'Laughing at me. Loonatics.'

Anouk has learned that, of all the doctors and specialists out there, you'll never meet a person more blunt than the transplant surgeon. The transplant surgeon deals in risks and percentages. The transplant surgeon deals in likelihoods. Her transplant surgeon, a tall woman in her fifties with shorn hair and smart stud earrings, loves percentages. In her comfortable office with cushioned chairs, she spoke about the percentage of patients who never make it out of the hospital. She spoke about the percentages of patients who make it through the first year, the second, the third. Not an especially high number. She listed, with one neat and tidy finger dabbing the palm of her opposite hand, the risks of post-operative infection, acute rejection, chronic rejection. Anouk's new lungs, she explained, won't be diseased like her old ones, but her immune system will slowly attack and injure them, and within a few years they too will become scarred and ineffectual.

'Lungs,' said the surgeon, 'are a difficult organ to transplant.'

'Why?'

'The tissue is extremely fragile. The alveoli, they're minuscule and easily damaged. The cells are metabolically very active so we have only a little time between harvest and transplant. A few hours. You'll be on call. It will be your responsibility to get to the hospital on time.'

There was talk of what recovery would be like, swapping the old

14

cystic fibrosis daily treatments, which Anouk has lived with all her life, for a new regime, new medications to deal with the complexities of rejection. 'This probably isn't what you wanted to hear,' the surgeon said.

These words, more than any of the others, made Anouk angry. As if she had been deluded all along and now here she was, hearing the truth for the first time.

Nora puts her hand on Anouk's knee. 'Are you tired?' she says. 'Long drive today.'

'I think I'll stay out a bit longer.'

'Then I'm going in for another beer,' says Nora, hoisting herself out of the chair.

Cold air on Anouk's legs from where Nora has lifted the blanket. 'Get me one too.'

Nora stops, looks at her. Considers.

'It's my birthday.'

They smile at each other, two smiles weighted and complicit. They were never sure until now they'd make it this far.

Before the transplant team would agree to put Anouk's name on the donor list, she and her mother were subjected to what felt like a trial. There were meetings with her surgeon and other surgeons, a nutritionist, a psychologist and a physiotherapist. Also, a doctor of bones. A doctor of kidneys. Nearly every body part represented. The team had to agree that Anouk and Nora would behave, could handle the pressures both pre- and post-op, would do what they were told. They had to determine whether she would put forth her best effort to survive. What she was going to be given was precious.

The dock pitches slightly with Nora's retreat and Anouk looks out across the water. About an hour ago she thought she saw a golden eagle. Nora thought it was a hawk but Anouk is pretty sure it's an eagle. And she knows of an island, out of the many islands in this river, she knows there's one close where eagles often nest. She used to see them when she was small, riding in the aluminum outboard with her dad, Red. They're rare, but they're here.

Someone is out there in the world breathing through a pair of healthy, pink lungs that are going to end up in Anouk's body. She inhales deeply, or tries to. Her lungs snag against their cavity walls like sandpaper. Healthy lungs, the CF specialist explained, are springy and spongy. If poked, they would give way and pop back like pillows. They have sharp-edged fissures that fill efficiently with air. Anouk's lungs have hardened. They're gnarled. Riddled with cysts and pockets of pus. They're the colour of dung. The description makes her think of a piece of gristle, or a wad of gum drying on the edge of a dinner plate.

Anouk eases herself out of her chair and spreads the blanket on the dock. She has to manoeuvre around the delicate tubing that runs from the oxygen canister to the cannula in her nose, and lies down on the blanket and presses her cheek into the cedar. The cedar, still warm from the day's sun, the smell of it, fills her. It topples her. It's in her blood, this smell, this river. She reaches over the edge of the dock and dips her fingers, caresses the cold water. She wants to swim but can't. She wants to immerse herself. Maybe she could just float, holding on to the edge of the dock, but she can't risk getting sick. The dock moves again and here is Nora, poking Anouk's bum with the tip of her sneaker.

'Skinny ass,' Nora says. 'Skinny, skinny ass.'

The echo of the loon is like air in her wasted lungs.

4

Anouk
Ottawa River, 1987

THAT SKY OF Anouk's youth, that sky over the Ottawa River Valley, over the river, over fields of corn and sunflowers, flax and blueberry – that sky stretched on for ever. Her house was on the river and the closest town was called Pembroke, where she went to school and where, deeply gouged into the weed-cracked sidewalk in front of the school, were the words: *Mr Morton is a azz-licker.* There was an IGA grocery store, a Canadian Tire, a movie theatre. In the summer, the roads were jammed with people from southern Ontario with canoes and kayaks strapped to the tops of their cars, bikes on racks with wheels spinning in the air. In the early months of winter, the snow banks that lined the streets, snow thrown up by 4 a.m. ploughing, were white and loafy; by February they were dark grey and ice-shiny. In the gas station you could buy fishing worms and leeches in neat, Styrofoam boxes, and next to the gas station there was a boutique that sold prettily painted mailboxes and scented candles and beaded wind chimes.

The Ottawa River was wide open for long stretches, then channelled and split by islands and arms of land that connected together to make a warren of small ponds and passages. Where the water ran wide, the current was slow. Early in the morning, the river, in some parts, was so calm and covered in mist that it disappeared. If it weren't for the striders skating to and fro, their fine legs bending the surface tension of the water, you'd scarcely know the river was there.

A few kilometres upriver from where its course squeezed and buckled over boulders and falls, where the water rushed white and frothy and deadly, there was a quiet pocket in the southern bank. A horseshoe bend in the land, a tiny bay. Not even a bay; a dimple. In the middle of this pocket there was a small island that, if viewed from the bank, looked like a tall ship. One lofty, spindled pine at the bow. At the other end of the island, the stern, a tapered deck of Canadian Shield igneous rock.

Anouk lived with her mother and father, Nora and Red, on the riverbank adjacent to the tall-ship island. The house, built of weather-darkened clapboard, sat on top of a gentle, grassy slope that rose from the bank. It was a split-level house, with a large ground floor where the kitchen and dining room opened to the living room, which was walled on its river-facing side by a vast window. So. You could see the river from almost anywhere in the house.

Nora came from Toronto and Red was from Pembroke. They met in 1971, in a three-storey brick house just off Spadina Avenue in Toronto, working with a charity that helped newly arrived American draft dodgers find jobs and places to live. Red was in teachers' college at the University of Toronto and Nora wasn't sure what she wanted to do. They fell in love surrounded by guys whom they considered heroes, who rode bikes or hid in the trunks of cars to cross the border into Canada so they wouldn't have to shoot people in a country about which they knew nothing. Nora and Red fell in love listening to Neil Young and Lynyrd Skynyrd and the Eagles. It was romantic. When Red's mother died in 1975, he inherited her house in Pembroke, sold it, and convinced Nora that they should buy the place on the river. At the time, she was taking a course to be a counsellor. It was her work with the draft dodgers that made her want to do this. She didn't really want to move to the river, but she was in love.

For the first week of August, the month before Anouk's tenth birthday, Nora's sister Mel came up from Toronto for a visit. The two sisters spent a lot of time by the river, lounging in deck chairs on their crescent of sand (too small really to be called a beach) with their legs stretched out and their feet in the water. They drank bottles of beer, which Anouk fetched for them from the kitchen. Anouk liked her aunt. Mel was a little bit bad. She smoked Rothmans Specials and swore and told dirty jokes, and she made Nora laugh. Anouk liked how her mom and her aunt looked like two different versions of the same thing. They both had long, slender legs and knobbly knees. Bodies wide at the hips, square torsos and flat chests. Both with broad shoulders and long necks. But Nora's hair was red-blonde, like Anouk's, and Mel's was dark brown. Nora's shoulders were covered in orange freckles in the summer. Mel's were smooth and tanned. Anouk had the same flamingo-like physique as her mother and aunt, but she would never be tall, and her shoulders and back were slightly hunched because of her cough, which she lived with every day. To hunch the shoulders, to roll the back, was to open the chest cavity, to ease the passage of air into the lungs. This was what her body did.

A few days into Mel's visit, Anouk sat in the sand near her mother and her aunt, ploughing a trough with her heels. She didn't sit too close to Nora because if she did, Nora would start pleating her hair, looking for louse eggs. Anouk had made the mistake of scratching behind her ears at breakfast the day before, and now Nora was obsessed. Anouk's scalp was indeed crawling with lice, and Anouk knew it. She wanted to scratch the shit out of it but didn't want to give Nora the satisfaction, so instead, she got up from the sand and walked into the river. For Anouk, in the summer, the river was the land was the river was everything. She moved effortlessly between the two, picking up her damp bathing suit first thing in the morning, picking it up from the floor next to her bed and uncoiling it from the pretzel shape it took on when she'd rolled it off her body before going to sleep. She waded into the water now until it was up to her scabby, mosquito-bitten knees and dunked herself, eyes open to the sting of freshwater the colour of tea. She exhaled all the air out of her lungs so she could sit on the silty bottom. Underwater, her skin looked melted-butter yellow, dotted with black particles of river matter. When she needed to breathe she resurfaced, turned to see if Nora was watching her.

Nora, speaking to Mel, held her hand above her head, as if shielding her eyes from the sun. She was doing this to keep the river midges away from her face; they were attracted to the highest point, like lightning. Mel had a T-shirt wrapped around her head against the bugs. She slapped her upper arm and plucked something dead from her skin, said to Nora, 'I don't know how the fuck you can stand living here.'

To which Nora replied, 'Who says I can stand it?'

Anouk dove under again, avoided a stand of water lilies with a few strong frog kicks, then resurfaced and flipped over to float on her back. Pedalling her feet lazily, sculling her hands, she peered up at the sky, so empty that it looked like there were swirling bubbles up there, like water in a pot the instant before boiling. She swam to the ledge of rock at the stern end of the island and pulled herself up, careful not to scrape her shins. The bald rock was sun-warm, and through the arches of her feet, she could feel her island buzz. She stood for a minute, catching her breath, then clambered up the rock, toeing the solid folds between the slabs, to where the island was a soft carpet of copper-coloured pine needles and moss and old leaves like brown paper. The frogs had been prolific this past spring and there was the rock pool in the middle of the island to be visited, amphibians to be counted. She picked two buttercups and a couple of delicate bluebells from the thin island soil, twisted their stems together and tucked the arrangement behind her ear. It was hot. Sweat pricked her itchy scalp. A yellow cricket javelined past her knee and was gone. She practised the fox-walk. Bare heel on the ground first, feeling for sticks or rocks. Roll the outside of the foot into the step and land gently on the ball of the foot. Repeat. Slow and methodical. If she were in a group, each person would step into the others' footprints, like voices overlapping in song. This was the way the first people did it, how they moved undetected through the bush.

In the swampy dip at the centre of the island she parted the cigar-headed bulrushes and squatted by the water, thick with globular algae. Lacy milkweed tickled her thighs; something else pricked underfoot. She became still. At first, nothing. Then she saw them. Seven frogs, no, eight. Silent and cool as marble, heads just visible poking out of puckered water. One, its skin dry and grey, perched regally on a stick. She had named the frogs earlier in the summer, made up stories about them. Wrote these stories down in a little book. The one on the stick, that was Redmond, named after her dad.

'Hello, Redmond,' she said.

What she wrote about Redmond in her little book was this: *Redmond was lonely, being the king. When you're a king, you don't get treated like a person, you get treated like a king.*

On the far side of the island she sat on a submerged sandbar streaked with black, iron-rich sand and clay deposits. The current had carved perfect wavelets into the sandbar, and the shallow water that now flowed over the sand glinted black and grey and gold. Anouk dug her fingers under a tablet of clay and prised it away, clouding the water. She mashed the clay between her palms until it became a paste, then lathered it up and down her arms and legs, across her cheeks and forehead. Left a handprint on her bony breastplate. She climbed on to a ledge of granite, the rock glinting with mica, and stretched out in the sun like a lizard, and soon her skin began to tighten as the clay dried a silvery, flaky blue. Her face a mask. She was island. She was river.

This had been a really bad summer for wasps. Worse than usual. The day after Mel went back to Toronto, Anouk and Nora and Red ate their dinner on the porch, plates of barbecued chicken and the end-of-season peaches 'n' cream corn balancing on their knees. Anouk watched a wasp land on her corn, searching with its antennae. Another two wasps danced around her chicken, bounced off her wrist.

Nora asked Red to install screening around the porch so that the following year, they wouldn't have to put up with all these god-damn wasps. She had been stung twice this summer, she said, and kept finding wasps in her drink cans.

'I'm afraid I'm going to swallow one,' she said.

'Just check the can before you drink,' he said. He swatted at a wasp that was investigating Anouk's hair.

'But I don't want to check the can before I drink.' She brought a cob of corn to her mouth, then put it on her plate again without taking a bite. 'This effing place,' she said. 'Sometimes.'

'Plenty of wasps in Toronto,' he said.

'Did I mention Toronto?'

The next day, Sunday, Anouk went with her mother into Pembroke, to the Canadian Tire, where Nora bought a wasp trap, a little plastic dome shaped like a cartoon hive. Since they were in town, they also stopped by the IGA for groceries, and walking back to the car they passed the movie theatre. Anouk stopped and looked up at the billboard. She called to Nora, already a few shops ahead, asked her to come back.

'Can we see that?' she asked her mother, pointing to the billboard.

'No way.'

'Look. It starts in twenty minutes. Please.'

'I've got milk here.' Nora raised one of the bags from the IGA and gave it an angry little rustle.

'I really want to see this.'

Bag still held aloft, Nora hesitated. Frowned. Anouk knew she had almost won. 'We don't have your Creon. So. No snacks,' she said, and told Anouk to wait while she put the groceries in the car.

Anouk stood under the shade of an awning and kicked off her flip-flop, and poked at a concave piece of glass on the sidewalk with her bare toe. August heat. No wind. Anouk's hair, the deep and layered orange of pottery glaze, was tied back in a long braid. Not a strand moved. The rev of a cicada rose, sawed the air, crescendoed and faded. She imagined that, if you could see this sound, it would spiral tightly into the air like a spark from a campfire, then burst and fizzle and disappear. She ground the glass into the pavement with her toe. On her foot, a black and sweaty band of dirt between her big toe and the next from where her flip-flop rubbed all summer long.

'What are you doing?' A lazy call from across the street.

Anouk looked up. It was Maggie, a girl from school, standing there holding a leash. At the other end of the leash, a small, wiry black dog pissed against a tree.

'Going to a movie.'

Maggie, bug-eyed, glanced briefly at the billboard. 'Seen it.'

Anouk shrugged.

'Aren't you going with anyone?'

'My mom.'

Maggie rolled her bulbous eyes. Rolled them so hard it was a miracle they didn't pop out of their sockets and land in the gutter.

Her dog shook his leg and spun about to sniff his own piss, then dragged at the leash, and Maggie carried on down the road.

'Go fuck yourself,' Anouk whispered.

Almost home, after the movie, Nora pulled off the paved road and on to the dirt track that rolled through the woods to their house. She stopped the car. Without discussion, she and Anouk got out and switched seats. Anouk put the car in gear and slowly drove, neck stretched to see out of the window. The woods here, delicate and mixed: thin-trunked maple saplings and jaunty, soft-needled pines. Silver birch trees peeling curls of papery bark to reveal salmon-pink flesh underneath. Anouk crept along the track, not wanting to kill a rabbit, a mouse. Not wanting to kill a garter snake or chipmunk or anything else. Halfway home, she stopped the car with a jolt and pointed out an oasis of sunlight a few metres into the woods, where a colony of buttercups grew in a patch of grass.

'Pretty,' she said.

'Come on. I need to get this milk in the fridge.'

At home, Anouk helped Nora set up the wasp trap. They poured cola into the tray at its base and hung the trap from a hook screwed into the top of the porch overhang. The trap was punctured with funnelled holes that tapered towards the inside of the dome. The idea was that the wasps would fly into the holes, attracted by the sugar in the cola and, once inside, wouldn't be able to get back out.

'Ingenious,' Nora said, standing back to admire her work.

'I think it's mean,' Anouk said.

'You've never been stung.'

'I don't think Dad will like it.'

Nora looked at her. Looked at her for a long time.

'What?' said Anouk.

'You and your dad,' said Nora.

'What?'

24

'Nothing.'

After a couple of days, Anouk inspected the trap. It was carnage. Most of the fated wasps were still alive, some boxing apoplectically against the inner walls of the dome, which was now sweaty with condensation. Others drifted drunkenly against each other. The tray at the bottom was a sluggish mixture of body parts and sugar.

She watched another wasp as it worked its way into a funnel, busily scrabbling its strong legs, its black-and-golden abdomen striped and sleek and doomed.

5

L'Inconnue
Paris, 1898

THE GARE DE Lyon grumbled and steamed. The train heaved into the station and I disembarked, my carpet bag light enough to be carried by one hand. It was a Wednesday afternoon and travellers swarmed the station, not just people from France but from other places as well. The platform clanged with languages I didn't understand, tongues rolling backwards, guttural sounds shifting in the throat like stones. Baffling combinations of consonants. A short, dark man who spoke French with a foreign accent offered to sell me a miniature wooden omnibus from a collection of buses and carts and coaches lined up on his stall table. He showed no emotion when I declined. A Roma woman pirouetted up and down the platform selling silk scarves. Perhaps fifty of them fluttered from her swiftly moving arms, the colours so bright and loud and uncoordinated it was as if the scarves were shouting. There was the smell of coal from the trains but there was also some other kind of burning, and there was the smell of wool, of perspiration and perfume.

The instructions Madame Debord had written to me in her final letter were to wait on the platform for the cocher, who would take me in his cab to her apartment building. He would be carrying a sign with my name written on it. I positioned myself so that my back was against an iron column, and waited, rubbing my thumb over the round, solid face of a rivet. Two well-dressed men passed by, very close, gesticulating aggressively. One of them knocked my bag to the ground with his elbow and didn't bother to stop. As I bent to collect it, I was approached by a man with no legs. He wheeled himself over on a small wooden platform, dirt-black rags wrapped thickly around his palms and up over his wrists. He smelled like piss and rot but had a friendly, gap-toothed smile. His thick black hair shone with grease and he spoke with a drooling crook at the side of his mouth.

'I apologize, Mademoiselle, for the indecency of those fellows.' His voice was an eloquent, dignified slur.

'Thank you,' I said, remaining crouched close to the floor. I was aware of the skirts and boots and trouser legs that flowed around us, but thought that to stand would be unkind. The man entwined his fingers across his chest and tapped his thumbs together, raised his chin and smiled, lids heavy over his dark eyes.

'We're not all as hostile as that.'

'I'm sure,' I said.

'First time to Paris?'

I nodded.

'Betrothed?'

'No.'

'Here to work, then. To make your small way in the big world.' He looked at my hat, at the cut of my coat. 'Shop girl,' he said, still smiling, 'or seamstress. Perhaps a lady's companion.'

I nodded at his last guess, amused.

'I couldn't think of a more uninspiring position than the lady's companion,' he said, 'but likely an improvement from whatever situation it is you've left.'

'Well.' My legs were going numb.

He continued to stare at me, and I felt obliged to open my bag and reach for the small satchel of money I carried. I took out a few sous and offered them to him. He rotated his hands to make a bowl shape, his fingers having already been laced together, and into this I dropped the coins. He then did the most amazing contortion with his arms, a sort of figure-of-eight twist where his hands disappeared into the folds of his ragged clothing, then came out empty.

I stood then, and with the straightening of my legs, the blood rushed to my feet. I felt as if I might topple over.

He began to turn his trolley and move away. 'Adieu,' he said, and made as if to tip his hat, though he wore none. As soon as he'd gone, swallowed up by commuters, I wondered if I'd imagined him.

The cocher and I soon found one another. He took my bag and bade me to follow him quickly through the station. His cab stood in the street, lined up in a row with several others, the horses lean and tired and resigned. It had rained earlier in the day and the hem of my skirt drew mud, but the sun was out now, its light reflecting off the limestone buildings. As soon as I was seated in the carriage we were underway. I stared out of the window like a baby peeking from its pram. Clermont-Ferrand was sizeable enough but this was my first city, and it was Paris. Stuck behind an endless line of omnibuses and carts and other cabs, we crawled slowly along Avenue Daumensil, towards Place de la Bastille. People were everywhere, everywhere. Women with babies, and girls hurrying with parcels stuck importantly under their arms. Slick, clever-eyed street merchants and workmen dusty with the remnants of hard labour. Gentlemen who seemed to just be strolling, doing nothing, stopping in the middle of the crowd to look in a shop window. These men seemed wholly unconcerned by anything, anything at all. All the cafes were full. Waiters pranced among outdoor tables, clearing cups away and setting down dishes of food. Women chirped to each other across the open air from every other balcony. On one corner, a group of elderly men had set up a semicircle of chairs, and seemed to sit and speak as casually as if they were in a parlour at home. Looking down a smaller street to my left, I thought I saw a dwarf-man riding a tricycle, but lost him in the crowd before I could be sure. Moments later I thought I saw Tante Huguette coming out of a milliner's, black lace up to her chin, but was of course mistaken.

Chestnut trees, gregarious with white blossoms, lined the avenue, and there was the perfume of a dozen flower stalls and the stink of mud and yeast and horse. At the steps of the Colonne de Juillet, a newspaper kiosk thrummed with people. On the Rue de Rivoli, a gleam of wealth I couldn't quite comprehend. The cream-white facades of the buildings, decorated with rosettes and vines and other ornate carvings I didn't have the language to describe, and the heads of gods and saints propped these buildings up, under mansard roofs of storm-grey slate. The northern sky beyond was almost the same colour as the slate, though darker, richer, and to the east the sky was a washed-out blue.

We eventually turned into a warren of smaller streets barely wide enough to accommodate two passing carriages, where there was less light and the noise was more acute. The whipping and snorting of horses and the creak of wooden wheels, the frustrations of a baby, the clattering of dishes. Boots on cobbles and someone with a wet, chesty cough. I lost all sense of direction as we turned several tight corners and finally stopped in front of the gated entrance to a courtyard, the courtyard hemmed by blocks of apartments six storeys high. Flower boxes hung off balconies; gas lights perched on flourished iron brackets, waiting for the dark. No dung in the road and a narrow, paved walk on one side.

Without dismounting, my cocher called out, 'Le cordon, s'il vous plaît,' and after a moment, by some unseen hand, the heavy bolt that had lain across the gate to the courtyard was lifted by cord and pulley. The cocher hopped down from his platform and pushed the gate open, then climbed back up and we advanced through the porte cochère. The courtyard was just big enough for him to turn his carriage, which he did before helping me out with my bag. Without a word, he climbed back up on his cab and was gone.

I stood unmoving, unsure at first what to do. The only other person in the courtyard was a young boy, dressed in thin but well-maintained clothes, filling a bucket with water from a communal tap.

At ground level, the buildings housed spaces of commerce: a wool carder, a milliner and a stationer. Clerical offices and an atelier for leatherworks. Next to the porte cochère, the office of the concierge. I approached the door and rang the bell. The man who answered reminded me of something fungal, mushroomy: grey skin that looked like it might darken and take the impression of your fingers if you applied pressure for too long. He was very short, and had a conical, bald head and the attitude of one who would prefer the dark and damp. Under a log, say. He motioned me inside, and returned to his position behind a tall wooden counter with nothing on it but a brass bell and heavy ledger.

I handed him my letter from Madame Debord and he looked down his stubby nose at it, took his time reading. Behind him, a wooden rack on the wall with several numbered slots stacked with letters. From the ceiling there draped an iron chain on a pulley and this, I assumed, was the mechanism for opening the gate.

'Has Mademoiselle journeyed far today?' the concierge asked, looking not at me but out of the window.

'Not far.'

'Where has Mademoiselle travelled from?'

I told him where I was from, though I could see from the flatness of his expression that he'd only asked for asking's sake. He pointed me to a stairwell, directing me to go up one flight to the second floor. I collected my bag and headed up the stairwell, which was narrow and smelled vaguely of onion broth and tobacco, but was well lit with gas lamps. The paint on the walls was fresh. On Madame Debord's door, a small brass plaque engraved with her name. I knocked twice, rapid and light. Quick footsteps and the door was answered by a girl only a few years younger than me, about fifteen years old. Her hair was twisted in a loose chignon at the base of her neck and she wore a simple cotton dress.

'It's you,' she whispered, and waved me into the vestibule with a jerk of the hand, then disappeared behind the vestibule door. I remained there, holding my bag against my knees. A gilded clock ticked loudly on a marble-topped side table. The girl came back carrying a laundry sack over her shoulder.

'Madame is having a nap but she'll wake in an hour. She'll want coffee and something sweet. You'll find what you need in the kitchen.' Without looking at me, she backed through the door and pulled it softly shut.

The clock ticked. To my left, a corridor with four closed doors and a kitchen at its end. From behind the door closest to the vestibule, gentle snoring, like a nesting pigeon. To my right, an oval mirror. I removed my hat and hung it from a hook next to the mirror, where other hats and scarves were hanging. My face shone with the grime of travel and my hair was a state, so I dropped my bag to the floor and tried to smooth it with my palms. This only made things worse.

I stepped out of the vestibule into the salon, which was high ceilinged and decorated with yellow wallpaper. Two tall windows adorned with heavy, dusty drapes. The room was comfortable, and not so choked with the gilt and knick-knackery I had been anticipating. Two simple settees and footstools, an odd collection of armchairs whose upholstery didn't match and yet, somehow, still looked tasteful. A mahogany writing desk by the window and faded, silk-covered cushions on the settees. All the cornicing that was to be expected and a large mirror above the marble fireplace. An expensive but worn rug on a tired parquet floor that could do with a waxing. A chandelier. Something peculiar too: piles of newspapers stacked into the corners of the room, under the side tables and up against some of the furniture. Some piles partially avalanched, others weighted down with heavy glass ornaments. The newspaper on the top of the pile closest to me was dated only two days prior. I made my way through the room to one of the windows and pulled back the drape. Outside, flower boxes of pink and red geraniums, slightly gone to seed and with the woody, arthritic stalks of an unpruned plant that had survived at least one winter.

At the far end of the salon lay a small dining room with a table big enough for six, a table that appeared vast and out of place as there were only two chairs. A glass-fronted cabinet filled with fine dishes and some tarnished silver. Two portraits in oil on the wall, darkly shaded.

I went back through the salon and vestibule, and down the corridor to the small kitchen. Copper pots, also tarnished, hung from hooks on the wall. There was a dark-grey cast-iron stove and oven, with four burners in various sizes to hold saucepans and casseroles. I opened the oven door and saw that it was fuelled by gas rather than wood – a novelty for me. A porcelain sink and lead tap with running water. The tap needed a polish. On the counter, a set of pewter canisters lined up by size. I lifted the hinged lid from the largest one: coffee beans. Others held hunks of sugar, salt, pepper, nutmeg, dried thyme and mace. The spices were old and ashy and only faintly aromatic.

The kitchen window overlooked the courtyard, and I glanced out and saw two men standing in the corner smoking pipes. One of the men looked up at me and I ducked. Under the window, the garde manger, breezy with the air that flowed through its open slats, where Madame had stored a jug of milk, some raw meat wrapped in waxed paper that looked a little suspect, a tomato and half an onion.

On the wall under the cupboards, a dark bruise of damp in the plaster. I pressed my finger to it, and it gave way softly and there was the fusty smell of mould. I located the coffee pot and searched the cupboards for something sugary, and found, to my delight, a tin of bergamot sweets. I stuck one amber crystal under my tongue and wandered back down the corridor, opened the door to the WC. A simple porcelain toilet decorated with fine blue flowers. I balled my fists, happy and a little giddy at the thought of having a flush toilet just down the hall from where I slept. In the bathroom, a sink adorned with the same blue flowers, an enamelled bathtub and gas water heater, which consisted of a copper chimney with a tap running into the bathtub. A water heater! I couldn't believe my luck.

I went back to the salon and sat in an armchair and waited. From the apartment across the road, the hard rainfall of a piano being played mezzo-forte. There was wealth here, more than I had ever known, but neglect, too. Only a few weeks would have passed since Madame's other girl had left the position, but the apartment was muted by a layer of dust that looked much older than that.

I knew almost nothing about Madame Debord, had only vague memories of my grandmother travelling to see her in Paris when I was very young. I remembered that there had once been a visit planned, when Madame Debord was going to come and stay with us, and that it had to be cancelled due to her poor health.

She woke up perhaps two hours later with a hoarse cough, just after 6 p.m. I hadn't been asleep, but I hadn't been entirely awake either, and I sat forward with a start, opening my eyes to an unfamiliar room that had become cut with shadow by the obtuse light of a spring evening. I rose quickly and stumbled, knocking my shin on a footstool, and, comically, propelled myself through the vestibule to the first door in the hallway. I knocked lightly.

'Audette?' Madame called, her voice tight, like wind passing through a tunnel.

I opened the door and stood at the threshold. The blinds were closed and the room so dark that Madame would have only been able to see my silhouette. I considered pretending to be Audette (whom I assumed, correctly, was the laundry girl who had let me into the apartment) to save her a shock.

The rasp of her breathing, then, stuttered again, 'Audette?'

I took a step into the room. 'It's me, Madame Debord,' I said, and whispered my name.

Shuffling blankets. Another, weaker cough. A match was struck and a lamp next to the bed was lit and there she was, propped upright, half sunk into a large pillow on a canopied bed that was partially recessed into the wall. She'd pulled the blankets up and was clutching them under her chin, and a cap was perched on her high forehead. She was petite and had glinting eyes, like those of a field mouse or squirrel.

'Did Audette let you in? Did you lock the door behind her?'

'I didn't,' I said. 'Shall I go and lock it now?'

'Always lock the door,' she said. 'The family who live on the third floor are Russian, and they are thieves. I'm sure of it. And that concierge, Monsieur Muller. He can't be trusted either. He holds back the post and he's cheap. I've been at him to repair the wall in my kitchen for over a year but he refuses.'

'He did look the type,' I said.

Her hard eyes widened with the surprise, I thought, of someone who was accustomed to being pooh-poohed. She nodded curtly.

'Will Madame take her coffee in bed?' I asked, assuming this was what I was expected to ask.

'Absolutely not,' she said. 'Lock the door, then come and help me dress and we'll take our coffee in the salon.'

The girl who had been my predecessor was, apparently, also a thief. Madame Debord confessed that she had lied when she'd written in her letter that the girl's position had been terminated because of a marriage proposal. In truth, I found out now, Madame had given her the sack because she'd been stealing. She didn't want to alarm me, she explained, by writing about the duplicitous sorts of people I might encounter in Paris, so she'd lied. When she told me this, as we sipped coffee in the sitting room with a deck of cards on the table that never got dealt, with the sky darkening and my stomach rumbling and no mention of an evening meal, she did not apologize for the fiction.

'What did she steal?' I asked.

'A silver salt cellar, which belonged to my mother. She also helped herself to a small sum of money. And I'm quite sure a pair of silk stockings.'

'How awful.'

'She took the spoon too. The one that belonged to the salt cellar. It was lovely. The spoon part of the spoon was scalloped and inlaid with gold.'

'I'm so sorry.'

'Trust is foolhardy,' she said.

I nodded.

'Believe me.'

My job was simple. I was to help Madame dress in the mornings and fix her petit déjeuner of milky coffee and toasted bread, sometimes a plate of fruit. Madame seldom left the apartment so it was up to me to buy the food, daily. We ate simply. Omelettes, crusty bread and cheese, charcuterie, beef stews, cassoulet, lamb's tongue on toast and fish with butter sauce. Or, what grew to be my favourite, garlic and bread soup. I cooked a little but Madame preferred food bought in shops and restaurants and carried home. She loved sweet things, pastries with cream and jam, candied fruit, tarts and confectionery. She loved cognacs and wine and sugary coffee with brandy. You could see these indulgences in her face – a soft, shiny richness to her skin, her plump jowls. More important to Madame than food, however, was the accounts book she insisted I keep. When her husband, who had been a partner in a trading firm that dealt in textiles and apparel, was still alive, she employed a cook, who, apparently, had been skimming francs off the top for years. Madame was convinced that no one but herself was above slipping a few unearned sous into their pockets. I kept a detailed tally of every centime she gave me and every centime I spent, and each evening after supper we went over these sums together. Sometimes, when I came back from buying food or medicine or newspapers, it was obvious that my dresser drawers had been inspected, the blanket pulled back on the bed and the pillows disturbed. The little drawer in the bedside table was sometimes left ajar. She was searching my room, and wanted me to know it.

Evenings, we played cards; we played dominoes. She drank a lot of wine and expected me to partake, so I partook, diluting my glass with water. She sat at the window and sometimes I wrote to Tante Huguette. I didn't recognize this at first but came to see after a few months that my letters to her were a test, to see if she would write back, not just to acknowledge the small portion of my wages I regularly sent, but to see if I was missing from her life. She did respond, a couple of times. She wrote that she was pleased to know I was making something of myself and that now, with my contributions added to the income she was earning from my vacated room, she had been granted relief. Tremendous relief, in fact, was what she wrote.

Madame had no visitors. No invitations. She owned no books

but was a fool for the gossip and sensation of the newspapers and the serialized dramas of les feuilletons. When I asked her about the newspapers stacked around the apartment, she told me they were to be taken to the butcher and sold for five centimes a kilogram. Madame Debord didn't need extra money, from what I could tell. Her husband had left her plenty and the partners in his firm faithfully sent her a small monthly dividend. But she was frugal, her clothes and furnishings years out of date. The apartment was in dire need of new wallpaper and paint. Or at least a good cleaning. When I suggested to her that maybe Audette, who lived with her mother in one of the small loft apartments, would do a good job at cleaning, she said Audette couldn't be trusted with anything more valuable than a soiled chemise. So, without being asked, I performed some light cleaning as well. Under surveillance, naturally.

Despite Madame's late, two-hour nap, which she took daily from 4 to 6 p.m., her bedtime was precisely nine-thirty. She asked only that I sit by her while she drank her warm brandy and fell asleep, which never took more than five or ten minutes. After that, the evenings were my own. I would turn down all the gas lamps in the salon and place a candle on the side table next to my favourite armchair, by the window. I would sit quietly. All day there was noise, either from the piano across the street or from a heated debate in the apartment above us. Always someone washing dishes, always feet on the stairs. From outside, the horse whip, the newspaper seller, someone hawking some new gadget one could not possibly live without. And laughter. People in Paris laughed endlessly. Not always mirthfully. But at night, in that narrow corner of the city, there was the hush that followed the end of noise, after the lamps were extinguished. I liked to stare out of the window at the darkness, the lack of light like a salve to my tired eyes. Sometimes I reread the day's papers – mainly gossip, mainly grisly.

Twice a week I helped Madame Debord bathe. It turned out the water heater that I had been so excited about leaked gas and wasn't safe to use, and Madame didn't think it necessary to spend the money to fix it. So I had to heat her water the regular way, on the stove. I had helped my grandmother to bathe so this wasn't new to me, but Madame hadn't been looking after herself at all and the first time, it took me an hour of scrubbing to remove the dead skin from her elbows and feet, to remove a black, gummy matter that had collected in the creases under her breasts. I could take care of her hair myself, but I convinced her to call in a manicurist, at least just the once, for her finger- and toenails.

I loved running errands outside the apartment. It was spring and Paris was blooming. Tree blossoms rained on to the boulevards and flowers spilled from stalls on so many street corners, and the people – those who had the means to do so – dressed in colours a little more fantastic than real. Rosy-cheeked and flamboyant in skirt and hat. Shiny shoes fresh from the cobbler. Ribbons, scarves and lace. Foreigners wore clothing I didn't then recognize: the turban, the fez. Scottish tartan and the embroidered Spanish cloak.

I meandered between boucherie and boulangerie and charcuterie. I varied my routes to get a taste of different parts of the city. I had to take care though. Madame grew anxious if I was gone for too long. Once, as I had just come in and was hanging my hat in the vestibule, she told me that she had become convinced I'd absconded with the day's food allowance and was only just, moments before I came through the door, preparing to go downstairs and ask Monsieur Muller to alert the gendarme. After that, when I left each morning, she got into the habit of leaning from the balcony of her bedroom and watching me walk down the road. I would turn and smile and wave, several times, until I reached the corner. Often, when I came home, she would be there again, waiting. Her claim was that she was out getting some air, but I knew better.

Paris, however, provided me with endless excuses for being late:

a dead horse in the middle of the road stopping traffic, construction, a crowd gathered around a fire eater or contortionist. A student protest, hundreds of young men marching, blocking the intersections, waving flags and singing 'La Marseillaise'. I had to detour, I would tell her. I couldn't face the crowds. Felt overwhelmed and had to sit down. She was very sympathetic.

It didn't matter that I couldn't afford entry to the theatres on the Boulevard des Italiens or Montmartre or any of the others. The streets were spectacular enough. A string quartet amongst the cafe tables, a man coming out of a courtyard on stilts, his face covered in blue grease. Vaudeville in the Place de la République. A woman in stage rags, her face grimy with charcoal, singing a gut-twisting aria under the glass-topped acoustics of a dark passage, pigeons cooing and shitting on the steel rafters above.

One morning in June, my basket heavy with bread, cheese, a bag of assorted sweets and a litre of wine, I stopped to watch a clairvoyant on the Rue de Rivoli, not far from the Hôtel de Ville. She sat stiffly on a tiny stool hidden by her skirt, her eyes blindfolded with a black kerchief. Her curly hair was unnaturally red and her neck queerly long, and she wore a simple yellow dress. Her companion, a much older man with a waxed moustache and an oily, black beard, walked amongst the crowd. He wore a smart purple jacket, too big, and under that a red waistcoat. Two young women who stood very near me, both leaning against bicycles, called out to him and he did a hop, a little half-twirl, and approached them. One of them dropped a few coins into the small wooden box he carried and the crowd hushed. He called to his lady in the yellow dress.

'Will Madame describe the person I'm standing next to?'

The clairvoyant sat straighter still and lifted her head, her odd neck extending. She brought one long-fingered hand up to her throat and placed it there in a kind of loose stranglehold, and thrummed her fingers just below the ear. She spoke calmly and with a foreign accent. I suspected her hair was a wig. 'She wears a heather blouse with blue stripes. An oyster-white skirt and wide black belt. A black ribbon adorns her hat.' She raised her hand to hush the crowd, which was now gasping. After a moment, she spoke again. 'Her bicycle is black. It once had a bell affixed to the front handlebars, but the bell became defunct so she removed it.'

People around the girl looked to her for confirmation. Her face had gone white and she was nodding, clutching the arm of her friend. The sound of hammering could be heard from somewhere else. The bell of a passing omnibus. No one spoke.

'Would Mademoiselle care to know her fortune?' the man prompted, jangling his box below the poor girl's nose. 'Only a sou. Always true.' Caught in the wax of his moustache, a crumb.

'She only wants to know one thing!' her friend honked, releasing another coin into the wooden box. The crowd laughed, perhaps relieved that some black-magic spell had been broken.

The girl gave her friend an elbow to the ribs, but faced the man with her chin up, determined. 'Should I or should I not accept the proposal I received just yesterday?'

The crowd jittered. The man held up his hand for silence and the people obeyed, and he turned to the clairvoyant, whose hand was again poised at her own throat.

'Yes,' she said. 'And there will be children. The first to be born in the autumn of next year.'

I left this debacle, smirking, anxious to bring Madame her lunch.

6

Nora
Ottawa River, 1977

NORA NAMED HER daughter Anouk two days after she was born, and by the fourth day she and her husband Red knew something was wrong with their child. She wasn't feeding, and had not yet passed the green-black sludge Nora was expecting, had read about. Meconium: earliest stool. Tar-like, odourless, composed of materials ingested in utero.

They went to the doctor in Pembroke, and were sent to the children's hospital a few hours away in Ottawa. Anouk was given a blood test, a cruel pinprick to her heel, purple and round as a plum. She was given a test where a gel was applied to her thigh to make her sweat, and her sweat collected by a square of paper so they could test its level of chloride.

Nora said to Red, while they waited for their baby to wake up from the surgery that was needed to remove the dry rocks of meconium and cut out a dying twist of bowel, Nora said: 'This is like that dream you have, when you can't get anywhere; the one where you're trying to run but your legs just won't.'

Red wasn't able to say much at all.

The test results came back, and Nora and Red learned this: they were both carriers of a faulty gene. When their child was conceived, she inherited this gene from both of them. Having this faulty gene meant that the mucus secretions in Anouk's lungs and pancreas were thicker than they were supposed to be. Her pancreas wasn't able to produce the enzymes her body needed to absorb the food she ate – she was getting very little nutrition. She cried all the time because she was always hungry. This faulty gene meant that the thread-like hairs in the branched pathways of her lungs, the cilia, were sticky and matted together, harbouring bacteria, trapping fluids, almost as if she were drowning. Her life would be marked by coughing fits, lung infections, malnutrition. A daily regime of antibiotics and physiotherapy, and later a nebulizing machine that would allow her to inhale her medications by mist. The condition was called cystic fibrosis and her life expectancy was twenty-six years.

After the surgery, Anouk stayed in the hospital until her bowels worked the way they were supposed to. This took two weeks. Nora pumped her breast milk and Anouk was fed safe, enzyme-rich food through a tube in her nose. People came to speak to Nora. This was a whole new education. She was visited by a CF specialist, a dietician, a psychologist and physiotherapist. This seemed an initiation. This esoteric world, and all those who populated it, had been there all along, and now Nora and Red and their baby were a part of it but their arrival hadn't made so much as a ripple. No one had been surprised or even impressed to see them. No one said: Hey, you're not supposed to be here, or, this shouldn't be happening to you. After two weeks in hospital, Anouk passed some kind of yellow jelly and the intensive care nurses said that was good, she could go home. Nora and Red were taught how to cup their hands and hit their baby on her chest, under her arms and around her back. This loosened and dislodged the gunk in her lungs, made it easier for her to cough the stuff out. Twice a day, five minutes each time. They had to be careful of bruising, of breaking a rib. They were shown how to lace fruit puree with tiny balls of Creon, the acid enzyme she would need to digest food. If they weren't careful, the Creon would burn her mouth.

When they took Anouk home from the hospital, Nora said, 'This is a different baby than the one we had two weeks ago.'

And Red said, 'No. She's the same. Everything else has changed.'

7

Pieter
Stavanger, 1951

MY SON. MY BEAR. There was a time, before you and your sister came along, when your mother and I didn't think we were going to get our family. We tried and we tried and nothing ever came of it. Your mother's heart was broken and I was just angry. After a while, you begin to accept your lot because there's nothing else you can do, and you learn to rewrite your future. And then, after almost eight years of trying, there was Tilda. And then not even two years later, you. You were born in the late summer of 1951 and I was not in the room with your mother when you drew your first, rattling breath. I was made to wait in some kind of family lounge. Your sister had been left with neighbours.

Your coming was long and it was complicated, which was unexpected – Tilda had been so straightforward. The first labour stabs came at three in the morning. Your mother woke me. She sat straight up in bed and spoke clearly, as if she hadn't been asleep at all. She ordered me to collect your sister and the bags and to meet her in the front hall.

It wasn't until the following evening that you finally emerged, grey and floppy, your mother later told me, as a dead frog. Your heart rate was low and each breath a task. Before she had a chance to see you properly, you were taken to the other end of the room and surrounded by medical staff. With rapid pulses, the doctor compressed your chest until your breathing became regular. In essence, he breathed for you, mechanically, until you could breathe on your own. You and your mother stayed in hospital for a week before we were able to take you home.

You were not an easy baby.

For two years we didn't sleep. You made sure of that. And you were tense. You were like – you were like grinding teeth. You were like a cramp in the calf muscle. All of this burden rested with your mother and for most of that time she was irritated with me, and with Tilda. And with you. I did what I always did when life became hard. I vacated. Our toy manufacturer was only just operating out of a simple factory; we hadn't yet branched away from Stavanger. But the company was growing, so it was easy to find reasons to stay away from home. I set up a bed in the back office and slept in it often, and I can tell you, it became a comfort to wake up to the smell of wood shavings, to wake up to the smell of glue and paint and the labours of craftsmen.

Once, I don't know how long I'd been away, maybe it was three or four nights, I returned to a house that was dark and quiet. It was early evening, late November, more than a year after your birth. It had been snowing all day and the world was quiet; the world was dusk-blue and crystalline. I was thinking I would help your mother by wrapping you and Tilda up snug and taking you both for a night walk. There was a hill not far from our house that was ideal for sledding. I'd already seen children on it a few minutes before, when I drove past; dark, thick-limbed creatures tumbling all over the face of the slope, screaming in the near dark.

So it was this I was thinking of as I opened the front door: taking you out with the sled. But the house was cold to the bone; the radiators had not been turned on for days. I called into the dark

45

even though I knew the house was empty. I looked on the kitchen table for a note and found no note. Your mother often took you to stay with her parents so I called there first, but they hadn't heard from her. I tried the neighbours. I tried our friends. No one knew where my family was.

What could I do? I turned on the heat and put the kettle on the stove. I sat at the kitchen table and leafed through a pile of unopened mail. This silent house that was usually clamorous with child-cry and footsteps pounding on stairs, with various objects being drummed upon and the hiss of a hot iron over cotton, the silence of this house was disconcerting. Where was my family? The silence perched on my shoulders and blew into my ear. It lifted the hairs at the back of my neck. It ticked.

After I don't know how long, I became hungry. The refrigerator contained a bottle of milk that had gone off and a hard block of cheese and a half-eaten loaf of soda bread. Cold stew gone fuzzy in a cold pot. I opened a can of oily smoked mussels and stood crookedly over the kitchen counter, spooning the mussels on to crackers and taking bites out of a wedge of the hard cheese. Dribbling oil down the front of my shirt.

I left crumbs everywhere and eventually shuffled up the stairs to bed, warming myself under the blankets with the heat of my own body.

Three more days your mother stayed away. No phone call, no letter. I thought about calling the police, but I knew I was being punished. I knew you were safe somewhere. For the first two days, I came home early from my work, expecting to find our house warm again and with a pulse. On the third day, driving past the sledding hill, I decided that I would go to your grandparents and confront them, confront your mother, because I was certain you were all there.

But you were home. She had come back. I knew this before I

pulled into the driveway, because once again the windows were lit and smoke rose from the chimney. One of Tilda's snow boots lay on the front walk and I knew why. She would have thrown one of her tantrums and had to have been dragged by the armpit from your grandfather's car and into the house.

I opened the door to the sound of your braying and to the smell of onions being fried in butter. Tilda had barricaded herself behind a wall of cushions on the floor in the front room and you were in your high chair at the kitchen table, your face shiny and red from crying, chewed pieces of carrot drying in your hair. Your mother stood at the stove, drawing a wooden spoon slowly around the pan of onions in a kitchen that was steamed with heat and fry and noise. The radio was on but I don't remember what was playing. It was just on.

'Merete,' I said.

She continued to stir.

'Tilda's boot was outside,' I said.

'She didn't want to come in.'

'That's what I thought.'

Your mother swayed in motion with the wooden spoon.

'How are your parents?' I asked.

'I wouldn't know.'

'Isn't that where you were?'

She laid the spoon aside and forked slices of gammon into the pan; she hissed and rubbed vigorously at her forearm with the back of her wrist where a spit of grease had landed.

We ate our meal in silence. I, with you in my lap, tolerating you even when you dug your pudgy hands into the food on my plate and threw it to the floor. I put Tilda to bed with a story while your mother bathed you and soothed you to sleep.

In the darkness of our room, your mother and I alone in our bed, I turned to her with intimacy and an acknowledgement that

47

the fault was mine. She took from me that night, with her body, in a way she hadn't before and wouldn't ever again. Afterwards, I searched for her but, even pressed against me, she was missing. It was clear she wasn't going to tell me where she'd been for those three days, or however long it was you'd been gone. Not that night or any other. For me, for the time being at least, it was enough to know and to be humbled by the knowledge of what I had come so close to losing for good.

8

Anouk
Ottawa River, 1987

ANOUK LAY PROSTRATE on The Cheese, a triangular wedge of hard yellow foam. With her hips elevated and her head down, she lay patiently while Red drummed with cupped palms up and down her back, between her shoulder blades. On the floor just by her head, a white, plastic cup. When she felt the urge to cough, she pushed herself up, coughed, and spat thick, sand-coloured sputum into the cup. She showed it to Red.

'We can get more out,' he said.

She bent again over The Cheese and propped her chin in her hands and looked out of the window to the yard where Nora was hanging wet towels on the line, which had been strung on pulleys from a tree to the house. It was early morning and sun hadn't yet hit the line; in the shade, the crisp white towels looked blue. Everything Anouk saw was distorted, jumpy, because of the pounding on her back, so Nora looked almost puppet-like, or robotic, pulling another towel out of the basket and snapping the wrinkles out of it and securing it to the line with two pegs. She advanced the line forward and there was the raking squeak of the pulley mechanism, loud enough for Anouk to hear through the window. Another wad of phlegm was working its way into the bottom of her throat. She

49

tensed her shoulders and her father stopped pounding. She spat into the cup again, showed him.

'Gorgeous,' he said.

Anouk stood up. 'Am I done?'

'You feel clear?'

'I guess.' She went outside and sat on the edge of the porch with her toes in the cool morning grass and watched her mother. Nora in jeans that had been cut off at the knees and a ribbed red halter top.

The tight sigh of the screen door opening behind her. 'Anouk,' Red said. 'Come on.'

He wasn't finished with her yet. In the kitchen there was a cupboard for Anouk's drugs. Neatly stacked white boxes with generic labels, enzymes and antibiotics and vitamins. Red rinsed the spit cup in the sink and turned it over to dry on the windowsill. He handed her a glass of water and a small bowl of pills. Variously coloured tablets of penicillin derivatives. She could swallow three pills in one go. Red prepared her enzymes, pulling apart five of the large, dark-green capsules of Creon and emptying the granules into a bowl. He mixed the granules with a generous slug of maple syrup and stirred. Anouk poured a bowl of cereal and put a chocolate muffin on a plate, always encouraged to eat foods that would help to fatten her up.

'Eat it all,' said Red, putting the dish of maple syrup on the table in front of her, handing her a teaspoon.

Even doused in sweet, thick syrup, some of the bitter granules stuck in her teeth and she worked them out with her tongue before they could dissolve and burn her gums.

Nora came into the kitchen, hands in her hair, twisting a bun on top of her head.

'You ready?' Red asked Anouk. He was packing a bag for the day: two water bottles and a box of pills, some fruit and cookies wrapped in foil.

'We'll be out of your way soon,' he said to Nora.

'You're not in the way,' she said.

At any given time, at least one room in their house was in a state of flux. That summer it was the kitchen. The robin's-egg blue on the walls was to be sanded in preparation for some other colour – Nora hadn't yet decided between a mustard yellow or just straight-up white. She was also restoring the cupboard doors and had stripped the tiles off the floor. Was considering a new set of taps.

The dust wasn't good for Anouk, so Red was taking her out for the day. For the work, Nora had recruited Jody, a friend they'd known for as long as they'd lived on the river.

'Do you know where that box of sandpaper is?' Nora asked. 'It wasn't in the shed.'

'It is in the shed.'

'Nope. Just looked.'

'I saw it two days ago.'

Nora shrugged.

Red made a move for the door.

'Don't you dare look in that shed,' said Nora. 'I'm telling you it's not there. Could it be in the basement?'

'It's in the shed,' Red called over his shoulder, as the screen door slammed behind him.

Nora leaned against the kitchen counter and crossed her arms over her chest. She frown-smiled at Anouk. Anouk knew, as necessary as the sandpaper was, her mother did not want her father to find it in the shed. Her mom was like a fish swimming against the current.

Nora spooned coffee grounds into a paper cone and put the cone in the coffee maker and pushed a button, slipped two pieces of bread into the toaster.

Anouk watched Red stride back across the lawn, empty-handed.

'I'm sure I saw that box the other day,' he said, coming into the

51

kitchen. He was slowly scratching his beard, the place he often looked for what bamboozled him.

Nora reached for the telephone mounted on the wall and dialled. The toast popped.

'Who're you calling?' Red asked.

'Jody might have some.'

Red smiled at Anouk. 'Got your shoes?'

Nora hung up the phone. 'He's not answering.'

'I'll pick some up for you,' said Red. 'I'll go now.'

'You'll be nearly an hour there and back.'

'Well.'

'This is stupid. There was a whole box. It's here somewhere.'

'I'll just go,' said Red, flipping his Toronto Blue Jays cap on to his head. He gave the peak a little shuffle left and right before settling it in the middle, the hair at the back of his head sloping into its usual ducktail.

'Red,' huffed Nora, staring into the sink.

As promised, Red returned less than an hour later with sandpaper, and now he and Anouk were bumping along a dirt road towards the home of Red's friend Fraser. Fraser was American. He was one of the draft dodgers Nora and Red had met in Toronto, and now he lived here and operated a sugar shack, where he boiled sugar-maple sap into syrup. Anouk's favourite time to visit the shack was late March, or early April, when the nights were still freezing but the days brought on the thaw. In those months, the sap flowed the clearest and with the greatest pressure from the trees, and that was when Fraser tapped them with metal spiles, collecting the sap in aluminum buckets that hung from hooks nailed into the trees. He tapped until the leaf buds unfurled. Over wood-fuelled fires in the shack he boiled the sap in stainless-steel vats, and the smoke, sometimes backlit from the sun and rimmed so fiercely with light it almost looked like the smoke itself was on fire, that smoke would rise up into the blue sky over the naked black branches of the sugar maples. That was when the snow was the prettiest, the spring snow, kind of oldish with a sparkling top crust of paper-thin ice, pocked with bits of black forest debris and sticks and the frozen stills of animal prints. There was the deep-cold smell of the ground defrosting and there was the soft spring light, caster of the long shadow through trees, ghosts' legs laid over the snow. When the tapping and the boiling was at its height, Fraser paid a guy with a horse and hay cart to take people for rides through the maple bush, and that was the best part of the whole thing, lying back on the moving planks of wood, bits of golden hay sticking into your neck, looking up at the sky and the black branches passing over you. The horses creaked leather and metal and other bits of tack; steam rose from their snouts and they shat hot apples of chewed hay into the snow. Outside the shack, Fraser would fill a trough with snow and pour into it wavy lines of hot, extra-thick syrup, and after a few seconds collect the cooled taffy on to popsicle sticks.

Red and Anouk arrived now to a very different place, maple trees green and summer-lush, ferns and shrubs knee-high from the forest floor. Sun reflected off the red tin roof of the sugar shack and the wood shelter that leaned next to it, which housed cords of neatly stacked firewood for the spring boiling.

Inside the shack, there was no one around, but the stainless-steel evaporator vats were a presence; cold and empty, waiting on top of ovens for the next sugaring season. Along the walls, shelves of glass bottles, amber-brown and golden. The cedar-plank walls preserved the smells of maple sugar reduction and smoke. This was not one of those mass-commercial outfits, where the sap was piped right from the trees into a network of machinery. Here, buckets were carried by hand from the trees to the shack. Wood was burned.

'You want dark or light?' Red asked. 'Or should we just get both?' He held up two bottles.

'Both.'

Fraser came in then from a door at the back. Denim overalls, bright-yellow T-shirt. He wore heavy boots and his burly arms, hairy and bare, were loaded with cardboard boxes. With a peach wedged between his teeth, juice on his chin, he regarded them with a waggle of his bushy eyebrows. He settled the boxes on a counter and took the peach out of his mouth, gently cuffed Anouk across the top of her head. 'You've grown,' he said to her. He looked at Red. 'I always hated when adults said that to me, like it's some big fucken surprise. But,' he turned back to Anouk, 'you have. Grown. You've gone from scrawny to not as scrawny.' He tapped the bottle of darker syrup in Red's hand. 'That one you eat over ice cream.'

'I can't eat ice cream,' said Anouk. 'It goes right through me.'

'Because of her medications,' said Red.

Fraser blew out his cheeks, shrugged. He sucked the last of the orange-yellow flesh off the peach pit and tossed the pit out the door. He looked at Red. 'Anything else you wanted?'

Red scratched his beard. Glanced at Anouk. 'Ah,' he said.

'Come out back,' said Fraser.

Anouk had seen this act before. They would be gone for a few minutes and when her father came back, he would stink of pot.

'Yep, yes. Okay.'

Now alone, Anouk checked out her reflection in one of the steel vats, moving from side to side so she was either thin as a whippet, collapsing into herself and disappearing, or wide as a house. Stretched and blurred. Eyes like peach pits. Soon bored, she went outside and kicked around in the dirt a little, picked at an amber crust of dried sap running down the scaly trunk of a white pine.

Red and Fraser came back around the side of the sugar shack, smelling like skunks. Anouk tried not to laugh when her father came close to her, thinking he'd gotten away with something, but she did laugh, so deep and good that it tickled her in the wrong

54

spot and set off a coughing fit. She held on to the tree, doubled over, consumed.

'Shit. Is she okay?' Fraser's voice, alarmed.

'It's fine,' said Red.

The more she tried to stop, the harder she wanted to laugh, and the coughing got worse. She coughed until she felt the release, and there was a great gob in her mouth.

Red, who'd left her alone, now handed her a tissue. Still hugging the tree with one arm, she spat into the tissue. Put it in her jeans pocket and drew the back of her hand across her lips, wiped her eyes. A few remnant coughs sputtered like an engine just turned off.

Fraser, one hand clasped over his forehead: 'Christ. You were hackin' like an old man.'

'People say I sound like a dog barking,' she said. 'Or a smoker.'

'That's a two-pack-a-day cough,' Fraser offered, 'at least.'

'At least,' Red agreed.

9

Nora
Ottawa River, 1987

NORA AND RED had argued that morning again, about moving south, back to Toronto. For Anouk, Nora reasoned, to avoid the cold winters. To be closer to the specialist clinic. But Red countered with the fact that Toronto could be just as cold as Pembroke, and why would they want to live where the air was less clean?

Because nobody in Toronto will ever be shocked that I've never driven a snowmobile, thought Nora. Or question why I would rather stay home and watch TV than go fishing, or cross-country skiing. No one would ever expect me to know about canning my own tomatoes. Because in Toronto, Nora thought, I could go to a party crammed with people I've never met, or I could ride the Queen Street car from where it starts to where it ends, and through my window see the different parts of the city pass by like rock strata. Big, leafy maples and Lake Ontario in the east, drunks cocooning themselves in sleeping bags on benches in Moss Park, the centre point of Yonge Street. I could keep riding, she thought, past the Eaton Centre and Sears and all the head shops and record stores on Queen West, the street vendors selling nuts and hot dogs with sauerkraut, past the suede tassels and leather boots and army surplus in the windows of the retro stores; I could just sit on the streetcar all the way west until I hit the Polish delis on Roncesvalles and then High Park, and then turn around and go back again.

She didn't say this though. Nostalgia was a weak argument. And she did appreciate Pembroke. She loved how her daughter was growing, this child of the river. Anouk's lungs were more robust for all the time she'd spent in the water. The river – its rhythms, its fluctuations and its pull – the river welcomed Anouk. It enveloped and accepted her. Absurd. But Nora believed it.

It made her spit though, Red's insistence that nothing ever change. That they stay here for ever. And why did every damn thing have to be about Anouk anyway?

As soon as the stones that spun off Red's truck tires could no longer be heard pinging the roadside trees, Nora and Jody moved to each other in the middle of the kitchen. It was a bit of a fumble; Jody was no romantic. A farmer of hops and sunflowers, and endearingly stupid. Two hours of hockey every Tuesday night in the old boys' league kept him fit as a fiddle. His face was beautiful and made more so by a partially missing front tooth that had been cracked by a flying hockey puck years before, and capped, then knocked loose again and left.

This thing had been going on for months, but never in her house. It was always at his place, or in his truck or her car down a dirt road. Once or twice, a motel.

She put her hand on his chest and pushed him away, the other hand on his belt. Anouk's dirty breakfast bowl was still on the table.

'You want to go for a drive?' he said, his eyes already heavy, drugged. 'I'll take you anywhere you want.'

She stepped away and straightened her top, tightened the elastic around her hair. 'I knew this was going to happen.'

'Isn't that why I'm here?'

'You're here to help me with the walls.'

He stared at her for a bit, as if hoping this were a joke. 'You sure?'

She reached for the bag of sandpaper and pulled it out and found that Red had bought plenty. Three different grains.

'I'm going for a swim first,' Jody said, and let the screen door bang on his way out.

This wasn't love. Far from it.

The sanding was done, the walls stripped, and the holes filled and smoothed over. And the dust, fine and powdery, was everywhere. Nora and Jody were both coated with it and there was still all the cleaning to do, but he came up behind her and slid his hand into her shorts. She dropped the rag she was holding and his tongue groped her ear (she never liked this much: hot and wet, the breathing cartoonishly loud) and she let him take her weight. Closed her eyes and got what she wanted, the only thing she wanted out of this: the illusion that she could have been anywhere, that her days were not inevitable. The newly sanded walls fell away and she floated up, over the river, over the choking trees, over the purple fields, the yellow fields. She never knew where she would land but this time it was the apartment she'd lived in, in Toronto, before Red. It was in a building just off the boardwalk along Lake Ontario. The building, gone now, was listing to the east, sinking into the soft ground. It was so dilapidated that to walk down the corridor was to stumble like a drunk. It was a shitty apartment. Dark. Small windows. Always someone else's television. Always someone else's dog. The odours of other people's lives.

Jody pulled her hand around to him and she obliged. Her knees felt weak. But only because this was awkward, standing up like this leaning against him.

There was too much space here. She missed the comfort of

close walls, or the incoherent mumble of a neighbour's radio. Her sister Mel lived near by, and they used to talk, all the time. Drinking coffee in her shitty apartment or walking out on the pier in winter, brown hunks of ice hanging off its edge like a beard. She didn't remember what they spoke about but if it had been fear, she wouldn't have known about fear then. Likewise for love. She wouldn't have known about love. She saw now that the two were inextricable.

Oh. But. The farmer certainly knew what to do with his hands. Nora brought herself back into the room, the back of her neck moist from his breath. She turned to him and finished it, and climbed the stairs to wash. He went outside to the river.

There was always guilt afterwards. Here in the bathroom, a cabinet in the corner for Anouk's medications. Nora, sitting on the toilet, stretched out her leg and prised open the cabinet with her toe. White boxes and cups stacked neatly, endlessly. There would always be a need for this stuff until there wasn't.

She finished, stood, watched Jody through the window. He had stripped down to the skin and was wading into the river. She lost sight of him behind trees but he soon reappeared and was now almost at Anouk's island. Don't get out, Nora pleaded, don't go there. But he did, pulled his long body up on to the rock, shook water from his hair like a dog. He'll go to the other side and piss into the river, Nora thought, disgusted.

That night, after dinner, Nora filled the bath with hot water and a few drops of lavender oil. She ran the tap and the shower too, to fill the bathroom with steam, and helped Anouk out of her clothes. Anouk's body, nine years old nearly ten, was still, to Nora, an extension of her own. That's my knee, she thought. Those fine white, perfect hairs that follow the curve of my daughter's forehead, the thick blue vein that travels across the pale inside of the wrist, the downy stuff that licks the hairline, and the subtle dip in the chin, as if pressed by a thumb when she was still in the mould, that's all me.

Nora dropped her own clothes on to the bathmat and stepped into the bath and reconciled her shoulder blades with the taps, settling in. Anouk got in too, winced with the heat and sat opposite, their legs entwined. She still showed no signs of puberty; the malnutrition she suffered from the CF stunted her development. Her bones and muscles were as evident under her skin as the borders on a map. She was growing though, and getting older, and room in the bath for the two of them was depleting. This nightly ritual would come to an end.

After the bath, wrapped tightly in towels fresh from the clothesline, Nora brushed Anouk's hair and braided it in one long rope and squeezed it until water dripped from the end of the wick. They went downstairs in their pyjamas and Anouk flopped on to The Cheese. Outside, the sun fell behind the trees on the far bank of the river and the world was muted.

The river hardly moved at all. Two or three stars in a sky not yet black. Nora cupped Anouk's back, and then Anouk stood at the window with a glass of water and handful of pills, wiped water from her chin with the sleeve of her pyjamas. This small gesture filled Nora with enough love to make her panic.

Nora glanced at the wall that she and Jody had used to hold themselves up only hours before. Sometimes she couldn't remember who she was or what she was supposed to be doing. Could have forgotten her own name.

10

Pieter
Stavanger, 1955

LITTLE BEAR, MY first swim the summer of your fourth birthday was on a Sunday in early June. I remember it well because even though the air temperature had been rising steadily over the previous weeks, the sea was burning cold. You were digging in the sand with your sister and your mother, and I could hear you laughing as I walked into the sea, the smooth stones sliding against each other under my feet. When water is that cold, I don't hesitate. I have to keep moving forward until it's deep enough that I can float, and then plunge in and go. It couldn't have been more than fourteen or fifteen degrees that day, and the sea took my breath from me. But my thoughts were pure and indivisible – this is why I love swimming in cold water. I plunged in and there was the first gasp, involuntary but familiar; then the chill-ache came right away to my eyes and forehead. I circled one arm over my head and pulled a pulse of that beautiful water down the length of my body, then the other, moving further and further away from you and your mother and your sister. I kicked hard and my calves balled up, and a cool spray of bubbles plumed from my toes. My skin began to burn and tingle across my cheeks and collarbone, down my arms and the barrel of my chest. As the blood left my extremities to warm my organs, my fingers and toes went numb and curled into claws, while the hearth of me remained warm and pumping. Then, all through me, electricity like the rainbow pulsations of a jellyfish, and tranquillity as the gasping subsided and my body learned to breathe again.

My thoughts meandered and soon I was thinking about wooden spinning tops, the manufacture of. The smooth running of a lathe over hardwood – solid, Norwegian maple. We used the heartwood for the manufacture of spinning tops because its quality wasn't as good as the sapwood used for furniture or musical instruments or what have you, so we got it cheap, and besides, it was richer in colour. It was prone to burn on the lathe but . . . none of this matters anyway. The point is, you were right there on the beach, your white-blond hair ignited by the sun, your soft, pink lips pursed in concentration as you dug your hole to who knows where, while I swam in the sea ruminating over spinning tops. I wasn't thinking about your mother, or Tilda; I wasn't thinking about you. I was thinking about red dust flying from a spindle, a floor covered in ragged wood chips, sawdust settling over everything.

The thing is, I was becoming restless. Our company had done well on spinning tops and building blocks and fighter planes, on small wooden copper-inlaid boxes for girls to keep their feathers or glass beads or bits of ribbon. I was getting bored of wood and my interest had turned to plastics, specifically soft plastics. I know you don't care about any of this, my Bear, but this is part of the story. And it's important. And I want you to know everything. I swam that cold day, saltwater pickling my tongue, causing it to swell, my arms passing by my vision like ghosts, I swam that day further and further from you and your sister and your mother, thinking about polymers. About ethylene and benzoyl peroxide. Chemistry, Bear. I had been reading about the development of a new kind of plastic that was soft and durable, and I thought about the toys I could design with this material: cars and trucks. Dolls with soft faces and pudgy, bendable knees.

I kept to my usual kilometre-long route, hugging a shoreline that dipped and crested like a waltz, then turned and came back. Before I reached the section of beach where you were, I felt my cold-water tolerance waning. It happens fast. To swim in water like this you have to pay close attention. The warmth in my core was slipping away, as if someone had opened a window to let the winter air in. I looked up to see how far away you were, my beacons – a bright blue blanket and two blond heads, you and your sister, bobbing about. I kicked my way back home to you, and came clumsily out of the sea on tumbling stones and bloodless feet.

You took no notice of me as I trudged and tripped my way back to our blanket. Your sister had buried you in a hole and there you were, just a head, with a wet rim of dark sand around your mouth and under your nose. Your mother, who'd been reading, who was always reading, carefully placed a strip of leather down the spine of her book to mark her place and put it on the blanket. (Books in your mother's hands were always precious things.) She passed me my post-swim clothing: a woollen, long-sleeved top, flannel trousers, a scarf and thick socks. She poured me a mug of hot coffee from a glass bottle kept warm under blankets and handed it to me once I was dressed, and handed me also a piece of apple cake, because nothing warms a cold body better than cake. I curled around my mug of coffee and took long, sweet and indulgent gulps while you ate sand, spitting it down your chin in gritty rivulets. Crying and laughing at the same time.

As my blood, lower in temperature due to its efforts to keep my core warm, returned to my extremities, it cooled me even more and I started to shiver violently. Your mother, used to this sort of business by now, ignored me and went back to reading her book. My teeth clattered, jangling the bones in my ears. I spilled coffee over my hands.

You wanted to show me something. You asked me many times to come and see. I didn't bother. I was cold, and I was thinking about something else.

At home under the pressure of a hot shower, I stood, swaying from side to side, warming my fingers and toes. This gentle rocking on the balls of both feet was a physical memory from when you and your sister were infants and needed to be held and moving, all the time. In those days, fathers didn't generally hold their children so much, but I did. I just couldn't believe the feel of you, the weight of you in my arms. You were the perfect, perfect design, in the way your smooth skin tightly contained the bones and the blood of you. The creases in your wrists and toes, the round knobs of your ankles, the sworls of your ears. Every inch of you was just as it should be.

I got out of the shower and cleared a circle of steam from the mirror so I could shave. When I opened the bathroom door, you were sitting on the hallway floor, holding your fat arm up for me to inspect. Just above your elbow, on the inside of your arm, there were the angry pink welts of a sharp pinch.

I knelt down to you. 'Did Tilda do that?'

Your blue eyes were wide, jewelled with tears. Your long white lashes were clumped together. You nodded yes.

'What did you do to antagonize her?' I asked.

Confused, you only continued to nod.

'Did you hit your sister? Did you ruin her game?' You were always knocking over her towers, chewing her puzzle pieces or stripping the clothing off her dolls.

You nodded yes, vigorously. Not yet old enough to lie. 'I hit Tilda,' you said.

'Why?'

'Yes.'

I picked you up and shifted you to my hip, and carried you into our bedroom. I put you down on the bed and took my underwear from where I'd slung it over the back of a chair, and stepped into it.

'You have fur,' you said to me, pointing to my groin.

'Yes I do,' I said. 'And one day you will too.' I put on my trousers and undershirt, and selected a fresh, short-sleeved shirt from the closet. I doused my palms with cologne and patted my cheeks and neck, then oiled my hair and combed it back. My skin, invigorated by the sea and then the hot shower, buzzed like music.

'Do me too,' you said, pointing to the bottle of cologne.

With the bottle sealed, I pretended to dab more cologne on to my hands, and patted your cheeks, still tear-damp. 'All better?' I asked.

'You didn't,' you said. 'You didn't put any.' You clumped the bedspread in your strong hands.

'Ah,' I said. 'You're right.' I pulled the top from the cologne bottle and measured the tiniest bit into my hand, and spread it on your cheek, admonishing myself for playing you for a fool.

11

L'Inconnue
Paris, 1898

SUNDAYS, THERE WAS the river. Of course it was always there, pumping through the city, involuntary and vital as a heartbeat, but on Sundays we would take the omnibus as far as the Jardin des Tuileries and walk along paths lined with rhododendrons and roses, then cross over the Pont Royal to the Quai d'Orsay. It was the only time Madame Debord would willingly leave the apartment. She may have been paranoid but she was still a Parisienne; watching people was sport. Seeing what they were wearing. Who was out. Passing judgement. Sometimes we would see people whom Madame knew, or used to know, and they would treat her with caution, as if she were feral. But as far as I could see, she was only a little touched with nerves. While we walked she stayed close to me, her fingers clamped to the crook of my arm. These walks got her talking. She spoke a little about her husband, about how they used to go to the theatre in the evenings, eat in restaurants. She told me that once, she too was new to Paris, that she had been born on the north coast, in Wissant. She told me that on a clear day, you could see across La Manche, all the way to England, to the white cliffs. She told me about how, when the tide was low, she and her brother would walk out on the mudflats with buckets and sticks, and she would hike her skirts up high and they would dig cockles out of the sand.

'I used to hunt for lucky stones on the shore,' she said, one Sunday in August. We were sitting on a bench close to the Pont Royal, the river air boggy and humid. Working boats passed on the water, powered by oar or steam or sail, carrying coal, linen, flour, timber. Birds made a racket of cheeps and squawks and there was the clop and ricket of carriages above us on the quay. 'A lucky stone is white and smooth; without any blemishes. It has a hole through its centre.'

'Did you find any?' I asked.

'One.'

'And did it bring good luck?'

'The perfect stone is meant to bring a husband. Children.'

It had rained all the night before, and this morning the sun was strong. Water dripped from the acacias and steamed from the veins between the cobbles. My scalp prickled under the weight of my hat.

Madame Debord pulled at the ruffles of her collar and stared out at the water for a long time, then began to speak again. She told me she had been pregnant seven times. Out of those seven, four babies died in the womb. Out of the three who were born, two died within hours. One, the only one whom she named, lived for twelve days. All of this before Madame Debord reached the age of twenty-six. During this time, Madame Debord told me, she tried everything to keep her babies alive. She travelled to Plombières-les-Bains to bathe in a pool fed from an underground spring. The water, naturally heated and iron-rich and rust-coloured, like diluted blood, was said to be a cure for barrenness or other faults in the reproductive system. She changed the whole of her lifestyle, stayed away from loud noises or ruckuses of any kind. She stayed away from crowds.

'Any excitement is bad for an unborn child,' she said. 'A woman is more prone to falling when she's pregnant. She's more sensitive to pandemonium and ill feelings of any kind. A baby in the womb is like uncooked bread, and any negative thoughts will affect him the same way the baker's hand can misshape his dough.'

One doctor told her the babies were dying because her womb was too hot, so she ate only blandly cooked food – chicken boiled down to broth, or stews of lettuce and sorrel and spinach. She bathed in ice water. But later, another doctor declared the womb was too cold so she switched to salted venison and hot, steamy baths.

She was fortunate to have survived any of this, fortunate that her husband could afford doctors at all. She told me about Ambrose, the baby who lived for twelve days.

'Mon chou,' she said, *my sweetie.*

All this talk reminded me of what I knew about the bloody howling of my own birth, and I stopped listening to Madame. On the river, a weave of rubbish – blackened vegetables and dirty foam, sticks and weeds – passed by, undulating over small waves. When I turned my attention back to Madame Debord, she had her hands at her chest, palpating the area above her breasts in the way a kitten might press its mother's abdomen to encourage the flow of milk.

'You cannot imagine the pain,' she said, her dark, nocturnal eyes looking somewhere I couldn't fathom. 'A day or two after Ambrose was gone, my breasts became inflamed with milk and something else much worse. I wanted so badly for this to kill me.'

I gently pulled her hands down to her lap.

'I was kept alive to furnish two more miscarriages and to watch my husband die.' She stopped talking, pulled at her pearl earring. After a few moments, she raised her chin, clasped her hands together in her lap. 'I suppose we should carry on,' she said, and lifted her hand to me so I could help her from the bench.

Not long after we started walking down the river path, a woman several paces away called out to Madame. She was coming quickly towards us, the hem of her lilac skirt damp with rainwater. Frantically, she waved a rolled newspaper in the air, trying to get our attention. She was very tall, several years younger than Madame, and moved as if there were a wooden board fastened along her back and neck. She approached us, smelling strongly of rosewater perfume. Madame Debord stiffened against my side as this woman placed both hands on Madame's shoulders and kissed the air beside each of her cheeks. The woman glanced at me, waiting to be introduced. When no introduction came, she spoke, breathless. 'So this is your new girl, then?'

Madame Debord nodded. Her expression was vacant, half formed, like a drawing that had been scribbled in charcoal by a toddler.

I was about to make an excuse, to get us away from this woman, whoever she was.

And then.

A girl, my age, appeared at the woman's shoulder. A little bit taller than me, a face broad and open, cheeks flushed. She wore a lime-green, checked blouse and a tie at her neck, and a simple, pearl-grey skirt, appropriate for walking. Her clothes were understated and respectful, but everything about her physical self was plush, exaggerated. Her eyes bigger than eyes should be and they were silty, liquid brown. Full lips, thick, dark hair pulled back into a chignon, but curly, difficult to keep under rule. She had the countenance of someone used to getting her way.

This. This was her. This was the moment we met.

The woman pivoted to the side and nudged the girl forward, towards Madame. 'May I introduce you to my niece, Axelle Paquet. Axelle has come from Provence to live with us. She's working in the perfumery department in La Samaritaine. Isn't that exciting? You enjoy it so much, don't you, Axelle?' The woman turned to me.

'Have you seen their window displays? La Samaritaine? They're extraordinary.'

I had. Impossible to miss. A lot of shine and glitter. Vacant busts displaying hairpieces – fountains of hair. Headless, hourglass torsos tied up to the point of suffocation in expensive corsets. Rows of brass-buckled boots, feathered hats, embroidered linens and sprays of silverware. I'd seen the displays of all the grands magasins and learned that their effect was to leave me feeling empty, regarding articles I would never possess, articles I hadn't even known I'd wanted to begin with. I looked at Axelle Paquet but her gaze was downwards, bored.

'It's so lovely to see you outside, Madame Debord, enjoying the fresh air,' the woman said. 'Cooped up indoors is bad for the circulation. I get out for at least an hour every day, even in poor weather.' She continued to prattle, her voice rising. She spoke further about the benefits of fresh air and demonstrated her point with a story about the ill health of a neighbour, a newspaperman, who was now dying of tuberculosis. 'Too much time in an office,' she said. Words cascaded from her mouth and I looked again at Axelle. This time, she looked back, widened her eyes in ridicule towards her aunt. I bit my bottom lip against a smile.

'Such a thing as excessive fresh air, though,' reported Madame Debord. Where her fingers rested on the inside of my arm I felt a gentle pinch. 'We really must be on our way.'

'Ah,' the woman said, 'of course.' She turned to me and smiled. 'Take care.'

We said our goodbyes and Madame pulled me away, and, after we'd walked for a minute, I looked back, if I could just see Axelle Paquet again. But they were gone.

That evening, as Madame sipped her brandy in bed, she told me the woman by the river was a cousin of her late husband, and she hadn't introduced me because she was, officially, no longer speaking to anyone in his family.

'They tried to send me to an asylum,' she said, her voice heavy. 'Once, after Ambrose, then again, after the others. They were all party to it.'

'I'm sure that's not true,' I said.

She looked at me, eyes drowsy from the liquor, slightly defeated. 'That niece of hers,' she said, 'Axelle What-Have-You. Coquette.'

'I hadn't noticed,' I said. Deep inside, somersaults.

The following Friday, though I was already late getting home, I stopped in front of La Samaritaine. My basket was heavy with bread, eggs, a bottle of cream and a head of lettuce, and I pushed with some awkwardness through a crowd that stood gaping at the front windows, gaping as if the mannequins behind the glass were not made of wood and plaster but were instead live actors on a stage. After some tussle, I passed through a heavy set of doors into the magasin. An atrium like a cathedral. Glass and iron railings and level upon level of commerce. An alarming array of pomp and shine. There were pairs of women floating along the aisles, dining together or sitting alone, reading. Chatting. None of it impressed me. I was approached by a young girl in a blue striped smock who offered assistance to my shopping experience, and I asked her the whereabouts of the perfumery. She insisted on walking me there, towards the back of the ground floor.

When I saw Axelle, I wasn't at first sure if it was her, but then she turned and there was her profile, the slope of her round cheek. She spoke to someone I couldn't see, then cocked her ear to listen and nodded, then bent low to some task. Shoppers brushed past me as I stood there, a fool, unable to breathe. She stood again and I was about to leave but she saw me, narrowed her eyes, then, recognition. A smile and a wave. I had no choice but to approach the counter.

71

The air was spicy with lavender, rose and the almondy whiff of heliotrope.

'You've come to see me,' she said. Behind her, shelves extended the height of the wall, stacked neatly with small glass vials of scent, each labelled with a rectangle of white paper.

'I was looking for stockings,' I said.

'Nonsense!' She pinched my elbow. 'You've come to see me. You want to make friends and I wouldn't blame you. Life with your Madame must be deadly boring.'

'On the contrary.'

'Hm.' She studied me for a moment, tapping one finger against her lips. She turned and walked up and down the aisle of perfumes, selected a bottle, then another, and then hovered over yet another but changed her mind and came back. She carefully pulled the wooden stoppers out of the two bottles and placed them on the counter between us. 'Hand?'

I gave her my hand. She undid the cuff buttons of my blouse and rolled it back to expose the white belly of my arm, then tipped one of the bottles just at the spot on my wrist where a thick, bluish vein branched off into smaller tributaries, and held the bottle there until a drop of amber oil fell from the spout. She rubbed the oil into my skin with the knuckle of her middle finger.

'Other hand,' she said.

On my other wrist, same procedure, different scent.

'It takes a moment for the oil to settle into the skin. On you, one scent will have a very different odour than it would on another woman. Stay here a little longer and we'll know which is best.'

So. I stayed a little longer.

12

Anouk
A Mennonite Farm, 1987

THE LAST WEEK of that summer, the summer of the wasp trap, Anouk and Nora and Red did the long drive to Toronto for Anouk's appointment at the specialist clinic. Red drove and Anouk watched the familiar pass by the window: craggy walls of Canadian Shield rock that had been blasted open with dynamite when the road was built, in some places painted with decades-old graffiti; mixed forest of birch and pine, fir and maple. Swamps and bog land where dead pines, which looked as if they'd been scorched then cooled to ash, protruded out of water that was clogged with algae, lilies and milfoil. They passed a hundred lakes and they passed gas stations where you could buy gun ammunition and marshmallows and beer; they passed hand-painted signs for fresh strawberries, blueberries and corn.

Somewhere in the farmland north of Peterborough, where the fields rolled with wheat and corn and where aluminum-sided barns glinted in the sun, Red stopped at the mouth of a long driveway, which led to a Mennonite farm, because there was a sign he hadn't seen before. *Duck Eggs For Sale Here*, the sign said.

'These folks usually stay away from the rest of us,' Red said, excited. 'We can't not go in.'

'They only want to sell eggs,' Nora said.

'It's an invitation,' said Red, reversing the car so he could make the tight turn into the driveway. 'And anyway, you've never had a duck egg. They're delicious.' Still reversing, his hand on the back of Nora's seat, he turned his face to Anouk. 'They're blue,' he said to her, as if this fact proved his point.

Later, Anouk wrote about the Mennonite farm in her notebook. She wrote about the closed gate at the top of the road, and how she had to get out of the car and use the entire weight of her body to open it. She wrote about the barn with a green roof, and the horse buggy in front of the barn with no horse. She wrote about the garden, the beefsteak tomatoes hanging heavy on the vine, and the purple, blooming cabbages.

She wrote: *Me and Dad stood at the bottom of the porch steps and there was not a single sound on that farm. No chickens or horses or wind. The world just stopped. I said Dad there's no one here but Dad walked up the steps anyway and knocked on the front door.*

She wrote about what she knew of Mennonites, what she'd seen. Horse buggies on the road. Men in neat black suits and hats and ties. Women in bonnets, no make-up, blue collars all the way up to their chins. About this, she wrote: *When we're stuck behind them in our cars we're like horseflies near their heads. They'll ignore us unless we get too close.*

She wrote about how she walked up on to the porch with her dad and stuck her nose against the screen door and smelled wood oil, and baking, and the wax of a candle recently blown out. This was the moment she decided that she would write about the Mennonite farm. It was those smells coming on a breeze from somewhere deep inside the house and the subsequent thoughts of sepia faces in old photographs. Women's tiny hands peeping out of puffy sleeves. Buckles and lace and men with sculpted facial hair. With her nose pressed against the screen door, Anouk touched time.

Red gave up. And when they turned around to go back to the car, there was a ghost. Anouk wrote about this too, a ghost standing at the bottom of the porch steps. She wore a cap over her hair, and the back of her cap was tied with ribbon. She wore a cotton dress down to her ankles, black leather boots and a blue apron with pockets.

The girl, not a ghost, led Anouk and Red around the side of the house to a pantry at the back, and Anouk wrote about the jars of peaches and pickles and jams, and she wrote about how the girl's leather boots scuffed on the soft, wooden floorboards. She wrote about the goosebumps that rose on her arms when she heard the sound of leather boots scuffing on soft, wooden floorboards.

The eggs cost two dollars for a dozen. Red didn't have any money and Anouk also wrote about this, about having to go back to the car and get money from her mom, who was sitting with the car door open, her leg stretched out and her bare heel in the dirt, and Bruce Springsteen playing on the car radio. She wrote about how, when the girl came around from the back of the house, Bruce Springsteen noise was being pitched about like the silver ball in a pinball machine. It pinged against the side of the barn, and against the front of the house. It pinged against the horse buggy with its horse bits resting in the dirt. It pinged against the tomatoes and the cabbages. And then Nora couldn't find any money in her pockets, so Red dove into the car and fumbled across her lap to look in the glove compartment, and Nora said *oh for fuck's sake* when Red yelled *eureka* and backed out of the car waving a two-dollar bill all over the place.

Anouk wrote about how, when all this was going on, she looked at the girl and the girl had turned her face towards the cornfield beyond the barn, looking as if she were prepared to stand there for all of time if she had to.

*

Twenty kilometres beyond the farm, they stopped at a roadside chip truck for poutine before turning on to the eight-lane highway that would drag them like a riptide into Toronto. Anouk took a handful of enzyme pills, and she and Nora and Red sat at a picnic table to eat, the glossy brown paint of it peeling off in tiny filings that stuck to the backs of their bare legs.

The sun was hot, the sky hazy and yellow. There was no wind, only the odd shush of a passing car and the creak of insects rubbing their legs together in the dry roadside grass.

Nora looked at her watch. 'We'll be late doing your physio.'

Anouk shrugged.

Nora stared at her. Swiped a gravy-soft fry, sloppy with cheese, from Anouk's paper cone of poutine. 'You feel Okay?'

'Fine.'

'She's fine,' Red said.

'You won't always have us around to check the time, you know.'

On the ground in front of the table, Anouk spotted the corpse of a dead mouse, pounded foetal into the cement like chewing gum. She slid off the picnic table and crouched down to inspect the mouse and all its parts, perfectly preserved as if under a glass plate. Precise claws, curved tail, the divots in the cheeks that sprouted white whiskers, and the whiskers themselves. Only things missing were the eyes. Dried out or pecked out. She pointed one finger out to touch it.

'Don't,' Nora snapped. 'That's disgusting.'

Back in the car, Anouk opened the carton of duck eggs. They could have been described as blue, she wrote later, but only because blue was the closest you could get. It was the same as describing the veins on the insides of your wrists as blue. There had to be a better name for that colour. She just didn't know yet what it was.

76

13

Anouk
Ottawa River, 1987

FIRST DAY OF school. Anouk walked the dirt path to the main road to meet the bus. She was dawdling, couldn't help it. September leaves. And the sun. Shining through the leaves. Close to the main road, she bent to undo her shoes – she was going to take them off and run through the leaves – but as she bent down she heard the impatient idling of the school bus engine.

'I'm still here,' said the driver, that sympathy smile pasted on his face.

She was often late. It was the medication, and then having to wait for the medication to work so her lungs would be ready for the physiotherapy. The year before, the driver had been instructed to wait whenever this happened, but it would have been better if he were mean about it. He was mean to everyone else.

'I was jumping in the leaves,' she said, climbing the stairs into the bus.

'Sure.'

Her teacher that year was Mr Chester. He was one of those teachers who preferred his students to sit in circled groups rather than rows, and who brought in muddy plastic bags full of plums and apples from the trees in his yard. Anouk was relieved to see,

77

when she walked into the classroom, that the seats had already been assigned. That she wouldn't have to be asked to join a group. Or not be asked.

The first day of school was unremarkable except for one thing: Mr Chester announced that they would each make their own time capsule, which he would keep, and deliver back to them in three years.

'Three years is a heck of a long time,' he said, rubbing his hands together, circling their tables. His shoes were as soft and floppy as dog ears.

'You'll choose a few objects that are significant to you. There's no rush. I'm giving you until Christmas to decide. Also, you'll write a letter.'

'To who?' someone asked.

'To whom,' Mr Chester corrected, one finger on his chin.

'To whom?'

'To yourselves.'

This is going to be good, Anouk thought.

By the end of the first week of school, Anouk had set aside three objects for her time capsule. One, a celluloid film in a manila envelope, a chest X-ray of her lungs that was taken after her last infection. She knew how to look at an X-ray, how to identify the smoky shading of scar tissue. Like thin clouds, the kind that looked as if they were about to disappear.

The second choice for the time capsule was a plastic pill bottle full of river water. Naturally.

The third thing, a fossil of some primordial shellfish, bought in the gift shop at the Royal Ontario Museum in Toronto. The fossil had been presented neatly on a square of yellow foam in a small plastic box, and with it, lost now, a written explanation of how the fossil had been formed. More or less, it read: this was not the actual animal turned to stone, but a copy. Any physical trace of the animal was gone, the soft parts, the muscles and skin and organs, eaten by other animals or bacteria. Then, millions of years after its death, the skeleton, buried deep in sedimentary rock, dissolved as well, leaving an empty space, a mould. Mineral-rich water eventually filled this vacancy and, under the pressure of layers and layers of rock, turned to stone. This was the fossil. Seas dried up and the earth's crust shifted, and what was underneath rose to the surface like an ancient book found and opened and deciphered.

So when you died, Anouk understood, you could leave an imprint of yourself behind. Even if no one ever found it. But if someone did, she might try to figure you out. Who you were and where you came from. How you lived.

Anouk had a coughing fit at lunchtime, in front of everyone. It lasted for about a hundred years. When she got home, she put on her swimsuit and went to the river. She stood on the little beach and watched a dead leaf float by on its back, pointed edges curled up like fingers. It was warm out, for September, but the water temperature had already begun to drop. Anouk didn't have a lot of time; Nora wasn't home but she would be, any minute, and this, an autumn swim, was not allowed.

Anouk walked right into the river without stopping, then dove in and frog-swam deep underwater until she couldn't anymore. The water was punchy. It beat the air out of her lungs. She turned on to her back and floated, ears submerged to the shush, and soon felt as if she were rising up through the fire of September trees and into the blue.

The fit at school had come out of nowhere. Sometimes that happened. Kids who'd been sitting close moved away, afraid they might catch it.

Too cold to float for long. She turned on to her front and swam to the island, pulled herself on to its sun-warm rock and pressed her body into the granite. Granite like the story of the earth, jewelled with nuggets of milky quartz and shining flecks of black and silver and pink mica. Hot stone, dry leaves and pine sap, and crisp air on her wet skin. She shivered.

She watched a rivulet of water run from her body, meander down the rock and back into the river.

'Anouk!'

Her mother on the beach, one hand on her hip, the other flapping in the air.

'What the hell are you doing?'

Her mother dressed in a wool sweater big enough to reach her knees, long jeans and leather boots. Nora stomped over to where the canoe rested on its gunnels under a tree and began to haul it towards the river. Anouk stood and watched, hugged her thin arms around her body against the cold. Couldn't feel the rock under her numb feet. Nora stumbled into the canoe, fought to free the paddle from where it was stored under the thwarts and then freed it, grabbed it by the neck and plunged the blade into the water. The cedar canoe jerked forward in crooked thrusts. As Nora pulled up to the island, her eyes wide and darkly clear, Anouk dove into the water and began to swim home. By the time Nora turned the canoe and caught up to her, she was halfway back.

At school, in the yard after lunch, some of the kids barked like dogs. Not in front of Anouk, but loud enough for her to hear.

Legs wobbly, her fingers numb and tingling, Anouk climbed the grassy hill back to the house. Nora ran ahead and came back with a towel, wrapped it tightly around Anouk's body, so angry and baffled she couldn't speak. She pushed Anouk into the house and on to the couch, where she pulled off her suit and cocooned her in soft pyjamas and a wool blanket. Outside fading to denim-dark, rich blue. Something small flew fast past the window and was gone from sight, then returned and then was gone again. A bat. Nora pushed a mug of hot water in Anouk's hands and instructed her to drink; she was shivering so much that water spilled over the rim of the cup. The drops settled into shining beads on the wool of the blanket, hovered there for an instant, then sunk into the wool.

14

Pieter
Ben Nevis, Scotland, 1931

BEAR. THERE WERE stories I wanted to tell you. My grandfather, he was a natural storyteller. My father, not so. People die and maybe they leave something behind, a wristwatch or a ring or a set of silver tableware, but none of that means anything without the story. It's what keeps us here after we're gone, and we're only truly dead when those who know our stories are also dead.

I'd like to tell you about the foolish thing I did when I was twenty-two years old, in 1931, when I was an apprentice making toys for another man. I was very lucky to have this position, Bear. It was my greatest ambition to one day have my own company, to manufacture my own toys, and working under this man, who was very good at what he did, was a good start. In the beginning, I was very happy working for him.

Every year, this man closed his workshop for the month of August to holiday with his family at their summer home, and so there I was with an empty month and nothing to do. One evening, a day or two into my break, I was eating a meal with an old school friend and he told me about Ben Nevis, the highest mountain in Scotland. He said it was relatively easy to reach the top, he'd been the summer before, and so I decided that is what I would do. I would go to Scotland and climb this mountain.

I had never been to Scotland. I had been walking in the hills in Norway but I was hardly an experienced mountaineer. One could purchase topographic maps from the Royal Geographical Society and I knew how to use a compass, to start a fire, to raise a tent, so I thought I would be well equipped. And when you're twenty-two years old, you tend not to recognize the things you should not do.

I borrowed, from this friend, a pair of sturdy leather boots, without taking the trouble to try them on for size, and very quickly organized rail and ferry travel. My efficiency at purchasing tickets, at organizing transfers, at selecting good-quality socks and a useful knife, lulled me into believing I knew exactly what I was doing. Instead of sailing on the Bergen Line from Stavanger into Newcastle, in the north of England, I arranged to travel by train to Calais, and from there boarded a ferry to Dover. It was a meandering, circuitous and frankly nonsensical route to take, which cost more than double, but I had always wanted to see the white cliffs.

This is something to see, Bear – the cliffs at Dover, across the Channel from France. The cliffs are composed of a white chalk, which is the compounded skeletal remains of billions of tiny sea creatures called plankton. Numbers you cannot even imagine. Looking at the cliffs is like witnessing a part of the earth's history, one which originated underwater and eventually broke the surface into the air. Quite something.

Anyway. Once I reached Dover, there was a train to London, and from there, another train to Edinburgh. I spent one night in Edinburgh – a very old and regal and windy city overlooked by a castle at its central point, a castle built of hulking dark stone that has been scored by weather and rain for hundreds of years – and in the morning I boarded yet another train to a small town called

Inverness. But still, Bear, I was not within walking distance of this mountain.

The further north I went, the closer I felt to home. Yet I had no idea what I was doing or where I was going, really. In England, my cobbled English had been sufficient to get what I needed, but in Scotland, people spoke with accents that were as strong and thick as the smoke from the peat they burned in their fireplaces, and much of the time I only half understood what I was being told. Friendly men warned me about the mountains, said the weather was moody and capricious. Warned me of cliffs hidden in cloud, evaporating trails and cold winds that could freeze the hairs in your nose, even in summer. But, I silently protested, I am from Norway. Norway! Where the mountains are bigger and the winters colder.

From Inverness, I travelled by foot or car or horse-powered tractor, often all three in the matter of a few hours. The boots I had borrowed from my friend? Too small. My feet burned, blisters weeping golden sap into my socks. Socks crusted to the blisters. It was hell, until it wasn't. You can get used to anything, Bear.

As I travelled, the land around me buckled into steeper and steeper mountains, snow-peaked and bare of trees but laden with violet and yellow and silver heather, spotted with sleepy white sheep and languid cows. The roads were narrow and potholed. They rose and fell and twisted on a hair, or cut long, sweeping incisions into the steep walls of valleys.

When I finally arrived at the mouth of the glen that would lead me to the mountain, I had already been travelling for two weeks. I greatly underestimated how long the trip would take me, and knew I would be returning late to my apprenticeship. But I carried on, moving forward as slowly and stubbornly as the ferry that had carried me across the English Channel.

The Highlands are a melancholic place. The mountains are almost always hidden in mist and the tongues of blue that lick the sky are watery and fleeting, but there is a ballad to the landscape that exists in everything. In the wind, you can hear battle. The bog that sucks keenly at your boots has memory. You climb an outcrop and look out over the valley to an endless horizon of overlapping peaks and it's like looking back in time, because you know that nothing about this view has changed for hundreds of years. Perhaps only the random placement of sheep on the opposite slope. That's the only thing that changes.

I was accosted, Bear, daily, by ticks and flies and midges. The midges, beasts! They got into my tent, into my mouth, into the corners of my eyes. I must have inhaled a thousand of them. There was a stony trail to follow but often it was swallowed by a bog or confused by rock, and several times I got lost. So much of the land there was like a wet sponge and my bleeding feet were never dry. My clothing was inadequate and so was my tent.

On the third afternoon, zigzagging my way along the face of a rocky traverse, the whole of the sky descended on me and I was lost in cloud. Knowing that below me there was a drop of several hundred metres, I decided to sit and wait for the cloud to pass. I was wearing a thin cotton shirt but was hot from walking and so I didn't bother to put on warmer clothing, even when the rain started to fall, so fine that it formed perfect, silver beads on the hairs of my arms. Steam rose hotly from my skin. I was content. In the mist, there was nothing at all to the world; it was like being underwater. I needed the rest anyway and I leaned back on the rock, water dribbling down my neck, and congratulated myself for being invincible. By the time I realized I was cold, it was too late. I dug through the damp clothes in my pack for my woollen trousers and top, and, with numbing fingers, jammed my limbs into the clothing. Remember, Bear, I had already spent my youth swimming in cold water – cold wasn't new to me – but I was on a mountain, far away from warmth and shelter. I was also trapped by the mist. I couldn't remain sitting in one spot so, going very slowly, I inched my way along the trail, blind, pushing my boots along the narrow path and not daring to break contact with the rock. My teeth were chattering and I shook from deep inside my body.

I knew I was in trouble but when you're in the midst of trouble, you haven't got time to think about the trouble you're in. So I kept going forward and this seemed to be working okay until, from somewhere beyond me, somewhere in the fog, I heard a harmonic, mournful lowing. I stopped. The sound continued, and it was getting closer. I don't go in for ghosts, Bear, but when you're socked in weather that seems to have no end, in a country as old and full of stories as Scotland, and when you're growing deliriously cold, you become a little more open to the romance of ghosts, of the ones who passed before and perhaps left a little of themselves behind. I'm not saying I was expecting some kind of spectre to appear, only that I considered the possibility of it. Even the appeal of it. Anyhow. The moaning sound continued to grow closer, but I kept moving forward because I certainly couldn't go back. After a few minutes, a figure did take shape. At first, I was perplexed. It was a hulking thing, low to the ground. As I got closer I could see more detail, a bulk covered in copious amounts of long, straggled hair, heavy with moisture. I thought: dog? Boar? But it moaned again and suddenly the mist between us dissolved, and there, in all apathy, a massive Highland cow. A bull, no less, sitting sideways on the trail and solid as a wall. He swung his great head slowly towards me and shifted a little, but clearly had no intention of moving. His eyes were concealed by his matted, dirty white coat and he smelled of bog water and peat and hot, bovine muscle. The particular way the trail was cut into the side of the mountain meant that I couldn't divert above or below him. What with my heavy bag, and considering I couldn't see more than a metre ahead, the bull was blocking my only way forward. I waved my arms and yelled. He swatted his small tail at me as if I were a flea. I sang the

86

national anthem of Norway, danced, unbuckled my trousers and urinated, thinking this might offend him into shifting. Nothing.

Meeting the bull had at first distracted me from how cold I was, but I soon remembered, as if the cold were a jealous companion and had tapped me on the shoulder and said: You're not leaving me behind. I needed to move forward and find a place to pitch my tent and light a fire. I searched the ground and found a few good-sized stones. With my heart in my throat and not sure how this would end, I threw the stones at the bull's rump. All this inspired from him was a grumble and an angry twitch. So, I found more stones and this time, lobbed them at his head. This got him up. He took a few steps towards me so I bent again for more stones, nearly losing my balance with the weight of my heavy bag strapped to my back. I scrabbled at the ground again and came up with a handful of grit, and threw this at the bull. Steam billowed from his wet, black nostrils. I screamed something low that hurt my throat and this inhuman sound echoed strangely in the mist, surprising both of us. With impressive agility, the bull danced a tight circle on the narrow trail and began to move slowly away, dumping as he went a glorious procession of green and steaming pats of shit. I gave him a few minutes' head start before I continued down the trail, cold and tired and humiliated.

I would have told you this story, Bear, when you were a little older; maybe I would have taken you on a similar trip. We wouldn't have had to go to another country. We could have found one of the wild places at home, rambled from one world into this other, and I could have built you a fire and told you this story and hoped you gleaned from it some sort of wisdom. Maybe you would have, or maybe, like most men, you would have ignored your father and gone off to make your own mistakes. Because these are the sorts of things that build a life: crossing water to another country and wondering about ghosts and suffering the humiliation of being bested by an animal dumber than you and with more time to lose.

15

Anouk
Ottawa River, 1987

M R CHESTER TROOPED Anouk's class to the school gymnasium on a morning when they weren't normally there, and everyone got excited. Thought they'd be doing something physical with balls or hula hoops or rope. But when they got to the gym, there was a woman from St John Ambulance waiting for them, and on the floor lay a manikin dressed in a blue-and-white tracksuit.

Someone said the manikin looked like the killer from a Halloween horror movie. Anouk thought she looked like Red when he fell asleep on the couch with the newspaper.

The class sat in a circle around the manikin and listened as the woman from St John Ambulance explained something called cardiopulmonary resuscitation. CPR. Cardio: relating to the heart. Pulmonary: of the lungs, or, the nature of the lungs. Resuscitation: to revive, especially from apparent death. She showed them how to check the victim for signs of breathing, to listen to the nose and mouth, to see if the chest was rising. She showed them how to tilt the head back with one hand on the forehead, to open the airway by lifting the chin, to check the mouth for food or debris. She showed them how to pinch the victim's nose and make a tight seal – rescuer's mouth around victim's mouth.

The class jittered.

She showed them rescue breaths, two together, steady. She showed them chest compressions. Arms straight, the heel of one hand on the breastbone, the other hand on top for added support. Fingers laced.

She asked for volunteers to practise on the manikin, and when Anouk raised her hand some of the kids groaned. Someone else said it wasn't fair if she went first. Because of the germs.

Mr Chester stood up in the middle of the circle, and held his palms up flat the way teachers did when they wanted everyone to shut the hell up and listen.

'I know something about this manikin that you don't,' he said. 'I have a story about where she came from. We're all going to have a turn and we're going to be kind to one another and afterwards, I'm going to tell you what I know.'

Which he did. Back in the classroom while he handed out pin badges supplied by the woman from St John Ambulance. The badges were white, with red hearts on them.

Later, at home, Anouk added the badge to her time capsule.

16

L'Inconnue
Paris, 1898

I QUICKLY LEARNED THAT Madame's mood was much improved if she spent time outdoors, so I encouraged her to accompany me one Saturday, the week after my wrists were oiled and perfumed at La Samaritaine, to have lunch with Axelle. It took some convincing. Madame was not at first enamoured with the idea of spending her Saturday with a member of her late husband's family, no matter how distant a cousin Axelle may have been. I suggested that, if Madame behaved herself, Axelle would bring a good report back to the family. Madame would shine.

'What do you mean: if I behave myself?' Madame asked.

'If Madame will pardon my saying.'

'Please, speak.'

Worried I may have ventured too far, but too late to turn back: 'Vous ne prenez pas de gants.'

For a moment she was silent, then said, to my relief, 'You've got me all wrong. I'm very careful in how I conduct myself with others; the problem lies with those who are so sensitive they need to be handled with kid gloves.' She tried to hide her smile with a face of stone, but I could see that she was pleased.

Having arranged to meet Axelle by the fountain in the Jardin du Luxembourg, Madame and I left the flat early and boarded an omnibus. We crossed the river at the Pont de Sully, under a sky that was low and heavy and somewhat threatening. Passing through La Sorbonne, we watched the students wandering the streets, gesticulating importantly and smoking their clay pipes. We disembarked on the Boulevard Saint-Michel, not far from the university, a five-minute walk from the entrance to the garden.

In a note delivered to me earlier in the week, Axelle had directed me to wait at the head of the fountain, where a statue of a man depicted in bronze spied over a pair of marble lovers, and Madame and I waited there now, the air balmy and still. Close to where we sat, a cheapjack set up his table of novelties under the shade of the plane trees that lined the grotto. He spoke his trade quickly, one dark eye roving for the gendarme. Among other oddities, he was selling men's ties which, he guaranteed, would not ride up.

The cloud broke and the facade of the Palais du Luxembourg was momentarily a brilliant cream-white, its windows flashing, dramatic against the slate sky. After a few seconds, the sun retreated and the stone faded again to a soft, ashy grey.

Axelle arrived several minutes late and, as we were all hungry, we went directly to a restaurant she and Madame both recommended, with a view of the gardens. Although rain was a possibility, we convinced Madame to sit outside because the air was fine and warm and there was the lovely aroma of late roses. We ordered omelettes with fresh herbs and cheese, a basket of bread and a small carafe of red wine. Our waiter suggested a bowl of fresh fruit and as I nodded yes, Madame grabbed my knee sharply under the table.

'No, Monsieur,' she said. She waited for him to leave before she said to me: 'You must ask the price of fruit before they bring it to the table.'

'Why?'

'They will charge you a king's ransom for it.'

Axelle brought her napkin to her mouth and pretended to wipe her lips.

Before our food arrived, a man approached wearing a smart coat with tails and a white cravat. Without saying a word, he placed a single, glazed cashew, which was nestled sweetly in a white paper cup, on the table between our wine glasses. He gazed at the nut as if it were the most beautiful object in all the world, as if it were his own child, and implored us with a long, searching look from his sad eyes to agree. I reached for the nut, but Madame put her hand over the cup and shook her head.

'No, thank you,' she said, her small eyes on him.

I glanced at Axelle, embarrassed, worried that Madame was ruining our day out. Axelle was glaring at Madame's hand, which lay like a stone slab over the swaddled cashew. The man left the nut on our table and turned to the couple sitting next to us, and placed another paper cup between their wine glasses.

'If you eat it,' Madame whispered, 'he won't let us alone until we each purchase a whole bag of nuts. We mustn't encourage the fellow.'

'But Madame,' said Axelle, 'what if they're delicious?'

'Don't be swindled. For these people it's only a game. Look, he's acting. It's all just an act.'

'That doesn't mean the nuts aren't tasty.'

'Be my guest,' said Madame, removing at last her hand from the paper cup. 'If you don't object to being manipulated.'

Axelle sulked, and did not touch the nut. I wanted to tuck behind her ear a dark curl that had fallen next to her eye. But then she straightened up, squared her chin. 'We are all actors, some of the time. We might not even realize we're doing it – it's in our nature. Don't you agree?' She looked at me.

'I would agree that we present different faces to the world,' I said, 'depending on the situation.'

'Depending on what one needs,' said Axelle.

'In any situation, you will find me to be the same person,' said Madame. 'This is a privilege reserved for the old.'

'You're not so old,' I said.

'Ah,' she said, looking past me. 'Here come the eggs.'

The food was delicious. Axelle did most of the talking while we ate. Among other morsels of gossip, she told us about her directeur at the perfumery who was flagrantly running amok with a young haberdashery girl. 'They barely try to hide it,' she said.

'At least it makes the day more interesting,' said Madame, whose tongue had loosened considerably after two glasses of wine.

Axelle also spoke about her wish to move from the perfumery to a different job, one which carried more prestige.

'Have you heard about the models?' she asked. 'The girls who work for the clothing designers?'

We hadn't.

'You can find a position at one of the couture houses,' she said in a near whisper, leaning closer, protective of this information, 'where your only task is to wear expensive garments all day and parade in front of women who have more money than sense, tempting them to buy what you're wearing. You have to make them believe that they will look as beautiful as you do, even if they're ugly. You have to make them imagine what their lives could be so you twirl around, or sit in a chair by a window and pretend to write a letter, or, if you're modelling an evening gown, you stand next to a painting or a bust or some other ornament and sip a glass of water that has been coloured to look like wine. You're selling more than just the clothing, you see. It's an act,' she said, turning to Madame, 'but it pays very well.'

'It would be a far superior act if they permitted you to drink real wine,' said Madame Debord.

'How strange to be regarded in that way,' I said. 'To be observed. As an object in a dress. You're far bolder than I.'

'People have been observing me my whole life,' said Axelle.

The waiter came back then, carrying the bill on a small silver tray. Madame scrutinized it from bottom to top and quibbled over an unexplained five-centime charge.

'La caissière,' said the waiter, 'is new. I apologize.' He took the bill away and returned a few moments later with a corrected version.

'You've got to be on top of them,' Madame said, loudly enough for his benefit, while she pinched coins out of her purse.

'Madame, do you trust no one?' Axelle asked.

'No one,' said Madame.

The following Saturday, I went alone to meet Axelle in the same part of the city, this time to visit a place that she had kept secret, but promised would be like nothing I'd seen before. We met in front of a confectioner's on the Boulevard Saint-Germain and walked towards Rue du Bac, stopping on a corner to watch a man who was selling mechanical tin toys. He stood just in the alcove of a large wooden door, its central brass knob like the eye of a Cyclops, and at his feet, a circus of wind-up toys. Monkeys playing the drums, waddling ducks and a somersaulting clown – each of its swinging parts being slowly pulled over by its own momentum. The automatons, a dozen of them at least, ambled sleepily about the cheapjack's feet, bumping into each other and into the stone walls of the doorway. When one strayed too far, he would pick it up gently, turn it the right way around, and place it back on the pavement.

'How much?' one onlooker asked.

'Twenty-five sous,' the cheapjack answered insouciantly, as if sale or no sale were nothing to him.

'I'll give you twenty.'

'Impossible, Monsieur,' the cheapjack said, without looking up from his toys. He scooped up a duck that had stopped moving and from his pocket procured a key, which he turned in a hole in the duck's back before setting it back on the ground. With a small pat to the head, he sent the toy on its way.

I loved this banter, this *act*, Madame would have called it, played out by two strangers who either didn't know they were performing or didn't care. Mocking frustration but clearly pleased, the onlooker took out a purse from his breast pocket, and paid the asking price for a bear that raised its arms again and again as if it were about to toss the red-and-white ball that balanced between its paws.

A few blocks down the Rue du Bac we came to our destination: Deyrolle's, a taxidermist. Two floors of exotic animals and other curiosities. This was a place of high ceilings and large windows that let in the bright afternoon light. Creaky wooden floors and the dusty smell of talc. The narrow showrooms were full of people, of rustling skirts and the scuff of boots on worn wood, full of people quiet and awestruck at what they saw displayed on long tables and behind glass. Axelle had been correct; this place was indeed like nothing I'd seen before. This was time itself, seized, and I had been transported. There were animals I had heard of but never seen and hadn't truly believed existed until now – all frozen in past-life's pose. Their glass eyes stared into the future or they stared at nothing. The cheetah, pink flamingo, deer and leopard, each exhibit labelled in perfect black script on a small white card, the French and Latin names of the specimens and their places of origin. A snow-white peacock from India on a pedestal, its tail feathers falling to the ground. A blue-faced vulture from Chile, and a furry Australian possum perched on a gnarled fork of marbled wood. From the Americas, a beaver, a mink, a jackrabbit the size of a dog. There was a metallic-green hummingbird and a platypus. What an animal that was, the platypus, adapted to land and water both!

There were rats as big as puppies, ostrich eggs cradled like jewels in nests of velvet, canaries of every colour imaginable. In one glass case, a bat, and next to it, the skeleton of a bat, its wing bones articulated like the veins of a leaf. I was enchanted. I paused to stare deeply into the pitch-black, perfectly round eyes of an owl. Axelle became enamoured with a tiny, white mouse no bigger than her thumb, its eyes glowing like little red coals. The larger animals – the enormous moose, the bear, the caribou, the kangaroo – were not behind glass and it was difficult to resist the urge to touch, to run my fingers through the coarse fur, or caress with my thumb the smooth tips of their hard, white teeth. I wanted to wrap my arms around the neck of the lioness, push my ear against her solid chest and listen to the beat of her heart.

Up on a high shelf, perhaps only for the eyes of those with the wherewithal to look, a desiccated human head screamed silently from within a bell jar, its teeth crusted with brown plaque. Hairless, nose mostly gone, the left side of the head was crept over by a dusty web, something fibrous. The head looked as if it would crumble to dust if the bell jar were to be lifted.

And there was more. In a back room, we discovered a gallery of wooden cabinets, their many drawers shallow and wide and easily pulled open to reveal trays of insects, perfectly preserved and held in place with fine metal pins. Butterflies of silvery blue and green, grasshoppers, termites, moths and dragonflies. Bees, wasps, scorpions and aphids. It was almost too much. Slick pincered beetles covered in intricate armour, dried larvae husks, a hairy tarantula bigger than my fist.

Looping her arm around mine, Axelle said something peculiar about female spiders.

'Pardon?' I said, turning to her. I had been distracted by a cabinet that displayed a series of ammonite fossils; small, shiny coils of ancient sea creatures, embedded in rough ears of rock. But then

Axelle's arm twisted with mine, and I quickly forgot about the fossils.

'There is a type of female spider,' she said. 'She kills her male companions after the act of mating.'

'C'est vrai?'

'Yes. I think they eat them too.'

'How awful.'

We carried on to the back of the room where a small man sat at a worktable, his left eye greatly magnified by a round glass strapped to his head. He was bent over his work, arranging the iridescent wings of a giant butterfly, lost in this task.

Axelle pulled me to lean against the wall and put her mouth to my ear. 'He lives with his mother,' she whispered. 'He's been obsessed with insects since he was a boy. He used to collect spiders from under his bed and would keep them in clay jars, feeding them house flies and ants. But they always died.' She looked at me, her shoulders shaking with silent laughter. 'He's been in love once but she wouldn't marry him. Too many dead moths and crickets in jars.'

I played along. 'His father wanted him to train to do something clerical. Something sensible with money, with numbers.'

'His father ran off with another woman. Mademoiselle Scarabée.' Axelle snorted, slapped her hand over her mouth.

The poor man looked at us, one eyebrow arched, his left eye swimming behind glass.

We left Deyrolle's feeling very wicked, and as I still had some time before Madame expected me home, and as the weather was lovely and mild, we decided to walk along the river. I didn't want to say goodbye yet, nor, I thought, did she. Crossing under the Pont Alexandre III, we stopped to watch a group of titis scampering over the iron girders like a pack of squirrels in the trees. Under the young boys' feet, the Seine flowed, and the September light that shone through the iron struts and arches penetrated the water, and the water was green and inviting.

One boy, who couldn't have been older than five or six, leapt athletically from one girder to the next, using the strength in his legs to maintain his balance and stop himself from tumbling into the river. Barefoot, he scrambled to the top of a pillar, using the large rivets as grips, and, hidden in shadows in the upper arches of the bridge, piped to his friends, 'Regardez-moi!' His voice echoed and the other boys, swinging and hanging upside down from their knees, hollered their appreciation, encouraged him to go higher. A deeper voice, likely an older brother, told him he was an ass.

I imagined dropping my skirts and my hat and shawl, right there on the path. Unlacing my tight boots and tossing them into the water and climbing into the guts of that great bridge, just like those boys, and hanging upside down until my temples throbbed.

'Street rats,' Axelle said, and pulled me by my hand.

'It looks fun,' I said, allowing her to drag me, watching the boys from over my shoulder. Though I hadn't so much as undone a single button, I was out of breath.

'You're a strange one,' Axelle said. We were out in the sun again, standing under the chestnut trees that formed a neat line all the way to the centre of the city. Axelle pressed her thumb into the palm of my hand while a woman passed close by, pushing a grizzling infant in a pram. My heart thumped *regardezmoiregardezmoi*.

'Nothing about you seems to fit,' Axelle said and held my arms out, examining me like a seamstress would. 'You are a collection of surprises.'

'I'm not sure if that's a good or bad thing.'

'Nor am I,' she said, and smiled.

17

Nora
Ottawa River, 1987

N ORA DREAMT SHE was falling and woke from this dream a little after dawn with the half-formed notion that the sensation of falling in sleep was actually the memory of being born. Or of dying. That total loss of control, that endless inhalation without the response of the exhale. She turned to face the window and through the gap in the curtains could see the first snow coming down, a universe of minuscule cogs, free-falling.

Red, asleep beside her, rolled over and mumbled. That face, the way his hair curled behind the ear, the smell of him. She would have touched him, but.

She put on a hefty wool sweater over her nightgown and pulled on a pair of Red's thick grey boot socks. Downstairs, she set the coffee machine and turned up the thermostat and stood in the middle of the kitchen staring at the floor, staring at nothing, waiting for the coffee. When it was ready, she poured it into a thermos and then went to the hall closet. Boots and coat on, scarf wrapped around the bottom half of her face, she took her coffee out to the porch. The cosmic silence of snow. There must have been five or six inches, and it was still falling. Hot coffee in the throat, down the gullet, and she stepped off the porch into airy snow that gave no resistance and filled her boots.

Open-mouthed, she turned her face up to the falling flakes, which seemed to form twenty metres above out of thin air then whirl chaotically to the earth. Flakes landed in the divots of her eyes and melted. Flakes landed in her mouth and tasted like paper. The sky, obliterated.

She ran as far as a big oak and stopped there. Each of its bare, dark branches, down to the thinnest, topped perfectly by a shadow of white. A blue jay, icy in its colouring, took off from high up in the tree and set off a cascade, and now there was snow melting under her scarf, melting hot. The yard, before she ran across it, had been flawless but now, with the trail she cut, a trail that was all blue shadows, it looked like some cumbersome, dead thing had been dragged through the snow. She was afraid of what she was going to do.

Anouk woke a few hours later, congested, nose red. Nora had to lug her through the nebulizing, the cupping and the medication. She made Anouk porridge with raisins and a scoop of peanut butter for extra fat, and a pot of hot chocolate. All these tasks she moved through as if today were a dream, her life already unrecognizable before she'd even done the thing that was going to change it. She built a fire for Anouk because, even though she couldn't stop the cold in her daughter's nose, in her sinuses, she could keep her warm.

The problem was, Anouk felt fine, like any kid with a minor cold would. She wanted to go out in the snow. A pitched whine crept into her voice; she rejected offers of books or games. So Nora turned on the television. Red came downstairs long after breakfast and together they monitored her temperature, pressed on her glasses of juice and water. Anything to battle infection. They did an extra session of physio to keep ahead of the mucus building up in her lungs, and outside the snow fell so steadily that at one point the trees on the far side of the yard were obscured.

Nora watched this through the kitchen window and Red came up beside her.

'You okay?' he said.

'I'm fine.' Fine: the meanest, deadest word uttered in marriage. 'I'm just worried about her. All this snow. What if we have to get her somewhere?'

'We follow the steps.'

'Maybe we should just go now. We can be in Toronto before it gets too bad and then, if we need the hospital, we're already there.'

He put his arm around her, spoke gently. 'Look at her in there,' he whispered. 'She's watching back-to-back reruns of that show where rich teenagers fuck each other all day in their beach cabanas. She's not even coughing.'

'There's no sex in that show.'

'It's implied.'

'You think she gets it?'

'No way.'

Later, Nora tucked Anouk into bed and turned off her bedside lamp. In the dark, she laid her hand firmly on Anouk's forehead.

'I won't be able to sleep,' said Anouk, turning her head from Nora's hand.

'It's been a lazy day.'

'It's not even eight yet.' The whine.

'That voice,' said Nora. 'You could clear a room with it.'

'You mean shatter glass with it.'

'Eh?'

'That's what you usually say. You could shatter glass with that voice.'

Nora kissed her forehead, made no move to get up from the bed.

Garlic and ground beef frying in a pan. The smell and sizzle of this reached Anouk's bedroom from downstairs. Red, cooking a meal. Unaware of this night. Outside the window, the sky was lofty and purple, turbulent like the underwater view of a breaking wave. The snow had stopped falling but the weather report warned of more to come, some time after midnight.

'Why aren't you going, Mom?'

'I'm going.'

When Red slammed the kitchen door on his way out, the clock slid down the wall to the floor and see-sawed for a moment on its lower rim, before tipping face down to totter and settle like a coin. The kitchen was charged with the cold air of his leaving. A moment later, across the yard, the shed window snapped yellow light and she knew at least he wasn't planning to wander in the snow all night. There was an electric floor heater in there, a couch. The heater was a hazard and the shed a tinder box, but.

She went to the small room off the side of the kitchen and pulled open the door of the hot and ticking dryer, loaded her arms with still-warm clothes, the milky smell of hot cotton. She carried this load into the living room and dumped it on the couch, the clothes a tangled mass of vacant feet and arms and legs. Solace in the repetition of the mundane, of everyday jobs: snapping socks, squaring shoulder seams, aligning the legs of pants.

She had said to him that she did it because she was lonely. But that wasn't true. She wasn't even a little bit lonely. Given the chance, she would have been more alone.

She paired socks together, their thready guts exposed, into ugly little balls, and laid the stray singles over the arm of the couch. She got down on her knees and pushed her face into the neatly folded clothes, warm and maternal. At least something was.

*

Red was not a heavy type of man but as soon as he came back into the house, some hours later, boots shucked off, coat dropped to the floor, the volume of the house halved. Nora had moved from the floor to the couch, not able to sleep, had swept the folded clothes on to the carpet. Red came in and sat down on the floor, his back against the armchair.

'In the movies the first thing people say is, how long has this been going on?' he said.

'Eh?'

'I don't know how, I . . . I'm embarrassed for you.'

She nodded.

'So. How long then?'

'Seven months. Eight.'

'Pretty fucking stupid bitch of a thing to do.'

'Red.'

'Get my name out of your mouth.' He stared hard at the floor.

'Do you want me to leave?'

A tight stretch of time like holding breath. 'No.'

They hadn't heard her come down the stairs but suddenly there was Anouk in the middle of the room. She had taken off her night-gown and was shivering in her underwear; her hair was damp with sweat. Nora moved quickly to pick her up, the girl hot and bony in her arms. She weighed so little. Then, Red's fingers dug deeply between the bones and tendons of Nora's elbow, hard enough to hurt.

'I'll take her,' he said, and gathered Anouk up like a doll. The only thing Nora could do was to follow them up the stairs and into Anouk's room. Nora turned on the light. Anouk's sheets and duvet were on the floor and the fitted sheet had been stripped from the mattress. Red looked at the bedding on the floor and he looked at Nora and then he looked away, so she picked the twisted sheet off the floor and spun it open and stretched it over the mattress. It seemed crucial now to align the corners of the sheet perfectly over the corners of the mattress. She collected the other sheet from the floor and tucked it neatly under the foot of the mattress and pulled it up to the head of the bed, smoothing it with her palms as she went, then folded the top edge back on itself, ready for Anouk. Red settled her into the bed and Nora ducked in beside him with the duvet and there was his smell, his winter skin and the grass he would have smoked earlier in the shed.

Anouk sat up, coughed wetly and spat a mouthful of sputum into the cup she kept next to her bed.

'The cough touches my throat if I lie down,' she said.

'Why didn't you call us earlier?' Red asked, stroking the wet hair off Anouk's forehead with his thumb. He propped the pillows behind her neck.

Nora, perched on the end of the bed, imagined she wasn't a part of this scene.

Anouk leaned over and coughed again and this cough led to another and another, a fit lasting several minutes. Her cup was full so Red took it and left the room. Afraid to disrupt the scene, Nora watched her from the end of the bed. Red came back with a box of tissues and a new cup and a wet cloth for Anouk's face.

'Go to bed, Nora,' he said, his back to her. 'I'll do the night.'

Nora opened the bedroom window to let in the cold air and lay in bed listening to the slow dance of wind and tree. Her heart kicked in her throat and ears, kicked so hard her whole body was exhausted. She was not going to be able to sleep tonight. In the dark she could just make out the contours of this room: Red's clothes hanging over the back of a chair, one sock and a pair of boxers on the floor beneath it. Closet door that never shut completely and a tumble of shoes at its base. Red's Jays hat on the bedpost, a stack of books on the bedside table. A stout, dusty candle on the bedside table too, which hadn't been lit in years. She pulled open the table drawer and scrabbled in it for a lighter. Found one and lit the candle and it sparked, smelled of burning dust. The room became shadows and it no longer belonged to her. She wondered where was the sense of relief she thought she had coming.

Anouk's cough, rattling down the hall, was wet and desperate. She wanted to go to her daughter but didn't dare. There was the sound of the cough and of the wind outside, and there was the sound of Red's voice too, deep and soothing and humble and kind.

18

Anouk
Ottawa River, 1987

Each cough was a punch. Too big for the ribcage, too big for the throat. Some were so violent, Anouk was afraid that if she fell asleep she would suffocate. She was afraid her ribs might break. This was possible; it had happened to other people. Experience had taught her not to cry because this only made things wetter and stuffier.

Her mom had gone to bed, but her dad was here and she was glad it was him. He kept his hands off her, didn't even look at her, didn't try to stop it. Only touched her to wipe the stuff off her chin. Once or twice he tried to coax her to sleep and she must have slept a little because there were dreams. Sticks and mud and half-eaten bits of fruit in the mud.

The hour finally came when the light through the window changed to grey, and her dad was asleep with his chin on his chest. She poked his knee and he opened one eye, lifted his head slowly.

'Oh my God, that hurts,' he whispered, rubbing his neck. He grimaced and smiled both. 'Good morning.'

Her throat was too pummelled to speak. Her ribs ached too.

'Did you sleep at all?'

She shrugged. Her chest was heavy with mucus. Breathing was difficult. She scratched a few words out. 'Don't you want to go to bed?'

'Nah.' His face had darkened, as if he just that moment realized how tired he was. 'We'll let your mother sleep.'

No school. Her dad stayed home from work too. Her parents watched her closely over the next few days and she watched them too. One afternoon, the light fading by three, Anouk watched her dad go out in the snow with no coat, and she watched him through the window as he stood next to the big fir tree with his hands on his hips and looked up into its branches. When he came back in and sat in the armchair across from her, she said, 'What were you doing just standing out there?'

'Thinking about that old fir.'

'What were you thinking about it?'

'I might get rid of it.'

'Why?'

Her mother came through the room then and just walked between them on her way to somewhere else, and his eyes followed her until she was gone.

'Why?' Anouk asked again.

He shrugged one shoulder.

Every time Anouk coughed, which was a lot, her parents checked the colour of what came up. As long as it stayed a light, oatmeal brown, she could stay home. If it looked green, hospital.

And then one morning, before dawn, she woke with dry eyes, lids creaking on hinges and a familiar, gritty tickle in her lungs, the sandpapery rub against her ribs. She was full of fluid and brought up a mouthful, spat it into a tissue. It was thick. A collection of tiny globes all nestled together like frog spawn, and green as pond scum. She called for her dad and he came quickly, hair on edge, and a rumple and sideways-ness to the clothes he'd slept in. She showed him the tissue, and he sat on the edge of the bed and searched his beard with thumb and forefinger.

'Well then,' he said.

'Can we wait another day? See what happens?' She coughed and spat again. A feverish, sidestep swoosh inside her skull.

Nora appeared in the doorway then, leaning against the door frame with her arms crossed over her chest and looking heavy. When she saw that Anouk was watching her, she bent to pick at something on the knee of her pyjamas.

'We have to bring her in,' Red said. 'We'll take her local.'

'I think we should go straight to Toronto,' Nora said. 'They'll just send us there anyway.' She took a big breath, filled her lungs right up, and went straight to Anouk's closet and opened it. Pulled things out – old boots, Lego, a deflated volleyball – and scattered them on the carpet.

'What are you doing?' Red asked.

'Where's her bag?'

'Hall closet.'

All the song was gone from their words, Anouk's parents, when they spoke to each other. They were beat. She was tiring them out. Nora left the room and came back a moment later with Anouk's bag, the one they used for long stays at the hospital.

They still did her regular physio, cupping her back, even though within the hour her lungs would be full of fluid again. Anouk in fever, almost pleasant, waited on the couch while Nora worried a trail around the kitchen, packing food and water for the car, stopping to look out of the window at the snow. Red was upstairs packing pills and the nebulizer – the motorized compressor, the tubing, the mouthpiece. To nebulize: to inhale the medicine by mist, to inhale it straight into the lungs, so that it would loosen the gunk that clogged the cilia, making it easier to expel.

The world outside the window was still and the sky a flat grey, and the pine trees that circled their yard like palisades were laden with white.

Nora came out of the kitchen and went to the bottom of the stairs and called up to Red. 'You nearly ready? Radio says more snow in the next few hours. I want to get south of it.'

Red answered with the heavy fall of his thick-socked feet on the stairs, the stairs stripped of carpet and splintery rough. He lumbered with a backpack hanging off one shoulder, a sleeping bag tucked under each arm, and gripped in one hand the hard-shelled case that held the nebulizer. He dumped it all by the front door and slowly his body rose.

'We've got to get a move on,' said Nora.

'What does it look like I'm doing?'

Anouk watched. She watched Red collect coats and hats and gloves, and pile them next to the bags. She watched Nora move from kitchen to living room and back again. She watched the first new flakes of snow reel and curl past the large living-room window, falling slowly and softly as if they'd been dropped accidentally and would not be followed by any more.

19

L'Inconnue
Paris, 1898

IT WAS TWO long weeks before I saw Axelle again. She came unannounced to Madame Debord's apartment in the afternoon, while Madame was sleeping. Axelle had gone that day with some of the other girls from La Samaritaine to a very odd place, the city's morgue, and she was desperate to tell me everything.

'You have a fascination with death,' I said.

'I haven't,' she said. She sat primly on the edge of Madame's sofa, having refused coffee or any other refreshments, and was pulling her gloves off, one finger at a time. 'What makes you say that?'

'Our last outing was to the taxidermist. Now you're touring the morgue.'

'Oh, everyone goes to the morgue.'

'Why would anyone want to see that?'

'I don't know. The entrance is free? And the show is. Well. You can't look away.'

'It seems intrusive.'

'Some say it's your civic duty to go. Bodies are found in this city all the time, especially in the river, and when no one knows who they are – who they were – their remains are exhibited in the

110

morgue for anyone to see and, with luck, identify. But it's a gruesome show. I had to go just to stop people asking me: have you been yet? Why haven't you been?'

'And? Was it worthwhile?'

'I won't soon forget it. The whole thing is like a carnival show. Outside on the street, in front of the building, there are hawkers selling all kinds of things, gingerbreads and apples, toys for children. I heard that once, a body was found in a chest, and on the day the chest was exhibited in the morgue, a hawker stood out front selling toy versions of the same. It's ghastly.

'You wouldn't think there were dead people just on the other side of the doors. The queue was enormous and you cannot imagine how nervous I became, just from having to wait. When we got to the front, there was a wooden partition set across the doorway, which blocked our view of the interior, and from inside there was a current of very cool air, and an odour that was like face powder. I almost turned away but the girls, they were determined.'

'Why?'

Axelle leaned towards me, whispering. 'A few weeks ago, two babies were pulled from the river. Dead. An infant and a child of two. Everyone believes them to be sisters. Thousands of people have come to see them. Only last week someone identified them so they took the poor things off display and thawed them out – they freeze the bodies, so they don't rot as quickly – they thawed them out and prepared them for burial. But then, a few days ago, someone else claimed the identification to be incorrect, that the children they'd been identified as were in fact alive and well and living with their mother in Chaillot. So the babes have been frozen again and put back on display.'

'You really wanted to see this?'

'Not exactly. But I told you. Everyone was going.'

'And?'

'Well, it was a unique experience. I suppose I have no regrets.'

I didn't want to hear any more, but here she was, her knees almost touching my own, and I wanted her to tell me stories until we were hungry or hoarse, until the sky grew dark and the street lamps burned. 'What was it like inside?' I asked.

'Oh. Something else. The viewing salon was dreary. Damp flagstone floor, lamps turned low. On one side of the room there was a window, wall-to-wall, and there were so many of us that at first I could see nothing. And the people were just plain rude, pushing to get a better view. One nasty little urchin mashed my toes with his dirty boots when he budged past me. But there was a guard at the door who moved the masses along, and before I could change my mind again I had been conveyed to the centre of the window and there I stood. Dead people just the other side of the glass, a mere two steps away.'

'You saw the babies?'

'I did. I saw them. Other bodies were laid out on tables but the babies were wrapped in red velvet, all dressed in bonnets and boots, sitting up in chairs. It was the saddest thing I've ever seen. Their skin was, I don't know how to describe it, it was falling apart, like cheese. Clearly some sort of theatre grease had been applied to hide this, but I suppose in the end, you can't deny death.'

A snore rumbled from Madame's room then, almost like a machine coming to life. Axelle giggled. 'Will she sleep for very long?' she asked.

'Another hour at least,' I said. From across the road, the hysteric trill-dance of piano. Axelle looked to the window, then to the clock on the mantel, and I feared that now she had finished with her story, she would leave. 'Are you sure you won't take coffee? Something sweet?' I asked. 'Madame always keeps a bit of chocolate or bergamot.'

'Wait, I almost forgot.' She opened her reticule and brought out a small paper bag, shiny with patches of oil. She patted the empty seat next to her. 'Come,' she said. 'Something for you.'

I moved to sit next to her and peered into the paper bag, which she held open. Inside, like baby mice nestled together, cashews. Lovely. Coated in oil and grains of sugar and salt.

'Not precisely the same as the ones we were forbidden by your Madame, but it was the closest I could find.'

I dipped my fingers into the bag, picked out a nut and put it in my mouth. I didn't like it. Bits of cashew stuck stubbornly in my teeth and there was too much salt, but Axelle had gone to the trouble. I reached for another cashew and, as I struggled to get it out of the bag without ripping the paper, Axelle touched my face. She touched my cheek with the backs of her fingers. Her lips on the tip of my nose, a kiss.

I kept my fingers in the bag, unsure of whether or not I had imagined this kiss and wondering if I should pull out another nut, and . . . My heart? It dissolved like sugar on the tongue.

'Have you ever been with a man?' she asked.

'I've never been with anyone.' In this moment I could smell everything. Everything. The salt the oil the morning coffee her skin.

'I see the way you look at me. You look at me as if you want to breathe me.'

'Do I?'

Her lips on my lips, so quickly it almost didn't happen. I couldn't breathe at all.

She moved away then. As if nothing. She asked for a bergamot sweet and, when I came back from the kitchen, carrying a small plate of them and feeling as if I'd been slapped or woken abruptly from deep sleep, she had put her gloves back on and was preparing to leave.

'Will you come again?' I asked her in the vestibule. The sounds of Madame from down the hall: a body rolling in layers of blanket and sheeting, a low moan.

Axelle glanced towards Madame Debord's room. 'You had better tend to that,' she said, 'and perhaps we'll see each other tomorrow.'

Axelle did not return the following day, though while Madame slept I read in the salon and pretended to myself that I wasn't waiting and that I wasn't looking for her out of the window. She didn't come the next day or the next, and it must have been a week before the grey face of Monsieur Muller appeared at the door with her letter, which explained that she had been very ill but that she was better now, and that she would like to visit the following afternoon.

Which she did. Sitting together on the sofa, her hands on my face smelled of October and almonds. Madame was asleep down the hall and Axelle, chewing on her lower lip, pulled my shawl from my shoulders and undid the buttons at the collar of my blouse, and she pressed her lips to my neck. She pulled her face away and looked at me as if I were something to be read.

'What are you looking at?' I asked.

'You. You're fortunate to have naturally pale skin.'

'Oh.'

Upstairs where the Russian family lived, something heavy dropped to the floor, and then panicked footsteps. The quick, muffled draft of an argument in a rhythm that had become familiar to me.

Axelle's hands were at my waist. 'You're covered in gooseflesh,' she said, and kissed me.

This time, this first time, was a fumble. We remained clothed, pecking at the edges of each other to where we were barred by buttons and petticoats and corsets. I was afraid – not of being caught; Madame Debord slept for hours and never got out of bed without my help. I was afraid of the way her touch triggered a kind of thickening inside my body, something like inebriation. When Axelle left that afternoon, I felt as if my own clothes could not contain me, and when I put my head on my pillow that night I found that my eyes would not close and that she had become everything. I stayed awake most of the night, sleeping a little at dawn, only to wake and be pummelled again by the sweetest thoughts of Axelle Paquet.

In the middle of October, Axelle and I sat outside together at a small cafe not far from La Samaritaine. Axelle, careful not to look me in the eye in public, read to me some gossip out of *La Presse* – a cuckolded man had been accused of pushing his wife down a flight of stairs – while I sipped my coffee and picked at an apple tart with the tines of a silly little dessert fork.

'I've been worrying,' she said, folding the newspaper on our pedestal table, 'that I've made a dreadful mistake.' She spoke with her eyes on the street and my heart kicked at my ribs.

'Oh?'

'Do you think,' she said, leaning towards me, 'that because I've seen those dead people, do you think I could have brought a curse upon myself? Do you think it was mocking of me to visit that place?'

'Mocking towards whom?' I asked, relieved that my heart, for now, was safe.

'The dead. I feel like I've seen something that can't be unseen.'

'That's true of everything you see.'

She nodded, pleating the edge of the newspaper like a fan. 'Do you think though,' Axelle went on, 'that I might have drawn the wrong sort of attention to myself, you know, from Death?'

'You do spend a lot of your time at its fringes,' I said.

She frowned. 'I'm being serious and you're making fun of me.'

I grabbed her hand, only to assure her that I had been joking, and she quickly pulled it away, shifted her eyes to the tables around us.

Because when we were *out there*, outside Madame's cosy, shabby salon, Axelle was not the same person as she was when we were alone; one ear, each of us, alert to the sleep of an old woman down the hall, when Axelle pressed her fingers to the sides of my face or when she unlocked me with a kiss, or when she peeled away my corset shell and lifted my chemise over my head and took my small breast, my beating heart, into her mouth. When her tongue was at my ear and her breath how I imagined the ocean would sound, when her fingers like a pestle stone found me.

When we lay naked together (very quickly we grew bold and naked and entitled) we compared our bodies. Axelle was curved and plump and warm, with shiny white tracks traversing the terrain of her thighs where the skin had stretched in growth. The hair at her pubic bone was tawny and rose freely from her body, whereas mine was black, wiry and slick. She had a beautiful potted belly, and if a hundred cakes would have given me a belly like that I would have eaten every one of them, but my body never held on to fat.

Outside the cafe where we sat that day and spoke of death, a chill wind blew up the boulevard, carrying bits of paper and leaves and the smell of leaves. On the road in front of us, a team of men unloaded large sacks of flour from the back of a sagging cart, a cart pulled by two muscular, black and shaggy horses. A pall of flour hung in the cold air about them, whisked into swirls by the horses' stamping hooves, and the sight of it, the flour dissipating in the air, made me feel mocked – reminded me how loose my hold was on this love I so badly wanted. I was partially, but not wholly, aware of my own stupidity.

Over the following weeks, as October moved into November, Paris lost its colour but I, I was in love. The river roiled brown

116

and, with weeks of rain, gained momentum like a whipped horse. After the rains, the clouds moved on and the temperature plummeted under a sky pale blue. At night, I shivered in my bed, barely able to sleep, and in the mornings, I would go to my window to see the city frosted white. The chimney smoke that hung over the slate rooftops would catch the early sun and the whole world glowed.

Axelle and I took whatever we could. Mostly in the salon, sometimes in my bedroom, always when Madame was having her nap. Once, only an hour into her sleep, Madame called for me while Axelle and I lay face to face on my bed. She was running her finger along my jawline and I was tumbling deep and blind, and then there was Madame's voice calling me back up to the surface, and I came up for breath and we both, Axelle and I, froze. Fish-eyed and dumb, we stared at one another, her fingers resting on the blood-pulse of my neck, her knee prodding in between my legs. I rose from the bed, shaking, and stumbled to Madame's dark bedroom, to the smell of flatulence and wine.

'What is it?' I asked her.

'I'm thirsty.'

'There's a glass of water next to your bed, Madame. Where it always is.'

'Well, it's been knocked over or something else. There is no water here.' Then, the sound of a drinking glass toppling, rolling, water dripping from the bedside table on to the floor. 'Oh,' she said.

I brought her another drink and a cloth to clean the spill, and, in the semi-darkness, mopped the water from the floor. 'Will you be getting up soon?'

'Not likely.'

'Is there anything else you need?'

There was a moment of silence while she considered this, and then a hesitant, 'No.' One tiny word loaded with the awareness that something wasn't right.

And it wasn't long after that, maybe a few days, that I answered the door to find Axelle flustered, flaring at the nostrils.

'That toad of a concierge,' she said, pushing past me. 'He was watching me strangely just now.' There was the smell of perfume on her but also wood smoke and leaves.

'He can't know anything. You're a friend who comes calling.'

'Well. We've got his attention. And he'll gossip. They all get together like hens. It'll come back to your Madame before we know it.'

'I'll tell her I'm teaching you how to sew.'

'I already know how to sew.'

'It's as good a story as any.'

That evening, sitting together in the salon and going over the day's expenses, I told Madame about Axelle's visits, and explained that she had been coming during Madame's naps because those were the hours I had free to give. I told her it had only been a few times, and apologized for having had a visitor without her consent.

'There's something unsavoury about that girl,' she muttered, squinting at my small print, the most recent entries on the accounts ledger. 'She's bold.'

'She's a friend who needs assistance.'

Her face remained sceptical. 'How can someone of her age and upbringing not know how to sew?' Madame said. 'Ridiculous.'

'Isn't it? I had to help. And I thought it might reflect well on you.' I poured a little more brandy into her glass and felt immediately guilty.

And what a peculiar thing it was, to become as familiar as we did with one another's bodies. The position of freckles and moles, the way the muscles moved with the bones, the curls of hair at the back of the neck or the particular odour of the skin after climax. The idea of nakedness became much more profound than the simple uncovering of skin. When, with my eyes closed, I kissed all the parts of Axelle's body, I imagined that I was painting her into existence, as if she hadn't been a part of the world until she was a part of the world with me.

A November Sunday. Walking along the river on a day that was crisp and sunny: Axelle, Madame Debord and I. After a short distance, Madame grew tired so we found a bench and settled her there. I left Madame and Axelle on the bench, and ventured a few paces upriver to where a vendor sold cakes and tarts and roasted nuts kept warm over a wood fire. I purchased three small pistachio cakes, dusted with powdered sugar and lovely green flakes, because they were pretty, and because I was happy and foolish. When I turned, Axelle was beside me, eyeing the cakes as the vendor wrapped them neatly in paper.

'I wouldn't generally eat cake this early in the day,' she said.

'Today you shall,' I said, pulling coins from my purse. I kept one eye on Madame, who watched us like a baby bird. 'I love you,' I whispered, handing her the parcel of cake.

She looked away, then shook her head and laughed. 'Qu'est-ce que je vais faire de toi?' she said. *What am I going to do with you?*

20

Nora
Ottawa River, 1987

NORA SAT COMFORTABLY in the high driver's seat of Red's truck. The truck was an obvious choice for the drive to the hospital in Toronto; safer, and there were chains in the flatbed if the snow got really bad. Before they got as far south as Fowlers Corners, the snow was already coming down strong, fists of it buffeting the windshield. The heat in the truck blasted dry air, making her drowsy, but Anouk, feverish and cocooned in a sleeping bag in the back seat, was cold. Nora cracked her window open an inch and the deep pulse of cold air hurt her ears.

After a few minutes of this, Red said, 'Can you close the window, please.'

'I'm sorry. The heating is putting me to sleep.'

'Should I drive?'

She glanced at him quickly. 'If you want to, but. My eyes are better than yours.'

Under all this snow the world was like the waiting womb. They passed a few cars but were otherwise alone, and then for several kilometres there were no other tracks on the road. Then, a faint double line of a vehicle having turned on from a side road, the track already mostly filled.

The radio was on and the voices began to deteriorate, to skip with static, so Nora reached over to turn it off and now the only sounds were the blow of the heater and the flap of air through the window. It had been a week since Nora told Red about Jody, and other than those few words the first night, nothing had been said.

Maybe life could be like this, like a finger broken and never treated, healed but crooked. Or a leg. You could walk with a limp for ever. You could get used to anything.

Red: 'I think we should put the chains on.' With Red now, everything was a statement, terminal.

'It's not that bad.'

'So we wait until it gets bad, then put them on.'

'No. I'm just saying. When we stop to eat, we'll put them on. Don't you think?'

'Whatever you think.' He shifted away and rested his head against the window and closed his eyes.

Not yet noon, but Nora had to turn on the headlights. She kept a steady foot on the accelerator and kilometres passed in silence. The land here was hilly. The road swerved around bends, up and over hills that broke one after the next. Nora took it slowly. Should have stopped to put on the chains when Red suggested it but now, with the visibility so poor, there was nowhere safe to pull over.

The road descended steeply and they came to a single-lane bridge that spanned a river, a cut of black water bleeding a track in the snow. Nora slowed to a crawl, beeped the horn to warn any oncoming vehicles of their approach, as she knew that the road on the other side took a sharp, hidden turn to the left. They crossed the bridge and took the left, which quickly inclined. Nora slipped the truck into first gear and hit the accelerator hard, and the truck fishtailed slightly, the engine whining. She lost the gear and stalled. Looked sideways at Red. He was sitting forward, shaking his head. Nora pulled the emergency brake and restarted the engine, then bit hard with first gear and eased off the brake. The truck jolted up and over the lip of the hill and swung towards the side ditch. Nora spun the wheel with the turn to avoid the skid and the truck straightened out. A tree in the middle of the road and she hit it square. And time stopped on the inhale. A crunch. Nora's head whipped forward. Her seat belt dug into her neck, and then there was the seize of inertia, then no thought or movement, only the exhale. Truck silent. Nora reached into the back seat to touch Anouk but couldn't feel her. She unclipped her seat belt and leaned over the seat and saw that Anouk had rolled on to the floor of the truck, still in her sleeping bag, eyes wide open.

'Are you hurt?'

Anouk shook her head. Laughed or made a sound that was almost a laugh.

'Are you hurt?' Nora asked again.

'No.'

Red unbuckled his seat belt and got out, left the door gaping.

'We hit a tree. You're sure you're not hurt?' Nora leaned further over, and felt up and down the length of Anouk.

Anouk, cumbersome in the sleeping bag, shuffled herself back on to the seat. 'We hit a tree?'

Nora turned back to the front and watched Red through the window. No tree. Red leaned over, inspecting the grille, something on the ground. He came back to the passenger side and got his coat.

'What did we hit?'

'A buck.'

'We didn't.'

He punched his arms through the sleeves of his coat, dug into the pockets for his gloves and hat. Without looking at her, 'Are you okay?'

'I'm fine. Are you okay?'

'I'm okay.'

'Wrap yourself up,' Nora said to Anouk. She shimmied into her own coat and turned the engine on again for the heat. As soon as she stepped out of the truck there was the smell of animal, the bitter, rank rustiness of blood and the musk of fear. First thing she saw, a spray of blood in the snow, and then there it was, forelegs bent and contorted under its body, hind legs spread out behind. Still alive, hot breath rising from its nostrils and gasping mouth. A low, tuneless moan. One antler, seasoned and woody, was caught in the grille, forcing the buck's head to hang awkwardly. It was trying to break loose, digging trenches in the snow with its hind hooves. Blood dripped thickly from its mouth and nose and its eyes rolled towards the bush, the road, towards Nora, not seeing her, and up to the falling snow.

'We're lucky we're not dead,' said Red. 'If that had been a moose.'

'What the fuck do we do?'

Red knelt in the snow behind the deer's head. He reached for the antler that was stuck in the grille, wrapped his gloved fingers around the thickness of it and tried to pull it away from the metal. The deer screamed and kicked, dark eyes rolling. The front hooves jerked, palsied, and the air filled with a strong snort of urine. Nothing ever sounded so loud as this animal's laboured breath, its dissonant moan. There was a break in the metal where the antler met the grille, and Red tried to pry back the jagged piece of steel but it wouldn't bend.

'Can he feel it?' she asked.

'Course he can feel it.'

'No. I mean, does he have feeling in the antlers? Can't we saw them off or something?'

Red sat back on his haunches and rubbed his beard. He touched the deer's shoulder, as if to calm it, and the animal tried to rear back, its movements weak and distorted. 'I don't have any tools,' he said. 'Fuck.' He put his hand on the back of the buck's head and gripped the antler again and tried to manoeuvre it one way, then another, but the antler had become even more wedged in the grille.

Anouk had crawled to the front seat and was raised up on her knees, trying to peer over the hood.

'We can't stay here, Red.'

Red, still kneeling in the snow, was looking down the road, listening for something. The sound the buck made seemed to come not from the buck but from somewhere older and collective and indescribable.

'Red?'

'Just please shut up for a second.'

'Are you kidding me?'

A layer of snow had accumulated on his hat and shoulders, and on the buck. It looked as if they'd been there together in the road for hours, Red at the animal's head, and the buck, its blood freezing blooms in the snow, the buck steaming and twisted out of shape.

'Red.'

'I wouldn't, Nora. You need to not talk right now.'

So much life in the dying buck, still. Nora thought if she listened hard enough, she would be able to hear its doomed heart beating against its ribcage. If only it would die, they could rip it loose and carry on.

'Get me the bag, please,' he said. 'The big backpack.'

'Why?'

'Nora.'

She went around to the back of the truck and opened the canopy flap. The backpack was wedged underneath everything else, and she could not think of one good reason he might want this bag, and she looked behind her, up the road; it was unbearable to be so hated.

She brought the bag back around to him and he positioned it under the buck's neck, at the base of its head for support. Blood dripped black on to the canvas of the bag. Nora went to the side of the truck and motioned to Anouk to roll the window down.

'You okay?' Nora asked.

'We hit a deer? Is it dead?' Anouk's voice bubbled, congested.

'Yes, but it's not dead.'

'Can I get out?'

'No way.'

'Will it die?'

'His legs are broken. He seems to be in a lot of pain. It would be better if he died.'

Anouk considered this.

'Are you hungry? Are you warm enough?'

'I'm scratchy.'

'We'll get out of here as soon as we can.' Nora put her hand on Anouk's forehead, down her neck, clammy.

Anouk pulled away. 'Your hands are cold.'

'It's cold out here.'

'Dad's mad at you.'

'Well. I crashed his truck into a deer.'

Nothing about the tableau at the grille had changed when Nora came back, except that now the buck seemed to have accepted Red's hand on its shoulder.

'He must have turned his head just as we hit him,' Red said. He stroked its fur. 'And we weren't even going that fast.'

'I'm sorry, Red.'

His eyes flashed and then he looked away again. 'Yep.'

It was cold and deeply quiet. Snow quiet. No wind and the snow fell straight as rope. Still, heat rose from the animal. Its winter-thin ribcage expanded and relaxed with each laboured breath and its haunch shivered and twitched.

'Red. You're not doing anything. We have to do something. Anouk's getting worse.'

'I'm thinking.'

'She's getting worse.'

'She's fine.'

Nora looked up the road, all but obliterated by snow that fell as if it would never stop as long as the world turned. She had half a mind to just get in the truck and start driving until the buck died, until the road wrenched him from the grille. She went again to the back of the truck and opened the tailgate and unloaded all their bags. She was looking for a shovel, something she could use to hit the thing over the head. Nothing in the flatbed. She lifted back the rug that lay on the bottom, and underneath was just sawdust and dirt and rust. Some tangled fishing line and a hook bent out of shape.

'Somebody's bound to come along soon,' she called out. Something to say at least. She repacked their things and closed the tailgate. Back to the deer and the man, and she repeated these words again. Somebody's bound to come along soon. Get the fuck up, she thought.

'Aren't your legs getting cold?' she asked, cajoling. She whisked her hands together, her knuckles raw pink. The deer's eyes were glazed and its face was set. Its movements now seemed involuntary.

Red looked down at his legs and brushed the snow from his jeans, but still did not get up.

'What's wrong with you, Red?'

He looked past her, up the road. 'I don't know what to do.'

She could use a rock to the head. It would be awful, but. 'Screw it,' she said, and tramped through the snow-filled ditch at the side of the road and into the trees, mainly birch and alder here, naked and spindly and asleep. A thousand branches nicked at her cheeks, caught her hair. She was looking for a rock small enough to carry; big enough for killing. No feeling in her fingers or toes. The afternoon light was so flat and the ground so uniformly white that it almost wasn't there. Only indications of the land underneath were the baby green yew branches and the odd yellow grass stalks poking through the snow, like breathing straws in water. There were no rocks here but she kept trudging forward and, when she turned to look back, the truck on the road looked like a photograph, scratched and worn. That dark hump on the road was Red. That deep hum was the sound of the engine keeping her daughter warm. She tripped on a root and landed with her arms buried, got back up angrily. Black dirt under her nails and a scraped knuckle.

Red was calling her name and so she pushed back towards the road and then there he was, standing over the deer. Nora organized her face into a confident smile for Anouk, watching through the windshield.

The deer's eyes were death-open.

'Did you kill it?' she asked.

'No.'

He knelt again and laid his palms flat on the dead animal's haunch, and Nora knelt beside him. He leaned closer, put his cheek on its shoulder.

'What are you doing?' Nora whispered. The smell of the animal was sharp and it was also beautiful. The rusty sound of Anouk coughing came from the truck. 'Red. We have to go.'

'I know that.'

The antler that was entangled in the grille had pulled slightly away from the buck's head, leaving a gap underneath that was ruddy and fleshy, like the blood-filled socket after a lost tooth. Nora straddled the deer's muscular shoulders, its thick neck, and there so close was the soft, white fur lining its ears. There were its long black lashes and the bony racks behind the ears from which the antlers, like polished, grainy wood, sprouted.

With one hand she gripped the trapped antler by its thorny base, and with the other hand she pushed the top of the deer's skull and in this way tried to separate the two. The flesh and skin at the base of the antler pulled like gum, but still held. Her mouth filled with spit. She gagged, her throat tight. She looked to Red for help, but he had moved away and was looking down the road at nothing.

This was too gentle. She shifted her weight and got a better purchase with her heels in the snow, and with this new leverage tightened her thighs around the animal's shoulders and pulled harder, eyes closed, pulled the head back until the antler began to crack away – a grinding sound and wet. She moved her hands closer together and gave a bit of a twist to the antler, and finally felt antler and head separate. She released the buck's head and it dropped heavily to the snow. The antler was still in the grille but could now be twisted easily from the bars.

'We should keep this,' she said, out of breath, a little nauseous, holding the antler up to Red. A shred of skin and brown-grey coat, and also a shard of bone, hung off its base.

Red turned. Looked at her face and then the thing she held in her hand and back at her as if she were a stranger.

Again, 'We should keep this.'

Red ran both gloved hands up and down his beard, then moved to the buck and gripped its back legs under each of his arms and began to haul it to the ditch, carving a guilty trail in the snow. Blood dripped thickly from the hole where the antler once was.

'I can't believe I did that,' Nora said, daring to be proud of

128

herself, and helped Red to kick snow over the carcass. A gesture of burial at least.

'Well. You killed it, so.'

She wiped her hands in the snow to get rid of the smell, but the smell stayed and maybe she didn't mind it so much. She loaded the antler into the back of the truck, careful not to soil their things with its bloody stump.

21

Pieter
Karmøy Island, 1942

I ALREADY TOLD YOU that my grandfather – my father's father – was the storyteller in our family. He was also the archivist, the keeper of records. He survived my grandmother by a decade and when he died, partway through the war, your mother and I packed up their little house on Karmøy, the house by the sea where I spent most of my summers as a boy.

The war had been a confusing time, Bear. Among other things, I was already thirty years old, considered by some too old to fight, considered by others to have had no excuse for doing nothing. There were men my age who chose a side and enlisted. Others joined the resistance. But this wasn't my plan. I hadn't yet managed to save the money I would need to start my own business, and I was still working for the man under whom I'd apprenticed. I was good at what I did – very good – and I could think of nothing else than to build something of my own. Naturally the war slowed everything down, so I stayed right where I was. I began to fear it would be this way for ever.

But then my grandfather died. And he'd left everything to me. Finally, there would be enough money that I could lease my first factory space as well as a bandsaw, a lathe and a sanding machine, and purchase most of the tools I would need, drawknives and whittling knives and mallets. The man I had been working for all those years helped by giving me a bargain on a lot of what I would need.

This makes me sound callous, as if I were more concerned with what I could get from the death of my grandfather than with what I had lost. It may sound that way but it wasn't. This was an opportunity, a way to honour and to remember.

Your mother and I had been married only a few months when he died, and I was lucky to have her with me on this trip to Karmøy to settle his affairs. The house had been sold and all that was left to do was to pack up what my father wanted (he wasn't sentimental and had asked for only a few things to be salvaged), to decide what to give away and what to throw out. A whole life, a marriage, in boxes and kitchen drawers and closets. In a cedar chest and a glass-fronted armoire. In a crawlspace under the stairs, I found my father's old binoculars. I prised open the rusty snap of the hard leather case and flipped up the top, and fastened to the underside of the lid, a yellowed and brittle slip of paper. On it my grandfather had written that these binoculars had been given to my father for his twentieth birthday by an uncle. Everything had been itemized, memorialized, in this way, as if in preparation for audit: a tennis racket, a jewellery box, a clock. All in my grandfather's tidy script. Your mother found a box of photos and we lost two hours drinking cheap wine out of the bottle, sifting through photographs labelled on their backs with dates and names that were known to me because of my grandfather's stories. There was the cousin who'd gone to America and married a Mexican on a horse ranch, and the fisherman who had been lost at sea and was believed by everyone in the village to be dead. But then who, two weeks later, washed up with his boat in some craggy Scottish cove. He'd been blind drunk on spirits the whole time.

Bed linens and clothing were to go to an orphanage. Furniture, dishes and cookware were to be donated to the church for their annual charity sale. For my father: a cracked-glaze teapot and tube radio. Some inexpensive jewellery, my grandfather's pocketknife, photographs and books. Also, my grandmother's paintings and the mask that hung on the wall. The milky one I used to want to lick when I was a little boy. According to my grandfather's labelling system, the radio had been a gift to my grandmother for their forty-fifth wedding anniversary. The mask had been a curio, a keepsake purchased at a flea market in Oslo. Apparently, my grandfather wrote, it had originally come from Paris.

The work was tedious and your mother and I were newlyweds. On the last night, amidst boxes and a house now cold and echoey in its new state of transition, we lit a fire and candles, and I threw a silk handkerchief over a standing lamp. When there is nothing but picture hooks and stains on the walls, when the carpets are rolled up and cushions packed away, a house becomes sharp and mean. I put the handkerchief over the lamp to soften the shadows and to make the room feel a little more inviting. And we were a bit drunk. We weren't thinking clearly. We ate our dinner on the floor in front of the fire and drank more wine and talked about our future, about my toy business and your mother's wish to go to university, and we talked about the children we were both eager to have. We schemed and we made love and then we fell asleep, tangled together like two puppies. It couldn't have been much later when I woke up to a burning, sweet smell. A room translucent with smoke. At first I thought a spark had come off the fire and ignited a box or some other old, flammable thing, but when I turned to wake your mother up I saw the lamp, alight, tip to the floor.

I stood unmoving, choking on smoke. My eyes, Bear. I have never forgotten the sting. Couldn't see for the tears. While I stood there like an ass, your mother attacked the lamp with a blanket, punching out the flames. If she hadn't acted so quickly, we would have lost everything. She burned the palms of both hands that night, and a dash of her wrist on the right side. Over time the scars faded so that you wouldn't know they'd ever been there unless you knew the right place to look, just on the nub of her wrist. A shiny redness, which only she and I knew was there, because she was my wife, and this was part of our story, and I knew where to look.

22

Nora
Toronto, 1987

NORA PLUCKED AT the coarse, white deer hairs stuck to her jeans, licked her thumb and rubbed a shadow of blood from the webbing between her other thumb and forefinger. In the hospital now, dim yellow lights and the smell of boiled chicken and Anouk asleep on a high, mechanized bed. Nora and Red had closed the curtain around them and sat in stiff metal chairs on the same side of the bed. Three other children asleep in this room but not children with CF, because children with this condition could not be mixed for the risk of the bacteria they might spread to one another. Nora watched Red, asleep also with his chin on his chest and his cap pulled over his eyes, and she looked at his hair, the way it curled up under his hat, then flowed over his ears like it always had and probably always would.

They were waiting for the blood results and cultures to tell them what bugs were growing in Anouk's lungs and which antibiotics she would have to receive intravenously. On the inside of Anouk's elbow, a wad of cotton secured by transparent tape. Nora, with breath held, carefully peeled the tape back from Anouk's skin and removed the cotton, which was stained with a perfect, heartbreaking pinprick of brown blood. Nora scrunched the cotton in her fist and tossed it to the garbage bin at the foot of the bed.

'Why'd you do that?' asked Red, rubbing his eyes under his glasses.

'Cotton balls give her the heebie-jeebies.'

'You could've woken her up. She only just stopped coughing.'

'I didn't wake her up.'

'Well.'

A porter passed in the hallway pushing a cart with wheels that squeaked. Some kind of jargon was spoken impassively over an intercom.

More time passed and then a man they knew well, Dr Atulewa, slipped through the gap in the curtain looking worn out but impeccable. Nora had always liked him (hero worship, but so what): the triangular tuck of his silk hankie that matched his tie, the strong cologne that was oak and vanilla and moss. Huge hands, and fingers tapered like fine candles.

'Hello again, family,' he said, a whispered and vibrating radio voice. He bent over Anouk and with one elegant finger gently stroked the back of her hand.

'She's so tired,' Nora said.

'We'll have to wake her,' he said, 'but in a moment.' His finger stopped moving, but he left it on her hand for one more beat before removing it, as if reading her. He sat on the edge of Anouk's bed, his knees almost touching Red's, and bent to a file in his hands. His glasses slipped to the end of his nose and stopped, seemingly on command, just short of the tip. He read Anouk's results quietly. A new bug, nothing ominous, but one that was resistant to penicillin so they would be going with some kind of macrolide. Nora nodded and Red rubbed his beard. Anouk would likely be in hospital for two weeks. He asked Nora and Red for permission to speak to Anouk about doing a blood gas, not essential for her treatment and quite painful, but imminently helpful for research. The team would be very grateful, he explained, over

135

the rim of his glasses, but would understand completely if Nora and Red declined.

'Sure,' said Nora. 'We can talk to her.'

'No way,' said Red.

'You don't have to decide tonight,' said Dr Atulewa, getting up from the bed. He closed the file and tucked it securely under his arm. 'We'll have to wake her now, I'm afraid, get this line in.' He excused himself while Red leaned over Anouk and, with both hands on her shoulders, shook her gently. She shrugged him off. He kissed her forehead, whispered something in her ear. Nora put one hand on Anouk's shin and nudged it side to side. Anouk kicked and rolled away but soon opened her eyes, dark with anger. Angrier still when they told her it was time to put the intravenous line in her arm.

Dr Atulewa returned, pushing a cart that held the tubes and needles for the IV. Anouk shifted her gaze towards him, didn't say hello. Her eyes followed his movements as he reached over her head and switched on a fluorescent wall lamp that spluttered and revved and cast them all in its mean, blue light.

'Would you mind if I sat?' he asked her.

She shrugged.

He pushed the cart out of the way and sat on the edge of the bed, facing her. 'You're cross with me,' he said. 'I don't blame you. You were sleeping well. But I've asked my colleagues who run the ward if I can do this procedure for you. Really, it's their job. I had to bargain with them a little.'

'Nurses are better at needles.'

'You're remembering the last time,' he said.

Anouk nodded. Nora remembered too, the student doctor who'd run the intravenous line into Anouk's arm and immediately Anouk saying it felt wrong, and the doctor assuring them all it was fine. Within hours, Anouk's arm was swollen and burning.

136

'My colleagues reminded me of that too,' he said, smiling. 'I told you, I had to bargain.'

'Why do you want to do it?'

'Ah,' he said, gesturing to her arm, 'may I?'

Anouk offered her arm and he turned it gently to expose the smooth, white underbelly. He cradled her elbow with one hand and traced the lines of her veins with his finger. 'You have perfect veins, do you see? Very easy to work with. Some people's veins burrow, deep down, and they wriggle out of sight. Like earthworms. They don't want to be found. Yours aren't like that at all.' He let go of her arm and she tucked it close to her body, under the blanket. 'Now. If you don't mind, we'll go ahead and be done with this business very quickly and you can go back to sleep. The anticipation of the thing is always far worse than the thing itself.'

'I don't know what that means.'

'It means we waste too much time worrying about the future,' said Red.

'Quite right,' said Dr Atulewa, pinching a couple of blue gloves from a box mounted on the wall, snapping them on. 'Now, Anouk. Shall we?'

She dragged her arm once more from under the blanket, as if it were some heavy load not part of her, and offered it. Dr Atulewa tied a tourniquet a few inches above the elbow, then with his fingers felt up and down the smooth path between her wrist and elbow and settled on a spot halfway between the two. He rubbed the area clean with an antiseptic cotton pad. Nora shuffled her chair closer to the head of the bed, and the sound it made as it scraped the floor was brash and unsettling.

'Sorry,' she whispered. She leaned close to Anouk and gave her a quick smile, and Anouk closed her eyes.

Red got up and stood at the end of the bed.

'Can you believe we hit a deer?' Nora asked Anouk, because

137

Anouk loved stories, and here was a whopper. 'Can you believe we have his antler in the back of our truck?'

'Is this supposed to be helping?' Red's voice from the end of the bed, a thousand miles away.

Dr Atulewa busied himself with tubes and a wide-gauge needle, filled a small plastic dish with saline, and flushed out a tube and catheter. He screwed bits together, removed caps, pulled fluid with a fat syringe from a glass bottle. 'What are you talking about?' he said. 'What deer?'

'Anouk, tell him,' said Nora. She put her hand on Anouk's cheek, to say: I'm here.

'I'm going to hold your arm now, Anouk,' said Dr Atulewa, gently gripping her stick-thin arm, pulling the blue vein taut with his thumb. 'I'm going to insert the needle. Small scratch.' He slid the needle into her arm, not far from the wrist, guiding it with the same thumb he used to hold the vein. 'Now. Tell me about the deer.'

Anouk, breath held, eyes shut tight against the pain, refused to give up the story.

Dr Atulewa removed the tourniquet and pulled the needle out of her arm, leaving the catheter inside and a plastic port dangling. He screwed more tubes together, flushed and primed, fastened the port and tubing to her arm with a transparent, skin-like tape. He removed his gloves and tossed them with a hook shot into the garbage. 'I'm dying of suspense,' he said. 'Tell me the story of the deer.'

'It's not pretty,' Red said.

'We hit it,' said Anouk, her eyes moving between Nora and Red, and in them some kind of fear or recognition. Clearly unsure how to present this story, which version would please or harm one of her parents or both.

'How awful.'

'My mom had to rip its antler off.'

'You don't hear that every day.'

138

'That's enough now,' said Red. He looked at Nora with eyes empty and sad.

At the very least? Nora took comfort in the night hospital. She left Red sleeping with his jacket over his shoulders, on the couch in the family room, and walked the darkened corridors to the elevator. Rode it to the ground floor where there was a cafe and stationery store, a pharmacy, a coffee and sandwich counter. There was also a flower shop that sold long-lasting carnations and metallic helium balloons, which, in the middle of the night, were pressed like faces against the shopfront glass. The hospital at night. A sleeping village, a film set. Everything closed and she was drawn to the hum of a vending machine, brightly lit in the semi-darkness. She slotted in a few coins and waited for the paper cup to drop. Night coffee. Skeleton-crew coffee. Anouk safe, for now.

These hours between shifts, with their red EXIT glow, these hours were exclusive in the hospital. A carnival after closing time. Carrying her tepid, third-rate coffee, she passed through the lobby, which was an atrium, lofty and echoey and dissected by elongated, geometric shadows. At the back end of the atrium she strode, stretching her legs, up a wheelchair ramp and turned a corner to another wing, walked down a corridor that was very dark, and came up against a locked door.

She wasn't going to drink the coffee, had only bought it because it was something to do, to witness the procedure of the cup dropping, the nozzle opening and the dark liquid spewing. Procedure was everything in this place and easier to think about than blood.

Here was another elevator. Which didn't stop at Anouk's floor. So a stairwell had to be located, more dark corridors and locked doors. Eventually she found Anouk's ward but didn't go into her room. Instead, she sat in a chair opposite the nurses' station and pretended to drink her coffee.

Night staff, they moved fluidly, in slow motion. Two nurses, a man and a woman, worked quietly behind their curved counter, like the watch on the bridge of a ship. His head was bent to something, the light from a desk lamp reflecting off his face, and she was going through a stack of files, checking things off. The man looked up from his work and asked Nora if she needed anything and she thought, sure: how about the night shift? I'll sit where you are and you sit where I am and then instead of this, I can just be at work right now.

She smiled at him and shook her head no, and repeated the gesture of pressing the paper cup to her lips. She rested her head against the wall and listened to the collective sleep-breathing of children. Some on this ward required machines to help them breathe, and so there was the beep and hum and mechanics of all that too. From where she sat, she could see through a half-open door someone else's child, asleep under a thick, floral-print duvet brought from home.

White deer hairs stuck to her jeans and the shadow of blood still marked her hand. A piece of deer antler in the back of the truck with bits of flesh still clinging, hardening, at its base. Red hadn't known what to do. But she had.

She stood up and dropped the full cup of coffee into the garbage and went to where her coat hung over the back of the chair in Anouk's room, and she put her coat on and she kissed her daughter on the forehead and whispered goodbye in her ear and stood there watching her for a moment, and then she turned around and, with body numb and electric, she walked out of the room, and there was her thumb on the elevator button, and there was the wait for the doors to close, and there were the metallic balloons with their faces trapped behind glass, and there was the revolving door that spat her out into the cold November night tarnished yellow with streetlight, tears freezing on her cheeks and the last flakes of snow drifting down from a sky night-purple and indifferent.

23

L'Inconnue
Paris, 1898

THERE WAS A time when I thought I could mark the point in my story where what followed was irreversible; this point like a hinge, where every moment leading up to it was inconsequential but everything after had its own momentum leading to one inevitable end.

This hinge moment, I once thought, could have occurred when my father died and Tante Huguette became my keeper. Or when my mother died, or when as a child I realized I was in love with a girl whose name was Emmanuelle.

It could have occurred before I was born, when my grandmother and Madame Debord met as young girls.

But, there again. Perhaps every moment, every single moment of our lives, is a pivot, a fulcrum. Perhaps the moment of which I should have been wary began with a patch of wood rot, with damp plaster and rusty nails. Maybe it was the morning Madame and I woke to what sounded like all the dishes in the world crashing to the floor.

That morning. I scrambled from my bed, wrapped my dressing gown around my shoulders and moved quickly through the apartment to the kitchen. There, I found the cupboards hanging crookedly off the wall, their doors open and Madame's everyday dishes in shards at my feet. A lone cup slid from a collapsed shelf to the floor, pirouetted on its rim for several rotations, before wobbling and eventually coming to rest while Madame cuckooed from her bedroom. Where the cupboards and shelves had come away from the wall, a wound gaped from the plaster, revealing thin wooden laths with dried mud and horsehair filling the gaps. On the floor, broken pieces of glass, ceramic and dust, and pieces of the mouldy plaster that had finally given way. I stood in the middle of all this, unsure what to do. Madame squawked.

A querulous rapping at the front door. I went quickly down the hall, and opened it a crack to find Monsieur Muller standing there with a face puffy and demented from sleep interrupted.

'What in God's name?' he asked, breathless. His fat hands twitched at his thighs.

'The kitchen wall,' I said, 'has fallen apart. The cupboards have come down.' I opened the door further and stepped back. 'Have a look for yourself.'

I left him to it and went to Madame Debord, who was standing in the middle of her bedroom, reaching around her back, wrestling with one arm of her dressing gown. She looked like a marionette dancing spastically under the strings of a mad puppeteer. I gently untwisted the garment and helped her into it, and brought her to the kitchen.

Her eyes, like holes, moved from the gash on the wall to the pile on the floor. 'This is a catastrophe.'

'It's not,' I said. 'It can be fixed.' I turned to Monsieur Muller, who was rubbing both hands up and down his bald head, the loose folds of his scalp wrinkling and stretching. 'You can call on someone for us, today?'

'My man is holed up in his bed with a broken leg, fell from a roof just last week. It'll be hard to find anyone good, and for the right price, at such short notice,' he said.

'I am not paying for this,' Madame Debord said, pointing a shaky finger at the concierge. 'I told you this had to be fixed. I told you many times.' She put her hands to her temples, trying, perhaps, to rub away the two large glasses of wine she'd consumed the night before.

Monsieur Muller grasped both hands at his waist, his stance suddenly formal. 'You're mistaken, Madame. I was not made aware of any problems in this apartment.'

She turned to me, incredulous, and back to him. 'I told you,' she cried. 'I told you about the dampness creeping up the wall, about the smell of mould.'

He pursed his lips, rocked on his heels. 'Written clearly into the lease of this apartment, I can assure you, you will find that you are responsible for any damages to the property.'

'But you, Monsieur,' I said, 'are surely responsible for the upkeep of the building? This is not Madame Debord's fault.'

'This is a result of Madame's neglect.'

Madame made the smallest noise then, and leaned against the door frame.

'We'd like to see a copy of the contract,' I said.

'Indeed.'

'Don't bother,' said Madame Debord, everything about her depleted. 'He's got every word of that contract engraved on the backs of his eyes.' She stepped carefully to the mess and stooped down, reached for a quarter-moon of salad plate.

'But he knew about this,' I said.

She stood by the counter, next to the sink, her small back to Monsieur Muller, and drew her finger along the cracked edge of the plate. The morning light through the window cast her face in blue pearl. I moved to stand next to her and put my arm around her shoulders. To the concierge I said: 'You'll call on someone for us, please.' From upstairs, I could hear footsteps.

From below us, water flowing through a pipe. We'd woken the entire building.

Monsieur Muller sighed, as if this weren't his job, as if he weren't enjoying this just a little bit. 'I'll let you know,' he said, and as he walked down the hall, unaccompanied, continued to utter something about how difficult it would be to find someone dependable.

We took our breakfast that morning in a restaurant: simple coffee, bread and cheese. I brought a pencil and notebook with us, and showed Madame how we might recoup her losses over the next few weeks by cutting certain luxuries, mainly sweets and cakes and wine. We could go without meat. It was also a good opportunity, I told her, to sell off the stacks of journals and feuilletons. Make more space.

'The butcher won't want all of that paper.'

'There are butchers all over Paris,' I said.

'You'll waste whatever you earn on the omnibus.'

'I'll walk.'

'You do know there is money? We don't need to do this. You know I'm mad, don't you?'

I reached across the table and covered her small hand with mine. 'We are all of us a little mad,' I said.

Later that afternoon, only minutes after I'd finished sweeping the mess of plaster and glass and porcelain into a corner of the kitchen, there was a knock at the door. I opened it to Monsieur Muller and a young man waiting with bucket and crowbar and other items of construction and repair. He was about seventeen or eighteen, tall with skinny arms that dangled awkwardly from broad shoulders and a barrel chest. His nose shone with grease and he wore a dirty cap over lank, auburn curls.

Monsieur Muller cleared his throat. 'A plasterer from the Compagnons. Name is Nicolas. Count yourself lucky we got him today.'

'Thank you, Monsieur Muller.' I turned to the young man. 'Can Monsieur do cabinets as well?'

He nodded.

I opened the door wide and pointed him down the hallway, and watched as he ferried his tools from the stairwell into the kitchen: a tin bucket loaded with speckled trowels and a brush, a broom, a heavy metal case and a large bundle of thick, dusty sheeting.

In a low, sour voice, close to my ear, Monsieur Muller: 'Do not pay him until the work is complete. He looks like he can't say no to a drink.'

'You're certain he's from the Compagnons?'

'Every institution has its rogues, non?'

'And I suppose this was the best you could do.'

'As I said. Count yourself lucky.'

Madame refused to leave her room. She sat on her bed, facing the window, fidgeting with her clothing – pulling at the neck of her blouse, twisting the fringe from her shawl tightly about her fingers. When I suggested we go for a walk, she baulked.

'He'll steal everything. We'll come home and there won't be a cushion to sit on.'

'What is your solution, then?' I asked, gently. 'You can't stay in your room all day, all week. We don't even know how long this is going to take.'

'You go out there with him. Find out how long he'll be, and how much this is going to cost. Blast that scoundrel Muller.'

In the kitchen, Nicolas had arranged the sheeting over the counter and was laying out his tools.

'This apartment has running water,' he said, his eyes on my forehead. 'Makes my job easier.'

'Well, I'm glad of that.'

'Mademoiselle should probably not be here.' He picked up his crowbar from where it lay on the floor and faced the wall with it poised next to his head. 'This work is dirty and loud.' He glanced over his shoulder at me.

'Please wait,' I said. 'We haven't yet agreed on your fee.'

'Didn't the concierge already tell you?'

'No.'

He leaned his crowbar against the wall, straightened his hat. Squared his shoulders. 'I won't discuss my fee with a woman,' he said.

'Well, we have a problem then, because it is only women who live here. You may as well pack up your things and count this as a wasted day.'

He tightened his mouth, tried to appear fierce. A boy.

I looked at him and said nothing more. If I learned one useful thing from Tante Huguette, it was the power of silence.

He lowered his face so that it was mainly hidden by the rim of his cap. 'Four francs per day. Plus materials.'

His wage, cheaper than I expected for Paris, betrayed his low rank in the Compagnons. 'And how many days do you predict this will take? Can you estimate the cost of materials?'

He kicked at the dusty floor before answering. 'Five or six days, at least. Have to let this wall dry out before I plaster it again, and it will take me at least half a day to source the materials for the shelving and cupboards.' He put his hand to his chin, stroked it where sparse, wiry hairs grew. Instead of forming a square jawline, the skin of his neck made a straight sloping run from the bottom of his chin to just above the sternum, like the sag of a crane. 'It should be about five, six francs for wood and nails, hinges and handles. You'll want treated wood and nails, of course.'

I had taken out the notebook and pencil I still carried in the pocket of my skirt and began to write.

'But that's only an estimate,' he said, glancing at the notebook. 'The final addition could be more.'

'Can't you use the hinges and handles from the old cabinets? The nails?'

He bent to the pile of rubble in the corner and sifted through it, collected a few small bits and showed me. In his palm lay two twisted and rusty nails, like a pair of dead insects. 'These were flimsy to begin with. Impossible to use again.' He went back to the pile and raised the corner of a fallen cabinet with the toe of his boot. 'I'll recover these hinges, but the handles are out of fashion. Wouldn't your Madame like to try something new? I can bring a catalogue, with drawings and everything.'

'Perhaps we can sell the old handles,' I said. 'I'll discuss it with Madame. Don't throw anything anyway or purchase any metal finishings without consulting us first.'

He tipped his hat to me.

Simply because he had told me not to, and also because I was emboldened by the haggle, feeling very much that I had won, I remained in the doorway and watched while he used the hammer and crowbar to break away the plaster at the edges of the scraggy hole. As he did this, he tapped the wall, searching for where the damp ended and the dry, sound plaster began. Dust rose in the small space and I covered my mouth with my shawl, suppressed a cough. The plasterer hummed a tune of his own making and soon, my nose and the back of my throat became dry with dust. I could taste it. Eventually, most of the wall was exposed to reveal weathered laths running in neat, horizontal rows. I ran my eyes over the wall. Walked up to it and touched the bitumen-hard mud, pulled at a few strands of horsehair, brittle and orange. I sniffed deeply and discovered I liked the smell of damp wood and cold mud. Wouldn't it be curious, I thought, to uncover something old and forgotten. A necklace that marked a betrayal, or bones, or a tooth. Something like that.

Nicolas spent the rest of the day filling sacks with rubble and clearing out the mess. I was grateful, dirty and worn out when he finally left at half past six in the evening. In spite of his belligerence, he'd swept and arranged his tools neatly in the corner of the kitchen, leaving nothing behind but some chalky boot prints.

On the fourth day, the new plaster dry and the cabinets almost complete, I asked Nicolas to give me the hinges and handles so I could sell them. The day before, I had asked Audette the laundry girl to sit with Madame, and had taken a stack of newspapers to five different boucheries, a walk that occupied most of the day. I asked each butcher if he knew where I might sell or trade old cupboard handles, and was given the name of a reputable metalworker whose workshop was not far away. Madame liked the idea of new handles for new cupboards, and I wanted to achieve this for her. And while doing all this I thought of Tante Huguette. Just watch how I can take care of things, I thought. And I thought of Axelle. Just watch how I can take care of you.

Nicolas, at first, pretended he couldn't hear me. I had to ask twice. 'The handles?' I said. 'I've got a man who might be interested in them.' I swept my hand over the new, smooth wall. It was cool and satisfying to touch, and smelled of the earth, of the parts of the earth that saw no light. The seam where new plaster met old was almost imperceptible. Work worthy of an aspirant in the Compagnons – in spite of his dishevelled look and seedy demeanour.

'They were worthless,' he said. 'I dumped them with the rest of the rubbish.' He pinched a few slender nails from a pot and held them between his lips, took one and held it to a length of wood.

I put my hand on his arm to stop him working.

He looked at my hand, as if it had scorched him, then at my face, then slowly removed the nails from his mouth. There was an inflamed red spot at the side of his nose.

'That's precisely the opposite of what I asked you to do,' I said. 'I know all about the Compagnons. I know what they do to thieves.'

'You don't know anything.'

'My father was a baker, a sédentaire. He spoke often of his tour and all the ceremony and the rules. He was very proud.'

'I didn't steal anything.'

'The handles,' I said, 'and the hinges, or perhaps the money you now carry in your pocket, will be returned to Madame Debord by this afternoon. If not, it won't be hard for me to find your Compagnon house. I could ask there for the handles?' I removed my hand from his arm. 'I only want this job done well. I have no desire to get you into trouble.'

He sniffed sharply, then looked up, alarmed. Madame Debord was standing in the doorway, watching us, watching me.

'I wonder,' she said, addressing me, 'if we might go for a walk. I cannot stand the dust for another minute, and I think we can leave Monsieur here on his own.'

In the vestibule, as I helped Madame with her coat, I asked her if she wasn't worried he might steal from us. She looked at me, with a respect no one had ever afforded me in all my life, and said, 'No. Somehow I don't think he will.'

When we returned a few hours later, Madame a little sleepy after a glass of wine in the charcuterie, I found that a small collection of francs and centimes had been left on the dusty kitchen counter, the money weighted in place by a triangular shard of porcelain.

That night, while Madame drank her liqueur in bed, we sat companionably in candlelight. She tucked in blankets and I in my dressing gown, darning a pair of stockings. The work soothed me, each pull of thread and tug of fabric, and the stitching fell into the rhythm of Madame's breathing as she settled into sleep, and soon the job was done and I laid the stockings in my lap.

I watched snow fall outside the window in large, airy, moonlit bundles, snow that would not be there in the morning. I thought about how I had come to this place, how it passed that I now sat alone in this room with a woman who had been, essentially, a stranger. A woman who depended on me wholly and whom, I realized, I enjoyed looking after. I was good at it. And I wondered: how had I travelled so, so far from home? I thought about Tante Huguette, a woman who had been given no choice but to raise me and whose life was now, it seemed, tremendously improved without me in it.

Snow tumbled, rolled softly, only to melt once it hit the wet ground, and I thought about my father, bones in a pine box sunk in the earth next to a similar box containing the bones of my mother. Who was dead because of me.

My family – my father, my grandmother, my dispassionate aunt – had never been good at remembering their dead. I knew almost nothing of my mother's parents or her parents' parents. I knew very little of my father's ancestry. My grandmother had a brother who'd been kicked in the head by a horse when he was six years old. I knew that the incident had left him blind, but I did not know his name.

Snow fell and I wondered: is it death when your heart stops beating? When you stop taking breath? Is it death when the rivers that run through your mind turn black? Is it death when the last living creature that feeds off your body has picked the bones dry? Or is it death, finally, when there is no one left alive who remembers you? It seemed not many generations needed to pass before one's existence was completely forgotten. As if she had never been.

Madame had fallen asleep with her liqueur glass in her hand. I slipped it from her fingers and set it on the table, and blew out the candle. The wick glowed red, then faded, then disappeared and there was nothing left but the sweet smell of paraffin wax.

Madame spoke, a bodiless voice in the dark. 'You won't leave, will you?'

'I'll stay until you're asleep.'

'That's not what I mean.'

I knew she was thinking about her babies. Her grief was there in the room with us – it always was. It came from a part of her that saw no light. I felt for her hand in the dark, took it in mine, and kissed it.

Neither Nicolas nor I said anything about the money, and I believed the matter was resolved. Soon enough the cabinets were ready to be mounted on the wall, complete with new hinges that I had purchased myself, forged by the metalworker who'd been recommended to me by the butcher. The handles, purchased from the same metalworker, would be delivered in a week's time. Madame had given me the responsibility of choosing them myself, and what I'd selected was simple and elegant. Nicolas had been right: new cupboards needed new handles.

It was half a day's work for Nicolas to put up the new cupboards and shelves, and I was glad to pay him and see him off, though he would be back the following week to fit the metal finishings. He was surly and greasy and arrogant and immature, and was as repelled by me as I was by him.

And then, Axelle. I hadn't seen her since the cupboards came down and I was aching. I wrote to her and asked her to come but heard nothing back. I wrote every day for a week to no reply, and I looked for her at La Samaritaine. I was told she had left the perfume counter for another position. Finally, on a Friday while Madame slept, a knock at the door. I knew it was Axelle and, as soon as I opened the door, I kissed her. Her whole body was rigid. She pulled away.

'Don't be such an idiot,' she whispered, her voice fierce, from the throat.

'Madame is fast asleep.'

'I don't mean her. Anyone could see us.'

'There's no one here but us.' I took hold of her hand and tried to pull her closer, but her body tensed like a cat.

'I'm not staying,' she said. 'I've only come to tell you. Stop writing, and for goodness' sake, don't come looking for me.'

'What?'

A creak on the stairs made us both freeze and we stared at one another, waiting for someone to come up. I listened for another moment, sure I could hear someone breathing. Axelle began to turn away, to leave.

'You can't just—'

'It's happening, chérie. The position I've wanted all this time. Modelling the dresses. I can't go running around playing these little-girl games anymore. Everything is different now.'

'It was never a game.'

She stared at me with a look that was shattering and horrendous and foul: pity. She shook my hand and turned, descended two or three steps, and stopped. Looked up at me over her shoulder. Half her face was concealed by the lilac ribbon that draped from her hat, the same shade of lilac I had once seen woven into the seams of her chemise. 'I won't forget you,' she said, and then she turned the corner of the stairs and was gone. I stood, holding on to the door frame, for a lot longer than any person should.

24

Pieter
The Koie, 1955

BEAR, FOR YOUR fourth birthday, we packed you and your sister into the car with blankets and pillows and boxes of food, with beach balls and paddles, fishing nets and poles, and we drove out of the city on the motorway that followed the river of Bjerkreim. You'd been on this drive before, but this was the first time you were old enough to appreciate what you were seeing out of the window; forest and lush summer farms, the deep gorge. I always loved this drive along the river; it was never boring. Sometimes the riverbed was so wide that the water ran smooth and still. In other places, where the land closed in on the river like a vice, the water surged and kicked and frothed.

We stopped at a rest spot on the side of the motorway for lunch, and, after we ate, we found a path through a cluster of trees that led to a small beach. Not really a beach, more a spit of coarse sand. The water here was deep and iron-red. It moved quickly, was ripped in a pattern of sharp ridges of white water. Your mother spread out a blanket and I lay on my back, rested my head on my arms. I closed my eyes and felt the hands of the sun settle on my face. I was just about to tip into sleep when you landed on my chest, forcing the breath out of me. You climbed me like a lion cub, pulling my nose and ears, your elbow in my face, your knee in my stomach. You travelled over my face and there was the tang of urine. I shrugged you off on to the sand.

'Bear,' I said, 'did you have an accident?'

You sat up, sand in your hair, trying to hide the wet patch between your legs. 'No,' you said.

'You did, I can smell it. Merete,' I said to your mother. 'He's pissed himself.'

'So take off his trousers,' she said. She was also lying on her back, holding a book up with one straight arm. 'You can wash him in the river.'

'Can you not do it?' I asked.

To this, I got no reply. I made a big deal of sighing and puffing, and picked you up by the waist and carried you over my shoulder like a sack of flour to the water's edge. Tilda had already made her way over to a low-hanging suspension bridge that crossed the river twenty or so metres upstream, and was halfway across, bouncing, the bridge rippling under her. As soon as you saw this, you tried to abscond, but I caught you by the waistband of your trousers.

'Come here, you rascal,' I said. You squirmed in my arms and began to cry, reaching your arms towards your sister, as if she could rescue you. I pulled off your shoes and socks, stuffed the socks carefully in the shoes, and placed them neatly side by side on the sand. This distracted you enough that I could pull off your wet trousers and underpants. You immediately covered your bits with both hands.

'Since when are you shy, Little Bear?' I asked, dousing your clothes in the cold water. I scooped a palmful of the pebbly sand to scrub the gusset of your trousers. 'Nobody's interested in your fishing tackle,' I said.

You looked at me doubtfully, and I scooped up more water to wash between your legs. You wouldn't let me though, and so I left it. 'Suit yourself,' I said.

'Pappa!' you squealed. Your modesty no longer important, you pointed with both hands at the river. You were jumping up and down. 'Look at the fish!'

I turned quickly to look, but of course, the fish you had seen was already gone. The jumping fish gives you one chance only. As does the shooting star. Or the baby kicking inside the womb. I stood staring at the moving water, hoping the fish would surface again, and when I looked back at you, you had gone up the beach towards the bridge. I watched you scramble up the bank and stand at the end of the bridge. I watched your sister run to the far side and I watched you try to follow her. But you fell, the motion of the bridge too much for your short legs. Tilda ran back to you and instead of helping you up, jumped with knees bent so that you bounced like a doll. I watched you two, your sister laughing and you crying and frustrated, and I knew I should go to you but you were both too beautiful and strange with the sun shining on you and the river surging past, not more than three metres below. I didn't want the moment to end.

I don't know precisely what time it was when we got to the town near our lake, but it was that golden part of the day when the sky would hold the summer sun just under the lip of the horizon very late into the night. We stopped at the market for milk and fruit, potatoes and bread. We bought a chicken and a side of cured pork from the butcher, and then crossed the centre of town and on to a wooded, winding road that brought us to our lake. At the north end of the lake, we turned on to the gravel road, potholed and meandering through a mixed forest of birch and alder, willow and pine, the western faces of the trunks a jewelled orange with the setting sun, small stones pinging the windows. This road took us higher and higher until we reached an even smaller track, so unused it was more like the ghost of a road, which you would be wary of following if you didn't know where it led.

My grandfather's koie. He built the cottage himself when my father was a little boy. We've sold it now, one of the hardest things I've ever had to do, Bear. But I'm sure you would understand. We couldn't go back there.

But I remember everything about the place. When you came to the end of that rough track there were the first glimpses of the lake in the distance and the purple hills beyond the water, then the trees familiar and the tall grass and wildflowers, and finally the koie itself, that tiny cedar building constructed by my grandfather's own boat-rough hands. Grass-roofed and A-framed with a crooked iron-pot chimney. You were asleep in the back of the car so we left you there while we unloaded, Tilda running from the koie to the car and back again, getting in our way, throwing her dolls on the single top bunk at the back of the koie. You, your mother and I would sleep on the bottom bunk. It was big enough for the three of us. We'd always thought we wouldn't have to worry about bunk space until later, when you grew too big to share.

We hadn't yet made it there that summer; it was our first visit, and your mother began the week as she always did, pulling back the curtains, clearing away from the windowsills the dead, grey spiders, their carcasses like paper, like dust. She wiped the winter settlement from the long wooden table, swept the floors. There was evidence of strangers having used the cottage: an oily candle stub on the windowsill and an unopened can of sardines that wasn't ours on the counter next to the sink. But we didn't mind. The koie provided good shelter, with a large wood stove and soft beds. Off-season walkers relied on this refuge. And these visitors hadn't done any damage, nor had they burned any of the wood we'd left piled neatly next to the stove.

When everything was unloaded, the food and blankets, oil lamps, fishing rods and clothes, I woke you and carried you, cocooned in a blanket, from the car over to a lichen-covered slab of rock behind the koie. We sat together and looked over the descending wood to the lake below. You weren't fully awake, and you curled your body into my chest and whimpered, displeased with having been disturbed. I rocked you back and forth and spoke about the fish we would catch in the morning, the fish we would catch before your mother and sister had even left their beds. I described how we would motor out on the glassy water to where a creek emptied into the lake, where the water was cool and shallow and where the trout, golden-green and spotted like leopards, were sure to be. You asked me if a fish knows it's been caught when it's been caught and I told you I didn't think so, and you asked if you would be allowed to hold the rod all by yourself and I promised you that you would. We sat together on the rock until your mother called us in to eat.

Dinner was chicken and potatoes cooked in the fire pit. Your mother put you and your sister, both silly with exhaustion, to bed at ten. She lay down with you and told you a new story about the girl all three of you had invented together. A girl named Anne who lived on an island that was shaped like a boat. This girl could climb trees without making a sound. She was the master of wasps. When it suited her, she could transform herself into a fish.

I wasn't yet tired. I lit candles and arranged them on the dining table, poured two glasses of wine and sat quietly, shuffling a deck of cards, waiting for your mother. Her storytelling voice was one of my favourite sounds: somnolent, but punctuated when there was tension, melodic when the dilemma was resolved. My attention was half on the story but also taken up by the night sounds of the koie and of the forest. Wind speaking through the pines, an owl. The pulse of countless crickets and night creatures.

Sometimes, out there, with the air so pure, it seemed possible that if we knew how to listen, we might hear the sound of the stars cutting across the sky.

Your mother's story was over yet still she didn't come. I waited, my hands lost in the rhythm of shuffling cards, then softly called to her. My voice hung alone in the middle of the room. She had fallen asleep, so I took a pack of cigarettes and my glass of wine and went outside to the rock I had shared with you, a few hours before. I was hoping for a show, for the soft glowing dome of northern lights, but they never came.

Cold, when I woke up in the morning. Condensation dripped down the window next to where my head lay. I slept with the alarm clock tucked in bed next to me so I could silence the squawk as soon as it rang. Didn't want to wake your mother and sister at five in the morning. Your mother turned in her sleep and pulled the blanket up over her shoulder. You. You were tucked closely into her body like a snail in its shell. Your white eyelashes lay on your cheek and you were safe. I didn't wake you up, Bear, as I had promised, not because I didn't want you to come with me, but because I didn't want to peel you away from where you slept. The moment was precious and I didn't want to break it, and I thought that I could take you out again in the evening. True, the fish that bite in the evenings are usually the bottom-feeders, the long-whiskered, flat-headed catfish, and though inedible, though they taste of mud, I thought you would have had just as much fun catching and releasing them. So I decided to go without you.

I dressed warmly in my wool fishing cap and multi-pocketed canvas jacket, and I packed a small bag with bread and cheese and an apple, and the pocketknife I always carried, my grandfather's, for cutting the cheese and the apple. I collected my tackle box from where I kept it under the firewood shelter. A pale wash of light the colour of beach stones was just beginning to rise in the east as I turned from the koie and walked downhill to the lake trail. Inside the cover of trees, all was dark, and the trail was steep and rocky and crossed with roots, but I knew every rock and I knew every root. The darkness chittered and sawed with insects, and the deep echo and relay of dawn birdsong carved out the shape of the forest.

I found the key to our small boathouse in the place I'd left it the year before, the place it had been left every year, hidden in a tin box under a flat rock next to the boathouse door. Inside the boathouse, the sweet smell of petrol, of damp wood and old, hairy rope. Our small, square-nosed aluminium outboard sat snugly in its carpeted dolly, covered neatly in a thick, oil-stained canvas sheet. When I pulled the sheet away from the boat, releasing the smell of dust and winter, I upset a mouse that had built her nest in one of its folds, a mother capped with her row of pink and hairless, suckling pups. She sprung from the canvas and landed on the floor. A few of the pups still clung tenaciously to her but the others were left behind, a trail of beans. The mother ran out of the door and I stood there, thinking what to do. Thinking the pups might make good bait. A trout would go for them, no question. On one wall of the boat-house there was a long shelf where I stored tools, rope, fishing line, toy boats and buckets that belonged to you and your sister. I looked there for something I could use to collect the baby mice and settled for one of your wooden beach spades. I carefully scooped up the mice from the fold – there were seven of them – and checked the rest of the canvas for any more, and made a silent deal with mother mouse. I would lay the pups next to the boathouse door, on the flat key rock, and do the rest of the things I needed to do – launch the boat, load my rods and tackle box, see to the business of setting up the motor and servicing it if it needed to be serviced. If any of the pups had died by the time I was ready to go, I would take only those and leave the rest for her.

When I was ready, I found that two of the pups had died. I put those in my tackle box and left the others, wishing them luck.

The sun had risen beyond the trees now and cast a glow on the lake mist, which hovered just above the flat surface of the water. This is the best time to be on the water, when it's so calm that you can spot the striders. So placid, water appears to be something other than water, like a surface you can walk on. When the water is settled in this way it quietly records all that it reflects, as if its purpose is to remember, to jot down the story of the world. The spray of pine needles. The arc of a passing hawk. Clouds. A man alone in a boat.

I untied the bow painter from its metal ring on the dock, pushed off with my foot and yanked the motor cord. The engine spewed a small burst of oily smoke and chucked into action, and I cut a lazy, wide turn away from the dock and headed across the water towards the mouth of the creek. I took my time, watched the V-shaped wake from my outboard spread and thin and disappear. When I got to my fishing spot, I dropped the anchor – a brick tied to a length of rope – and pulled my rod from its bag and assembled the parts, strung the line and fastened a hook to its end with a bowline knot.

I can't remember now if I was thinking about you, Bear, or not. If I was feeling guilty for having left you behind. I don't think I was. What I remember now is the feeling of a dead infant mouse between my fingers, delicate and yielding as an overripe berry. I studied it: a little bit gruesome, a little bit fascinating. Translucent skin textured like a scrotum. Purple shadows of organs and veins and tiny, clawed paws. Black buds of eyes sealed in milky skin, ears not yet unfurled, white filaments for whiskers. It was perfect.

I hooked the pup through the neck and cast the line.

My first trout was a good size, about a kilo. And the mouse was still intact so I used it again. And then once more. When I opened the tackle box to get the other pup, I found that it was alive, nudging its soft, blunt nose blindly into the side of the box. Maybe this was cruel, Bear, but I was a different man then. Stronger and more resilient. Not as prone to symbolism or prophetic thinking. Knowing that the lethargic movements of a live mouse would make even better bait, I hooked this pup through the hind leg and cast my line. I reeled it slowly in and, when I lifted it into the air to cast again, it arched its back and its legs clawed at nothing. I cast again and reeled and noticed that there was now a little wind blowing, skating across the water. I watched the lake's surface change and darken, like something coming for me. I caught one last fish and, because I was beginning to feel hungry, turned the boat for home.

I was thinking about breakfast as I cruised sideways up to the dock, about how I'd fry the fish plainly with butter, salt and pepper. I knew you and your mother and sister would have eaten already. You would have had fruit and oatmeal, something like that. I would be eating fish alone.

I noticed something small and yellow bobbing in the water a few metres from the dock. It was one of your toy boats. I stepped up on to the dock and tied my bow up by the painter, and used an oar from the boat to retrieve your toy. In the little yellow boat were the remaining mice I had left on the rock, inching together. I figured your mother must have brought you and your sister down to the water for a play after breakfast, and that you must have seen the pups and thought them great passengers. You would have been delighted. I felt a little guilty, now being responsible for the death of an entire mouse family. There was no way the mother would care for these pups now, so I put the boat aside thinking we could use them for our evening fishing trip.

I strung my catch through their cheeks on to a willow branch and carried them up to the house.

'We'll never eat all those,' your mother said. She was peeling an apple at the table, the skin falling like ribbon in one, unbroken spiral.

'We'll eat the big one for lunch.'

'And more for dinner?'

'I can salt the others.'

She shrugged.

I put the fish in the sink and washed my hands. I wanted to show you and your sister how to gut and clean them, and looked in the drawer for my filleting knife. 'Where are the children?' I asked.

'Tilda's out back.'

'Bear's with her?' I asked.

Your mother put the apple and knife on the table. The careful click of metal against wood, the knife being laid down. 'Bear's with you,' she said.

Bear. It is a very long fall, from one life to the next. It's hard to find the words. I want to communicate this to you, to make you understand how much. How hard. How. What I have learned is that the world can suddenly and with impunity open up and swallow a man whole. His stomach is the first to plummet, and there follows the rest of his body, his torso his arms his fingers.

The sound that came out of your mother when I pulled your cold body from under the dock was ancient. It was thousands of years old and it was the collective cry made by a history of mothers falling. Older than memory. If I made any noise, I wasn't aware of it. Pink froth bubbled from your lips and when I wiped it away, more came. I stood in the lake, chest-deep, and continued to wipe the froth from your nose and mouth. I hoisted you out of the water and laid you on the dock and pulled myself up too, and there must have been a crooked nail jutting out from the wood because several hours later I discovered a gash in my shin that would have taken stitches had I cared to have it seen to. The scar, now white and shiny, is the speared and feathery shape of a willow leaf.

I straddled your small body and slapped your face. We both knew you were dead, but there's knowing and there's the heart and these

162

two entities don't always act as one. The dock rocked up and down as I threw you over my knees and hit your back with the heel of my hand, as if trying to dislodge food stuck in your windpipe. Your mother pulled you away from me and settled you into her lap, and I watched as the blue cotton of her skirt darkened with water. She was shaking you, and your arm bounced up and down and clear water dripped from the tips of your perfect fingers. This moment very quickly became a series of details. Your toes, bone white. Your hair drying quickly in the breeze. A stranger paddling over in a green canoe, his face a paper cut-out of a face. The toy yellow boat where I'd left it on the end of the dock with its cargo of dead mice.

25

Anouk
Toronto, 1989

LAKE ONTARIO WAS shrinking. At one time, when Toronto was still called the City of York, the shore lay several blocks north, in terms of the city. Front Street was named so because it originally fronted the northern shore of the lake. The Royal York, the finest hotel in town, was built facing Union Station, just by the water, but as the lake receded, exposing more and more land, the city developed until, lying between the hotel and the lake, there were two highways, more hotels, and a quayside shopping district.

East of the city, which, when Front Street was first established, would have been forest and farmland, there were the Scarborough Highlands, which later became known as the Scarborough Bluffs, sand cliffs bordering the lake that were more than a hundred metres tall at their highest point. They were compared to the cliffs of Dover by English colonialists, albeit a much smaller version, and they were eroding, little by little. In the 1940s, as Toronto's population grew, it became fashionable to build large houses on the clifftops, where the air was fresh and the views across the lake incomparable. The construction of the houses increased the rate of erosion of the land they were built on, and, by the time Anouk's mother moved back to Toronto in 1987, leaving Red without a wife and Anouk with a

164

choice, an abandoned bluff-top cottage that once belonged to an artist had already crashed into the lake. The city was busily planting trees and boulders at the base of the cliffs to slow the effects of erosion, to save the homes, but the lake, and its shore ever-changing, was eating away at the bluffs. Try as they might, they could not stop what the water was doing.

Anouk's mother moved to the part of Toronto just west of the bluffs, where every street running north–south ended at the lake. Nora had always lived in this part of Toronto; it was where she was born. And this was where Anouk's aunt Mel also lived. This was where the water was. But Anouk found the beach sand to be gritty with dirt, riddled with bottle tops and cigarette butts, sand that left your feet grey and dusty. It wasn't a junkyard, it wasn't that bad, but it wasn't the same as home. Lake Ontario didn't smell the way water should; there were no hints of cedar sap or mineral or dirt. It smelled more like cold tin.

Close to the water, the shore was stony – a slip and scatter of smooth, broad stones, perfect for skipping. And the temperature, even in the middle of the summer, was breath-taking cold. Red once told Anouk that this was because the lake was dead, nothing living in it to warm it up. But when Anouk told Nora this, Nora said that wasn't true. Plenty alive in there. There were trout, catfish and carp. There were weeds. And in the middle, where the water was deep, there were eels.

Anouk's mother left the family when Anouk was in the hospital with a lung infection. Just walked out, in the middle of the night. She stayed away for nine days. And then, she called, with a decision and a choice. Anouk chose her father. Anouk chose the deep winters, the sky, the river. All Nora asked for, out of everything the family possessed, were a few record albums, photographs and books, and the antler she'd ripped from the head of the buck she'd killed.

Lake Ontario was polluted and sometimes, when the wind was right, there was the ripe smell of sewage from the filtration plant at Ashbridges Bay, west of where Anouk now stood, on the beach. Staying with Nora for July and August. Anouk thought her mother had decided to live in this part of Toronto so that Anouk would have chosen to live here with her, but Anouk wasn't even allowed to swim in the lake. Anouk of the water. Anouk of the river. Here, on this beach, looking out across one of the Great Lakes, which, if you didn't know better, you'd think was the ocean; at her back was the splintery old boardwalk that ran all the way from the bay to the bluffs. In those months, the two hottest of the year, Anouk was banned from the water. Too polluted. Anouk of the gunky lungs. Anouk of the cystic fibrosis.

That summer, when Anouk was a few months shy of twelve, a fourteen-year-old girl named Carolina Cho was preparing to swim across the whole of Lake Ontario. The crossing was going to happen on the last weekend of August, and Anouk and her mother were following Carolina Cho's story as it was being recounted in a weekly column of the local newspaper. The portrait of Carolina Cho that ran with the column showed her standing on Cherry Beach, which was west of where Nora lived, practically downtown, in her cap and goggles, legs spread in superhero stance with her hands on her hips.

As part of her training, the column described, the girl got in the water at Cherry Beach and swam out into the open lake, along the length of the Leslie Street Spit: a sandbank landmass that consisted, mostly, of landfill that was dumped when the city was being developed, but also of sand that was being sluiced off the Scarborough Bluffs and carried west by the water. She would hug the spit up its west side and down its east, cross the wide mouth of Ashbridges Bay and carry on eastwards, passing beaches and parks that shuddered and breathed with maples and oaks. Carolina Cho's father, who was coaching her and always wore a red cap that was faded to pink, paddled alongside her in an aluminum canoe.

Anouk and Nora read that Carolina Cho swam in all kinds of weather. She swam in the dark. She swam when the waves were white-peaked, when they leapt on to shore, each wave like a hand reaching out and grabbing the shoulder of the wave in front of it. She swam in the early-morning fog when the surface of the lake was still, when there was nothing but an almost imperceptible roll and her body cut through the water like a blade through silk.

Some days, Lake Ontario was coloured a rich, navy blue. After rain, it was the colour of stale, milky coffee. Some days, it was pond green. Once, Nora told Anouk, something went wrong at the filtration plant, and from out of Ashbridges Bay there crept a black and bubbly slick of stuff unnamed. It licked up on to the beach for a week before a good rain finally washed it away.

Each week that summer, Anouk cut the Carolina Cho column out of the newspaper. She kept the cuttings in the drawer of her bedside table and imagined what it would be like to be friends with Carolina Cho.

Anouk was bored. Nora was at work most days, as a receptionist in a dental office on Queen Street, a few blocks east of her apartment, and Anouk didn't have a lot to do. After her meds and physio, she would walk to the beach and hunt for mermaid stones, pieces of glass that had been ground and smoothed over time by the movement of waves over pebbles.

Some days she would walk to where Nora worked, and they would eat lunch together at a restaurant on Queen Street. Some days, there was just the TV. On Friday nights, they would go to a movie at The Fox, a seventy-year-old theatre where the seats (several of them broken) were soft, springy and covered in tattered red velvet, and the popcorn was cheap. After the movie, they would cross the street to the Chinese diner for grilled cheese sandwiches and fries served by waiters who were tired and uninterested and famously rude.

'Isn't this great?' Nora asked Anouk the first time, after their plates were slammed down and half of Anouk's fries slid across the Formica table, coming to a rest under the tableside jukebox.

'It's great,' Anouk tried.

On a Wednesday in the last week of July, after Nora left for work, Anouk got on her bike and took the bike path, which ran parallel to the boardwalk, to the Olympic pool. She locked her bike and went through the turnstile to the pool building. The entranceway smelled of wet concrete, piss and chlorine. It was dark, and echoed the sounds of the pool, which was above. She bypassed the changing rooms and climbed the concrete stairs into the sunshine, where the pool deck was crowded with kids and wet towels that were plastered by sun-warmth on to the cement. She found a dry spot to lay out her towel and sat down, got a book out of her bag and pulled off her T-shirt and shorts. Stretched out her legs, wriggled her toes. A toddler leapt over her legs, spraying her with his water shake.

The pool deck was a suntrap and the walls around it blocked any wind that was coming off the lake. She was supposed to be careful of the sun, because the antibiotics made her skin sensitive, but instead she lay right back in it, the sun's hands all up and down her body, and she read for as long as she could stand it. When she thought she might ignite from heat, she hotfooted it to the edge of the pool.

This wasn't really swimming. Not really. The water boiled with too many kids. She jumped in, body pole-rigid, and was grateful for its cooling, but there was nowhere to swim *to*. The water was sterile, almost dry with chlorine. She dunked under, opened her eyes to the sting and pulled herself along the bottom, fingers gripping blue tiles. Legs everywhere. A foot jabbed into the small of her back. A nebula of hair drifted past her face. She got out, knowing it had been a waste of time but glad she'd at least tried, and padded wetly over to the wall that faced the lake. She was just tall enough that she could rest her arms on its top ledge and look out. The wind lifted her hair, dried the chlorinated water from her face, tightening the skin. On the horizon where lake-hazy blue met sky, a line of pale-white sails paused, like commas. Today the lake was rough and dark, and the big lofty trees in front of the beach stretched their arms and made music in the wind. A few people were there in the lake, windsurfers and bathers. But generally, other than Carolina Cho of course, people didn't bother. Too many stories having to do with the pollution, or of weird stomach bugs and infections.

Off to the right, the rocky, curved arm of Ashbridges Bay, where sailboats docked and sometimes the filtration plant spilled its shit. Anouk imagined the girl swimming, her red-capped father following in the canoe. She, Carolina, she could have been out there in the chop, just then. Swimming right through all of it.

The next day, Anouk packed a bag with a towel, water, a jam sandwich and a packet of Creon pills. On her bike again, this time she continued west along the trail past the Olympic pool, and through the park that lay to the north of the bay. Beyond this, the path moved inland and ran parallel to an expressway and a sad-looking greenbelt. She'd never ridden this far before, and when she came to a fork in the path, she took the left turn down Leslie Street, assuming this would take her to the spit.

She was riding through an area that she would write about when she was older. This story would be part of a series about Lake Ontario, which would also include a piece about the Scarborough Bluffs, and about the Toronto Islands. And these stories would not be written in a private notebook kept in a little girl's desk, but would be run in a national magazine.

But here she was, now. Riding through a kind of purgatory that was once one of the biggest marshlands in eastern Canada. Mallards, mosquitoes, reeds and terrapins. Miles of flat, insect-pocked water, home to lake salmon, bass and pickerel. Pit-stop for migratory birds from all over the northern hemisphere. The city grew around it and up against it. For decades, it was used as a raw sewage dump for a pig and cattle operation, but then people started dying of cholera and so forget the egrets, forget the swans. The swamp was drained and filled.

Now, the area was an industrial wasteland, with squat, square buildings on hard, grey earth darkened and mottled by motor oil stains. City dirt. Shreds of plastic caught and fluttering in chainlink fences and rusty padlocks hanging from heavy, metal gates.

Anouk rode for a long time through this and she wondered if she'd gone the wrong way. There was no respite from the sun. A drop of sweat travelled down in front of her ear and, defying gravity, settled behind the lobe.

At last, a sign for Cherry Beach appeared, and she took the turn to the right and the landscape changed again. Trees. A lot of them. Not like the big ones close to home but a good showing of poplars and birch, alders. She passed a small marina and boat club and the cheerful clink of halyards on masts. Here, there were people with dogs and books and bicycles. The grass along the side of the bike path was long and untended, spotted with furry dandelions gone to seed and tiny white daisies. She followed the signs to Cherry Beach and when she got there, propped her bike against the trunk of a tree and stretched her legs. Longest bike ride she'd ever done. The backs of her knees were sweating and her bum hurt. As her sweat, extra salty, dried on her forehead, it left a residue on her brow. As if she'd been swimming in the ocean.

Already in her bathing suit, she stripped off her clothes and pulled the towel out of her bag. She walked barefoot across the prickly grass, dodging acorns and goose shit, and shuffled through the sand to the edge of the lake. Today, no wind, yet still, cool relief coming off the water. Directly north of where she stood, an electricity plant. To the right, downtown, the CN Tower.

Dead-eyed gulls swooped and landed and, habituated, ticked right up to her on red stick feet, expecting scraps. Black, skittering squirrels with scavenging paws stalked her from bench railings, and chipmunks raced fluidly up and down beachside tree trunks. Fat Canadian geese waddled in and amongst the trees, casually dropping their long, green turds in the grass. City wildlife.

So. This was where Carolina Cho disembarked on her swims. If Anouk could, she would have stepped into the water alongside and followed her out to the open water until their strokes synchronized and their breathing did too.

Built into the sand there was a red lifeguard stand. A raised platform just big enough for a chair and sun umbrella. No lifeguard, but a white sign screwed into the frame warning people of the high pollution levels in the water, advising potential swimmers, strongly, not to do it. In so many words. Anouk took a deep breath. Even in this humidity, her lungs felt relatively clear. She stepped into the water.

Chill-ache up to the ankles. Up to the knees. The girl with the swampy lungs. The soles of her feet buzzed over lake stones that shifted with each step, and she dug her toes into the gaps between the stones. *Bathers swim at your own risk.* She dove in. The cold was a shock and when she came up, had to fight for breath. She stood again, breathed until she was calm, and dove again under this water that was unknown. She took a few strokes, feeling strong, towards the end of the spit that curled a few hundred metres away. Dove again, deeper, colder and darker, and opened her eyes. Nothing to

171

see but a green-grey haze. The river at home tasted like grass but Lake Ontario tasted more like the meltwater that might drip from a defrosting fish. But still. This was fresh water. Open water. Why did she listen to Nora? She was grinning now, dog-paddling in circles. She somersaulted and came up giggling as her insides continued to flip. She turned back to a shore that was further away than she'd expected and then spun and duck-dived and resurfaced, and did this again and again and came up in a front crawl. The spit wasn't so far now so she carried on towards it, keeping an eye out for sailboats that might be crossing from the marina.

Close to the spit, the water shallowed again and then she reached the man-made bank of rubble, geometric chunks of pocked and stony concrete, rusty rebar tunnelling through some of the concrete pieces like worms through apples. She climbed the bank, grazing her elbows, her knees, and stepped up on to the spit. Flat and grassy, young trees in full, bright leaf. The grass had been left to grow wild and there was a lattice of paths running through it, and there were people here too. Dogs. Benches and garbage bins. It wasn't like her island but still, it was a destination. She picked her way along the periphery, barefoot and agile, a skinny, sunburnt girl in a green bathing suit, and plucked a stem of tall, woody grass and chewed it. She picked a bouquet of soft-headed dandelions and sent the umbrella seeds floating with one deep puff, and her palms were left sticky with dandelion milk.

Standing at the end of the spit, she looked west towards the CN Tower and Toronto Island but to the south, out to the left, nothing but water. Birds here, plenty. Geese and gulls and slate-grey pigeons. Sparrows and chickadees and warblers, and she thought she saw a junco, fat and dark-eyed, but couldn't be sure.

Later, when Anouk got home, Nora was in the backyard, snoozing in a lawn chair with the newspaper laid across her stomach. Anouk watched her, for a moment, from the kitchen door. A pot of spaghetti sauce simmered on the stove and the whole house smelled of hot tomato and beef and garlic. Anouk went to the bathroom and peeled off her suit and emptied into the toilet the pale, pebbly sand that had collected in the gusset. She ran a hot bath and looked at herself in the mirror until it was obscured with steam. She looked through the window and could see that Nora was no longer asleep in the backyard, and then there was a soft knock on the door.

'You having a bath? Now?'

'Yes.'

'Where've you been? Today was my early, I thought we could do something fun.'

'The pool.'

'Oh, again? I'm glad.'

'Why?'

'Yesterday you said it was awful. I didn't think you liked pools.'

Anouk imagined her mother on the other side of the door, one hand flat against the wood panel. Guilt in her voice, in her face.

'Was it okay? Was it fun?'

'It was fine.'

'Did you swim with other kids?'

'Yep.'

That evening, a movie on TV and Nora cupping Anouk's back up and down. There was hardly any mucus and Anouk was convinced this was because of her swim in open water. Her body was happy. The heavy night air circulated freely about the house through open windows and from somewhere, the sweet smell of jasmine. Somewhere there was honeysuckle, and somewhere a lawn had been cut. They drank cola out of chilled beer mugs and shared a bowl of dill-pickle-flavoured chips.

Halfway through the movie, thunder grumbled from far away and deeply.

'Come,' Nora said, her hand on Anouk's knee. 'Come on.'

Anouk's mother leapt from the couch, and then she was out of the front door and Anouk followed. They sat on the porch and watched the people on Queen Street pick up the pace, go for cover. That feeling of the sky about to open up and plummet, a drop in pressure, a sincerity to the quietness of the world, and the whole world waiting felt like a guitar string being wound too tightly. On the trees, the pale undersides of leaves had turned belly-up, desperate for a drink.

'This is the best thing. It's just the best,' said Nora. This was a new Nora, happier away from the river, from Red and from her. 'This reminds me of my mother,' Nora said.

'Rain?'

'Ya. The porch, the rain. Can you smell it?'

Anouk sniffed. Storm smell, similar to blood. Goosebumps on her arms.

First, wind. In the movement of the trees they could see it coming up the street from the lake. The temperature dropped instantly and the khaki sky rushed with sound. A few fat drops of rain appeared on the sidewalk and on the parked cars, and then the deluge. Spray off the porch steps kissed their feet, the fronts of their legs. On the other side of Queen Street, a cat darted out from under a car and clawed manically up a tree. Lightning cracked the sky copper.

'Isn't it exciting?' Nora said, her voice barely audible over the sound of rain. 'The air is, I don't know, it's . . .'

'We get storms like this at home, too.'

'I know. And I loved them there too. It's just different in the city. Smells different. Feels closer.'

Anouk shrugged. 'Can we watch the end of the movie now?'

Later, while they slept, their garbage cans were burgled by

black-masked raccoons with nimble fingers. Later still, the yowls of cat fights at dawn.

Cherry Beach became a daily thing. Anouk would swim out to the spit and scramble up and over its bank. One day, she thought she saw the head of a turtle, but it was a shampoo bottle. Another day, she found a dead chipmunk with its eyes pecked out and its body sunken like a squashed can. Maybe there wasn't a lot of life under the surface of the lake, like Red said. But stuff was happening on top. Sailboats and windsurfers and motorboats. Long, cumbersome war canoes paddled by fourteen people in perfect unison, a cox yelling orders from the back. Every day, she sat on a rock at the end of the spit and scanned the water for Carolina Cho and the father in the faded cap, and she would look out at the waves, across the long, long summer where nothing much was happening.

26

L'Inconnue
Paris, 1898

NOT LONG AFTER Axelle left me in the doorway, perhaps two or three days, I was coming out of the apartment with a basket and shopping list, heading for the Boulevard de Sébastopol, when I came nose to nose with Nicolas. In that moment, I had been ruminating. It was only a meaningless thing: a pair of pale freckles at the base of Axelle's right ear, one smaller than the other like the moon orbiting earth. It was these, the smallest, sweetest things, that hurt the most. And then there he was, and he had the look of someone who'd had a lot more liquor than sleep. His eyes were bloodshot and without any spark, and his lips hung dumb and wet. I carried on walking and he lurched beside me as if, in his mind, the whole world were tilted and he was walking perfectly upright. I tried not to be afraid but my toes curled, grabbing for balance. We came to the corner, busy with road traffic, and had to wait to cross.

'You promised you wouldn't get me into trouble,' Nicolas said. His eyes wandered to a spot on the top of my forehead and he licked his upper lip.

'And I didn't,' I said. A carriage passed, and I stepped into the road to cross to the other side. On the opposite corner, a man stood watering a horse. Passing very closely to the animal, I tried to use it as a barrier to cut Nicolas off, but he managed a clumsy, drunken spin and kept pace with me.

'I'm deep into the shit with the Compagnons.'

'That has nothing to do with me.'

It was a beautiful day, cold, with a scorched-blue sky, and the dark-grey shadows cast by the bare winter branches on the limestone looked as if they'd been sketched on. The streets were busy and crowded. Nicolas bumped into a cafe table, upsetting a cup of coffee, and the clink of the china cup on the table was loud and unending. Nicolas proffered a sloppy apology to the man who was sitting there with his newspaper and pipe.

'I've been betrayed,' Nicolas said, regaining his balance. 'They know I stole.'

I ignored him, and stopped to let pass a group of men in work overalls. Nicolas took my elbow. It wasn't rough; it didn't hurt, but he wasn't going to let go until I listened to him. He pulled me into a recessed doorway.

'I'm going to lose everything,' he said, 'and I have nowhere to go. This was my last chance.'

'I'm sorry to hear that. However, I kept my word. I don't even know where to find the Compagnon house and I've said nothing to those men. You must have told someone else. Perhaps you were too drunk to remember.' I looked out towards the road just as a passing horse stopped to urinate, its piss potent and billowing steam in the cold air.

He stared into my face, trying to focus, and his hot breath reeked. Stubble grew in uneven patches on his pimpled jaw. 'You're like one of those girls on the postcards that the paper vendors sell.'

'What are you talking about?' I shifted my basket from one elbow to the other, looked from his face to the street and back to his face again. I could taste the smell of horse piss.

Nicolas laughed then. Not a mirthful, belly sound – more of a jab from the back of the throat. He kept his eyes on my face and reached for something in his back pocket, a rectangular piece of card, softened and creased many times over. He unfolded the card and made it smooth by rubbing it with an open palm against his chest, then turned it over to reveal the image. Two naked, creamy women in heeled shoes, one on a bed, the other crouched over her. I pushed the card away.

'I saw you kiss that lady,' he said. 'When I came to finish the handles. I saw you.'

'You saw nothing,' I said.

'I was there, I saw you in the doorway. You and a lady with a purple ribbon on her hat.'

'You don't know what you saw.'

'They're going to kick me out,' he said, leaning back against the stone wall of the doorway. 'I've got nothing.'

'I can't help you.'

'What do you think would happen if your sweet Madame knew what kind of girl you really were?'

'She would never believe you.'

Nicolas took a step towards me, suddenly very sober. 'Would make a good story though, wouldn't it? Perfect fodder for that concierge or the girl who takes the laundry. Truth or rumour, makes no difference to them.'

'What do you want from me? Do you want me to go and speak to the men at your house? Tell them there was never a theft?'

Nicolas held up the postcard again and leaned even closer to me. With his thumb and forefinger, he pulled gently on the lobe of my ear.

'Never,' I said, and pushed him by the chest. He laughed at me as I walked away.

*

But it wasn't going to be as easy as walking away from a drunk boy. I lived the next few days in terror. I watched Monsieur Muller, who was as sour as always but whose attitude towards me remained unchanged, and I watched Audette, who was busy and friendly and disinterested. Everywhere I went, to purchase bread or vegetables or wine, I was like an animal stalked. I had no appetite and, instead of sleeping at night, I composed horror stories that grew worse as morning drew closer: Nicolas confronting Axelle at her place of work, or even more awful, where she lived; Madame sending me home, shamed, back to Tante Huguette, to being told my presence was a burden.

Not knowing what was going to happen, or when, was far worse than anything he could have done to me.

So. It was a relief when, on a Saturday morning, I found an envelope addressed to me on the floor of the vestibule. It had been pushed under the door. Inside, the postcard of the two women. This time, I looked at it. The one on the bed, she had an arm bent behind her head, exposing a thatch of dark hair in the pit of the arm. The other woman who leaned above, as if about to mount the one lying down, was tied at the upper thighs and hips with some kind of wooden phallus, which dangled from her crotch like a puppet. The woman on her back lay with neck arched, legs open, other arm loosely around the shoulders of her dominant mistress, whose face was concealed. On the back of the card, scrawled in blunt pencil, the name of a cheap Montmartre hotel, a date and hour.

I exhaled for what seemed the first time in days.

27

Nora
Toronto, 1989

AT SIX IN the morning, Nora pulled herself out of bed and, on legs still dumb with sleep, walked down the windowless hallway. She stopped at Anouk's bedroom, door mostly closed, put her ear to the crack in the doorway and listened to Anouk's breathing. Smooth and clear. She smiled, carried on to the bathroom.

Nora had moved into this apartment a year and a half before, only a few weeks after the night of the hospital. The night of the buck. And it was so good to be home. Mel had helped her to find this place, on the ground floor of a four-plex on Queen Street, a few minutes from the beach. It was small and creaked with imperfections. The window in the bathroom was painted shut and some of the tiles in the kitchen were coming up. The storm windows in the living room, at the front of the apartment, looked like they hadn't been removed in years and were coated with dust and grime. The oven took an age to warm up and there was very little pressure in the shower.

But then. She had access to the backyard, and also the front porch, where she spent most evenings when the weather was warm; a bottle of Labatt's and a book, or the radio, or the mayhem and spray of a hot Toronto thunderstorm. Also, Mel lived right around the corner, that was good, and the streetcar stopped just in front of the house. Handy.

Nora sat on the toilet in the airless bathroom and rolled her neck, eyes closed. Waking up slowly, sweetly. July that year had been hot, but August was hotter. It was humid and stifling. Toronto heat moved in cycles, building upon itself until the lake pushed a storm across the city, only to begin the cycle again. They were in a heatwave now. It had been strangling the city since the middle of July and Toronto was thirsty. Leaves sagged from the trees and the grass in the parks had crisped to a yellow-brown. Flowers in hanging baskets drooped like mourners and people moved languidly, sweating after their morning showers.

Toronto's civic staff had been threatening to strike all summer. The talk that monopolized the waiting room in the dental office was all about rats and raccoons and squirrels. Three summers before, so Nora learned at work, the civic staff were on strike for two months, and the urban wildlife feasted and procreated on the garbage that piled up into banks that lined the streets. Weeds and grass grew thigh-high in the parks, and the gutters swam with plastic and greasy paper and empty cans. Rats everywhere. The city looked post-apocalyptic.

Nora pulled toilet paper from the roll. Still sleep-numb, she stared at the wall, painted a glossy cream. A water stain in the sink. A hardened knob of toothpaste in the bottom corner of the mirror.

Did she still think about the river? Did she think about the tall firs bending and lowing in a high wind, the fire and crackle of autumn? Did she miss walking barefoot over soft pine needles, toes wet with dew, before Red and Anouk woke up? The rough-hiss of June bugs, the warbler, the chickadee whistling *comeplaywithme*. Red and Anouk never knew that sometimes she did this, didn't matter what the weather was doing, that sometimes she went outside, very early mornings, to listen.

Did she think about Red? Of course she did.

In the kitchen, Nora set the coffee maker and dropped two pieces of bread in the toaster. She waited, looking out of the window to the backyard, grass spangled with tall weeds and in need of a cut. A scatter of newspapers wrinkling and thickening in the grass under her abandoned deck chair. She took her breakfast out to the front porch and sat with a copy of yesterday's local paper, turned to the column about the girl swimmer. Fourteen years old and was going to attempt to swim over fifty kilometres across Lake Ontario, starting from Niagara in the south-west and finishing in Toronto, not far from where Nora lived.

Anouk. Of the water; of the river. Her daughter who was about as different from Nora as a person could have been (though not in looks, no. Same legs too long for the rest of the body, same swan-like neck, same autumn hair). Her daughter loved nothing more than a good story. She was fascinated by this girl and what she was going to attempt.

Anouk. Did not come willingly to the city; pleaded with Nora to come north for the summer instead. Child of the river. A feral thing with sandy toes, cedar sap knotting her unbrushed hair, splinters in the flesh of her palms. Maybe in her pocket a paper-light chipmunk skull, shell fragments from a robin's egg or a couple of acorns. She was a child who could tell the difference between the calls of the swift and of the sapsucker. She was not afraid of spiders.

A streetcar, the first of the morning, passed without stopping. Empty. Across the street and up a few doors, the Korean man who owned the corner store came out of the store in a bright white T-shirt tucked neatly into high-waisted jeans. He carried a tray stacked with containers of raspberries, his brown arms lean and strong. When he saw Nora, he waved and jogged across the street with a palm full of berries.

'Thank you,' she said, meeting him on her porch steps.

'Nah,' he said, his attention on the street as he crossed back again to his work.

The raspberries, wine-red, so sweet the taste caught in the back of Nora's throat. Anouk. Had been going off every morning on her bike to swim in the Olympic pool. The exercise was good for her lungs but Nora worried about the humidity. And her skin was getting sun-pink – she wasn't being careful. But Nora only had her for two months and she wasn't going to spend it nagging.

Another streetcar wheeled up and stopped and swayed in its tracks, brakes exhaling, bell duh-ding. One person got off, and there was the electric whine as the streetcar powered up and moved on. Nora read about the swimmer. Today's article, a round-up of what she had been eating to keep her calories high, to maintain a layer of fat for warmth in the cold water. For breakfast every morning, pancakes and four eggs. Doughnuts for snacks, homogenized milk on her cereal. The column quoted the girl as saying that, while she didn't think other kids would believe her, sometimes she didn't want the doughnuts. Or the cake. There wasn't much fun in it when it had to be consumed in doses, like medicine.

Anouk, too, had to be convinced to eat more fatty foods, to keep the calories up because her body, her pancreas, was unable to process nutrients, to take the good stuff.

Anouk had been a long-limbed, skinny baby, always fractious with hunger. Couldn't be fed by the breast because enzymes had to be added to the milk.

Here was a scene: Anouk at the breakfast table, three years old. In front of her, the bowl of maple syrup with her dose of Creon. A red plastic spoon gripped in one tiny, angry hand, and here she was flicking the maple syrup across the table, round eyes fixed on Nora and combative, and here was Nora sitting on the kitchen floor, hair in her eyes, angry enough to want to strike the child, hard, but reasoned enough not to. Two bowls on the floor, flipped over. Nora engaged in a battle that she knew, the harder fought, the harder lost. The kitchen walls, the cupboards, dripping with maple syrup. Like some manic gingerbread house. Anouk hadn't eaten anything for three days.

Another scene: Anouk, six years old, perched on the edge of a hard chair in the office of her dietician. Cartoon posters on the wall of fruits and grains and fish, and a toy box of plastic foods. Plastic fried egg. Plastic chicken leg. Plastic bundle of green beans.

'Can you tell me about your poo?' the dietician asked.

Anouk, who'd been through this before, squirmed and looked at Nora. Anouk hated this.

'Go on,' Nora said, not wanting to speak for her daughter.

'What's the consistency?' said the dietician. 'Does it look hard or soft?'

'Soft.'

'And how does it smell?'

Anouk took a deep breath. Nora wanted to take her out of this room. 'It smells like poo?' Anouk suggested.

The dietician wrote something down. Smiled at Anouk. 'Is it oily? Are you getting caught out at all?'

What she was asking was: have you shit your pants recently? The answer was yes. Anouk got caught out a lot, another perk of the condition. Nora answered this one for her.

Last scene: Late September 1977, early evening. Nora in a chair by the river. Anouk was one week old, swaddled, sleeping. Across the lake, one rogue alder, bright fire-red amongst evergreens and other trees only just beginning to turn. The sky was settling into a lilac dusk, and the river, this night, was swift and speckled with wood and leaves and other debris after a day of rain. Nora gazed at the puckered face of the stranger she held in her arms. This, a day or two before Anouk was diagnosed. This was the baby who first touched her in the womb, that moth-wing quiver, soft as powder, that. There but not there. This baby could have been healthy. Lived without medication. Swum across a body of water so vast you couldn't see the opposite shore, couldn't even see where you were swimming *to*. This baby could have lived to an old, old age.

28

L'Inconnue
Paris, 1898

THE HOTEL NICOLAS chose in Montmartre was tucked into the end of a tiny cul-de-sac, midway up a steep and garbage-strewn lane where several of the cobbles were loose and moss-covered and rotting like bad teeth. This was a place that would have been damp even in a drought. The concierge at the hotel took me for a whore, and there was nothing I could say to this so I said nothing. In the room, the walls were papered yellow and peeling. The sheets, grey and stiff, and the smell, sour and lingering and shameful.

When Nicolas lay on top of me, I thought of Axelle, and how it felt when we kissed, when her soft mouth moved against mine. Her lips. Our kiss ebbed and flowed and, when Axelle slipped her fingers into parts of my body, and I into hers, we absorbed one another.

This act with Nicolas was repellent. His rough face, his darting tongue. Penetration was a demolition. With hammer and chisel he tore away at my walls, filling the air with the dust of me.

After the first time, Nicolas wasn't satisfied and so I was summoned again and again, half a dozen times at least, always under threat of exposure. Each time, I would leave the apartment with a stack of newspapers to sell, my alibi, and then there I would be, unresponsive beneath this boy-man who was scrawny and sweat-damp and quaking, with a body practically hairless and clammy skin that smelled of cold ham. His penis was like a blind, infant bird.

My body remained in the bed, but I. I sailed out of the window and over the slate rooftops of Paris, where the long buildings looked from above like an armada of ships adrift. I passed over Sacré-Coeur and the glass houses of La Villette where strawberries and cucumbers and cabbages grew in winter, warmed by beds of horse manure. I continued east, beyond the fortification wall, where horses cantered in the cropped and frosty winter fields and crystal ponds mirrored the sun in fractured light. Stands of leafless trees cast their skeleton shadows on the ground, bones scattered, and I.

And I. Smoke billowed from village chimneys and I flew right through it, cleansed.

Eventually, I would find the river again. Find it and follow it back into the city. The clanking, clopping, chuffing, dancing, steaming, caterwauling city. I wheeled and tumbled, spat, swore, leapt from chimney pot to chimney pot. I hovered by a balcony where a little girl sat, plucking white petals off a daisy, reciting the prophetic verse: *Il m'aime un peu, beaucoup, passionnément, à la folie, pas du tout.* The daisy head was scalped bald and the girl dispassionately flicked the limp, unadorned flower over the balcony railing, as it appeared the object of her desire loved her not at all. The naked, dead-body flower turned slowly as it fell to the maelstrom below, where it was caught in the hooves of a passing horse and stamped into the shit.

The last time we were together in that hotel, Nicolas cried, pressing his beak into my neck, claiming his tortured love. He was going away. The Compagnons had decided to give him another chance, and were sending him to Marseille. I almost felt sorry for him, his cheeks grisly with spots. Trembling, he promised that when his tour was complete, he would come back to Paris and marry me. I remained silent and kept my face to the wall, while he sloppily pecked at my ear. And when we parted that day, I walked home through the streets of Montmartre, elevated above the city, thinking I would never have to see him again. Thinking, like an idiot, that Axelle might love me if I told her what I'd done for us.

A few days later Nicolas was knocking at the door of Madame's flat.

'You've come to check your work?' I said, a warning. Madame was in the salon, reading her feuilleton.

'My train leaves in an hour,' he whispered. 'I had to see you again.'

I pulled my shawl tightly around my shoulders. Loudly, I said, 'We're quite satisfied, there's no need for you to come in.'

He cleared his throat, looked beyond me into the apartment. This time, without whispering: 'Say you'll wait for me. Say you're done with that woman.'

There he stood in dirty boots, his hands stuffed deeply into his pockets as if he were being reprimanded instead of giving orders. He carried a small leather bag over his shoulder, which most likely contained everything he owned. I had been fooled. Had been a fool to believe such a wretch would have had the power to undo me.

'I'll wait for you,' I said, knowing I would never see him again.

'And?'

'And I'm done with that woman. Now, go.'

He smiled, the first of his I'd seen; it was like dry plaster cracking.

29

Nora
Toronto, 1989

SATURDAY MORNING, THE last weekend of August and the final hours of Carolina Cho's Lake Ontario crossing. Nora, up at 5 a.m. She pulled herself from the bed, and from Anouk's bedroom could hear the hum of the nebulizer. Anouk, up without an alarm, into her routine early so they wouldn't be late to the beach.

Nora poured milk into a pan on the stove and prepared Anouk's Creon with maple syrup. She also set on the table Anouk's vitamins, liver pills and steroid puffer, and in her head a voice both mocking and kind: See? You can do this. See?

The only light in the kitchen was the stove light, and she stood at its edge stirring the milk, got a little lost and sleepy with the gentle scrape of the wooden spoon circling the bottom of the pan and the sweet smell of warming milk. Outside, the sky was indigo. The whole world in this muted moment was the nebulizer engine burring down the hall, and the froth just bubbling up on the surface of the milk, and the tick of a hot stove element. Linoleum tiles under bare, thick-skinned summer feet. She stirred three heaping teaspoons of chocolate powder into the milk and filled a thermos for the beach.

She went out of the kitchen door and across the backyard to the shed, which housed the lawnmower, a rusty rake, a shovel and crack-handled hoe. Also in the shed, on a dusty shelf and behind a stack of terracotta pots laced with cobwebs, Nora kept her cigarettes. With feet dew-wet and the smell of damp wood and cool earth, she retrieved her stash along with a lighter and an ashtray full of stubbed-out butts leaning against each other like sinking gravestones. She stepped outside the shed, behind it so Anouk couldn't see, and lit one up, blew the smoke sky-high. She looked up at those few morning stars, and felt the shunt of smoke going down the windpipe and curling into the furthest corners of her lungs. The guilt was as pungent as the smell. She revelled in guilt. She was wandering wife. She was mother.

On the Friday evening news, the day before, Nora and Anouk watched a clip of Carolina Cho's departure from Niagara, the other side of the lake. The girl, strong bare legs showing from under a large winter coat, red cap on her head, stood next to her father, who gave a short speech about the years of hard work that led to this one day. He expected the fifty-plus-kilometre swim, a distance that would vary depending on the wind and waves, would take approximately twenty-four hours, and he explained how the support team on the accompanying boat would feed his daughter every thirty minutes by passing food out on a cup attached to a pole. The water temperature, he said, out in the middle of the lake, would be about seventeen or eighteen degrees.

'Do you think she's worried about the eels?' Anouk asked.

'I'd be more worried about having to swim for twenty-four hours. Jesus.'

Carolina Cho, on the TV, kicked off her flip-flops and carefully removed her jacket, folded it and passed it along with her shoes to her father. She whipped her arms in wide circles and slapped her lateral muscles, slapped the backs of her solid thighs. She bent over and hung her arms loosely, shook them out, right down to the fingertips. Nobody so young had accomplished this swim before, the newscaster explained. The first person to do the crossing had been a swimmer called Marilyn Bell, thirty-five years before, who at the time was sixteen.

'Go, girl!' Nora yelled at the TV.

'Shh,' said Anouk.

Carolina Cho stood where the water was just past her ankles and looked out to the horizon. Her chest heaved. She adjusted her goggles, pushing them tightly into her eye sockets, and ran her fingers within the rubber strap at the back of her head and, with a snap, adjusted that too. She turned slightly to the beach, to the camera, and waved politely, then turned back towards the horizon and lifted her shoulders vigorously a few times, rolled her neck. She raised her right arm straight up and, from the support boat a few metres off, a horn blasted. Short and definitive. The girl, moving quickly now after the last few minutes of careful deliberation, splashed a few steps deeper, stumbled a little on the stones, and dove in.

The next scene of the news clip, filmed from the boat a few hours after the crossing began: Carolina Cho alone in calm water. Bright sun, minimal splash. With almost no kick, she trailed her legs behind the power of her arms and hips, and flicked her streamlined feet efficiently like tail fins only once every three or four strokes. She was water. She was lake. Her breathing rhythm, the newscaster said, was something she'd perfected over years: two breaths over two consecutive strokes, head down for two strokes then breathe again twice to the opposite side.

She'll repeat this pattern for twenty-four hours, Nora thought, until she gets to the end. What would go through your mind, with nothing to think about but your breath? Nora knew all about lungs and how they were supposed to work. The air would travel smoothly into the healthy lungs of this girl Carolina Cho, and branch off into the bronchi where her cilia flowed as freely as river weed, then slip without resistance into the smaller bronchioles, and deeper still into the air-sac clusters of microscopic alveoli where the oxygen would be transferred into her blood. Pathways clear and unscarred.

The final words of the newscaster: When Carolina Cho exhaled into the water, her father had reported earlier, she hummed. This, as far as her father understood, sent her into a state of bliss.

By 7 a.m. Nora and Anouk were on their bikes and getting close to the spot where Carolina Cho was meant to land at Ashbridges Bay. The lake was ribbed and pulsing with an insistent chop from a wind that had built overnight. On the beach, a gathering of fanfare. A television van and locals who had come to welcome the swimmer ashore. It was a perfect day. Still August, but the rising blue of the morning sky and the shifting broad leaves of the beach maples promised September cool. Anouk would be going back to her father in a few days.

Nora laid out a blanket and some food she had packed for breakfast: cream cheese and sweet grape jelly on bagels, sliced apples and bananas, cold sausages. Thermos of hot chocolate. Balloons jogged from where they'd been tethered to the lifeguard stand, and a few boats were anchored in the bay. A man bobbed alone in a Laser, mainsail pulled down and relaxed over the boom, with a pair of binoculars around his neck.

Anouk perched on the blanket like a meerkat. From under her white T-shirt, Nora could see the blue straps of her bathing suit and this, these stupid little straps, broke her heart.

Nora spilled hot chocolate on the blanket, and Anouk fed her bagel to a mob of dull-eyed seagulls who squawked and brayed and refused to leave. Eight o'clock became nine o'clock and Anouk, funnelling sand through the heel of her fist on to her legs, asked shouldn't she be here by now, and the TV woman paced around her van with a walkie-talkie pushed against the side of her face.

The man out in the sailboat scanned the horizon with his binoculars.

Starting at the television van, the news travelled from one end of the bay to the other like wind. Carolina Cho had been pulled out of the water. And like wind, the story was impossible to capture. Someone said she'd been bitten by a lamprey. Someone else said it was too windy and wavy out in the middle of the lake. And another: she'd become nauseous either from the bite or the waves, and couldn't keep her food down.

Anouk. Baffled. Nora poured the remaining hot chocolate into the sand and they packed their bag and rode home.

30

L'Inconnue
Paris, 1898–9

SOME WEEKS AFTER Nicolas left on a train for Marseille, I still bore Axelle like a scar, and had come to the conclusion that life would be more bearable lived quietly and without love. Because within me, in the place where my body breathed, a sort of melancholy had settled, like ash. This wasn't sadness or outrage or even heartache. Whatever it was, it was far worse than those trivial things. I chose to ignore this feeling and continue what I had been doing before, to brew coffee for Madame. Heat water for her bath. Eat what little I could.

A few days before Christmas, Madame and I went for a stroll along the Boulevard Beaumarchais, which, for the season, had been converted into an outdoor market, lined with dozens of little rough-wood baraques. All the things you could buy. Or even just touch. Chocolate perfumed with orange or lavender, bronze ornaments, silks from China or just a good pair of bootlaces. Madame and I made up a game where, at one shed or another, we both guessed at items we believed the other would choose to possess, if we could only choose one, then revealed our guesses. Madame chose correctly for me almost every time. She bought me sticky sweets that came in a cardboard funnel, and I ate every one of them because all morning, the taste of something like stale coffee had lingered on my tongue and I wanted rid of it.

We came to a wall of stacked birdcages, right there in the street. Each cage vibrated with tiny, delicate songbirds and their fragile, perfectly formed heads ticked like the hands of a hundred clocks. They had beaks of vibrant blue and yellow and orange. Madame's favourite was the yellow canary. I preferred the house finches, their muted, pastel feathers untidy and their movements less mechanical than those of the other birds. I watched them for such a long time that Madame offered to buy me one.

'What would I do with a bird?' I asked.

'I don't think one *does* anything with a bird. Admire it? Set it free and see if it returns?'

'I don't know how to care for it.'

'I shouldn't think there's much to it. Feed it some seeds every once in a while; make sure it has clean water to drink. It could be a companion to you.'

'A bird as a companion.'

Madame grasped my hand then. 'You're not happy here anymore. I keep expecting that you're going to tell me you wish to return home.'

I couldn't speak. All the vile things I had done. A hot ache steamed behind my eyes.

'Let me buy you the bird,' she said, and raised her arm stiffly to get the attention of the vendor. In that moment, a humidity settled over me and nausea swelled in the bottom of my stomach. I took a few steps towards a cafe table and sat, heavily, and slowed my breathing. Concentrated very hard on not vomiting.

Determined to possess the bird, Madame hadn't noticed that I'd sat down, and when she realized I was no longer standing next to her, she pivoted back and forth like a lost child.

'Here,' I said, 'I'm here.' My mouth was dangerously full of saliva and my guts rolled.

'Ah,' she said, working her way past a pair of men who stared and pointed at a cage of tuft-headed cardinals. She beckoned with her small, gloved hand. 'Quickly now, we need to choose a colour. I was considering the grey-and-violet one, but I'm not so sure. It has a queer look.'

I inhaled, my lips shaking, and exhaled, towards the ground. I pinched the bridge of my nose but this did not stop the tears. Madame Debord stood at my shoulder and cupped my chin, lifted my face towards hers. 'What on earth is wrong with you?'

'The sweets,' I said, trying very hard to smile. A tear ran down the side of my nose and came to rest at the corner of my mouth. 'All the sugar. My heart's beating madly.'

She blew her cheeks out. 'Well. They weren't meant to be eaten all at once, were they?'

I shook my head. 'If you don't mind, Madame, could we go home?'

'Now? What about the little bird?'

Nausea blew through me again and this time I couldn't stop it. I vomited the sweets into the lap of my skirt: putrid pink and orange and a shade of purple too purple to be believed.

And then. More weeks dredged past. I was constipated and vomiting bile out of an empty stomach most days, and it became nearly impossible to fit my tender bust into even my loosest chemise. I thought I was diseased but Madame knew better.

Late afternoon, cloudy. The dining room was darkening in the space between Madame and me, but I didn't dare move from my seat to light the lamps.

'I thought I dreamt it,' Madame said. Her lips were quivering and even the sight of that unsteadiness made me want to purge. We

196

faced each other across the dining table. The stew in our bowls grew cold and the back of my throat was tight with the smell of the beef. 'I'd forgotten all about it, but that boy, the one who fixed the cupboards, he was here again, wasn't he?' She couldn't look at me and spoke as if she were searching the memories of sleep. 'You told him you would wait for him. I heard you say the words.' She looked from her bowl to the window and back to her bowl. 'He asked you to leave me and you promised him you would. I didn't think it was real. I heard the words but they were so unexpected, and . . . it was so easy to convince myself I'd heard nothing at all.'

'I only told him what he wanted to hear, Madame,' I said.

'We can force him to come back,' she said, sitting taller in her chair. 'We'll contact the Compagnons. You'll be married within the week and no one will ever know.' She laughed then, a sound soft and bitter. 'Well. Everyone will know. But they won't have the right to say a thing about it. At least, not to you directly. You and your family can live here, with me.'

'I can't marry him, Madame.'

'Why ever not? You've already given yourself to him.'

'I don't love him.'

'Love has nothing to do with it.' She fiddled with her spoon, rubbing her thumb up and down the edge of its cupped face. She looked at me with eyes that were bright and jittery. 'I don't give a damn what people think,' she said. 'We can do this. I can help you. A baby, really, is a wonderful, wonderful thing. It's another chance.'

With a throat dry as paper, I wished only for the dark to fall faster.

Madame became carer and I. The cared for. Some things I welcomed, for example, the gentle purgatives she urged me to try (they had to be gentle, she said, so as not to dislodge the baby while they did the work of dislodging me): leeks and spinach with fresh butter, honey, purslane with dock leaves, stewed prunes. These foods worked. She also indulged my cravings (salted nuts, goat's cheese, candied fruit of any kind) because she said that to deny them would be to deny the baby, to deny you. She said that you would be born craving what you had lacked in the womb so badly, you would enter the world carping and whining like a little devil.

She had other ideas that I didn't like so much – foolhardy, provincial superstitions. She warned against grinding coffee, or unwinding thread from a skein, or even plaiting my hair because, she believed, the circular motion could result in the birth cord winding its way around your neck, suffocating you. For the sake of peace I indulged her in this, but I refused to rub her suggested con-coction of St John's wort and brandy into the skin of my thighs, a procedure she believed would protect me from clumsy falls.

In the beginning, I concerned myself only with myself. You were simply the problem growing inside me, until one night in March, while I lay in bed, I felt the quickening. A moth at the win-dow. So subtle I wasn't convinced anything out of the ordinary had happened until, a moment later, it happened again. I sat up, sweat-ing. Next to my bed, the wicker berceau Madame had already placed in the bedroom. Ambrose, the baby who'd lived for twelve days, had slept in this basket, which was lined with stiff, yellowing lace. As I sat up, it came again. A twitch in the deepest part of me.

This. This was the moment. This was you.

But I was so, so tired. I could scarcely get out of bed in the mornings yet I still had a job to do. As much as Madame wanted to coddle me, there was food to be shopped for, meals to be cooked and companion-ship to be made. There was always that. I felt as if I were wilting but Madame, she was blossoming. From old clothing she kept in a trunk in her room, she pulled out the layette she'd sewn herself: long slips and swaddling, night caps and undershirts, napkins, nightgowns, socks. All unworn, a little yellowed with age but with embroidery so fine and delicate, it touched my empty heart.

The season did what seasons do. Soft green buds appeared on the acacia trees and my belly grew. The hump of it was still concealed under my skirt but I could feel it there, hardening. You fighting already for your own space in the world. Everything changed, everything. The smell of fresh bread or the sound of horses on hard-packed mud. The well-dressed gentleman reading his news or the old woman selling her copper pots. Even the way the spring sun shone off the Paris stone – all different, unfamiliar again. It wasn't that things had become worse, particularly. The world had been stained like wood. I had been stained.

I felt nervous, all the time. All the time.

One morning, late March, I sat on a park bench and stared at the twiggy black branches of a dwarfish tree. Small silver-green buds, still packed solid as stones, protruded from the tree's multitude of tough little knuckles. One shrivelled, yellow leaf clung to the tip of a branch, and I watched this leaf for a very long time. The wind blew and the leaf danced in a shifty, awkward way, yet still it held on, as it had done throughout the winter. Unperturbed by the new year's growth. My body was pulling itself inwards, wrapping itself into a dense nut, and I did not interpret the leaf as some sign that I should persevere. It meant nothing.

On a busy street in Montparnasse (it might have been that same day or it might have been another), I saw a different man selling those mechanical toys made of painted tin. As before, onlookers watched the toys meander and jerk pointlessly around his feet. They looked like a horde of gargantuan, nocturnal insects that had been taken against their will from under a rock and were now blindly trying to find their way home. I thought of the man with his magnified eye in Deyrolle's, impaling butterflies with straight pins. I thought of Axelle.

The air in the street was smoky and full of the steam of horses, and I became distracted by a wedding party passing by. The bride, if she was the bride – it was difficult to tell – looked young and unprepared. People shouted salutations. One man drank freely from a jug of wine and offered it to a young boy. There was a gentle prodding on the toe of my boot and I looked down to find one of the toys bumping up against my foot, trying to mount it. The toy, at first glance, looked like a man and woman copulating, but of course it wasn't. This was a plaything composed of two acrobats locked hands-to-feet in a perpetual somersault.

This, too, meant nothing.

Nor did the ricochet sound of a woman beating a rug with a broom on a second-floor balcony mean anything.

Nor did the church entrance that swayed with black funeral drapery mean anything.

Nor did the wooden lasts hanging in the cobbler's window, like pigs' trotters, mean anything.

There was something else my Tante Huguette told me about my mother.

I was fifteen years old when, undressing for bed one evening, in winter, I discovered my first blood. This was long after the death of my grandmother, so it was to Tante Huguette that I brought my stained bloomers. Put up with one of her headaches, which made her as mean and dangerous as hot iron, she was sitting in a chair in front of the hearth with a blanket over her knees and her knuckles shining around a glass of brandy. Her chin was tucked into the ruffle of her collar as if she were sheltering from an icy wind. The room was nervous with fire shadow.

I twisted my bloomers in my fists, cleared my throat to get her attention. She opened one small, roving eye.

'What could be so important? Can you not see that I'm suffering?'

'Something happened.'

Tante Huguette opened her other eye and glanced at the fabric in my hands. I untwisted the bloomers and the stain in the gusset appeared, like a rusted flower unfolding.

She leaned forward to examine it. 'Ah,' she said, and settled back into her chair. Closed her eyes once more, slowly, as if even that tiny movement exacerbated her headache. 'I've been waiting for this.'

'Is there something wrong with me?'

'It's your womanhood. The blood will flow monthly, or thereabouts. You can now bear children. Congratulations.'

I stood, swaying on my feet, no less confused than when I entered the room.

'A man, hopefully one you are wed to, will plant a seed in your field whether you like it or not,' she said. 'Or two. Or three or four.' She opened her eyes and turned her head towards me. She smiled. 'I feel it would be remiss of me not to tell you that you do have a choice in these matters. There is the medicinal douche. There is arsenic. There is pennyroyal. Your mother attempted pennyroyal when she was carrying you. Your father had just begun his apprenticeship in another town and she had an intuition he was never coming back. Anyway.' She took a careful sip of brandy and, with one hand straddling her forehead, she rubbed both temples, her smallest finger jutting out like a dirty word. 'Evidently she did not take enough.'

31

L'Inconnue
Paris, 1899

'WE COULD MOVE away,' Madame Debord said one evening in the salon. Expenses ledger balanced, liqueur poured. 'We could go to some other city where nobody knows us. Toulouse or Nîmes or Nice. Why not live by the sea? I ought to be living by the sea, it's in my blood, and the further one moves from Paris, the cheaper the rent. Our story is simple: I am your grandmother. Your husband, the child's father, died. In a fight. No, no. That's sordid. He died of consumption or a weakness of the heart or some other fault with an organ. People will be suspicious – people love to believe the worst – but there will be no way to determine the truth.' She touched the side of my face then, gently, with the backs of her fingers. 'You may even find someone else willing to marry you. You're thin but you're pretty enough.'

I listened and tried very hard not to scream. To live the rest of my life behind a fiction that was as badly constructed as those old kitchen cabinets. As shabby a lie as teaching a friend to sew.

But then one morning in April there were swallows. Queeping and trilling in wide arcs outside my bedroom window. I woke and, without my commanding it, both my hands found my stomach, round and tight and with an odd, dark line running from its centre down to the pubis. Somewhere deep inside, the shock-jab of a knee, or elbow or foot. That was you. That was your knee. Your elbow. Your foot.

I was hungry. For the first time in months, I woke thinking of something other than Axelle. I was ravenous. Not wanting to wake Madame, I walked softly on the balls of my feet to the kitchen and poured milk into a bowl, and sat at the table with the milk and a triangle of hard cheese and a hunk of bread. I dipped the bread into the milk and broke off crumbs of cheese with my fingers and savoured every bite. When I was finished, I went into the salon and pulled the drapes back from the windows. The geraniums in their boxes were bursting pink and red. I pulled open the windows to the fresh morning air and leaned out to pinch off the old brown, gnarled leaves from woody stalks, making way for new blossom. This left my fingers sticky and smelling of bitter nut.

I'd never seen the sea. To live by it, I thought, that morning, could be something.

I dressed and put on my spring hat, a soft, white woven hat with a wide brim, fastened with a water lily I'd sewn myself. I told Madame I'd be gone less than an hour. In my pocket, just the right amount of money to purchase food for the day. I went to a certain charcuterie, and a particular boulangerie, where I could get cold, cooked meats and bread for a little less than what I usually paid, leaving me with enough money to buy daffodils. I wanted something yellow, something bright.

The flower vendors in the Place de la Bastille were loud and competitive. Mostly women, women in comfortable skirts and wide-armed, cotton blouses, displaying their goods in large woven baskets on the ground, or flat baskets in their arms, or big-wheeled barrows. They were no-nonsense and jolly and wore their hair tied loosely on top of their heads, fuzzy locks around their ears, cheeks rough and rosy.

At least, those were the women I noticed that day. They wouldn't all have been no-nonsense. They wouldn't all have been jolly.

The flowers and plants were artfully choreographed. White lilies spraying like fountains, bleeding nasturtiums, delicate white daisies and stiff hyacinths not yet blooming. Everything spilling to the ground, baby's breath and fern and feathered plumes of conifer stems. Underfoot, a carpet of cuttings and discarded fronds and cartwheeling petals.

I walked the gamut of sellers, each daring me to buy, until I found the freshest daffodils, their heads still swaddled tightly in their husks. I bought ten, wrapped in brown, waxy paper. Water from the stems seeped through the paper and dripped on to my skirt as I walked, and I imagined the daffodils opening in the vase on my bedside table like the horn section of an orchestra. I almost felt happy.

And, queerly, the perfume of flowers, the earthy smells of dirt and roughage, made me want to fill my mouth with dirt, to feel the grit of it in my teeth and along the plane of my tongue.

On my way home, in the shelter of a passage, its glass roof darkened by dust and muck, I saw someone I recognized, the legless man from the Gare de Lyon. He was begging at the outdoor tables of a restaurant. I stopped to watch him, considering whose lot was worse, his or mine. He caught me spying and palmed his way slowly towards me. His movements, they were slow, soporific. I could have stood in that spot for a hundred years watching him approach while everything else in the world flowed around us, we two pieces of flotsam. As he drew close, I recognized the awkward hang of his lip, his contorted mouth. He smiled.

'Monsieur,' I said, my voice high and silly with complicity. 'Comment allez-vous?' I thought he might confide in me some precious, private thing. But from the look on his face it was evident he didn't remember me at all.

'What could be so terrible, Mademoiselle, from way up there?'

'What makes you say that?'

'Your sadness is palpable,' he said, with great difficulty. 'Perhaps Mademoiselle is weighed down by her condition?' He directed his gaze just below the waistline of my skirt.

I knelt to him as I had before, though my balance was off and I nearly tumbled on to my backside. I laid the daffodils by my knees and steadied myself with my palms on the ground, and a woman passing in a red velvet hat looked down her nose at me and frowned. Thin peacock feathers pranced from where they were fastened at the top of the hat, an indictment. And then she and her hat were gone.

'You would be amazed at what can be seen from my perspective, Mademoiselle,' he said, drawing out his final syllable like taffy.

'Monsieur is bold to address a stranger with such familiarity.'

'But here you are, on your knees. Quite familiar.'

'You don't remember me,' I said. 'We met, a year ago, in the train station.'

His eyes fluttered and he pressed one dirty finger to his lips. 'I meet a lot of strays.'

'I had a husband. He died,' I said, shuffling my feet. My toes were going numb and my knees were close to buckling. 'He had a sickness in his heart.'

'Son coeur. En effet.' *Indeed.*

'He had a condition.'

The legless man closed his eyes, very slowly, then opened them again. 'You're not in mourning dress.'

I raised my eyes towards the brim of my hat.

'You ought to get yourself some black muslin,' he said, as evenly as he could. 'And a wedding band.'

What a fool I was. My mouth went dry and my ankles ached. I stood up, dusted my hands on my skirt, then brushed the dirt away and smoothed the pleats with my palms.

The legless man watched me, closely. 'Mustn't be soiled,' he slurred. With one filthy hand, he pulled at a thick forelock of greasy hair and tucked it elegantly behind his ear, then smoothed it with two fingers until it shone like metal. 'Your story needs work,' he said.

'The story is all I have.'

'Then you must learn to believe it,' he said, and stretched out both arms to me, creating with his hands a bowl into which, I understood, should be placed a few sous. I had spent the last of the money on the daffodils. I looked through my basket for an apple, a roll of bread, anything, and offered him a wedge of soft cheese wrapped tightly in paper. 'I have nothing else to give.'

His face darkened.

'I'm terribly sorry.'

He spat on the ground next to the hem of my skirt and his spit was pearly with phlegm. 'Pute,' he said, spitting again. Some of it landed on his chin and this made me retch. He rotated his platform and, as he rolled away, gathering speed, he called again over his shoulder, 'Putain!' Everyone in the passage stared.

I pulled my hat over my eyes and quickly retreated; the end of the passage seeming a mile away. The daffodils. I left them in the dirt. It had been a ridiculous idea to buy them in the first place, with money that wasn't mine to spend.

I did not want to go back to Madame Debord's apartment, believing that if I walked far enough and fast enough, I could leave shame behind. And so I walked without direction and was soon crossing the river at the Pont de l'Alma, where I descended the stairs to the riverbank and continued east. Mounted on the side of the next bridge, the Pont des Invalides, was a stone carving of a woman's face. I had passed this bridge before but this was the first time I noticed her, and, oh. She was cruel. Her face sculpted in ashy-grey stone, protruding from a coat of arms that was covered in amphibious scales. White streaks of bird shit ran down her cheeks, and the creases of her features were blackened with mould. Wavy hair, parted down the middle of her head, framed a look that was seething. Her mouth was a black gash, forced open by some silent lament. I imagined, though, that I *could* hear her, and the sound was mournful, unchanging in pitch and volume. It carried all the weight of the bridge and the people passing over it, and it carried the darkness in their hearts, too.

A bunch of yellow daffodils. Pah.

The next bridge along the river was the Pont Alexandre III, the place where Axelle and I, a lifetime before this, had stopped to watch the ambling boys. It was now two in the afternoon and growing cloudy, the sun just a dull hum in the sky. Normally this would have been unthinkable and scandalous, to be alone and skulking under a bridge, but, if nothing else, the apathy I felt was certainly freeing. I remembered that feeling I had the first time I'd been here, with Axelle, when I wanted to take off my boots and do what the boys were doing. This second time, I believed I was that person who could shed herself and just. Climb. I placed my basket on the ground and took one tentative step on to an iron rib, wrapped my arms around the nearest support and pressed the side of my face against it. The metal was cold and rough with rivets that were hard and reassuring against my cheekbone. Feeling stronger than I had in weeks, I skirted around this pillar and reached for the next, grasping it with one hand before letting go the first, and slid my boots flatly along the rib, too afraid to break the connection between my feet and the bridge. Afraid I might get tangled in my skirts and fall. With both arms, I hugged the second pillar, and, once again, repeated the manoeuvre pillar-to-pillar until I was a quarter of the way out over the river. I lowered myself into a sitting position and dangled my legs over the water, a mumble of murky green licks, a good drop below my sturdy black boots. The river.

Intoxicating, ceaseless ripples like tongues whispering incoherently. And the wind passing under the bridge was a doleful answer to the stone woman howling from the Pont des Invalides several hundred metres away. I stared into the water and remembered what it felt like when once, Axelle rested her head on my naked stomach and her eyelashes brushed my skin. And I stared into the water and remembered the dark warmth of Madame Debord's bedroom, which smelled of wood and woman and wax and sleep. I hadn't expected to grow so fond of her.

And then there was you. The stranger growing inside me. You were a gift I neither wanted nor deserved, and I felt very strongly you weren't mine to keep.

Below my dangling feet, the river.

32

Anouk
Toronto, 1989

ON HER SECOND-TO-LAST day in Toronto, less than a week after Carolina Cho did not make it across the width of Lake Ontario, Anouk went again to Cherry Beach. Yellow leaves tumbled across the grass and there was a change in the wind – a fresh cold, the edge of fall. And the sky was for ever blue. Not a cloud.

An infection was coming; the low-down rumble and scratch was there. This itch happened when the lining of the lungs became inflamed and rubbed against the lining of the cavity in which they sat. It didn't hurt, but it was annoying, like hearing your own voice in your head when your ears were clogged with water. Or like an involuntary twitch. The last thing she should have done was to get into the lake.

She swam out to the spit and climbed up on to it and walked across to the other side, goose pimples on her arms and legs, and climbed right back into the water. Open, windy lake now, nothing ahead of her but horizon, two blues fading into each other at the seam. She pretended that she was Carolina Cho out in the middle of this great water.

She put her head down and swam, and when she turned her face to breathe, the air clawed through her system, inhalation rough and gritty. With heavy limbs she carried on; it wasn't supposed to be easy to get to the other side of the lake. The cold crept inside and her blood shivered. She kicked harder. Battered a little by waves. She turned to look back and saw that she was further out than she'd expected, and that the waves had carried her a little way up the length of the spit. But she turned again, face down and arms trundling, to see how close she could get to being in the middle of nothing. To really see what it was like. As she took her next breath, a wave caught her in the face, and her throat and nose were swamped with cold, foul-tasting water. She swallowed some but inhaled some too, and so she choked and sputtered. Coughed. Coughed again.

Before it really began, the fit, she knew it was coming, and within seconds the cough was a live thing acting alone. Simultaneously it was of her and not of her, this millstone she had carried since birth. Each retch required the work of her upper body and so her legs had to keep her afloat. She began an awkward paddle back towards the spit, which seemed to have moved further away. Her head went under just as another cough came up and she inhaled what felt like all the water in the world. So she turned on to her back and drew her legs up and kicked like a frog, and with arms out straight, scalloped the water with cupped palms. This worked for a short time, but being on her back antagonized the cough so she spun again on to her front and paddled like a dog would, trying to keep her head above the waves. Every few strokes she had to stop, hug her body and let the cough come, beating her legs to stop from sinking. She paddled as much as she could between coughs, so that it felt like she was pulling the land towards her by a thin cord. But with each cough, the cord snapped and the spit, released, bobbed away again like a balloon. The calf muscles in her legs had balled tightly into iron cramps and she was very tired.

Panic, at first, sparked in the pit of her throat. It travelled through her body outwards, from her sternum to the tips of her fingers. No direction or control over her limbs. Her head went under, and when she resurfaced her face was angled towards the sky, mouth gaping. She went under again, into the murk, bubbles rushing and tight fists pale and was she actually drowning?

She came up again and here was her body, racked with its interminable, wet cough. This was familiar. This she could do. The cough killed the panic because the cough took everything, and, as the panic drained from her, she was able to take control of her exhausted limbs and clumsily propel herself towards land.

Eventually her hand hit rock and she pulled herself up out of the water like some kind of newt, dripping and spent. She scraped her knee on a rock and pink, watery blood ran down her leg. She sat in the grass, hunched forward to ease the tightness in her chest cavity. Aftershocks of cough. Something felt wrong in her ribcage, as if she'd cracked a bone. A woman stopped and asked her if she was okay and Anouk told her she was fine. The woman asked where her parents were and Anouk waved towards the beach. 'Over there,' she said.

No one would have noticed Anouk's drowning. She knew this. Had seen it on television. Contrary to what most people believed, a drowning person didn't make much of a splash. A drowning person was there one moment, and then she was not. Drowning was private. Unremarkable. Drowning was quiet.

33

L'Inconnue
Paris, 1899

MADAME DEBORD WAS frantic when I returned home from my antics under the bridge, several hours late. My hair had come loose and somewhere along the way I'd discarded my hat. She was hungry and she was afraid, and she made me sit down on the sofa in the salon with a blanket over my knees. I wasn't able to explain to her where I had been and she was too anxious to investigate.

'Carrying a child can do peculiar things to a woman,' she said, flapping like a caged bird about the room. She knocked a pile of newspapers and they fanned out across the floor. I started to gather myself from the sofa to pick them up, but she snapped at me to stay seated and so I watched, helpless, as she tried to reorganize a bunch of old newspapers that refused to be piled, and so they slipped and slipped and slipped a hundred times to the floor. Eventually she gave up and, on to some other mystery, began going through the drawers of a sideboard with alarming aggression, flinging things that had been stowed for years to the floor: a pair of scissors, pencil stubs, a man's leather glove, a lone cufflink and a snuff box. This was the most evidence I'd yet seen of her deceased husband. It occurred to me to ask her what she was doing, but I simply didn't care.

'I was sure I had a pair of beeswax candles somewhere,' she said. 'They smell lovely, and their effect is soothing. But, I—'

'They're in the third drawer, in the kitchen. Wrapped in brown paper.'

'Ah.' She disappeared down the hallway and there was the dry shuck of stiff wooden drawers being opened, and she soon returned with the candles, whispering to herself and picking at the paper in which they were tightly wrapped. After an age, the candles were twisted into a pair of brass holders and lit and placed on the mantelpiece, and Madame was sitting in the armchair opposite me.

'Each time I was with child,' she began, 'I used to cry. Often and without obvious cause. My husband thought I was suffering from hysteria.' She leaned closer to me and tucked the blanket more neatly around my stomach. 'I can feel it,' she said, and placed her palm on my body. 'We need to make arrangements before you become incapacitated.' She kept her hand on my stomach, and she was so close I could smell the powder on her skin. 'We travelled to Nice once, not long after we were married. The sea was a shade of blue I don't even have the words for, so much prettier than how it is at home. La Manche is the colour of storm. And the rain in Wissant. So much, worse even than Paris. But Nice is very different. We walked on the promenade, every evening we walked, eating some delicacy freshly plucked from a tree, almonds or apricots, and one minute you would catch that briny smell off the sea and the next turn it would be some wild, lemony herb. I could hardly believe we were in France. And,' she moved her hand from my stomach to my knee, 'the children are healthier there. I'm certain of it. More sun. Finer air.'

I couldn't speak. My tongue was curling, again, with the oddest desire to consume grit, dirt, coal. All reason was abandoning me.

'I probably was hysterical,' she said, and smiled, kindly. I could scarcely follow what she was saying. 'But now,' her eyes flitted to my stomach. 'We have another chance.'

I licked my dry lips and there was the shiver of candlelight on the walls. A snag of thoughts. Packing and transport, finding new lodgings. A disgraced lady's maid and her invalid mistress and a bogus story.

Madame was smiling but her skirt quivered with the obsessive jerking of her knee. 'We will overcome this,' she said.

In that moment. The future was a black gash forced open by rancid breath, a tongue licking my ear. 'Pennyroyal,' I said.

'What?'

'Do you know about it?'

Her smile set, like wax. She took her hand from my knee and smoothed her skirt over her lap with exaggerated gestures, as if she were a child playing at being an adult.

'Have you heard of it? Do you know if it works?' I asked.

She stood and went to the window and ran her fingers up and down a pleat in the drape. 'I saw, today, how carefully you tended the geraniums,' she said.

'Madame. Please.'

'They look so much healthier without all those dead leaves.'

214

34

Pieter
Stavanger, 1956

SOMEHOW, BEAR, A year passed after we lost you. It passed in the way one might cut through metal sheeting with blunt scissors.

Consider how it would be to move through the world but not be a part of the world. This is what grief is. A wasteland, dusty and infertile. The wind is gritty, the food tastes of nothing and there is no music, and in the distance some dark, unknowable thing is waiting. This is what grief is. Hollow as a tin can.

Food stuck in my throat and so did words. Sleep was like, it was like: trying to solve a puzzle without the comprehension that half the pieces were missing. Three, four, five in the morning, I would wake up with rage beating a hole in my wasted heart.

Your mother was given tablets to calm her nerves but they turned her to stone. I should have taken them too, but in those days men didn't suffer from nerves.

The passing of the year didn't end the grief but, as I've said, a man can get used to anything. You can learn to live on a few mouthfuls of bread and little sleep. You can interact with the world and yet still be separate from it. And we had your sister to consider. We had her, too.

Chemistry. This, at least, I could consume. The summer you

died, your mother and sister left Stavanger to stay with your mother's parents, and I was left alone to experiment with soft plastics in the kitchen oven. I baked glycerol and gelatin and corn starch, polyvinyl chloride and phthalate esters. I burned every pot and pan in the house, set the oven on fire and produced gallons of useless glue before I came up with anything useful. And the smell. It lived in my hair, on my clothes. It lived in the food. I could taste plastic when I brushed my teeth, and when I battled with sleep, my skin sweated plastic on to the bed sheets. Sometimes it addled my brain and I found it hard to concentrate, my thoughts coming apart atom by atom. I lost the cat. We had a cat and I lost him. I called your mother most days and I don't remember what we spoke about, or if we said much at all. I may have only spoken to your sister.

The difficulty with making soft plastic was in the pouring of the liquid resin into the moulds, for which I was using metal ice trays, without creating air bubbles. And consistency was a problem. It didn't seem to matter how vigorously I recorded measurements and procedure, I couldn't replicate one batch to the next. I wanted to create a soft plastic with a smooth, impermeable finish. Easy to clean, durable plastic that would hold its shape with just the right amount of plushness to give the impression of life.

During this time, I swam every evening. This was an attempt to clear my head and rinse the smell of burnt plastic from my hair and skin. It's dangerous to swim a long distance in the North Sea alone, or without someone on the beach waiting for you to return, so I kept close to the shore, never more than a hundred or so metres from land. The water temperature that summer never reached higher than sixteen or seventeen degrees and, because I wasn't eating very much, I was thinner and less able to deal with the low temperatures. I swam for short bursts, lacking the energy to do more.

But one day, a bad day, I kept my head down. I breathed seaward and didn't pay attention to the course I was swimming, to where the beach was. The water was calm but cloudy. I don't remember feeling particularly one way or another. Or caring much about anything. One way or another.

Drowning, the possibility that I could drown, had never been a consideration for me. The sea was as much a part of me as grief had become, and drowning would have been an act of defiance. I thought about it though, that day. The struggle between wanting to die and wanting to live. Press the muzzle of a gun to your temple and pull the trigger and it's pretty simple. But being a strong swimmer, I didn't think it was possible to drown, even if I'd wanted to.

This was torture, Bear, foolhardy, a type of self-mutilation. I was leading myself to you. Deep in the cold water, already shivering after ten minutes out, I told myself a story. It was about you. About how, one summer morning, you woke up as soon as the sun hit your face; your eyelids, your cheeks, your lips warm and rich and full with sleep. You nudged your mother's neck until she turned away from you. Then you remembered, we were supposed to go fishing. You stepped with bare feet out of the bed, expecting to find me at the table, to find breakfast at the table. Fruit and bread and a cup of warm milk. I wasn't there though, and you were mad that I had forgotten you.

So. You found your leather sandals just next to the door and sat on the front step to buckle them over your feet, your pink tongue poking out of your mouth and your hair sticking up and your pyjamas still on. You knew the way to the lake, down the path to the boathouse. You got there and called out for me, and looked through the boathouse door expecting to find me there, waiting for you. I wasn't. And then you made a discovery. On the flat rock, just outside the boathouse door, you found five baby mice. You didn't know what they were. Five pink and hairless creatures, blind and curled like cashew nuts. You went back into the boathouse and got your toy boat, and you scooped the mice up and put them into the boat. You probably spoke to them, named them, told them they were going on a trip. There was no question that this boat would be launched – live passengers! Very carefully, in both hands you carried the boat to the end of the dock, your eyes on the mice and nothing else. You launched the boat into the water and watched it float, and as it started to bob away, you crouched down and tried to reach for it, further, further out, until your equilibrium crossed an invisible line and you fell in. Your splash was silent and insignificant in that vast lake. You turned for the dock but there was nothing for your small hands to grab, only a flat surface of wood that was bright green and slippery with algae. And anyway you were too small to figure out this problem; you called out for me and water filled your mouth.

You sank without fanfare. Your silky hair flowed about your head. Your pyjamas billowed from your scrabbling limbs.

I know what it means to drown. I've read about it. You would have struggled at first as you sank, holding your breath, growing exhausted. When your respiratory system reached a certain saturation of carbon dioxide, your muscles would have involuntarily aspirated. You would have inhaled a great deal of lake water and you would have convulsed, continuing to swallow and inhale more water. You may have vomited. You would have, mercifully, lost consciousness, and succumbed to pulmonary oedema, which is an accumulation of fluid in the air pockets of your lungs, and ultimately, you died of suffocation, which means you asphyxiated, which means there was a lack of oxygen in your blood, which stopped the beating of your beautiful, beautiful heart. All of this – the breakdown of your perfect body, the final shudder of your young heart – would have taken less than three minutes.

I didn't know about this stuff then, that day I swam in the sea not paying attention to where I was going, telling myself this story about you. I hadn't done my research yet. That day, my story ended with the image of you sinking in your pyjamas. At that point, saltwater filled my mouth and burned the canals at the back of my nose. This was the result of surprise wash from a large leisure boat. I stopped swimming to cough and spit and emptied my nose of saltwater, stinging and hot. I turned to shore to see where I was, and saw that the closest point of land was hundreds of metres away, perhaps half a kilometre. I picked a point of reference on land, a church spire, so that I would swim in a straight line. I put my head back down and began to kick. I was very cold. You were there in the water with me, too deep for me to reach. I tried to think of other things: the melting point of glycerol, the whereabouts of the cat.

Raising my head every few strokes to sight the church spire, I settled into an awkward rhythm. My teeth chattered, my fingers had curled into bloodless claws, and my feet were like blocks of wood. No energy, I hadn't eaten much for days. With each breath, I grunted, trying to create heat. Here is a man who could drown, I thought. See how close a man can get.

I touched land at a rocky spit where a couple sat on a bench and watched me crawl pathetically from the water, a creature drenched through. It was a long walk back to my car, to my towel and warm clothes and jug of coffee. My numb feet bled on sharp stones that I didn't bother to avoid. If it were possible, I would have walked deep into the ground that day, just dug in with my heels and burrowed under the dirt.

But then I figured out the plastic and, within a year, I had refitted the factory and we started producing a new line of toys.

Anne was the first doll I designed. She was for Tilda. She was named after the little girl who featured in the stories your mother

219

used to tell you, the girl who lived on an island that was shaped like a boat. Anne who silently climbed trees, who was the master of wasps, and who could transform herself into a fish.

The doll Anne had a stubby nose and fat chin, a mouth open for the bottle. Her cheeks were blushed and her curly hair was painted on, fawn brown, and she had small, pudgy arms that stuck out as if she were asking to be picked up. When a bottle was put into her mouth, it could be moved up and down so that it looked as if the lips were sucking. You could press her cheeks inwards and they would pop back out. The impression of life. She was popular not just in Norway but all across Europe.

We also made toy cars, Volkswagen pick-ups and Mercedes-Benz. American Chryslers with oversized hoods. Tractors and buses, Beetles and racing cars. All cast in thick, durable rubber, solid primary colours. We kept it very simple. Convertibles with passengers sitting front and back. Indestructible, and easy on walls and furniture legs.

There is nothing original or admirable in how I conducted the next few years of my life. I avoided home, your mother and sister, moulded plastic into toys, and repeated to myself the story of your drowning and how it never would have happened if only I.

I was an automaton. Instead of a beating heart and flowing blood, I was a vessel spinning with sharp-toothed cogs and springs. If you lifted my shirt you would have seen a hole in my back where the key was meant to turn. I don't know why your mother didn't leave me, but, and this was something we only talked about in her final days (and she was happy again, by the end of her life, I want you to know that, because despair – because loss – can turn into a thing that is precious and beautiful; it can grow into something you cherish, a part of the stronger person you have become), she wasn't thinking about me either, nor did she care that I was never present. In those years after we lost you, while I did whatever it was I was doing, she was slowly finding her own path out of the black. I wasn't important enough to be left.

I could have carried on like this until death. I would have, Bear. I would have let life fester until this body dropped and the black swallowed me and there was nothing but black. I would have missed so many things: your mother finally attaining her university degree when she turned fifty-five, or the birth of Tilda's children, or standing in the silver shadows of a solar eclipse on a hillside in America one summer while that country was sending its youth to fight in another war. The man who'd taken me to see the eclipse? He had just bundled his son away, Bear, hidden him under the back seat of a car bound for Canada to save the boy from being killed in a war that made no sense to anybody. I would have missed it all had I not received something unexpected in the autumn of 1959. Only a small thing, Bear, a letter. But. It was a letter that changed everything.

35

L'Inconnue
Paris, 1899

I HADN'T, AFTER ALL, the courage to end you. You were a strong force, and you sensed you might not get your chance in this world. Any thoughts I had of pennyroyal or arsenic or tossing myself down a flight of stairs, and you became a flurry of hiccups and elbows and heels.

By June, there was no more hiding. My belly swelled outwards from the rest of my body, part of me and also not part of me. Every time I stood, I felt the weight of you pulsing on my thighs and undercarriage. Delicate purple veins laced across my chest and enlarged breasts, and thick blue veins bulged up against the skin of my thighs, twisted like worms. My calf muscles spasmed inexplicably in the middle of the night, so painful I would call out, and I had to urinate all the time. There was no more peace in sleep. Most of the day my stomach was contracted into a dense, tight ball, which made breathing difficult.

Madame Debord no longer trusted me, and all talk of Nice came to an end. She stayed by my side though, accompanying me outside the flat, walking with her arm linked through mine past the desk of Monsieur Muller, smug in his stiff, high collar. People could get used to (or grow bored of) anything, and even those who knew us – the office workers and milliners' girls in the courtyard, the butcher – lost interest soon enough.

Madame did what she could, even paying for a doctor. And though he pooh-poohed most of her ideas and superstitions pertaining to the confined, he was kind enough. At least, he pretended to believe us when we told him the father of the child had died. I was sure he could sense no man had lived in that apartment for a very long time.

Camille. You were born on the last Tuesday in July, 1899. The twenty-fifth. In the sky, a gibbous moon. Early that morning, I was woken in the dark by a pulsating starburst of pressure in my lower back and anus. The pain subsided as quickly as it had arrived, leaving me with the most urgent need to evacuate my bowels. Which I did, and on my way back to my bed, the pain shot through me again. And perhaps twenty minutes later, again. I had spent my whole life believing that childbirth was a dark and bloody, potentially lethal ordeal, and so I was prepared to die if it came to that. And maybe it was you or maybe it was me, but as soon as the birthing began that morning, in the dark, I wanted only one thing: to bring you safely into the world.

After a few hours of increasing discomfort, as the sun cast its light across my bedroom floor, the pains became a clenching vice-grip. I called for Madame and she called for Audette and Audette sent her mother for the doctor. I crouched in my bed while Madame and Audette prepared the apartment. Audette built a large fire in the bedroom and also in the salon to keep away any cold, because you and I both would be prone to the flux. She also closed all the windows and shutters and bolted the front door.

'But we have to let the doctor in,' I said.

'Don't worry about him,' Audette said, stopping at my bed long enough to cup her hand on my forehead. Her cheeks were flushed, excited. She disappeared out of the door to some other task.

'It's so hot,' I whined. 'Can we not open one window?'

Madame in my room and Audette, down the hall, answered no, in unison.

'It may be the stuff of the old sages-femmes,' said Madame, laying a stack of clean linen on the chest of drawers, 'but better to be safe.'

'Safe from what?'

'Witches. Devils. Peoples of the water. If they come at all, they'll come for your child at the moment of birth.'

'For heaven's sake.'

'All the clean rags you can find, Audette,' Madame called through my bedroom door. 'And start the water boiling.'

By the time the doctor arrived, I was on all fours over the seat of a chair, my stomach hanging low and my nightdress damp and slick against my body. The doctor compelled me to lie on my back, on a nest of old sheets Audette had prepared for me on the floor. Being on my back felt unnatural, and though he was the doctor, I wanted to tell him he was wrong. He muttered something about stale air and left the room, and then there was some sort of conflict on the other side of my bedroom door, in which I had little interest, until he came back in and flung open the window, letting the outside air blow gently over my skin. For this I was grateful, and willing to take my chances with these peoples of the water.

Each time I tried to return to my earlier position, on my knees, the doctor reprimanded me. Lying down, all the weight of you settled into my spine. After hours of this, I lost much of my will and had only the energy to do what I was told. I was offered a mask to wear, which, ignorant of its purpose, I accepted, and allowed it to be placed over my nose and mouth. The doctor administered a liquid by dripping it from a glass pipette into a wad of cotton folded into the mask, which I then inhaled. The liquid smelled sweet but made me feel as if my head were going to detach from my body and float out of the window. I pulled the mask from my face and vomited on to the floor, and no one asked me to wear it again.

More hours passed and I was permitted to walk around the apartment, to ease your progress. Audette kept the fires raging and Madame stayed as close to me as a shadow. I wanted this to end and it felt like it never would. I was imprisoned and I was possessed by pain. Each surge was like. Each one was like. All the bones of the lower back and pelvis and thighs contracting in size and density to that of a bullet. Not once though, not once did I wish you dead. And in these agonizing hours, and after all the years of having believed what Tante Huguette had told me, in these hours I learned that my own mother would never have wanted me to die.

And then. You came. With a warm gush of swampy water and hot blood, you came. I felt you, your head, the hard, solid skull of you pushing eagerly towards this brand-new life. I felt your slick and sticky warmth when you were placed on my chest, you with movements that were slow, like cloth billowing underwater, as if you hadn't yet realized this great transition. As if you thought you were still in the womb. The doctor tied two ligatures around the cord that united us, and with blunt-ended scissors it was cut. And you were cast adrift. He ignored Audette's cries that the cord must be severed at a certain distance from your small body – something having to do with the potential of your singing voice, she claimed – and he tied off the end with a clean strip of cloth. Madame covered your head with a sweet little cap and then you were taken from me. The white paste that greased your skin was removed with linens doused in water that had been warmed to the same temperature in which you had lived for those nine months before. Madame even cleaned your little ears, and all your orifices, with linen twisted into small tents, and, in spite of this intrusion, you made no complaint. Cocooned tightly in white, you were finally returned to me with your red, pinched face, asleep. Audette fed me a brew of some horrid mixture to prevent haemorrhage and, after the doctor left (because he wouldn't have approved), we gave you a spoonful of warm red wine doused with treacle to cut through the birth-phlegm in your throat; to comfort your stomach and cleanse it of any filth you might have ingested during your journey; to strengthen your brain against madness. On these points, Madame Debord was emphatic.

I, it must be said, was lovingly washed from head to foot by Madame Debord and Audette. They placed a warm cloth between my legs to absorb the flow of blood, and bandaged my abdomen tightly with a towel.

You. Had a shock of black hair that grew in a cowlick from the left side of your head to the right. Your toes were extraordinarily long and your legs bent up either side of your belly like a frog. Your gums were rigid against my breast when you fed, which was all you did for the first week of your life. You were attached to me, and I was attached to the bed with the blood of the lochia and with fatigue.

You weren't the only newborn in the apartment. Madame. She was enraptured, empowered. She went outside alone, to do the shopping, for the first time in fifteen years. She fed me stewed partridge as it was easy to digest, but denied me fruit against the risk of flatulence. I was given plenty of white wine and brandy.

'Food that will stick to the ribs,' Madame said, watching me eat a bowl of thick bread soup with vegetables and chicken fat. 'Fill the hole that's been left inside you.'

And I. You came with the gift of respite and, for a short time, I believed that I, we, had a chance at happiness. I was inebriated, high. Which made it all the worse when, two weeks after you arrived, I fell.

I couldn't, for some reason, settle you on to the breast, even though we'd had no trouble at first. Coaxing you to feed put both of us in such an anxious state that I had visions of slamming either my head, or worse, your good body, into the wall. It was the pitch of your scream. Your braying sent me into a frenzy. You screamed yourself purple and you hadn't any tears and I didn't know how to make it stop.

All I wanted to do was sleep, but when I slept, I dreamt of pushing your head underwater, or of losing you in a pit of suckling mud. When I was awake, my thoughts were darker still.

And the whole affair with Axelle. Compared to this? Vaudeville. I was ashamed to have ever felt anything for her at all.

I stopped being a part of the world. You and Madame Debord were somewhere over *there*, safe on the other side of a plate of glass that separated us. I could see you both but couldn't touch you. Through my half-closed bedroom door I could hear Madame singing and clapping and making a fuss. I would stutter-sleep until your lamb-cry, and then you would be placed in my arms and my nightdress pulled down to expose a nipple, dark and sore and split, and we would look at each other and then fight and fight until you latched on, for at least a moment. The prickle would come and the let-down of milk and a brief, brief moment of relief as I heard the sounds of your quiet swallowing, but then your body would tense, your legs curl up, and you, still tightly latched, would abruptly turn your head away, tearing my skin with your strong gums.

We called for the doctor. He informed me that my troubles were a result of my traumatized womb, a sort of shock, and that all would be well in time. He presented us with a feeding bottle. The rubber teat smelled like something burning, and I didn't think you would take to it, nor to the pap, the clouded mixture of flour and water we put in the bottle. And you didn't. You refused it with vehemence and the misery continued.

The first time I left the apartment with you, you were five weeks old. It was the end of August, the same season as, a year before, I had met Axelle. The smell of the streets, the sultry hang of the leaves on the trees, and the way the light fell through those leaves on to the pavement, reminded me of her. I was overdressed with petticoats and thick stockings and felt as heavy and uncoordinated as a barge. Just to breathe evenly was a task. You started crying and I envisioned letting go of the pram, like casting a boat off the end of a pier, and watching it sail into the middle of the road to be smashed by an omnibus. The feeling was akin to looking down from the edge of a great height, wanting and not wanting to jump. I went home, trembling, and left the apartment only once more in my life.

It was simple, Camille. This world had become intolerable and there was a chance I could hurt you, so I made a decision, and this decision unburdened my heart. Early October, a Saturday evening. I went to bed as soon as Madame was asleep. I didn't undress, but lit a candle and lay beside you, you asleep and fidgeting in your berceau. You sighed and sucked your lips with the memory of my breast, and your breathing was a messy gargle of stops and starts. I curled on to my side and watched the flicker of candlelight on the wall. I lay there, awake, until the candle burned to nothing, and then for quite a while longer. Twice you woke, and both times I fed you until you slept again. I was your mother still, this last night. When I was ready, I got out of bed and put on my boots and coat. I kissed you, very quickly, on your soft mouth. As I passed Madame's bedroom, I stood at her door, partially open, and listened to the rhythms of her sleep.

A letter. Left on the dining table. Madame had to believe I was never coming back, and that I could not be found. I wrote what was true, that I was not made of the mothering stuff but that she was, and that you deserved at least that much. And I wrote what was not true, that I was going to try and make a life somewhere else. I signed the letter with all my love and gratitude.

Paris. Deepest, coldest night. I consumed the air like wine, and walked at a brisk pace towards the river. All my senses buzzed. Extinguished gas lamps glowed with the ghosts of remembered light. I thought I could hear laughter and music and the rumble of the underground train tunnel that was being constructed for the World's Fair. Empty hooks in the butcher's window. Horse-less carriages lined up in courtyards. The locksmith locked up tight. All the things of life but not the lives to animate them. This. Time of night. Was a clandestine peek into a world known only to rats and bakers and bargemen. Cut-throats and prostitutes. I half expected to be confronted, and anticipated a murderer's hands at my throat, but also felt queerly untouchable. Here was a new day. And it was unspoiled, still wrapped in smooth brown paper. What a freedom it was, to know you were about to die.

My toes and fingers were numb by the time I reached the Pont Alexandre III. The river at the bank here was shallow, and I would have to climb a good way into the bridge to reach deep water. It was a job untying my bootlaces with dull fingers. In the end I had to prise my feet loose, but then placed my boots neatly, toes pointed to the river, and upon them lay my coat that I had folded as prudently as an apology. All this time, there was the call of the stone woman perched on the Pont des Invalides, warped and distorted by the wind.

In so many words, she was telling me to get on with it.

Which is what I did. I climbed, as I had done before, and once I reached the right spot, I spent very little time there. I waited for a sign but, as I already told you, none came. There was nothing sensational in this act; from the outside, very little drama. I stood, leaned forward, expelled the last of my breath and let myself fall.

The black water. Accommodating. Closed over my head.

36

Anouk
Ottawa River, 1996

ANOUK WAS EIGHTEEN years old and driving Red's truck with the windows down, and feeling pretty good because in the empty seat next to her, a copy of the local newspaper. And in those pages, her first printed feature article. A revisiting of the story of a tornado that had hit a nearby town ten years before, and the efforts of the local Mennonite community to help in the aftermath. Her pitch. Her work. First summer out of high school, first money she had ever earned, in the bank.

She stopped at a roadside farm stall to buy six ears of peaches 'n' cream corn. The stall also carried pints of blueberries and cherries, plastic jugs of apple cider and pies. A black goat cleaved at the gravel at the side of the road where it was tethered to a stake, and the farmer gave Anouk a couple of cherries to feed to the goat.

'Watch what he does with the pits,' he said, and then, as if he were duty bound: 'The cherries aren't local, they come up from Niagara.'

Anouk offered the cherries to the goat and indeed, it worked each one with its long, bearded muzzle, and eventually a bone-clean pit was ejected out of the side of its mouth by a tongue that was as grey and shiny as steel.

Back in the car, the milky smell of corn husk. The clouds were fast moving and passed over the sun so quickly that the road ahead snapped from light to dark and back to light again, shadows from rock or tree at once sharp as the edge of a piece of paper, then faded, then gone. Today, everything was beautiful.

She got home just as the sun was beginning to set. Great wedges of deep-orange light branded the side of the house, the lawn, the west faces of the trees. Red wasn't around, so she left the newspaper and the corn on the kitchen counter and went straight to the river, swam out to the island and climbed on to a slab of rock and lay there, stomach-down, and picked at a splat of dry, mint-green moss that was spread over the surface of the rock like scales. This rock. She pressed her cheek close into it. This rock striated fluidly with layers of black and purple and orange, and flecks of gold and silver. She wasn't supposed to be out here, just now. This hour of the day, she should have been back at the house taking her pills. Nebulizer. Physio. Repeat.

But today, everything was beautiful.

Early in the morning, the rev and cough and dying sputter of a chainsaw. Anouk pulled herself out of bed and went to her window and there was Red, standing by the house in a hover of bluish fumes. He pressed the body of the saw against his side and wrenched the cord. The motor started again, cutting savagely into the soft morning. It was a little after 7 a.m. She turned from the window just as Red lifted the saw to a lower bough of the biggest tree in their yard.

In the kitchen, she swallowed her pills and inhaled her steroids. While she waited for the steroids to work, she tidied the kitchen, her days like a jigsaw puzzle, slotting life into meticulous curves and divots between treatments. Her dad must have cooked for himself late at night because there was a sauce-crusted pot on the

231

stove and a bowl full of pasta in the sink, a half-mown ear of corn. Greasy residue on the cutting board, and the newspaper she'd left out and opened to the page that carried her piece, untouched. There was a dirty cup and plate of orange peels on the table, and she cleared this up too while her coffee brewed.

A firefly of worry there. A recognition that lately, over the last few months, there was a carelessness to the way her father did things.

She took her cup outside and walked around the house to where Red now stood in a dune of golden sawdust, the air thick with the rich smell of freshly cut wood. The saw whined to a crescendo as another bough fell from the tree. He didn't seem to know she was there and so she waited a while, watched him brace under the weight of the saw, the upper bones in his back jabbing at his thin plaid shirt. Without her noticing he had become smaller, and she wondered how this could happen. He switched off the saw and put it on the ground and shook out his arms, lifted a pair of plastic goggles from his face and settled them on the top of his head. His face was marked red with the impression of the shape of the goggles.

'Why are you cutting the tree?' she asked. This was the tree, she remembered, he was going to get rid of years before, around the time Nora left.

'I like the smell,' he said.

'You're cutting it because you like the smell?'

'Yes.'

'Are you going to cut the whole thing down?'

'Just these lower branches. Lets more sun into the house.' Sweat dripped from his nose and he wiped his forehead with the back of his arm.

When Anouk came back into the kitchen after doing her physio, for which she now used a tight, motorized vest which shook and agitated her chest to dislodge the mucus from her lungs (The Cheese now relegated to the shed, too sentimental a piece to throw away), Fraser and Red were sitting together at the table, both with plates of eggs and bacon, both with a bottle of beer.

'It's not even nine in the morning,' Anouk said, nodding at Red's bottle.

'I've been up since five,' said Red, taking a swig.

'Ah.'

'Fraser's been telling me about the priest and the mountain.'

'The monk and the mountain,' said Fraser, his mouth full of eggs.

'Get a load of this,' said Red. He patted the chair next to him and Anouk sat. 'So there's this Buddhist monk or whatever, he starts climbing a mountain at sunrise, he wants to get to his temple at the very top. Sometimes he walks quickly, sometimes he slows down. He takes breaks. Maybe once or twice he has a nap. He's a monk; there's no rush. Eventually he gets to the top though, just before sunset. He stays up there maybe a week, and then when it's time to go down, he leaves again at sunrise.' Red stopped, hand aloft and hovering by the temple at the top of the mountain, and looked at Fraser. 'He stays about a week?'

'Doesn't matter how long he stays.'

'Right. So when he's ready, he leaves again at sunrise and walks back down to the bottom, average speed faster because he's descending.' Red stopped talking, took another sloop of beer and grinned at Anouk.

'So?'

'So,' he said, 'Fraser showed me the solution to prove that there is one spot precisely, along that mountain path, one spot the monk will have occupied on both ascent and descent, at the exact same time of day. You think it's impossible, right? Without knowing the monk's speed or the length of either journey?'

233

Anouk shrugged. Her father's eyes sparkled with nonsense and she was confused. She looked to Fraser for help, but Fraser was folding bacon into his mouth and offered none.

'He proved it with a graph.' Red reached across the table, and pulled towards him a napkin on which was scribbled a series of black lines. He waved it at her. 'Bisecting lines and some calculus that I vaguely remember from school.'

Anouk raised her eyebrows at Fraser.

'I've been reading a bit of mathematics,' he said, without apology. 'You guys got any ketchup?'

'In the fridge,' said Anouk.

'You've gone all moody,' Red said. 'Is it because of the tree?'

'I don't care about the tree,' she said.

'Fraser, tell her the rest about the monk.'

Fraser rummaged in the refrigerator door and sat back at the table with a bottle of ketchup. He held it above his plate and turned it over, slapped its base definitively with his palm. 'If the monk were two, if you could track his original journey up the mountain, as if there were an apparition of him hiking up from the bottom at the same moment the real guy hikes down from the top, the monk and his apparition would have to cross paths at some point along the path, regardless of their variable speeds, proving there is a point on the mountain he would occupy at exactly the same time of day on both trips.'

Red leaned back in his chair and clapped. 'I love it,' he said. He reached for his beer and tipped the bottle to his mouth, then rested the bottle on his stomach. 'It seems really complex but it's just so simple. Two guys crossing paths. One the shadow of himself.'

'Where were you last night anyway?' Anouk asked.

'One the memory of himself,' said Red, picking at the label on his bottle with quick, tiny scrapes.

'Dad?'

'Eh?'

'Where were you last night?'

'Karaoke night at The Harp.'

'Are you serious?'

'Yep.'

'Look,' she said, and gestured with her chin to the counter where the newspaper still lay. She got up, grabbed the paper and dropped it in his lap. She draped her arms around his neck and leaned over his shoulder while he smoothed the pages.

'It's out?' he said, scanning the page. He found her name and moved his finger over it, as if it were braille, as if it might disappear. 'Well, fuck me,' he said, swallowing hard, his voice wet.

'Are you crying?'

'Of course I'm crying. This is stupendous.' He folded the paper carefully and turned it towards Fraser. 'Look at this.'

Fraser looked.

Anouk hugged her father tighter and he felt too small in her arms.

On Saturday, Red asked Anouk to do a dump run for him, something she'd never done on her own before. He was worn out, he said. After an early dinner, after her meds and physio, she loaded the flatbed with the stuff Red wanted to throw away: a stack of boxes and her old tricycle, rusted. A defunct computer keyboard, a broken clock, a broken radio, the wasp trap that once hung from the back porch. She drove half an hour to the dump road, a hard-packed track that led off the concession road into the bush. She could smell the dump before she could see it: sour, faecal. Up ahead, carrion crows swooped and hovered, dirty against the darkening sky.

She parked the truck in a gravel lot and went into the office, a white trailer on concrete blocks. Inside, Canadian pop music on the radio. Anouk dinged the dome bell on the counter and waited. On the wall opposite the counter there was the mini taxidermy museum that never changed, pet project of the man who used to manage the dump: dusty glass cabinets displaying the yellowed skulls of deer and marten, bear and squirrel, some intact and others decrepit, as if moth-eaten. There was a collection of birds' nests, twiggy and feathered with bits of string and moss and shards of pale, spotted shell.

Holding court on top of a wooden barrel in the corner of the room, a wolf. Claws yellow and chipped, brittle fur, the stitching showing through in places on the black hide. One paw was raised as if the wolf were about to say something important.

A woman came in through a ply-panelled door, and gave Anouk a key for a trolley and told her to watch out for bears. She told her to load the trolley and weigh it on the scales and then dump in an area marked B.

On the other side of a heap of broken and discarded armchairs, atop an eroding mountain of garbage bags, three scruffy black bears. A few hundred metres away from where Anouk now stood with her trolley of junk. Administrative in their movements, the bears looked as if they were employed by the municipality to sort through the garbage, item by item. They expertly pulled at plastic, systematically discarding what lacked potential for the more luxurious items. Spoiled for choice. All at once, answering some silent communication, they stopped what they were doing and gazed at Anouk. Even from a distance she could see the resignation in their eyes, which were as lightless as coal. These bears were corpulent and old, habituated and made lazy by this food source. They were not beautiful.

The dumping area marked B would have brought her closer to the bears, so she ignored her instructions and jerked the trolley around, difficult with one dicky wheel on the uneven ground, and headed back closer to the truck. Some of the boxes were flimsy, poorly packed, and fell apart as she unloaded them. Papers and school folders and old scrolls of artwork on faded construction paper, flaking with powdery pre-school paint, fanned to the ground. Among this detritus, a large Manila, bubbled envelope, creased and softened with years. Unopened. Anouk's name and address on the front, written in her own, years-ago handwriting. She picked it up and balanced it in both hands, remembered Mr Chester and his soft shoes. Remembered an X-ray but nothing else. She tossed the envelope on to the passenger seat of the truck and finished unloading the rest of the junk.

The only light on in the house when Anouk got home was a reading lamp, directing its yellow glow on to her father, who slept in his armchair by the living-room window. Three empty beer bottles lay at his feet like discarded toys. Another, mostly full, rested in between his legs. His head was thrown back and his mouth sleep-gaping. The skin of his neck, unshaven, sagged in a way that made him look old, and his glasses hung, monkey-like, off one ear. Anouk eased the bottle from the half-curl of his grip, and went into the kitchen and poured the beer down the sink.

She sat at the kitchen table under the hanging lamp, and pulled the Manila envelope towards her and slit it open with her little finger. First, she pulled out the chest X-ray and held it up to the light. A silver-and-black impression, a shadow; her chest her bones her arms spread wide. A ten-year-old girl lying on a hard slab under a suspended box that whirred loudly with the mechanics of medical investigation.

Black lung cavity. The areas of scar tissue, as insubstantial as cottony wisps of cirrocumulus cloud. Now, her X-rays revealed more damage, like water stains from rising damp.

Next, she pulled out an empty pill bottle that once held, she remembered, river water. Other objects: a desiccated leaf, brown and brittle and flaky as dried blood. A pin badge with a red heart on it, which meant nothing to her now, and an ammonite fossil in a plastic case. A rough grey rock shaped like an ear with a coil relief. Pressurized stone. Mineral-rich water had once filled the cast left by the disintegrated skeleton of some small beast, and then there was great pressure and aeons of time and then there was this fossil. She'd forgotten all about it.

She went into the living room and woke her father and sent him shuffling up to his bedroom. Halfway up the stairs (stairs which were rough and splintery and without carpet, the carpet still not replaced after having been ripped up, years before, by Nora) his glasses fell from his ear and he stepped on them, breaking an arm off the frame. He didn't stop to pick them up. Anouk found a spare pair in their old leather case in a kitchen drawer, and left them out on the counter in front of the toaster. She went out to the porch and sat. Time passed. Time was passing. Something was changing. There was the sound of crickets and frogs and the titch and scratch of some small, sharp-clawed rodent.

And the wind in the trees was the sound made by the currents of the earth.

In the morning, Anouk got out of bed close to dawn, woken by a snag: she should have been feeling good about having a story published in a newspaper, but she was not feeling good at all. She was groggy in the lungs. Creaky in the bones. Anxiety like an up-note, unresolved. She wanted to get up and walk out of the house right now, walk out of the kitchen door and barefoot it down the grassy slope to the sand. To the water. But cystic fibrosis owned the first hour and a half of every day. So before anything else, she did all that.

By the time she did get outside, around eight, the sun hadn't yet had the chance to take the night's coolness out of the air, out of the grass, and the grass was still dew-wet. Goosebumps rose on her arms. There was the mossy smell of river water, of rich dirt and cedar resin. This was the particular smell of the morning and it existed nowhere else but here, at this hour. The oak leaves – that tree where her tire swing once hung – the leaves on that tree were clapping now in a cool blue breeze. Not enough wind to touch the river though; its surface made only of light.

The phantom call of a loon echoed as if there were no echo in the world until there were loons in the world.

Somewhere in the trees there was the unsettling chirp of a bird that sounded like the snip of scissors cutting quick, short pieces of stiff ribbon. The lament was incessant and followed Anouk to the river.

She wanted to be in the water but the rasp in her lungs told her she probably shouldn't, and experience had taught her, at last, to listen. So instead she dragged the cedar canoe from its resting spot on the grass and rolled it over and pushed it into the water, stepping in with one foot in the centre of the hull as it launched off the sandy bottom. A daddy-long-legs rode on the canoe's gunnel, its prancing, articulated legs as delicate as fibres, the sun reflecting butter-yellow on its grey, speckled back. She tried to catch it. But the spider was agile, and escaped over the gunnel and down the outside of the curved hull. She leaned over, hunting it, and saw that it clung to the hull by the stern, out of reach and just above the surface of the water.

'Fucker,' she said.

'I think we should go picking,' said Red. He'd come out on to the porch, where Anouk now sat with a bowl of yoghurt topped with discs of banana and a cowlick of peanut butter.

'Now?'

'Just up the road.' He wore his Jays cap and his glasses, the broken ones. They hung crooked and to the left.

'I left your spare glasses out,' she said.

'Don't like those ones.' With one finger he tried to straighten the glasses, but they slid back to crook. He swung an empty ice cream container from its plastic handle. 'Don't bother with your shoes,' he said.

She looked down to his bare, fish-belly-white feet, his hairy toes.

This was how they picked berries in the woods when Anouk was little, feet bare to the ground, stabbed by sharp pebbles and stuck by old coniferous needles, but cushioned by them too. The dread of thorns and acorn caps, nettles and goose shit. The mash of slugs or the stubbing of toes on exposed roots. But there was also cool mud between the toes and the gratification of the earth, the dirt, the rock, right up there in the bridge of the foot. It left the soles of the feet tingling with pain, but also scraped clean and raw and good.

The wild raspberries that grew along the side of the trail were no bigger than garden peas. Anouk and Red worked beside each other, hunched over the berries, which were abundant, causing the pickers' progression along the trail to be slow. The raspberries were abundant and the pickers' progression along the trail was slow. Each time Anouk filled her palm she rolled the berries into Red's bucket, gently so they wouldn't bruise, and they carried on this way in silence until the bucket was full. It was shady along the side of the road and a little cool, and Anouk wanted to go back to the house. She watched a corn-yellow butterfly land on a waxy choke-cherry leaf, alight, circle, land. Alight again. A honey bee, its leg panniers packed with bright pollen, honed in on a violet honey-suckle horn, nestled, sucked, detached and bumped along to the next blossom. She wanted to go back. Something was happening, but she didn't yet know what it was and she didn't want to know. A ladybug left a thick trail of dark-orange shit on a fern plume.

'Where have you gone?' Red asked. He stood in the middle of

the road, where sunlight pooled. His grip on the bucket handle was tight, and the bucket was so full that tiny raspberries tumbled over the sides like passengers abandoning a sinking ship. 'You look lost.'

Anouk shrugged.

'That was great, your story, you know. I can't even tell you, how great it is.' He tapped his hand to his heart. 'You need to start the next one.'

'I know.'

Red tilted his face to the sky. More berries fell from the bucket and bumped along the ground. A procession of tiny, decapitated heads.

'You're losing all the berries,' she said. The world was beginning to tilt.

He lowered his head and took off his glasses and dropped them into the pocket of his shirt and, without his glasses, his eyes looked small and tight. 'I'm not well, Anouk.'

These words, like storm wind coming towards her across the surface of the water.

'I'm so used to it being you,' he said. 'This is a huge relief. You just wouldn't believe.' He smiled and his body seemed to relax.

'What are you talking about?'

'Your whole life, I've worried that I would have to watch you die. Finally, it's me and not you.'

A horsefly cruised around her head and she swatted it away, but it only tightened its flight path, tenacious and mean.

'I feel like, for eighteen years I've been stretching this rubber band tighter and tighter, waiting for it to snap. But you're doing so well. You don't need me. You're exploding into this. Woman. I can breathe now.'

'Make sense, Dad.' The horsefly lunged at her shoulder, retreated. Lunged again.

'I'm sick. Nothing they can do.'

'They who?'

'They who. Who do you think? Oncologists. Surgeons. Bunch of others. It's the pancreas. Worst cancer you can get. Top of the charts.' He smiled, his face apologetic and relieved.

She went to him and pulled the plastic bucket from his hand and swung it in the air by the handle. Released it and watched it fly into the trees. Berries soared. She turned and walked up the road a few paces to where it bent to the left and rose steeply; a sharp, short hill. She took the incline, grinding the balls of her feet into the hard-packed, stony grit of the road. The horsefly followed her. She stood at the top breathing heavily against the rasp of her pugnacious fucking lungs. Her pathetic lungs expanding and retracting, out of tune, a rusty harmonica. She put her hands on her knees and leaned over and took a deep breath and coughed and coughed and coughed, a sound like rocks tumbling in the dryer. Coughed again and spat a pearly globe into the dirt.

Everything was different now.

Suddenly, a concentrated strike in the flesh between her shoulder blades. A searing, mandible rip. Fucking horsefly. Roaring, she reached over her shoulder and felt the blood. Got her good.

She turned back down the hill, still coughing, and Red was thigh-deep in roadside ferns, collecting the berries out of the dirt. She wanted to crawl inside his body and curl up and sleep. He ignored her, and she sat in the middle of the road until the coughing stopped and all that was left were shudders of the cough. She went to him in the bracken and apologized, and he put his arms around her and she took in the old-sweat smell of his hat, felt his beard on her forehead. His body was soft; loose flesh gave way easily over bone. He held her face in his hands and asked her to help him find all the berries.

'It would be an unforgivable waste,' he said.

She parted fern leaves, scraped her shins and forearms on a thousand thorns. Berries squashed in her toes, soft and jammy and wet.

'You're bleeding,' he said, and pressed his palm into the middle of her back.

'Horsefly,' she said.

He shrugged, popped a handful of raspberries into his mouth and closed his eyes, worked the fruit around his mouth with his tongue. 'These taste so fucking good,' he said.

37

Pieter
Flight to Baltimore, 1959

I WAS ON A flight to Baltimore, Bear, four years after you died. I
had never been to the United States before. I had never been on
an aeroplane. Your mother packed my bag and she'd forgotten the
cigarettes, or I'd forgotten to remind her about cigarettes, and halfway into the flight I smoked the last one from the pack I kept in my
jacket pocket. Frustrated, I stared through the plexiglass window
at the bottomless, boiling white, at an air bubble caught in the
plastic. When you stare at so much nothing for too long, you start
to see things: an aeroplane on a collision course with your own;
the faces of your wife and daughter; the face of your son. I was
exhausted, and I was anxious, so I unbuckled my seat belt and
walked, grasping the seats hand over hand up the aisle, until I got
to the front of the plane where another passenger was smoking. I
tapped her on the shoulder, a well-dressed woman, older, and I
asked her if she could spare a cigarette.

'Of course,' she told me, and rummaged in her handbag, and
pulled out a silver case. She opened it, and I saw that it was full,
the cigarettes lined up and kept neat by a thin metal frame. How
simple, how easy. It made me feel unequipped.

'Could you possibly make it two?' I said.

She handed me three, setting them delicately in my palm, and smiled. Her lips were painted a bright pink, and the pink, I saw, had been transferred to the cigarette she was smoking.

Back in my seat, I lit a cigarette and inhaled deeply. Remember I told you, Bear, there had been a letter. It had arrived six weeks before this flight and remained unopened on my desk, buried under orders and invoices, and the only reason I'd found it was because I had been throwing things away.

I took it out of my jacket pocket, and read it for what was probably the fifteenth time. The letter was from two men, anaesthetists – Dr Miller, an American, and an Austrian, Dr Wolf – who were working together in Baltimore, and it explained a brief history of something that I had never come across before. A subject I would have had very little interest in had my life been any different than it was. Meaning: if you hadn't drowned. The letter was about artificial respiration, which I want to tell you about now.

Artificial respiration, in its earliest form, was described thus: for the purpose of restoring persons apparently drowned or dead. In the middle of the nineteenth century, medical practitioners recognized that any method used for resuscitation should require no more than one person and no medical equipment. Think about it. You break out in a rash, fracture a bone, you receive a wound, you succumb to disease . . . all of these things afford a victim time to be taken to hospital. Time for the doctor to be called. But if somebody stops breathing, say he has a cardiac arrest or has been pulled from the water, there are minutes only to save his life. The procedure had to be accessible to anyone present – doctor or not.

The early developers of artificial respiration advocated certain manipulations of the body. They understood that some sort of manual inspiration and expiration of air was required to get oxygen back into the lungs, into the blood.

These men knew that the cessation of breath didn't have to mean the end of life.

Experimenting on dogs and cadavers, a physician by the name of Silvester developed a technique wherein the victim was laid on his back with his arms at his sides. To force inhalation of air, the arms were raised above the victim's head, expanding the ribcage and creating a vacuum, forcing outside air to rush into the lungs. To expire this air, the arms of the victim were crossed over his chest and great pressure was applied there. The biggest problem with this method was that the victim's relaxed tongue filled the mouth, blocking the movement of air.

Some forty years later, another doctor, a Mr Schafer (who had moved on from dogs and dead bodies to live, hyperventilated test subjects) turned his victim on to the front and applied pressure to the lower part of the back, just above the buttocks, forcing air out of the thorax. This helped alleviate, in part, the problem of the tongue, but reduced the volume of air exchange.

Having no better alternatives, both the Silvester and Schafer methods were taught and employed across Europe and overseas. Of course, there would have been people residing in either camp, and I'm sure arguments over which method was superior reached religious heights, but nothing much changed until, in the 1930s, a fitness instructor in the Danish army cunningly blended both methods to create the Nielsen method, which was eventually accepted by the International Red Cross. Nielsen's method required one operator positioned at the prone victim's head. The arms of the victim would be raised and bent at the elbows, so that the hands were under the head. Pressure would be applied to the shoulder blades to expel air, and the arms would be grasped at the elbows and raised for inhalation. This method could be applied for hours, was straightforward and seemed to be the final answer.

But the midwives, Bear, as far back as the sixteenth century, knew better than all of these men. They knew that to save the life of a non-breathing infant you had to create a seal around the infant's mouth and nose with your own mouth and to exhale directly into the infant's lungs. This was natural and effective, but was never accepted by any medical bodies as official procedure because it was considered vulgar. And all through those decades that the learned men argued over arm positioning and whether a victim should be prone or facing the sky, the midwives continued to save lives this way.

Mouth to nose. Mouth to mouth.

Others tried to introduce mouth-to-mouth into the medical mainstream, but it was repeatedly ignored. Too sexual. Too disgusting. Who would want to put his lips around the mouth of another who is so close to death?

Bear, the authors of this letter that I carried in my breast pocket, Miller and Wolf, the anaesthetists in Baltimore, explained that they had experimented on live patients, administering mouth-to-mouth and measuring the gases in their blood. Their data proved that expelled air from a rescuer, delivered straight into the lungs of the victim via the mouth, resulted in significantly higher levels of blood oxygenation than that produced by the push–pull method, the Nielsen method.

Because this is everything. This is what it's about, Bear. Oxygen. Water flooded your respiratory system. You asphyxiated. Which meant there was a lack of oxygen in your blood. Which stopped the beating of your beautiful, beautiful heart.

By the time they contacted me, Miller and Wolf's recommendations for formalizing mouth-to-mouth as the official method of resuscitation had already been accepted by the American Medical Association. It had yet to be accepted by any international medical governing bodies, and they knew that for this to happen, they would have to demonstrate that the method was simple and that it could be performed by anyone, even women and children. Practising on live victims on a larger scale wasn't feasible, and they wanted to design a training manikin. A doll that looked unconscious but not morbid. Made out of a material that could be manipulated, that would resist but also yield a little to touch. The impression of life. This is why they wrote to me, Bear. Because of what I could do with soft plastics. Because of the Anne doll. They hadn't even known about what happened to you.

38

L'Inconnue
Paris, 1899

I WAS STILL ALIVE when I was pulled from the black water. The batelier who hauled me out slapped my face once or twice and, when he got no response, assumed I was dead. I seemed dead, and anyway moments later, I was. Besides, he wouldn't have been able to resuscitate me had he known there was still a beat to my heart — he wouldn't have known that was possible.

The chances of his having come upon me in the moment that he did — in the seconds I stopped struggling but before I would have sunk — were minuscule. But this was the way it happened. He became aware of me in that navy light because of one flap of my arm. He thought he'd come upon an enormous bass, and was fixing to drop a line when he saw the moon-pale flesh of my hands, my arms suspended in the yoke of the dead man's hang. The deep was claiming me fast, and it was only because he had the bargepole in his hand that he was able to catch me. After hooking me at my collar, he hoisted me up by the waistband of my skirt. Bemoaning the loss of a good fish supper, he dragged my sopping bulk over the side of the boat and covered me with an oil-stained, sooty blanket. He tucked me between two barrels and carried on with the morning deliveries that stood between us and the morgue. And I. Lay there, dead. A frothy mixture of air, water, blood and mucus issued from my mouth and nose, and water dribbled thinly from my ears. One unseeing eye casually open like a door somebody forgot to close.

The morgue was located at the south-eastern tip of the Île de la Cité, and was like most other administrative buildings in Paris: a stone box fronted by Grecian pillars, mansard roof, a facade screaming post-revolutionary idealism engraved with the words: Liberté! Egalité! Fraternité! The building backed on to the river, its stone wall almost flush with the bank, where the bodies of the drowned – and there were many – could be delivered by boat.

This wasn't the city's first morgue. The original, a stinking black hole dug underneath Le Châtelet, the prison, was nothing more than a cadaver dump. Deceased prisoners were shunted down that hole but also Paris's anonymous dead; men and women like I had been, pulled by their shirt collars from the river, or loners from the streets, or lost children. More murdered than not. Scores of suicides. The dead were piled like bricks on the floor, uncovered. It was a place you would go if someone in your life had disappeared and you hoped (or hoped not) to find her there, in the pestilent fug, with only the oily flicker of the warden's lantern to guide you.

When the prison was demolished, the medical inspector insisted on a new morgue that would be much improved upon the old, including better light, ventilation, cooling systems and a salle publique more suitable for viewing, separated from the dead by a wall of glass.

I was delivered to the morgue in the purple smog of early morning. My arrival was one insignificant and regular detail out of a million details in a city waking up for another day. A gang of workers was crossing the Pont de la Tournelle, shovels slung over strong, bent shoulders. Smoke rose from a thousand chimneys and street by street, alley by alley, people living on top of one another were swinging their legs out of bed, their feet landing on cold, waxed floors. Boiling water for coffee or standing in front of shaving mirrors or darning stockings that they hadn't had time to repair the day before.

Towering over the morgue there was of course Notre-Dame, white birds circling and screaming around its spire.

Mine was the only body to be delivered to the morgue that day. I was received by the pathologist on duty, Laurent Tardieu, a man who daily wore a fragrant sprig of dried lavender (tied tightly and sent in batches by his sister, who lived in his native Provence) in the buttonhole of his jacket to help ward off the stench of death. The lavender was no match for the fumes in which Laurent Tardieu worked – an odour like syrupy fruit from the fresh corpses, like rotting fish from the overripe ones – but all the same, he wore it.

Laurent Tardieu laid me out on a marble slab in the examination room and, as a formality, felt for my pulse with the pad of his middle finger pressed against the inside of my wrist. He listened for my heart through a small brass stethoscope shaped like a trumpet. After officially confirming my death, he logged my arrival into the morgue records, which were reviewed regularly by the gendarmes. He then peeled off what remained of my outer clothing. My linen petticoat and skirt, my blouse and cardigan. My stockings. He was not surprised that I wore no boots, and assumed that they had been left by the riverbank. (Later that morning they would be found, where I'd left them with my coat, by a young bookbinder, and taken home to his sister. She would, in turn, pass the boots on to a friend and get great use out of the coat for many years after.)

Laurent Tardieu left me in my chemise and culotte while he checked the pockets of my skirt for anything that might help to identify me. He found nothing. He then inspected my clothing for laundry marks, initials sewn with cotton thread on lapels or inside collars or waistbands. He did find initials on my blouse, which he added to the log, but on their own, meant not a lot. As far as he knew, my clothing could have been second- or even third-hand. He took note of the condition of my belongings: everything inexpensive but well looked-after. A tightly sewn patch on the elbow of my cardigan, neat darn tracks on the heels of my stockings. He noted that I wore no wedding ring nor any other jewellery. No lace or ribbon adorned my underclothing. Though my hair had become tangled and undone under the water, he could see that it had recently been washed. From my hands he retrieved one brown leaf and a slippery tangle of river weed. Common, he knew, from the struggle of the drowned. The residue of bloody foam in my mouth told him that I had inhaled water into my lungs, which meant that, when I entered the water, I was still alive. The lack of trauma to my body told him that, most likely, the water had been my choice.

Yet, I eluded him. My corpse and what I wore revealed very little about who I might have been, other than the assumption that, at some point in my life, I must have had some claim on the future, otherwise why the careful darning? Why the effort to make an item of clothing last just that little bit longer? This, more than anything else in his work, was what touched Laurent Tardieu's heart the deepest. Jackets worn down to the seams, elbows reinforced with leather. It was the ingenuity, the bringing out of thimble and thread that represented some will to survive, but then, in the case of suicide, the evidence before him on the slab that this woman or that man had, at last, given up.

Laurent Tardieu was a wonder at recognizing professional darning and leather patchwork, and sometimes traced the dead through the establishments that performed these services. He knew where certain silks, velvets and satins were sold, the signature styles of lace and needlework, of seams and cuffs and collars. He knew the craftsmanship of several cobblers in Paris, and had identified more than a few victims with the help of these artisans.

Meticulously, in tight, slanted handwriting, Laurent Tardieu added to his log every blouse, shawl, boot and bonnet. Every scar, tattoo, broken bone or missing digit. Wounds or blemishes on the body were attributed with their size, severity, location and possible cause.

He had observed that most river suicides were carried out by single women. Often on a Sunday. Often in the spring. It was the blooms and the stench of reproduction, he believed, that spurred a certain melancholy in unwed women of a particular age and social standing. These women were alone in the world, or at least alone in Paris, and proof of this was the fact that they usually went unclaimed, their corpses blackened and split like rotting plums after days of submersion. They would have known the river, these women. Perhaps they lived close by. They had spent time walking its bridges and embankments. They imagined what the cold water would have felt like, or what would have waited for them down in the dark. They imagined their own loose hair and skirts flowing with the current, down there with the weeds and the silt and the other unknowable things.

Laurent Tardieu's logbooks read like a saga but the real drama existed within him, within the stories he imagined beyond the physical clues.

There was the boy who had been dragged from the river the year before, and in his pocket were found a few bits of string and a rat's tail. Laurent Tardieu composed a life for this boy that played out in a tiny attic flat, looked after by a single mother with raw, laundry-house knuckles. The boy, about seven years old, only wanted to be with the other children who, in summer, bathed off the Quai de la Rapée. Not knowing how to swim, he dipped into the water and lost his purchase, and no one noticed when the river drew him, lovingly, into her body.

Or what about the elderly man who, before drowning himself, dressed in layers of clothing? Shirts and collars, waistcoats and trousers, top boots over his woollen slippers. His torso, thighs and chest were pocked with the ghost scars of syphilitic papules, a decade healed. In his pockets: a silver snuff box, a leather pouch of tobacco, keys and spectacles. A foreigner, obvious from the cut of his clothes, who, Laurent Tardieu concluded, lived a few steps below the position he would have liked to have occupied in life. Probably widowed. Likely confused and stumbling through the tertiary stage of his venereal disease, demented or insane.

Though he found no signs of trauma on my body, Laurent Tardieu did discover a familiar bilateral bruising along the muscles of my neck and chest, further evidence of drowning, or rather, the thrash and struggle of the drowning victim to survive. He began to create my story. Suicide, naturally. I was the right gender, the right age. He inferred correctly that my missing boots had been placed deliberately on the bank. Apparently quite common.

He palpated my abdomen, and determined from the shiny, pale lines that branded my skin where it had stretched, and from the dark rawness of my nipples, that I was a new mother. I was employed, he decided, with work unsatisfying to me. I hadn't really wanted to die, those bruises told him as much, and was probably downtrodden by the baby or a lack of love or too much of its unhealthy sort. With a cold sponge and a bowl of warm, soapy water, he washed the bloody foam from my chin and neck, inspected my fingernails.

Being the fresh specimen that my corpse was, Laurent Tardieu knew that any number of the anatomy labs in Paris would pay a good few francs for it, and he considered this option carefully, as his daughter was engaged to be married and the money would have helped a great deal. But there was something about me that intrigued him. He wanted to give me a chance to be found, and presumed that even after a few days in the viewing salon, and with enough care, my body would still be worth a small sum.

He laid my arms across my chest, and covered my body from the chin down with a linen drape. He could barely believe I'd drowned as my face wasn't bloated, nor my skin sullied. My high cheekbones and the shadows cast by the dim electric light gave the impression that I was smiling, and in that smile Laurent Tardieu sensed a secret, a hint of wisdom, or, more accurately, cynicism. It was this that prompted him to send his courier out with a letter for his nephew, an apprentice mouleur who worked in a model shop on the Left Bank that produced, among other things, death masks. His nephew had been failing to impress his master mouleurs and, though I wasn't any sort of important person at all, Laurent Tardieu knew instinctively that my face – the smile, the beguilement, the youthfulness – was a good candidate for a striking mask. He also knew that, with every hour that passed, as the fluids in my body pooled with gravity, my face would sink deeper and deeper into the grotesque. He implored his courier to be quick.

39

Anouk
Toronto, 2000

STORIES WERE EASY enough to find in Toronto. And living with Nora after Red died, for the few months Anouk did live with Nora, hadn't been so bad. There were trips to Dundas Street and Spadina Avenue on Sundays for dim sum. Coming home and snoozing together, while on TV the Blue Jays hit fly balls and spat brown geysers of chewing tobacco on to the dugout floor. The distant thwop of a baseball and the soporific voices of sports commentators.

There was the city dirt and the choke of exhaust and drivers getting nippy with each other. There was the woman with no teeth and eyes like snakebites who'd taken root in a pile of greasy sleeping bags in the recess of a garage door on Kingston Road. There were sleek glass buildings fingering the sky, buildings that burned at sunset, and there was the endless throng of Yonge Street, the head shops, Korean restaurants and Polish bakeries, and big trucks idling at red lights, and redundant corner stores and bargain book stores and squeegee kids in dirty sneakers, and hot chicken wings served with blue-cheese dip and celery sticks in wax-papered baskets at outdoor tables under the dapple of urban poplars, and in the parks downtown, amidst all of it, in the parks downtown, there were the tai chi people. Men and women, mostly Chinese, mostly old. In any weather. Swaying and firmly rooted like trees. There were open-air movies on towering inflatable screens in local parks on a summer Saturday night. Secret wine and takeaway pizza on picnic blankets. Toronto was good.

A white lilac tree grew in a neighbour's front yard, across the street from Nora's house. In the spring, Anouk and Nora made a stealth trip in the dark with sharp scissors and pilfered a few sprigs. Put them in a vase in the kitchen, and the whole house smelled of lilac until the blossoms browned and dropped to the table.

Anouk was writing regularly and waiting tables in a pizza restaurant, so less than a year after Red died, she moved into a basement apartment, not far from Nora. There were a few boys, or men. There were a few men. Once, possibly, love. He had these Van Gogh sworls of hair on the back of his neck that destroyed her. Or it could have been his eyes, the colour of dark sand at the bottom of the river, spurring dangerous thoughts of leeches and cold water, or something that would disperse in a puff if you tried to capture it in your hand. But also silky, silty, invitingly soft between the toes.

The first time she took him home he wanted to learn about cystic fibrosis, so she told him. Told him about her medical regime and told him about the diabetes she was sure to develop because her scarred pancreas was unable to produce insulin. She told him about the depression she sometimes suffered due to the strong steroids she took. She told him about how, when she was young, she didn't think she could die from it, and she told him about how it felt when she realized she would.

This was her first sex. When he pulled off his jeans a clutch of coins fell from his pocket and rolled loudly across the floor, and then he kissed the soft lobe of her ear and stroked her hair. From upstairs, from the family who lived upstairs, the bump of some heavy thing falling. Small feet pattered in retreat and someone yelled. There was crying and the tunnel voices of TV.

257

After, he said to her, with his head resting on her chest: 'Your lungs may be shit but your heart is strong as fuck.'

Anyway. It probably wasn't love.

Here was Anouk now, hurrying down Bay Street to the Queens Quay ferry terminal on a Tuesday morning, late for the 8 a.m. Toronto Islands ferry. By the skin of her teeth she made it, bought a ticket and hopped through the rolling gates to the boat just before they shut.

The foot-passenger ferry, open-aired and bullish, looked like something out of another century. Heavily varnished wooden deck and ironwork painted navy blue. Sturdy lines and miles of pop rivets.

The ferry ploughed through the inner harbour and she stood on the deck, leaned over the wooden railing and watched the downtown skyline retreat. The air smelled of gasoline and suntan lotion, wood varnish and dead freshwater fish. A small sailboat bobbed across the froth of the ferry's wake, barely enough wind to fill its mainsail. The ferry completed its fifteen-minute crossing and the passengers gathered at the box-nosed stern, crowding on to the wide staircase that led from the upper deck to the gangway. Anouk sat on a double-sided bench while everyone got off, waiting for the stairs to clear. Above her head, hundreds of faded orange lifejackets strapped to the inner roof, the kind that slipped over the head, the kind that resembled old locks.

She came slowly off the ferry, distancing herself from the crowd. She wanted to feel as if she were alone. She wanted to cross time. She followed a wide, tree-lined path past a small amusement park, just visible through the trees – the circus peak of the merry-go-round, the flume tower – and soon came to a low stone, arched bridge that crossed over an inlet. To the left of the bridge, a docked enclosure of water where pedal boats shaped like swans were corralled together against the bank and held in place by a floating tether. A gust of wind travelled up the Long Pond inlet from the harbour, scribbling the water into darker blue as it came, like the shadow of some great whale moving under the surface. When the wind hit the plastic swans they came alive, clacked their wings together, jostled for space.

Eventually she came to the beach on the far side of the island, where a stone breakwater thirty metres out from shore created a quiet cove. One girl playing in the sand in a red bathing suit. Bucket. Spade. Beyond the breakwater, Lake Ontario opened up and rolled unimpeded to the horizon. Anouk walked westwards along the beach, then came up off the pebbly sand on to another path. Soon, she left the water and walked through an area thick with buckthorn and elm, with scattered houses mostly hidden by trees. Up ahead, the island school, a long, low building. Children from the city went there during school months to study subjects like bird watching and orienteering, pinhole photography, pond life and stars.

Further on, she came to the lighthouse at Gibraltar Point and in front of it stood Lucas, the man she had come to see. The founder of the school; an expert on the history of the island. She was writing a piece for a travel magazine and was here to talk to him about the formation of the islands, about how they began much further east along the lake as sand and rock from the Scarborough Bluffs, sand and rock that eroded and was carried west by the water and deposited here. A warren of shifting sandbars and wetlands. Now connected by bridges and carriageways built a hundred and seventy years before.

Lucas was short, bald and fit, relaxed in a pair of cut-off denim shorts and flip-flops. They shook hands and walked west along Hanlan's Point Beach, towards the island airport, and Lucas told Anouk a ghost story – Victorian, spooky – about a girl who'd come to work as a chambermaid at the Hanlan Hotel, a hundred years before, and had been killed accidentally over a petty theft.

They walked slowly up the beach, and Lucas showed Anouk where the old resort hotel, now decades gone, used to store its bathing machines; squat, caboose-like structures on wheels. Private changing rooms for swimmers.

'They'd drag the machines out to the water by horse so the swimmers could get in straight from the cabins,' Lucas told her. 'Mainly they were used by women; they'd swim behind the cabins, so that they were hidden from other people on the beach.'

Anouk remembered the Mennonite farm, her father, blue duck eggs. The stroke of leather boots on a dry, wooden floor. Here was time, folding over on itself. Now, on the beach, she imagined hooves grinding over stones and sand, wood and iron wheels creaking and straining. A thick-clothed bathing suit, down to the ankles and up to the chin. The self-conscious laughter of women swimming carefully so as not to wet their hair. She could hear it.

'The girl who was killed, the chambermaid, she was caught stealing from one of the hotel guests,' said Lucas. 'I'll show you something at the lighthouse.'

They turned around and, with the airport at their backs, cut across the point.

'Story goes, she was caught with something like two or three coins. Not a lot. She's put under guard until the York police can pick her up, but at some point in the night she escapes, gets chased by the island constable to the top of the lighthouse, and there's a scuffle. She ends up getting tossed down the stairs.'

'Shit.'

'Neck breaks, she dies, leaving a bloody handprint on the twenty-third step. No matter how often they scrub it, bleach it, whatever, the handprint won't go away. It's still there.'

'Get outta town.'

'I'll show you.'

It was a few degrees cooler inside the lighthouse, and it smelled of mud and wet stone, like a cellar. Anouk followed Lucas up the spiral stairs, which disappeared like a lick with the curved wall of the tower. Going slowly, respectful of the legend, Anouk counted each step.

'It must have been dark that night,' she said.

'Yes, it would have been very dark.'

'There must have been torches.'

'Imagine that light jittering on the walls,' he said.

The staircase was narrow, turning into itself at each shallow step. Light from above, from the nest, cascaded down the close walls. Lucas jumped up a few steps then stopped and turned. He pointed to the step just level with Anouk's face. 'Do you see it?'

She leaned towards the step, propping her weight against the outside wall, which was smooth and cool against her shoulder. On the step, the suggestion of three splayed fingers and a horseshoe wedge of palm, a crescent tip of thumb. Tea-brown, grabbing the edge of the step. Obviously paint.

'We take the school kids up here with flashlights at night,' said Lucas. 'Scare the living shit out of them. They love it.'

'Do they believe it?'

'Sure. More fun if you believe it.'

40

L'Inconnue
Paris, 1899

LAURENT TARDIEU'S NEPHEW, the young mouleur, arrived at the morgue directly after his breakfast, and was indeed impressed with his uncle's judgement of the contours and plumpness of my cold, dead face. They both agreed that I had been decent-looking in life, and that now, the face of my corpse provided an ideal model for a death mask that might just help the nephew make his name at last.

So. In an examination room in the morgue on the south-eastern tip of the Île de la Cité, my body was prepared. The young mouleur handled my corpse carefully, using a bolt of linen to prop my head in a line of equilibrium with the rest of my body. This step was necessary to avoid displacement of my skin and facial muscles, which had relaxed to putty. With needle and thread he sewed shut my mouth and eyes, then spent a moment in silence resting his hands gently on my shoulders, trying to get a sense of my true expression. Already the fiction, the myth, was taking shape. Solidifying before the plaster had even been applied. He and Laurent Tardieu both saw a victim. Feeble. Scorned and wet.

The mouleur took a comb to my hair and styled it in the conventional way, parted in the middle across my forehead like drapes tied back from a window. He was careful not to touch my face, careful not to distort the features. Any rearrangement would be irrevocable, and I. Would be lost. He believed that he could capture something of who I had been, but frankly, how could he? Regardless, he had to work quickly, to complete the job before rigor mortis set in, as a mould taken from hardened flesh would not be as good as one taken from soft. He had been taught that upon death, the smile of the soul was released, but that it would only remain until the mortis. After that, nothing of the living remained in the face of the dead.

He painted my hair with a lubricant so that the plaster wouldn't adhere to it, but left my skin as it was; coated already with enough of its own natural oil. He then placed thin, damp paper at my neck and up behind my ears, as a barrier to form the outer limit of the mask. While he was doing this, Laurent Tardieu assisted him by preparing the plaster in a large bowl, a lime powder solution the consistency of soup. This the mouleur ladled over my face, the thickness of a few millimetres. This was the moment I. Became separate from the story.

Deep in concentration, the mouleur laid down a thick linen thread, starting from the top of the mould, above my forehead, drawing a path along the middle of my face: the bridge of my nose, the divot under my nose, my mouth, chin, neck. Another layer of a more solid plaster, much like pulp, was then laid over the first, providing a firm outer shell. Before both layers of the plaster set, the thread was drawn away, dividing the whole into two halves.

Once the outer layer hardened, the halved mould was eased apart slowly, and carefully lifted away from my head. If the whole thing were to fall apart, it would have happened at this point, as the seal between my face and the plaster was airtight and difficult to break. My face would have no longer been viable and I would have been rolled out to the viewing salon, rotting with the others and then forgotten. But he managed this delicate step without so much as a crack.

The young mouleur was finished with the skin and bones of me. He concentrated now on the cast, clamping the two halves of the mould together, creating the negative aspect of the mask. An empty cavern carved in the precise contours of my dead face. My nose, cheeks, lips and eyes, eyelashes resting, all concave, yet like an optical illusion, appeared in relief. The mouleur, with Laurent Tardieu standing at his shoulder, admired his own work. With the two halves connected, he could see that the seam between them was undetectable. There were no air bubbles, the finish smooth. The eyelashes were slightly clumped but that sort of thing was expected and, otherwise, he deemed this to be a perfect impression of me. In fact, these were the very words he said to Laurent Tardieu when he kissed both the pathologist's cheeks in gratitude: 'This is a perfect impression.' And Laurent Tardieu enthusiastically agreed. But. To impress is to imitate, and so it was never perfect. It was never me.

He cushioned the mould with hay in a wooden crate and covered the top of the crate with an ill-fitting lid, then packed his tools into a leather sack. He carried everything outside, joined by Laurent Tardieu, and set the crate on the pavement where people were already lining up for the viewing salon. Both men pinched tobacco from Laurent's stash and lit their pipes, and watched as more people crossed the bridges from the left and right banks to join the queue. A pack of skinny, dirty boys came running and spinning one another like tops from the direction of the Pont de l'Archevêché. One of them hurdled the mouleur's crate, knocking the lid askew and sending the crate skidding. Fists raised, the young mouleur yelled after him and was told, in so many words, to go fuck himself.

As the pipes were smoked down to ash, the mouleur tried to convince his uncle to join him for a coffee in his favourite cafe, not five minutes away on Rue Beautreillis, but Laurent Tardieu declined, deciding instead to ready my corpse for the day's first viewing. The mouleur's last words to his uncle as he heaved his bag of tools on to his back and collected his crate: 'Do you ever rid yourself of the smell, Uncle?'

Laurent Tardieu's wry answer: 'What smell?'

Laurent returned to where he'd left me alone, stripped a few strands of plaster from my hair, and washed the skin that had been crusted with white when the cast was set. With the help of a porter, he moved me on to a wheeled gurney and covered the lower half of my body with a linen sheet. The clothes I had been wearing, still damp with the memory of the river, were laid gently across my legs. I was pushed down a long corridor and through a set of double doors into the viewing salon.

Two rows of six marble slabs, black marble, seven of them already occupied. Five men, two women. Low-hanging lamps over the bodies and also over each, ice-cold water dribbled from swan-necked faucets, an effort to slow the process of decay. On the back wall, their clothing hung from metal hooks, wilted and empty. Jackets, waistcoats, leather belts. Woollen cummerbunds, breeches and blouses and dresses and trousers – a form of identification to speak for bodies that had become distorted beyond obvious recognition.

Four of these people had been pulled from the river, the other three found alone on the streets. I was laid out next to a young man whose bloated body had been found butting up against the middle arch of the Viaduc d'Auteuil, the bridge that crossed the Seine at the fortification wall on the western edge of the city. This day would be his last in the viewing salon. His eyelids, lips and nose were gone, eaten by fish and crabs. The skin had come off his hands like gloves and his gut was bovine, stretched to its limit. His testicles had swollen to three times their normal size and his tongue, tumescent and grotesque, had forced its way through the opening of his lipless mouth, and hung, defeated, like a mouse dead in a trap. Inside, his organs were already putrefying, dissolving into soup. Later that day he would be buried in the cemetery beyond the fortification walls with all the other unclaimed, in a grave unmarked.

On my other side, a woman in her sixties who had been discovered in a dirty, rarely used passage in Montparnasse, her neck bruised black from strangulation. Dents in the fingers of both hands where once there were rings. Hers was an unusual scenario in that she had been well dressed and well fed, unlikely to be without relations in Paris. But as yet, three days on the slab, no one had come to claim her. The bruising on her neck had spread like a storm cloud, rolling up into her jowls and down across her shoulders. Her skin was waxy and grey, and her lips drawn back to reveal several missing teeth. Her head was tilted back and slightly to the side, as if she were trying to detect the notes of distant, familiar music.

The coat in which she was discovered, a cornflower blue, was decorated at the collar and cuffs with a fine embroidery in white thread, the pattern so delicate you wouldn't notice the stitching unless it had been pointed out to you. The coat hung behind her, a loyal sentry.

Next to them, I looked like a pretty doll in the window of a grand magasin.

My muscles, my bones. My hair, skin, fingers, heart, kidneys, spleen. My lungs. My airless lungs. My cartilage, tendons, bowels, liver, my traumatized uterus, fallopian tubes, labia, clitoris. The small black mole between my breasts, once kissed by Axelle. My lips, my nipples, my eyelashes. The hairs in my nose, the cilia in my inner ears, my trachea, my tongue, appendix, intestines, anus, stomach, teeth. My blood and my water. My water. This body was either bound for the anatomist's scalpel, or this body would be buried and all its parts devoured and digested and liquefied by a billion living things until there were only bones.

A heavy green curtain dressed the glass that stood between the dead and the people who came to view the dead. This was pulled back perhaps minutes after I was deposited on the slab and my clothing hung up behind me, and very soon they came. They pressed their warm noses to the glass, and their eyes were wet with pity or revulsion or both. Not one of us lying there had died peacefully, and we each were the last word of a story that must have been gruesome or, at least, sensational. They came for free theatre but what they got was posthumous physiology. Missing limbs. Exposed bones. Bodies marbled white and wine-black because the blood had stopped circulating, then pooled and coagulated. What they saw were fingers the same as their own fingers that once struggled with a buckle or held a pen or scraped a spot of dirt from a mirror.

One visitor, a woman exquisitely dressed, stood stricken and pale with her hand to her neck, as if reassuring herself of her own pulse. She took no notice of the grubby boy who pushed in front of her, mingling his filth with her skirts, or of the errand girls standing next to her who gaped at the male genitals, or of the flâneur positioned just behind her, a regular to the morgue, who was getting hot in the pants. Every constituent of Paris was represented and there wasn't a moment the viewing salon was not packed. A child was held aloft to be given a better vantage point. A man in clay-smeared corduroy munched on a slab of cake he'd bought from a vendor just before coming in. He hadn't even planned on visiting that day; had stopped in on a whim, on his way home from work.

And then. Axelle. She appeared at the glass like a beautiful, rare fish in a tank. She wore the same coat she had been wearing the last time I saw her, and the same hat with the lilac ribbon. Standing beside her, a woman I didn't know. This woman, pretty in the typical way, was one of the other girls who modelled the dresses for rich women. Axelle and her typically pretty friend both looked bored. My love saw my body but she did not see me, and so I. Remained unidentified.

The Mouleur Statuaire was located on the Left Bank along Quai Saint-Bernard, not a long walk from the morgue. The day was sunny and crisp. The sky was a brilliant, boundless blue and the leaves on the plane trees bright yellow and chattering like canaries. The young mouleur was grateful to be walking in such fine weather, but he was eager to get back to the atelier to show off the best cast he had ever taken.

The premises were made up of a collection of small stone buildings set around a central cobbled courtyard. Headless, unfinished plaster statues, moulds for statues and cornicing, plinths, rosettes and garden tools were all stacked together against the walls that lined the yard. Everything was coated in yellowish powder, including a three-legged mutt who spent most of his time asleep under an outdoor table.

First for the mouleur, a bowl of coffee and a fist of crusty bread ripped from a loaf in the kitchenette. Dropping a trail of crumbs and slopping coffee across the floor as he walked and ate, he gestured, with a lift of his eyebrows, a half-hearted apology to the simple-minded girl who stood by the door with her broom, clearly put out but too feeble to say so. He went back through the courtyard, dipping his bread in the coffee and sidestepping a mob of cantankerous chickens, and into the main workshop. Inside, the walls and every surface, every tool, encrusted with powder. A long, waist-high workbench ran the length of the room, and at this bench a senior mouleur was bent to his work, wearing a stiff leather apron. His bald, liver-spotted head bobbed over a series of statuettes of some saint. On the table in front of him, a small hammer and set of chisels, speckled with dried plaster. Tools also hung from nails on the walls, and shelves that looked ready to fall were stacked with moulds and mixing bowls, sacks of pulverized lime and gypsum, broken chunks of statues and masks. On the back wall hung masks of the dead, mostly people unknown, the death masks having been commissioned by their families, but also a few notable poets, painters and long-dead members of the aristocracy. In the centre of the wall loomed the long and narrow face of Napoleon, his countenance sombre and authoritative, even in death.

A pall of plaster dust in the air. The old man at work on the statuettes whistled something sporty and out of tune. The young mouleur placed the crate on the table, opposite his companion, letting it fall a touch more heavily than necessary. The old man looked up, one red-rimmed eye squinting against the rise of swirling dust that the crate had disturbed. He very slowly scratched the side of his large nose with his crooked little finger, a finger disfigured in youth having been smashed with a hammer. The young mouleur shifted the lid from the crate and lifted out the mould, putting it on the table face down, rough-side up. It looked like something dredged from the bottom of the sea. A limpet, or an oversized oyster shell. He collected his apron from where it hung and crossed the leather straps behind his back and tied them snugly in the front, one eye on the old man, who was now concentrating again on his statuettes. From one of the shelves, the young mouleur selected a wooden bowl and set of paddle-like spoons, and carried these over to a large cask in the corner of the room. He scooped from the cask three heaping ladles of gypsum powder into the bowl, the gypsum having been mined from the quarries in Montmartre, crushed on site and dehydrated in a nearby factory. He brought the bowl back over to the table and turned the mould right-side up, and gazed into the recessed image of my face. He eyed the old man.

'Very fresh corpse today,' he said, rubbing his thumbs into the

269

depressions my cheeks had made. 'I believe I captured this one perfectly.'

'Hm.'

The mouleur tilted the mould towards the old man. 'Would you like to see?'

With a fine, stone-handled pick, the old man continued to scratch at a detail in the draping on a single statuette. He snorted. Eventually, he set down his tool very carefully and looked at the young mouleur. Bearing his weight with both hands on the table, he slowly, with much creaking, leaned across to peer inside the mould. His expression did not change. 'Is she anyone?' he asked.

'No. But wait. This will be special.'

'Is this what you're meant to be doing today?'

This was not what the young mouleur was meant to be doing that day. His list of jobs was long and tedious. But nonetheless he proceeded with the mould. First, with a clean rag, he applied a thin coat of oil to the inside surface. He then added water to the gypsum powder and stirred the mixture to a thin soup, its colour a pale, pollen-yellow. Working quickly, he tipped the plaster into the mould and then, cradling it between his forearms, he rotated the mould in all directions to drive out any air bubbles and ensure that the plaster coated the mould evenly as it thickened. He continued this motion until the plaster was dry enough that it wouldn't sag when he set the mould down. He quickly scraped the remaining plaster out of the bowl, now thick as butter, prepared another gypsum mixture, and repeated the same process. This was done three times before he propped the mould between two blocks of wood so that it would set evenly.

He walked back across the courtyard to the kitchenette and brewed another pot of coffee, ripped more bread from the loaf. He sat on a sunny bench in the courtyard and stretched out his legs, crossing his boots over the cobbles. He dipped the bread into his coffee and lit his pipe, while in the workshop, the mask was setting beautifully. A whole century was coming to an end, and there would not be many more days as mild and satisfying as this one.

After a few hours and the completion of some of his other, more mundane tasks, the young mouleur deemed it time to separate the mask from the mould. The old man had moved off somewhere for a smoke or a sleep in the sun, and so the workshop was empty. How the mouleur wished for an audience. Even the dog was nowhere to be found, nor the simple-minded girl and her broom, nor any of the other artisans. So he set about his work silently, first unclamping the two halves of the mould. With hammer and chisel, he carefully broke the back seal along the top edges, then gently prised each half of the mould, one at a time, away from the mask.

And there it was. I. Balanced in the young mouleur's chalky, work-rough hands. Not I. Nothing to do with me.

His pride was fit to pop the buttons from his shirt. And the mask was impressive. Smooth and detailed, nuanced, blemish-free. So lifelike, in fact, that decades later, people who knew about this sort of thing would be sceptical about whether or not I had been dead when the cast was taken. They were adamant that, if indeed dead, I couldn't have drowned. Drowning victims were never discovered right away. Drowning victims sank like rocks. And they didn't rise to the surface again until enough gases had built up in their rotting bodies to render them buoyant. This was not the face of someone who had spent days or weeks submerged, drifting along the silt and mud of the river bottom, swelling, peeling, feeding fish and crustaceans.

The young mouleur clamped the mould together again and laid it back in its crate, and propped the mask against the crate so that anyone who came into the room might stop to admire it. Soon after, the old man walked in, glanced at the mask but said nothing, and instructed the young mouleur to pack up the statuettes in preparation for delivery to the artist's studio, where they would be polished and painted.

I attracted a lot of attention in the morgue. Too pretty to be dead, people said. There had to be some scandal. By the end of the first day, Laurent Tardieu had to concede his plans to sell my body to a laboratory. The gendarmes had shown some interest, and they demanded I stay on the slab for as long as possible. The price, literally for my head, would not be worth the trouble.

Laurent did his best to preserve my body, sewing the splits together and applying powder to my face as it became more and more discoloured, trying to maintain my identity as he was certain someone would show up to claim me. But after nine days, my body more closely resembled a stuffed pig than a pretty doll. Abdomen bloated, skin waxy and white. My eyeballs had dried out and my face, first bloated but then drained, was pinched, all life gone and the skin sucked into the angles of the skull.

On a Wednesday morning, bright and cold, my body was buried alongside two other unclaimed corpses, in the corner of a cemetery reserved for souls such as ours. Swaddled in cheap muslin, my remains were placed in a pine box that was lowered by rope and pulley into the ground. By the graveside: a pair of dirt-encrusted fossoyeurs leaning over their dirt-encrusted shovels, a handful of porters from the morgue (there to carry the coffins), the morgue clerk, and a priest in a black cassock with a battered bible and somnolent tone. There the company stood, together alone, while a couple of rooks made a nuisance of themselves in the lower branches of an acacia tree. There was just enough wind to pick up the bright-yellow leaves on the ground and send them tumbling past the men's boots, and over the root-rough edges of the graves into the stillness and beyond. The pulleys whined and the ropes creaked and jacked against the pine box that contained my body, a satisfying and resonant sound. The box reached the bottom of the dark hole and, while the priest hummed the rites with great disinterest, the fossoyeurs, in deft and fluid movements, shovelled in the rich, black earth. The dirt landed at first with a percussive clop, which then softened to a crumbling, the weight on the coffin lid growing heavier and heavier still – everlasting.

Later, a moon three-quarters full. Autumn moon. White-blue light and long shadows. Three new mounds of dirt marked at their heads by small, unadorned wooden crosses. Beneath one of those mounds, I. Under all that indiscriminate weight, a cheaply made pine box containing my skin my blood my lungs et cetera.

And. That part about Axelle seeing me in the morgue? Wasn't true.

She was never there.

41

Anouk
Toronto, 2015

ANOUK SAT ALONE in an unremarkable waiting room at the CF clinic, Sunnybrook Hospital. Her lungs felt like the barrel of a cement truck. She'd been coughing continuously for a week and her ribs felt bruised. She ignored the messages pinging on her phone from her mother, and also from a magazine editor who was expecting three thousand words on a Toronto artisan who had trained in Belgium as a master cheesemaker. She'd interviewed the artisan the week before and now all she had to do was write the thing, and she liked to think it was her fatigue that was stopping her, but it wasn't. It was because the article was about cheese. And compared to everything else, compared to a pair of lungs that were on the brink, she didn't care about cheese.

She was a collector of stories without a story to tell.

She got up from her chair and went to the small, hermetically sealed window and leaned on the sill, rearranged her scarf around her neck. Chicken neck. Everything now felt scrawny; she'd lost fifteen pounds over the last few months and was always cold. Far below, between the hospital and the lakeshore, an artery of cars coursed east–west on the Queen Elizabeth Way. A white-and-green commuter train trundled past. Trees swayed. Cables and wires criss-crossed a sky that was a brilliant and searing autumn blue; the lake was a sparkling rich navy, choppy under the midday sun. All that life out there and not a sound of it passed through the window into this room.

This would be the third time Anouk needed intravenous antibiotics over the past year. The treatment would be like a deep-cleaning for the lungs, flowing into the tributaries and creeks that her oral medications couldn't reach. She waited now for a specialist who would insert a large catheter into a vein in her arm.

What did she have to say about cheese. For the last two years her ability to find stories she wanted to tell was waning, along with her energy. She was thirty-eight years old, and having to live again with Nora because she wasn't making enough money to live on her own. That's how they talked about it – she and her mother – their story was one of finance, not of ill health. Because she had by now developed diabetes, and the IV treatments were playing with her memory, making it hard to keep track of other medications along with the blood sugar and all the rest of it. What seemed to be a beginning felt a lot like an end.

Anouk pressed her nose to the glass, which smelled of dust, and said to the treetops, said to the cars, said to a flap of small black birds tumbling bungling by: 'Cheese.'

Soon after, a light knock at the door. A specialist nurse Anouk hadn't met before peeked her head in and invited Anouk to another room, where she was asked to lie on an examination bed. Next to the bed, a trolley with several drawers. On top of the trolley, a metal tray of sterile instruments and tubing and all the detritus needed to insert the catheter that would be threaded through a vein in her arm and travel all the way to her heart. Anouk could tell by the way the nurse practitioner handled the components that she knew what she was doing. Sometimes, these people weren't so confident, and their hands shook. They dropped things. Sometimes they would pick up one piece of kit and put it down before finding the right one, or they would make bad jokes or ask about where she had been on holiday, and in their eyes Anouk could see the need for her to make them feel okay, because they knew, after all, that it was really she, Anouk, who was the expert in the room.

This woman. Her face was serious. Her hands solid and cold as metal. She moved the ultrasound wand over the inside of Anouk's arm with one quick flourish, and tied the tourniquet tightly so that Anouk could feel her pulse blipping against the rubber sash. The nurse cleaned the area with an antiseptic-wet cotton swab and laid a sterile drape over Anouk's arm. She was a marvel with the local anaesthetic; Anouk scarcely felt the needle going in. While they waited for the numbing, the nurse unwrapped the blue paper from the instruments, and, when she was finished doing that, she told Anouk about the risks and side-effects, which Anouk already knew by heart. Infection, clots, bleeding and bruising. She asked if Anouk had any questions. No questions, but Anouk had to sit up so she could cough, and spit into a cup. The nurse waited patiently until she finished and was lying still again.

Anouk stared at the wall, aware of the proximity of the nurse. Could smell her soap, the detergent in her clothes. Could hear her breathing deeply through her nose. No pain, only pressure. There was a rectangle of slightly paler paint on the wall where some poster or frame once hung. Again, the plastic covering of the ultrasound wand circling the inside of her arm.

'Huh,' said the nurse. The room filled with a pause.

'What?'

'Your veins are being tricky.'

'They're tired.'

The veins always got the blame. More pressure, another hole pierced in her flesh. It wasn't painful, only grating. Like the whine of a mosquito in the ear. There were many steps to the process: the insertion of a thick needle, a guide wire through the needle, and then the catheter pushed along the guide wire. Once that was done, the needle and guide wire were removed and the catheter flushed with saline and capped. Five or ten minutes staring at the wall, and finally Anouk looked at what the nurse was doing. Blooms of dark blood decorated the green drape and still no needle in her arm.

'I'm sorry,' said the nurse. 'Luck is not with me today.'

So at least Anouk's veins were not to be blamed. Now it was fortune.

Being on her back made the lungs worse, so Anouk had to sit up again and cough. This time, the fit lasted for several minutes. And then the whole procedure had to be repeated from the beginning because her arm was no longer sterile, nor was the drape or anything else. The nurse was beginning to crack.

Success took an hour. The anaesthesia was fading and Anouk could feel the bruises of the failed attempts at threading her vein. She was exhausted and this wasn't over. There would be another room, another specialist. An antibiotics test and instructions on how and when to administer, doing it herself, at home. At home. That's why all of this was worth it.

And days later, antibiotics still pumped through Anouk's body, expedited by the large vein next to her heart into which the catheter delivered the drugs. She was itchy, all over; a bleeding, gritty rash had developed in her armpit. She was propped up on the couch with a blanket in her mother's living room and staring at the ugly, broken branch of deer antler Nora kept on the mantelpiece. Computer on her lap, another attempt at the artisan and his cheese. He worked out of a warehouse on Ontario Street, a few blocks west of Parliament. The area had for many years been derelict. This, at least, was interesting. Empty warehouses and small, defunct factory spaces being taken over and converted into studios. There was a story to this part of the city. Toronto a hundred years ago. Steam issuing from factory stacks and maybe an organ-grinder on the corner with a monkey. A boy selling newspapers plastered with gossip. Horses and whalebone corsets and cholera. Here now. The snap of a story just visible, a silver belly-flash from a fish deep down. But the drugs she took, they were strong. And what was the point anyway.

The cheesemaker used vinegar instead of rennet in the curdling process, and therefore his cheese was suitable for vegetarians. To concentrate made her sweat. The harsh, white fug of the antibiotics. The front window was open a crack and, even with the cool air coming through the room, she was hot. But also she was cold. She kicked the blanket from her legs and listened to the sounds from outside. An airplane somewhere. Or maybe not. A streetcar. Always a streetcar. Birds. A strange crackling she couldn't place.

In the autumn when Anouk was six years old, Jody, the guy with the chipped tooth, the guy who. Showed up to the house on the river with what looked like a wooden phone booth strapped upright in the back of his truck. It was an old ice-fishing shack that he'd repurposed into a sauna, and he wanted Anouk's parents to try it out. He planted it on the sand next to the water and showed Red how to load the small, cast-iron oven with wood and heat the metal cask of stones. Anouk and Red spent the whole day in the sauna. She could remember, even now, the hot, wet smell of cedar. The beads of sweat falling from her dad's beard, his rosy cheeks. Over and over, they ran between the sweltering sauna and the river, and the cold water was like music on the skin.

Now her legs bristled with the sensation of running through the sand, tiny pebbles grinding into her feet. Water travelled down the coiled rope of her long braid, dripping on to the backs of her thighs.

She touched her hair, dirty now, cut just below her ears.

That day. The movement of the river was reflected on the yellow undersides of maple leaves; the thick, resin scent of pine was everywhere, and Red was there was there was there. His hair, even when it was wet, maintained the ducktail moulded by his hat.

Red died in the beginning of October, a few weeks after Anouk's nineteenth birthday, only months after he told her he was sick. In the hospital in Pembroke, during his last weeks, she watched her father disappear. The morphine made him do queer things, like pinch an imaginary joint to his mouth, which she had to pretend to light. Sometimes he called her Nora, or Mom. Anouk helped him drink water through a straw, and washed away the spit that coagulated to yellow paste at the corners of his mouth.

No funeral but two weeks after he died, a remembrance gathering at his house. Friends from the river valley came, as well as Fraser, and Nora. Jody was there, and cousins and teachers and students from the school where Red taught. They made sure it was a celebration. There was a ukulele, a guitar and a French horn. They stood together and kicked at crisp leaves and told stories, releasing the papery smell of dying leaves into the air. Beers and joints were passed around a fire while the sun sank behind the trees, while the light, palpable, changed to gold and then indigo dusk. From someplace distant, the howling and yip of a coyote. So distant that its veracity was undetermined and some of the more drunken of the group speculated that it could have been a spirit howl, that it could have been Red. That solace, that tendency for the bereaved to see signs, to take ownership, in and of everything: this was meant for us, this snowstorm, this sunrise, this song that played on the radio at just the right time. Hand in hand, because Red would have loved that, hand in hand the friends sat still and listened, cock-eared, while the fire snapped and single leaves silently spiralled to the ground around them. It was enough. When the air became too cold, they moved inside and continued to drink, and many went home until only a few were left, and enough time had passed that someone suggested they swim in the river while the sun came up and do the ashes. It was Fraser who first stripped down to his underwear and ran into the water. His hoots echoed north and south up the bank, frightening a pair of finches off their perch. He dove down and came back up dancing, water spraying off his beard and his long hair. Someone else ran in, and then someone else, and Anouk, hugging a cardboard canister to her body, joined them. Down to her underpants, she stepped in fast and walked out until the water was up to her thighs, and lifted the lid of the canister. Inside, a sealed plastic bag. She opened this and looked inside to the ashy brown grit that was her father. His eyes, his hair, his teeth. His bones, skin, nose, fingers, heart, lungs.

'Do I do handfuls, or . . . ?' She looked to the others in the water. Her body spasmed with cold and her teeth clacked.

'All in one,' said Fraser.

She emptied the canister with a swing of the arm, and the fragments of her father arced through the air and landed on the surface of the water, and seemed to hang suspended there for a moment before they sank. Absorbed by river.

'Did you get it all?' Fraser asked. 'Make sure you get it all.'

She pulled out the plastic bag and turned it upside down and shook out whatever was left. A little drunk, deliriously tired, she said, to no one in particular: 'I would like you all to do the same for me one day.'

'It's a good place to end up!' hollered a cousin.

Anouk folded the bag back into the canister and tossed it on the beach, then splashed out to the water again and swam to where Fraser was. The water was so cold, it reached into her with two hands and stole her breath. Fraser looked at her and his face squared with worry, and she found just enough air to tell him she was okay. She took the black, blood-iron water into her mouth like wine. Felt every marvellous bubble that passed between her toes and crept up her thighs. She ducked under and opened her eyes to the murk, resurfaced and smelled what her river offered up: sand and clay and lily and bulrush and weed, warm granite and coniferous sap and rot and the silver-green glint of a dragonfly's diaphanous wing, and the life and death and the deep-winter freeze that was coming. She thanked her father for giving her this. River.

Fraser said, 'You need to get out now, girl.'

And she said, 'Don't tell my mother.'

But Nora had disappeared hours before, and so had Jody. And everyone noticed this, but the story was dog-eared by then and nobody cared.

Nora was sitting with Anouk now, in the living room in Toronto where the deer antler collected dust on the mantel. At some point Mel had arrived and they were watching Anouk. Mel was cradling a cup of something hot and she was smiling over the rim of the cup.

'Let me in on the joke,' Anouk said.

'You were talking in your sleep,' said Mel.

'I wasn't asleep.'

'You were howling.'

'Bullshit.'

'What were you writing?' Mel asked, nodding to the computer that was still balanced on Anouk's lap.

'Nothing.'

42

Pieter
Baltimore, 1959

I MET WITH MILLER and Wolf in a sparse office in a Baltimore hospital. The room was clean, a typewriter on the desk, a metal filing cabinet by the door. A few chairs and a film projector on a low table, pushed against the wall. Outside the window, November wind worried at the last brown leaves clinging on to the wet, black branches of the trees that lined the hospital car park. Clouds moved quickly across an ash-grey sky.

Wolf, a few years younger than Miller, had the hooked nose and flat forehead of an eagle. Jet-black hair. He sat casually in one of the chairs, elbows resting on his knees, while Miller, much broader in the shoulders and thinner in hair, sat at his desk. They were both younger than I, bright-eyed. Miller was a joker, told me he'd expected a Norwegian toymaker to look more like Geppetto, perhaps bearded, wearing a leather apron and smelling of wood and glue. They wanted to compare stories of transatlantic travel – air travel was a novelty in those days – as only months before they'd also been on a plane, to a conference in Norway in fact. That's where they'd learned about me.

I told them about my near disaster, having run out of cigarettes halfway through the flight.

282

It was small talk. We three were earnest and a little nervous.

Miller's assistant brought me a coffee – weak, American coffee. Miller asked me if, prior to having received their letter, I'd known anything about artificial respiration. I wondered then if I ought to tell them about you. Instead, I told them I hadn't, and that their story interested me very much. Wolf rose from his chair and pulled down a white screen that was mounted on the wall. He then moved quickly to the film projector, and fiddled with knobs and such until it whizzed into action. Miller turned off the lights and we watched a flickering film that showed a man, topless, lying prone on a surface of wooden boards, his arms bent up along either side of his head. The victim. Visible near his head was one knee and also one black shoe belonging to another man, the rescuer, who pushed with flat hands on the victim's shoulder blades while alternating that manoeuvre with another: grabbing the prone man under his biceps and pulling up on both arms so that his chest was raised off the wooden boards. I recognized that this was the Nielsen method of artificial respiration. The film jumped and the victim was now played by a young boy, and the rescuer, a woman. The camera panned out, giving a wider view, revealing that the demonstration was being performed outside, on a wooden dock, calm black water slipping gently along its edges.

'You can turn it off,' I said. 'I understand.'

The film reel whined down to silence and Miller switched the lights back on.

'Works, sometimes. And only if performed well,' said Wolf. 'But highly inferior to mouth-to-mouth.'

'All of my data, the blood gases and tidal volumes, was taken from live volunteers,' said Miller. He told me how he paid medical students to allow him to sedate and paralyse them in order to resuscitate them.

'Sounds dangerous,' I said.

283

'It is. And expensive.'

'So you want a manikin.'

'Something pliable and humanlike,' said Miller, 'where you can get air right into the chest cavity and see it rise. Some sort of balloon would expand where the lungs are meant to be.'

'It has to be female,' I said, already imagining what she might look like.

Miller and Wolf smiled at each other. 'We think so too,' Miller said. 'This isn't for data anymore, or medical folks. This is for members of the public, for teaching. People have to feel comfortable.'

'She can't be too beautiful,' said Wolf.

'Or too ugly,' said Miller.

'And she mustn't look like she's dead. Only unconscious, like there is a chance she can be brought back,' said Wolf. He explained that this, the notion that someone could be brought back from the edge, from that point where life tips over into death, was what attracted him to resuscitation. It's why he became an anaesthetist. He described how during surgery, the anaesthetist dulls the patient's vital reflexes, his breathing and circulation, and virtually keeps him alive until the surgery is finished, when the reflexes are restored, and the living body pulled back to the surface.

I was taken for lunch, and a tour of the city. I was shown around a medical laboratory. We met for a few more days and talked over how the manikin should work. I made sketches. I promised I would return in no longer than six months with a working prototype.

Back home in Stavanger, when I wasn't in the workshop designing the manikin's body, I was searching for her face. I studied women's magazines, newspapers. I looked for her image on the street, on billboards where lifelike drawings of women advertised cleaning solvents and toothpaste, automobiles and shampoo. She wasn't in any of these places. I looked for weeks until the faces became

284

meaningless and I began to feel desperate. Winter melted into an early spring and in April, at a Saturday party thrown by neighbours, I turned on their new television set and searched the faces I saw there. But the images on the screen were flat and emotionless and revealed nothing.

I spent a sunny afternoon in the library and found a table in a corner, hidden by stacks, and built a wall of heavily bound books on classical art, hoping I would find her there. Balthus's Thérèse was too suggestive and Da Vinci's lady with an ermine seemed to know too much. Manet's Olympia was too confrontational. The black lace around her neck and the silky, low-heeled slippers on her otherwise naked body suggested she was a prostitute. Schiele's Edith – too old. The Mona Lisa – too smug.

Botticelli's Venus made me pause. What I liked about her was the context of the sea at her back and the muscular presence of the wind god Zephyr, puff-cheeked and determined, blowing her to shore. But she was too forlorn, too sexual. I drew her face many times and imagined it in three-dimensional form. And it wasn't right.

By June 1960, the body of the manikin was finished, including the tube system that would transport the blown air through the mouth and nose to the inflatable chest cavity. Miller and Wolf telephoned me several times over this period, anxious to know when I would be returning with the prototype. But I still hadn't settled on a face. I took sketches of your mother, your sister. I even sketched your face, wondering if I could somehow interpret it on to the face of the manikin. But your mother forbade this. The idea that yours would represent the face of someone who might be brought back was intolerable to her. I don't know what I had been thinking.

Where are you, Bear? Does any of it matter, where you are? Do you miss being alive? Do you feel cheated by the things you'll never do, by what you've lost, this. Food-in-your-mouth life, this. Biting into the flesh of an apple, or melting ice cream on the tongue, life. This. Sand-in-your-toes life. Your mother kissing your sleeping eyes. You could never have known how much we loved you.

Should I be afraid? Is there memory, where you are? Is there an echo?

Where you are, I think it's like a river, and you're the flow. And every so often, out of the flow, you, me – all of us – we crawl up on to the bank and we do life. That life may be rich and long or it may be tedious. It may be a disaster – it's a gamble. But the only certainty is that it will end, and when it does, you find yourself the river again.

River is life and death both.

43

Nora
Toronto, 2018

THREE WEEKS AFTER her fortieth birthday, Nora's daughter is called in for surgery. Nora and Anouk arrive at the hospital just after 8 p.m. and Anouk signs the forms she needs to sign and her sputum is analysed for bugs. She's fitted with a cannula, and then her transplant surgeon comes into the room and tells her it's not going to happen tonight after all. The surgeon who removed the donor's lungs has determined they're not viable.

One month later, another pair of lungs become available and they're sweet as peaches, but Anouk is in the hospital, immobile with pulmonary infection. It's hardly her daughter lying there in that bed, and there's a chance she won't ever be well enough again for transplant.

But Anouk does recover enough to go home, and eight more weeks pass. Once again, the call comes, and Nora and Anouk are in a taxi bound for St Michael's Hospital.

'I don't know if I can take this again,' says Nora.

They sit at either window in the back seat, looking out, but their arms are extended towards each other, fingers grasped loosely together. It's January, just after 7 a.m. They have stopped at a red light. The city is peaceful. It's dark and it's stone frigid. The sky is the colour of copper and the streetlights cast a yellow glow on the ground, and in each of their halos can be seen a cascade of frozen crystals sifting to the earth. This is the consummate moment. If the surgery goes ahead today, Nora will either still have a daughter at the end of it or she won't. This truth is as definitive and indivisible as each one of those goddamn snowflakes falling to the ground.

The hospital is transforming from night to day when they arrive. The heavy main doors swing with people arriving to their shifts, but many of the corridors remain dark. As they pass through the main foyer, there is the grating squeak of a metal grille opening, revealing the coffee-shop counter. A stack of newspapers bound tightly with plastic waits in front of the still-closed stationery store. A young doctor in green scrubs and rubber shoes walks past thumbing her phone. All of these details are acute and frightening. Whatever happens, these are the last hours the world will feel exactly. Like this.

There won't be a lot of waiting. If this is going to work, the lungs need to be connected to Anouk's blood supply within a few hours. This is the sort of language Nora uses, the language of medicine, of mechanics.

The medical team won't disclose how the donor died, only that the lungs were helicoptered into the Toronto Island airport. The donor will only have died hours ago and the lungs are probably here now. There won't be a lot of waiting at all.

Another metal chair by another tightly made bed in another room with lights that hum. Consent forms to receive blood, to receive the organ itself, have been signed already but they have to go through the rigmarole again. General risks of surgery. Possible bypass during the procedure and the risks of. Risks of being anaesthetized. Risk of stroke, of bleeding, of needing a transfusion. Anouk nods and nods and nods. They're briefly left alone.

'I think it's happening this time,' says Nora.

Anouk is still nodding, like some kind of mechanical toy wind-ing down. Nora checks her phone. Eleven messages from Mel.

'What are you going to do for breakfast?' Anouk asks.

'Don't know.'

'Did you remember your book?'

Nora looks in her bag. No book. The clock on the wall has a white face with plain numbers and no second hand. 'No more coughing,' she says.

'No more physio,' says Anouk.

'All that free time you're going to have.' Nora thinks she should say something else, something more significant than this chatter, something maternal. And then a nurse comes in, wheeling at her hip a trolley of instruments for inserting a cannula. She pulls a green curtain around the bed to separate Anouk from the other patients in the room. She tells Anouk that one of the specialists from the CF clinic phoned and sends her best wishes.

The nurse offers Anouk a pill. 'This is a mild sedative,' she says, holding out a tiny paper cup, 'to take the edge off. It'll relax you. You don't have to take it.'

'I'll take it,' says Anouk.

'Slip it under your tongue,' says the nurse. 'Just let it dissolve.'

These are the last hours the world will feel exactly. Like this.

With two fingers, her hand shaking, Anouk places the pill under her tongue. She closes her eyes, presses her lips together. The nurse begins to prepare Anouk's hand for the cannula and there's some-thing, Nora knows it, something she should say that will help or guide or instruct, something like that, but all she can manage: 'My baby. I love you.'

Anouk

The operating theatre smells like metal and antiseptic. It smells like rubber. Anouk wears a blue paper cap, and its elasticated hem is hot and itchy against her forehead and the paper smells like disinfectant. The ceiling seems very far away. She's thinking of a poem she knows, can't remember the name of the poet, she's thinking of the words to a poem she knows where the poet is on the operating table and starts to hallucinate about the hairs on the anaesthetist's arms, hairs that are thick, red and curly like *little coppery ferns*. He wants to reach up and touch the hairs because, he thinks, it may be the last thing he ever sees. But he's afraid that if he does something like that, does something so irrational as to reach up and curl his fingers into the thick hair of the anaesthetist's arms, and then survives, he'll be laughed at later on. But very soon, he stops caring about whether or not people are going to laugh at him, and when he tries to reach up to touch the hairs, which have now become *little jets of fire*, he discovers that his arms have been strapped to the table.

Anouk, drugged, lifts one limp wrist to ensure she has not been strapped to the table. A radio plays somewhere, jazz. A saxophone requires great physical effort, she thinks. The stretching of the cheeks, the trachea, the flexing of the tongue. The strength of the arms, the abdomen muscles and diaphragm. The lungs. The lungs. Her legs are lovely and warm and the smell of detergent, of sterilized metal, is also lovely and warm.

The anaesthetist comes into view, and he's speaking but she can't concentrate on what he says. This is the person who will cast her away to sleep, who will do her breathing for her and then. This is the person who will bring her back. Now, he asks her to do something and she isn't quite sure what he's asked, but, seeing as her life is in his hands, she feels obliged to react in some way, to *do* some *thing*, so she sings.

'Michael row the boat ashore, hallelujah. Michael row the boat ashore, hallelu-u-jah.' This is the song the anaesthetist sings in the poem, and it's the last thing the poet hears before he loses consciousness. 'The River Jordan is muddy and cold, hallelujah.'

The anaesthetist's eyes crescent as if he's smiling – he has no mouth – and he says something to someone standing on the other side of the bed. No, he's speaking to her.

'. . . going to sting. The propofol. It's coming now. You'll feel it burning but only for a short time.'

She raises her hand, the cannulated hand, and as she does she sees a white liquid travelling up the plastic tube that is attached to her hand. It hurts a goddamn lot. And then a mask is placed over her nose and mouth. It smells like rubber.

'Breathe deeply,' says the anaesthetist. His voice is river silt. Move to capture it and it's gone.

Anouk tries to turn her head but she is drowning.

44

L'Inconnue
Paris, 1903

THE ORIGINAL MASK that depicted my dead face, having attracted no attention whatsoever, was packed away with the mould on a bottom shelf in the messy storage shack of the Mouleur Statuaire. The crate in which it was entombed gathered dust for four years amongst the detritus of broken and rejected statuary: half an angel's wing, a bust of Montesquieu missing its nose, stacks of crumbled cornicing. The young mouleur eventually moved on to another, more senior position in Reims, and forgot all about the death mask of the unknown woman.

It was the girl who swept, the girl who'd been mistaken as simple-minded by the young mouleur, who eventually found the box and opened it. Seventeen by this time, her mind was riotous with schemes and ingenuity. One wet Sunday morning a few days after her discovery, while everyone else was either sleeping or at church, she let herself into the atelier and stole the crate – mask and mould together – and brought it home to show her mother, father and four brothers. While the spring rain misted the windows of their cramped loft apartment, she lovingly dusted the mask, turning it in her hands and explaining to her family the technique required to produce such a perfect, unblemished piece of plasterwork (the young mouleur would have been so proud had he known this, because praise, even from a girl cleaner of the lowest order, was, for him, like catnip). She lied, naturally, telling her parents it was going to be thrown out anyway, and that she had asked as a favour if she could take it home.

'C'est morbide,' said the mother, crossing herself. 'I don't want it here.'

'There are no such things as favours,' said the father.

'I'll keep it next to my bed,' said one of the brothers.

'I bet you will,' said another.

'I'm selling it,' said the girl who swept.

Because when she had first seen it, she sensed an opportunity. She saw a face that would, with its laconic smile, transcend time and fact. Smooth as cream, a face on to which anyone could paint anything they wanted. It was pretty but not too pretty. Innocent but also wise. The girl who swept was a person whose instincts were sharp. She was someone who knew. The girl had toiled under rag and broom for years, looking up at the pale and the serious, the death masks of Napoleon, Dante, Voltaire, Goethe, etc., and here, finally, was somebody else who, to put it simply, knew.

The girl who swept used a wooden trolley, also pilfered from the mouleur statuaire (and which also closely resembled the wheeled platform used by that foul-mouthed vagabond with no legs), to transport the crate from model shop to model shop. At her first stop she told the keeper that the face depicted by the mask belonged to a poor, innocent shop girl who had fallen in love with a philandering rentier. The rentier, in turn, had assured her he had the connections necessary to catapult her dream career as a (and the girl who swept stumbled on this detail, as the story had taken an unexpected twist; she hadn't understood until that moment the whimsical nature of story to spontaneously awaken in this way, to live and to breathe. She quickly settled on *singer* as there'd been a playbill advertising a concert plastered on the wall outside the model shop). The rentier, she continued, had the connections necessary to catapult her dream career as a singer. When the innocent girl fell too much in love, according to the girl who swept, the rentier bolted out of Paris like a whipped horse, leaving no forwarding address, and the heartsick songbird threw her wretched self into the river. The girl who swept didn't think I would object to this fiction. She had seen it in my dead face: transcendence.

When asked the name of the innocent drowned woman, the girl replied that the incident had occurred several years before, and that the identity of the victim had been – another flourish of poetry here – lost, left at the bottom of the river. 'All the more intrigue, Monsieur,' she added, holding the mask aloft and stroking the waves of plaster hair lovingly with her rough, callused thumb.

With every shop she visited, the story was edited in small and unimportant ways. The dead woman was an orphan. Her lover an absinthe-addicted revolutionary. Or she was a model for a semi-famous painter; she was a Parisienne grisette. A milliner's assistant. A seamstress. It didn't matter. What mattered were the parts of the story that were unknowable. This, the girl knew, was the strongest selling point. This and the inarguable presence of the river, tumbling and spilling through the heart of the city, through the heart of the story. Rippler of breath. Catcher of light. Taker of lives.

She finally sold the mask and mould to a model shop not far from Madame Debord's flat, the owner in agreement that indeed, there was something intriguing about the unknown woman. The girl who swept was paid an amount that was equal to what she earned over several weeks of sweeping floors and scraping dried plaster off wooden spatulas and bowls. She walked out of the shop clapping dust off her hands and feeling wholly satisfied. She would hand the money over to her mother, minus the amount needed to buy herself her first-ever, grown-up hat.

*

The mask was hung in the centre of the model-shop window by a delicate piece of twine, and labelled with the placard L'Inconnue de la Seine, *The Unknown Woman of the Seine*, and was ignored for several weeks. The proprietor was about to move it to the back of his shop when along came a moderately successful Romanian artist, who had been living and painting street scenes in the Latin Quarter for several years. He purchased the mask and hung it on the wall of his studio, and, from that point on, every street scene he painted included a woman with my face – so small it was undetectable to anyone but him, yet still. The model-shop proprietor cast another mask and sold it within a week to the manager of the Théâtre des Folies-Dramatiques, who hung it in one of his dressing rooms. The next to purchase the mask was a poet, a woman, and after that, another painter. It followed that the mask became very fashionable for artists and intellectuals in Paris, which led, as these things always did, to it gaining the attention of the bourgeoisie. Twenty years after my death, the mask, reproduced en masse, hung over the stone mantelpieces of textile manufacturers and factory owners, alcohol agents and landlords, and then regular, working-class people too, not just in France but also Germany, Italy, England, Norway. The story, by then as generic as the lower-quality plaster used to spin out the hundreds of reproductions, had been boiled down to the obvious main points: peasant woman impregnated by a man who outclassed her. River. Identity unknown. Somewhere along the line, interestingly, a new element had been added. Apparently, some said, the mask had originally been commissioned by a lonely pathologist working in the city morgue who empathized with the innocence and beauty of the drowned woman and fell instantly in love. Close to the truth, yet still, not the truth. The girl who swept (who, by the time she died in 1965, was running her own, very successful theatre company in New York City, and who still kept her first-ever, grown-up hat in a box in a closet in a ground-floor apartment on Bleecker Street) would have appreciated that embellishment, and been vexed that she hadn't thought of it herself.

And neither she, nor I, nor Laurent Tardieu, nor the young mouleur would ever have expected that the mask would become muse to so many. And the words that were used to describe this inconnue de la Seine? Well. She was often portrayed as pure and innocent (no). Jilted (perhaps). Seductress (if only). She was compared to the river-borne Ophelia and moved the pens of Anaïs Nin and Vladimir Nabokov. Nabokov, like the rest of them, assumed I had been seduced and let down by a man. Suggested that maybe this man was a womanizer, or some kind of drunken artiste. He called L'Inconnue the palest and sweetest of all. He accused her of having frail shoulders. An English novelist wrote a bit of schmaltz about a poet locking himself away with the mask and losing everything because of his devotion to it. The melancholic poet referred to the mask as le Silencieux.

The silenced.

Ha.

45

Pieter
Stavanger, 1960

O N A SATURDAY evening in early August, I drove out of town to the beach at Orrestranda, where you used to paddle in the shallows and eat the sand. I changed into my swimming costume in the back of the car, and left my shoes stacked together over my folded clothes. Barefoot, with a towel slung across my shoulders, I took the sandy trail from the parking lot and climbed over the grassy dunes to the beach. Children played there, hurdling the small waves, and the dark heads of swimmers bobbed further out. Without breaking stride, I dropped my towel to the sand and walked into the water and kept moving forward until I was past the breaking waves and standing chest-deep. I fanned my arms along the surface of the water and let the swell rock me back and forth, sometimes lifting my feet off the seabed. My Bear. How many times had I done this? How much was the sea part of me? I was salt. I was sea. Water had been my element since I was a boy, staying with my grandparents on Karmøy in that house of white clapboard with a red roof, a house that was now occupied by strangers.

I floated on my back and let myself be blinded by sky. Nothing up there but more nothing, and when you stare at nothing for too long, you start to see things.

My grandmother kept dogs and cats. The cats always seemed to hang with bulging pink teats, with kittens. The dogs were usually ill or deformed. Rhubarb, strawberries and blackberries grew wild in my grandmother's garden, and once I ate so many blackberries my faeces looked like pie filling. My grandfather: the fisherman who told mariners' tales and other tales too, stories that I could never really be sure came from his own experience or fantasy or what – on this the old man was ambiguous.

Hundreds of metres up from where I floated, a gull coasted in from the right side of my vision, passed, then seconds later, circled back again from the left. I shivered. I hadn't thought about my grandparents' house in a very long time: the blackened kettle on the stove, the top drawer in the kitchen that contained balls of string, pencil nubs, candles and errant nuts and bolts, ledger pads and tobacco tins full of wooden buttons. Treasure for a young boy. I remembered how I nearly burned the house down, and I remembered the wallpaper that lined the stairway, a diamond pattern of soft, yellow blossoms. I remembered listening to the radio and eating home-pickled onions out of a jar, and the wind blasting my bedroom window, where on the sill I kept my collection of stones and shells and other ocean-worn rubbish. I remembered the heavy, cut-glass sweets dish on the low table in the front room. It was impossible, after nicking a sweet, to replace the lid silently, the ring of crystal infinitely loud and lingering in that small house.

I remembered lying on the rug in front of the fireplace with my arms folded under my head, sucking a stolen sweet, staring at my grandmother's paintings on the wall: a dry-docked fishing boat, a bunch of flowers, and the koie my grandfather built above the lake where you died, Bear.

And then.

I remembered her. I saw her face as clearly as the empty sky above me – every contour, every small blemish in the plaster. The round, youthful cheeks, smooth as buttermilk. The clumped eyelashes. The smile. I saw her and it was as if she saw me back, and it was as if she said: Well. Here you are, Pieter. At last.

46

Anouk
Toronto, 2018

ANOUK HAS A strong urge to move her hand and thinks for a
long time about doing so, but it feels as if it's been replaced by
a block of wood. She tries the other hand. It's become wood too.
That, or her hands have been bound to the sides of her body.
There's singing. *Michael row the boat ashore, hallelujah. The River
Jordan is. The River Jordan. The River. Is. It's something. It's bloody
and old. Hallelu-u-jah.*

Forget moving one piddly hand. Instead, swim.

She dives like a whale. She is fathoms-deep and placid. Salty.
Briny. Body warm. Somewhere, a heart beats. This isn't just water;
this, whatever it is, this. Fluid can be inhaled. This fluid is more
viscous than water and it fills Anouk's nose, mouth, trachea, lungs.
It breathes for her. Her blood flows rich and scarlet and is more
saturated with oxygen than she's ever known. She looks up towards
the surface. There is a cloudy, marbled, out-of-focus world beyond
where she is now. Voices are hush, hush, hushing. Or. That sound
could be the wind in the trees. Or. It could be the sound of loamy
waves rolling up a pebbly shore, losing momentum, and falling
back into the milky bosom of a gentle sea.

Anouk rolls and dives even deeper until she's pulling herself along a muddy riverbed. She grapples with weeds, gets tangled and then is released. A long-whiskered, flat-headed catfish glides in and out of her peripheral vision. It's the same colour as the riverbed and almost impossible to see, but she knows it's there by the clouds of sand it blasts into the current with every flick of its tail fin. She propels herself along the river bottom by clutching at rocks and using them for momentum to drive herself forward, and she's moving at such a clip that her clothes are slipping from her body and soon she's naked, and the water is breath against her skin. It should be cold but it's warm. Body-warm.

Up ahead, a bend in the river and around the bend, a submerged tree. Its black, leafless branches flow with cottony green witch's hair and frogspawn, soft river growth so abundant it's as if the tree has lain here for a hundred years. There's enough space between the prone trunk and the riverbed for Anouk to fit, so she shimmies under there, hugging the tree, and sees that on the underside of the trunk, a patch of bark has been stripped away and there are words etched into the bare wood.

There's a story here. Her body trembles with it.

Hush, hush, hushing voices coming from beyond the surface of the river, from the diaphanous elsewhere. Someone is calling her name. A cool hand cups her forehead.

But there's a story here.

She peers harder at the words scratched into the tree but can't make them out.

Her own voice in her head: Remember? Mr Chester's class. CPR. Pinch the nose. Tilt the head. Breathe. Count. Repeat. A manikin lying on the floor in the school gymnasium and everyone is embarrassed because they have to blow into her mouth. No one wants to take a turn after Anouk because they don't want to catch her germs. Remember? Mr Chester says: I know something you don't know. Be kind and I'll tell you a secret. He says: This is the face of a woman who drowned. He tells the story of a river and a woman with no name and a toymaker. Every manikin who has ever been made to teach people. How to breathe. How to save. Everyone knows this face. It's always been her and it will always be. After the lesson they each receive a pin badge with a red heart on it.

Anouk stares harder at the words etched into the wood. Maybe that's what has been written there, the name of that manikin.

Someone is calling her, Anouk, gently, but with persistence. Open your eyes, a voice tells her.

The river is breathing for her.

I give you my breath.

Anouk, wake up and see. See how you can breathe.

It's not the name of the manikin etched in the wood. Anouk runs her fingers along the worn fissures, trying to read them like braille, afraid they'll disappear. This is the name of the drowned woman, but she can't make out what it says. Anyway, it doesn't matter if she can't read it now, because this is, at last. A story worth telling.

She's buoyant. She holds on to the tree but it's slimy with algae, and whatever it is that's pulling her to the surface is stronger than her. Upwards, pulled, she keeps her eyes on the tree, but as she moves away from it the water darkens, and soon the tree is just a shadow and then it's gone.

Anouk opens her eyes. Hard to focus. The room is yellow-dark, it must be night. Someone is doing something to her hand. From out of the dark a quiet voice: she's awake.

There's something in her mouth, in her throat.

'We're going to try again, Okay? We're going to get this tube out so you can breathe on your own. You've been fighting us all day.'

She looks around the room and her eyes hurt. They feel rusty.

'Your mom's waiting down the hall. We'll call her in as soon as this is done. Now. Give us a big cough.'

302

Anouk coughs and there is a sliding. She wants to swallow so badly but can't. The endotracheal tube is out and another tube is pressing on her tongue, suctioning. Someone else is wiping her mouth.

'There. Done.'

Throat sore, new lungs. Anouk opens her mouth, and, as if coming up from deep water, inhales.

END

Epilogue

Camille Debord
Une Caserne de Pompiers, Nice, France, 1967

IN A SMALL community room at the local fire department, Camille Debord sits in a semicircle with ten other students, here to learn the latest method of artificial respiration that could, promises her family doctor, save her heart-sick husband were he to suffer cardiac arrest and stop breathing at home. Her and her husband's lives have changed utterly since he was diagnosed, and Camille is not going to take this sitting down.

The instructor looks like he should be in the army – probably he was. Wearing a soft-grey shirt and dark-blue slacks, he sits on the matted floor so that all the students can see what he's doing to the manikin that lies next to him. The doll has been introduced as Resusci Anne and she looks like she could be sleeping, lying there stiffly with her arms at her sides. Her hair, her wig, is curly-soft and light brown, and she's dressed respectfully in a white blouse and blue cardigan, and also wears loose-fitting slacks. She's even got shoes, white tennis shoes. From where Camille sits, it's difficult to get a good look at the manikin's face.

The instructor goes through the method step by step, demonstrating the precise way to tilt the head back in order to clear the airway, and how to achieve a tight seal around the mouth. It all looks a bit intimate. Camille is grateful the manikin is female. Once the demonstration is over, the instructor invites someone to volunteer to go first.

'I will,' says Camille, standing from her chair. Camille is the oldest person in the room by a good few decades.

The other students watch as the old woman, petite and with an open face, makes her way to the centre of the mat and kneels down alongside the manikin. Her movements are mechanical and quick, like a bird. Like a swallow.

She strokes a curl of hair off the manikin's forehead. 'Salut, Anne,' she whispers. Now close up, Camille takes a moment to study the manikin's face. It's moon-round and soft, perfectly symmetrical, the high, round cheeks of a young girl. There's a hint of life behind the closed eyelids. The mouth is open and there are holes in the nostrils.

'Maintenant,' says the instructor, 'what's the first thing we do?'

Camille nudges the manikin's shoulder and asks if she's all right, trying to elicit a response that of course will never come. It feels a little ridiculous to be doing this, but it could save her husband's life. It's important. She continues. She puts her hand under the manikin's neck and angles it so that her chin is raised. Path open. Airway cleared.

Camille presses down on the manikin's chin with one thumb, and squeezes the manikin's nose shut with her other thumb and forefinger. She gently tilts the head back further so the mouth opens, draws breath from deep down in her diaphragm and leans forward. She closes her eyes, wraps her dry lips around the waiting mouth of the doll named Anne, and exhales. The doll's chest rises with Camille's own breath.

Author's Note

THIS STORY IS inspired by true events.

The death mask of L'Inconnue de la Seine exists. Hundreds of copies once hung from hundreds of walls across Europe during the first half of the twentieth century. Nabokov really did write about L'Inconnue, and so did Rilke. Albert Camus compared her to the Mona Lisa. You can still purchase a copy of the mask from a dusty atelier in the southern suburbs of Paris.

The mask – or rather, the unknown woman who (*may have*) drowned in the Seine in 1890-something and whose absence defines its contours – has a knack for getting people's attention.

Something else: there was a Norwegian toymaker called Asmund Laerdal. In the 1950s, Laerdal was a successful manufacturer with an advanced knowledge of soft plastics who designed a lifelike play doll named Anne. He also designed toy cars, and imitation wounds for the Norwegian Civil Defence.

True: Asmund Laerdal had a son named Tore. When Tore was two years old, he nearly drowned. Laerdal saved his son's life before he knew anything about artificial respiration. Tore Laerdal still lives in Norway.

In 1958, Asmund Laerdal was introduced to a research team

made up of Peter Safar, an anaesthesiologist, and the physician James Elam. Safar and Elam were conducting studies on the efficacy of mouth-to-mouth cardiopulmonary resuscitation in the US, in Baltimore. They needed a manikin to continue their research, and to use as a training aid to teach CPR to the general public.

Asmund Laerdal, adept with the necessary materials and branded with the memory of what he nearly lost to the water, designed the life-saving manikin using the deathmask of L'Inconnue de la Seine for her face. He called her Resusci Anne and since her inception in 1960, this face has not changed. Hundreds of millions of people have wrapped their lips snugly around hers, given her their breath. Perhaps, so have you.

Everything else in this book: invention.

Acknowledgements

Thank you Clare Alexander, my secret weapon, and all of you at Aitken Alexander.

Thank you to my editors Alice Youell and Michelle MacAleese, for your faith and enthusiasm, and thank you to the wonderful teams at Doubleday UK and House of Anansi. Thank you especially to Sarah MacLachlan, Marianne Velmans, Claire Gatzen, Vivien Thompson, Alison Barrow and Antonia Whitton.

With all my heart, thank you Jo Willacy, Alison Brockway and Libby Anderson for allowing me into your unique world. I hope I got it right, or at least as close as possible to right.

Thank you so very much to Loic Boinet, Isabelle Gaultier and everyone at Atelier Lorenzi. Thank you also to Josephine Duval and Virginie Borsa.

For explaining the medical bits and your patience in doing so, thank you to Anna Bendzsak, Stephen Tsui, Alexandra Lamond and James Napier.

Thank you to my petits choux, Stevie Anouk Lindell and Camille Avarello Stone.

Thank you to the readers, and to the writers, who graciously shone their bright light into the corners I couldn't see: Merrill Brescia and Colleen Anderson, Joanna Quinn and Peggy Riley. And thank you Théo Gazeu, for the French. À la folie.

Bibliography

In writing *Coming Up for Air*, I relied very much on the insights and richness gleaned from several resources, particularly:

Death in Paris: Records of the Basse-Geôle de la Seine, Richard Cobb (Oxford University Press, 1978)

Fighting With Crib Gloves: My Battle with Cystic Fibrosis, Richard Keane (Tate Publishing, 2014)

History of Childbirth: Fertility, Pregnancy and Birth in Early Modern Europe, Jacques Gélis (Polity Press, 1991)

How Have I Cheated Death? A Short and Merry Life with Cystic Fibrosis, Tim Wotton (Austin Macauley Publishers Ltd, 2014)

In Paris: A Handbook for Visitors to Paris in the Year 1900, Katherine and Gilbert Macquoid, 1900

My Parisian Year: A Woman's Point of View, Maude Annesley (Mills & Boon Ltd, 1912)

Stiff, Mary Roach (Penguin Books, 2003)

Undying Faces: A Collection of Death Masks, Ernst Berkard (Hogarth Press, 1929)

About the Author

Born and raised in Canada, **Sarah Leipciger** lives in London with her three children and teaches creative writing to prisoners. Her short fiction has been shortlisted for the Asham Award, the Fish Prize and the Bridport Prize. Her first novel, the critically acclaimed *The Mountain Can Wait*, was published in 2015. *Coming Up for Air* is her second novel.